Caiseal Mór was born into a rich tradition of Irish storytelling and music. As a child he learned to play the brass-strung harp, carrying on a long family tradition. He spent several years collecting stories, songs and music of the Celtic lands during many visits to Ireland, Scotland and Brittany. He has a degree in performing arts from the University of Western Sydney and has worked as an actor, a teacher and as a musician.

ALSO BY CAISEAL MÓR

The Wanderers series:
The Circle and the Cross
The Song of the Earth
The Water of Life

Scratches in the Margin
The Moon on the Lake

The Tilecutter's Penny

CAISEAL MÓR

ARROW

If you would like to write to Caiseal Mór, he can be contacted at the following e-mail address: cais@s054.aone.net.au or visit Caiseal's website at http://www.home.aone.net.au/caismor/caiseal.html

An Arrow book published by
Random House Australia Pty Ltd
20 Alfred Street, Milsons Point, NSW 2061
http://www.randomhouse.com.au

Sydney New York Toronto
London Auckland Johannesburg
and agencies throughout the world

First published 1998
This Arrow edition published 1999

National Library of Australia
Cataloguing-in-Publication Data

Mór Caiseal, 1961– .
The tilecutter's penny.

ISBN 0 091 83492 9.

I. Title.

A821.3

Maps and artwork by Caiseal Mór
The Eilish typeface used on the cover and for the headings within the text was specially designed by Caiseal Mór for *The Tilecutter's Penny*.
Typeset by Midland Typesetters, Maryborough, Victoria
Printed by Griffin Paperbacks, Adelaide

10 9 8 7 6 5 4 3 2 1

Here begins
the tale of your descent.
Here begins the story
of the Holy Grail.
Here begin the marvels.
Here begin the terrors.

Acknowledgements

Selwa, thank you for your wonderful support and friendship. A guardian angel must have been watching over me the day I met you.

Likewise I have been blessed with the guiding hand of a gifted editor who I am also privileged to count among my friends. Thank you, Julia.

The team at Random House Australia have, as always, put a thousand per cent into getting this novel published. Thank you to everyone at Milsons Point and around Australia.

To patient friends who read and reread drafts of this manuscript go special thanks. There is nothing like an objective opinion now and then to keep you on track.

My web-site receives literally hundreds of visits each week. E-mails and letters from readers who have enjoyed my novels, music and other books arrive every day. This truly amazes me. My gratitude for all your kind words and your enthusiasm for my stories. I hope you will enjoy this tale just as much.

Last of all I would like to thank Angus, my ginger cat, for reaching up from his spot on my lap to tap the keyboard every now and then. If only he could spell.

CONTENTS

MAP OF THE WORLD

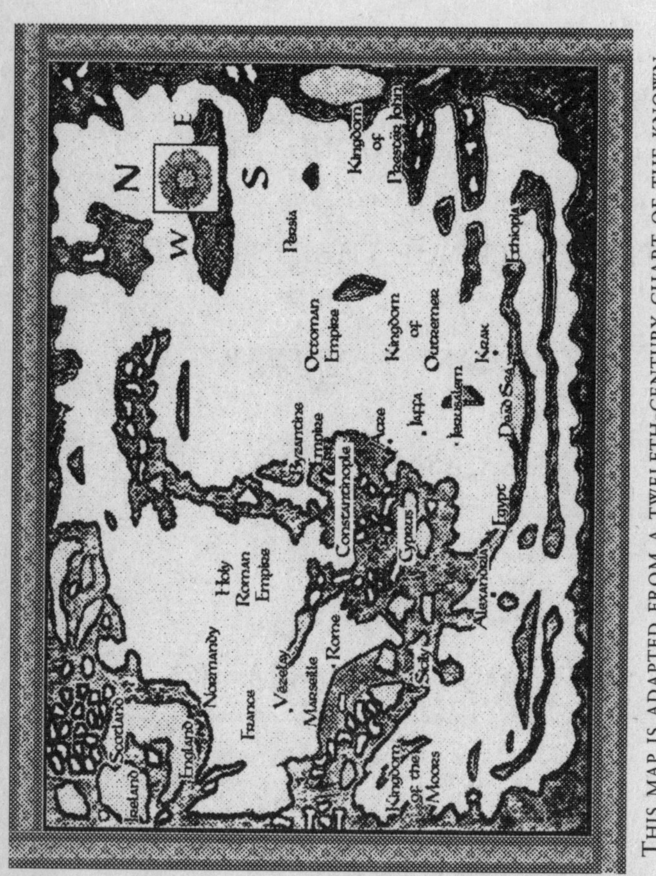

THIS MAP IS ADAPTED FROM A TWELFTH-CENTURY CHART OF THE KNOWN WORLD. THE ORIGINAL WAS A GUIDE FOR PILGRIMS.

MAP OF BALLY RAINE

THE NORMAN KINGDOM OF IRELAND

THE FITZWILLIAM ESTATES

Prologue

Do not judge me by the filthy sackcloth garments I am wearing. I am not a heretic. I am a Knight of the Temple of Solomon. When I was younger I liked to think of myself as a crusading Templar warrior in the service of Christ. These days I am not quite so pretentious or proud.

My fortunes have turned full circle. My guardian angel has deserted me. Now I face the end of my life lodged in a filthy royal prison awaiting the pleasure of the Bishop of Tournai. And whilst I tarry, that devious cleric eagerly embellishes the tale of my misdeeds against Church and Crown to ensure I remain here a little longer.

The bishop's long list of unfounded allegations is a cunning deception, part of a shrewd and subtle strategy. The seat he holds on the Inquisition gives him authority to investigate matters privately which he dare not discuss in public. If the King's Counsellors suspected his motives, they would surely condemn him.

My host is renowned for his cruelty. His cells are overflowing with the victims of his craft. I have witnessed his skill as an inquisitor and I can attest that, truly, he has a talent for torture. The elaborate spectacles of pain and horror I have seen here would make any hardened warrior flinch in dismay. No battle I ever took part in was so bloody; no enemy so vicious and merciless.

This butcher has displayed the suffering of others for me in the belief that I will succumb more easily to his interrogation. But his show of brutality has hardened my resolve. Though the bishop believes I will tell him everthing I know about the treasures of the Temple, I will not utter a sound, no matter how he threatens me. I will not betray my brothers in the order. I will not relinquish my soul to the inquisitors. Torture holds no terror for me. I will take my holy secret to the grave.

To strengthen this determination, I often turn to dreaming. I send my thoughts flying far beyond the bounds of this dank stone cell. In the long lonely hours while I await destiny, my spirit soars free. I call on all my memories. I review the miracles I have witnessed in my time. My wandering soul revisits the places and people I once held dear.

When I crave peace I recall the Tabernacle Church of the Holy Sepulchre in the city at the centre of the world. Jerusalem. When I need to hear a friendly voice I imagine I sit in the taverns of that town, listening to epic tales. I remember many of the stories even now: chronicles of knightly quests, songs of valorous deeds, verses from the holy books and, strangely, the exotic legends of the Saracens.

These infidel peoples from the east who venerate Mohammed as the only true prophet were once the greatest enemies of Christendom. Yet the Temple learned much from them. The Saracens long ago mastered the secrets of music, science, art and poetry. And their fantastic sagas are among the finest ever conceived.

It is claimed the chronicle of the Holy Cup of the Grail originated with the eastern people. In the version of the story I remember, the Grail was the sacred cup with which Christ served the Last Supper. There are innumerable accounts of its alleged attributes. The chalice is said to derive its magical properties from the touch of Our Lord. Water is turned to wine, salt changed into diamonds, and clods of earth transformed into gold. But the chief virtue of the vessel is the restoration of youth to any who drink from it. It is the means to eternal life.

Inspired by the chronicles of the Grail, there are men who have spent their entire lives searching sacred Jerusalem for traces of this artefact. Two generations ago the hidden passageways of the Holy City were exhaustively excavated and systematically plundered. All in the quest for the chalice of the Last Supper.

And even after all this time the maze of tunnels beneath the ancient ruined Temple of Solomon have not yielded all their secrets. Dark passages still remain unearthed to this day. Many mysteries lie buried deep in the vaults, yet to be brought to light. The fabled Ark of the Covenant is said to be secreted somewhere in the dusty crypts of Jerusalem. Blessed books transcribed by the holy hand of Christ are rumoured to be concealed under the great city.

I do not know whether there ever were such relics. There was a time when I believed in the Grail Cup with all my heart. But some tales are woven for the purpose of disguising profound truths.

When I first voyaged to the Saracen lands of Outremer I was certain these tales were true. In my understanding they were as infallible as the Gospels. I did not know then that I was born of an ancient bloodline. Or that it was not my fate merely to listen to the legends, but instead I was destined to play a part in these great tales.

When I arrived in Acre I had no idea this was the first stage of a long journey which would one day lead me to this very cell, accused of heresy, treachery and murder. I did not imagine I would sit in chains squandering the hours, conjuring long-dead comrades from the ether.

At last I think I am beginning to understand the mystery of the eternal circle of life.

THE CASTLE OF THE MYSTERIES

Chapter One

The massive two-wheeled wagon lurched to one side as the team of horses recklessly rounded a sharp bend in the narrow road. The driver swore loudly as he struggled to keep the precious cargo from spilling over into the ditch. But he did not spare the whip for he had no mind to slow down if he could help it.

The draughthorses strained with their load for it was heavier than any they had ever hauled. Under his breath the driver cursed his master for insisting the team take such an unwieldy cart on this journey. To the rear, in urgent pursuit, he could hear the thundering gallop of half-a-dozen warhorses pounding along like the relentless cloven-hooved horses of the Devil himself.

Sweat streamed down the driver's face as he glanced anxiously back over his shoulder. No more than a hundred lengths behind he could clearly see six knights clad all in black. To his dismay, they were steadily gaining ground on his team.

It would only be a matter of a few minutes, he reckoned, before the warriors were upon him. They obviously wanted to get their hands on the precious goods he carried. If he did not do his best to outrun them, there would be no escaping the wrath of his lord, the Grand Master of the Temple. The man cracked his whip urgently. The Grand Master was a man who rarely accepted excuses.

'Mary in Heaven,' the driver cried, panic taking hold of

him, 'spare me and my ponies from those evil black warriors.'

His prayer went unheeded. A matter of seconds later the wagon came to a part of the road that had been washed away in a recent rainstorm. Deep ruts had been transformed by the tempest into treacherous boggy holes. The driver had no choice but to slow down or risk the loss of his entire load. As if that were not enough of a concern, the cargo shifted dangerously. One of the ropes securing the heavy chest to the floor of the cart had worked its way loose.

'They'll murder me!' the driver screamed, certain these knights meant him nothing but harm. 'And if they don't do for me, the master will.'

Hastily he made the sign of the cross, anxious that even the Blessed Virgin Mary may have deserted him in his hour of need. As he completed the gesture the cart lurched to a halt, one wheel stuck firmly in the mud.

The driver leaned over the side of his stranded vehicle and quickly inspected the wheel; he knew straightaway that he would have to give up the chase. He would not be able to save the box of precious treasures now.

With a final glance at the large chest, he sighed and jumped from the cart. If he had any hope of saving his own life, he had to act quickly. His only chance was to make a hasty escape on foot.

'It's not me they're after,' he reminded himself, 'it's this bloody box. Best I let them have it and I go on my way as peaceably as I can.'

The draughthorses cried out in anguish, sensing their master's fear. It was then the driver noticed another group of horsemen ahead of him on the road. They were riding at a gallop in his direction. By the white surcoats they wore and the broad red crosses stitched upon their breasts, he recognised them immediately as friends and protectors.

Knights of the Temple.

The driver hauled on the wheel stop to ensure his horses did not work the cart loose from the mud in their panic. Behind him the party of black-clad knights was only a short distance away. The panicked man ran out in front of his great flat cart and waved his arms about wildly to get the attention of the Temple Knights.

Then a selfish thought crossed his mind. For his own safety he decided it might be best to seek the shelter of the bushes at the side of the road.

'I'll wait until these two bands of warriors have finished their business with one another,' he told his horses. 'Don't fret, I'll be back.'

With that he bounded across the road and rushed into the trees, far enough to be out of harm's way but not too far away to observe what happened next.

The two parties of warriors reached the abandoned wagon at almost the same moment. When they had reined in their warhorses, one knight from each group immediately dismounted and moved to inspect the great cart.

'Guy d'Alville,' the leader of the black knights grunted, grudgingly introducing himself. His black painted helm had a large flat faceplate across the front, concealing his features and muffling his voice. He had not removed his head covering, as was the usual custom when two strangers met on the road. Obviously unimpressed by the Templars, d'Alville stood with his hands on his hips, his head upright and proud.

'Theobald Larmenius,' the white Temple knight shot back, removing the helm from his head so the other man could look into his eyes.

'What is your business here?' the black knight demanded. 'This road belongs to the Prefect of the Order of the Hospital of Saint John.'

'Forgive me,' the Templar flashed. 'I was led to believe the King owned all the roads in this land, not the Hospital. Has Prefect-Brother Albert been elevated to the Crown?'

'I do not wish you any ill will,' d'Alville stated tersely. 'I am not seeking any trouble. I am here on the business of the prefect. I am sure you understand I have orders which I must carry out. Now move away from my wagon and be on your way.'

'There has been a mistake,' Theobald rejoined, inspecting the flank of one of the horses. 'These animals are the property of the Order of the Temple.' He pointed to a brand mark in the shape of two crossed human thighbones surmounted by a skull, which had been burned upon the left flank of each horse. 'This is a Temple brand,' he stated. 'Therefore it follows that this cart also belongs to my order.'

'Stand away from my wagon,' the black knight insisted, his commanding voice sounding strained and angered. 'The captain of a trading ship does not necessarily own the cargo in the hold.'

The Templar shrugged his shoulders. 'And what cargo are we speaking of?' he laughed.

'Holy relics from the Outremer,' d'Alville explained, 'stolen from the Hospital months ago.'

'The Order of Saint John claims possession of the Grail!' the Templar exclaimed mockingly.

'What do you know of the Grail Cup?' the black knight hissed.

'Only what the troubadours tell.'

The smile fell away from d'Alville's face. 'Take care, brother,' he warned. 'You do not know what you are saying.'

The Temple knight slipped his helm back onto his head. Then he placed a gloved hand upon the hilt of his sword.

'Or perhaps you do have some knowledge of the Grail,' d'Alville added, noting the white knight was preparing to fight.

'If we are fighting for possession of the Holy Cup of Life,' Larmenius countered, 'then I will battle you the harder. The Grail rightfully belongs to my order.'

'There are six of us,' the black knight warned, 'and only four of you. I have a great respect for the warriors of the white surcoat. But I feel I should warn you that I have been fighting for the last three years against the English in the north of France. My knights are all veterans of the Saracen wars. Please do not imagine you will be able to prevent me taking what is mine.'

'I congratulate you all on surviving the sharp swords of the heathen unscathed,' the Templar replied with mock politeness, 'but I beg you not to assume that I or my knights would surrender to you meekly. Or that I would allow you to pilfer that which is clearly the property of the Temple.'

In a moment both men had drawn their swords and levelled them ready for combat. Their comrades dismounted amid a great clatter of arms, eager to stand beside their masters. In this confined muddy space it would have been almost impossible to fight on horseback. There was simply not enough room to manoeuvre the warhorses around the wagon.

From the bushes the driver watched in terror, praying for his own safety and that of the gallant white knights who had come to his rescue. As he looked on, the first blows were struck. Within minutes two black knights fell, mortally wounded. Then a white-clad Templar succumbed to his attacker. It looked to the driver as if the Templars had the upper hand and would surely win this dispute.

But just then, to his horror, the cowering man heard an ominous sound behind him in the forest. It was the unmistakable noise of armed men moving through the bushes, making for the road. The driver lay as flat as he could under a low spreading tree, in the desperate hope he would not be seen.

Either his luck returned then suddenly or his prayers were answered. Twenty crossbowmen dressed all in black passed by without noticing him. Their sights were set on other targets. The man's heart sank when he saw them surround the three remaining Templar knights.

In seconds the brutal sound of swords clashing had ceased and all was quiet again. But the driver did not dare emerge from his safe hiding place. He still feared the Hospitaller knights would treat him with the same ferocity they had dealt out to the Templars. So he waited.

Not until all noise had ceased and he guessed more than an hour had gone by did the driver carefully and quietly get to his feet. Stealthily he made his way towards the wagon, checking every movement in the surrounding bushes like a frightened animal trying to sniff out the hunter.

The first thing he noticed as he reached the roadside was that his cart was still where he had left it. But the horses had been unhitched and most likely stolen. Four white-clad bodies had been laid out in a row along the ditch, their faces covered with their own surcoats. The bloodstains on their clothes told the story of their defeat at the hands of the archers. There was no-one else about and no sign of what had become of the thieving Hospitallers.

Still very cautious, the driver approached his cart to see whether any of the precious cargo had been stolen. To his surprise it seemed as if the treasure had not been touched at all. He looked about him again to make sure there was no-one lurking nearby. Then he climbed on top of the wagon to lift the cover off the treasure.

He raised the canvas sheet by one corner and saw underneath, to his surprise, a long black shield with a white cross painted on it. Suddenly the shield moved, and before the driver knew what had happened, there was a long knife pressed against his throat. The leader of the black knights had been lying in wait for him. Now there were warriors dressed in black all around him.

'Where is the treasure?' d'Alville demanded. 'What have you done with it?'

'I don't know what you mean,' the driver stuttered, scared half out of his wits. 'The treasure has not been touched.'

The black knight growled under his breath. One of his warriors pulled back the canvas to reveal a long flat chest. Two knights set to the lid and quickly removed it. Still holding the knife at his captive's throat, d'Alville thrust his free hand in among the contents and rummaged around.

'What is this?' d'Alville bellowed, tipping a handful of black powder over his victim's head and face.

The driver coughed violently, choking as the powder filled his nostrils. The black knight let his captive suffer for a short while before he carefully brushed the fine grains away from the man's face. Then he repeated his earlier question.

'Where is the treasure?'

The gasping man spat out saliva. Tears streamed down his cheeks. Finally he managed to sob a reply, certain it was not what the knight wanted to hear. 'This is the treasure with which I was entrusted. I swear it.'

'What is it?' d'Alville bawled.

'The finest black pepper from the lands of Prester John,' the driver cried, 'a gift from the Grand Master of the Temple to the King. It is bound for the royal kitchens.'

The knight abruptly released the pressure of his blade against the trembling man's throat and stood up. Then he slowly sheathed the small weapon into the belt hook at his side. D'Alville had still not removed his helm. It was impossible for the frightened driver to read what the knight might be thinking.

'I believe you,' the Hospitaller declared. 'Now get off the cart,' he ordered in a gentler tone. The driver quickly did as he was told.

'Please, my lord,' the driver begged, certain his precious

cargo was about to be redistributed amongst these Hospitallers, 'the Grand Master will skin me alive if I do not bring this treasure safely to the King.'

D'Alville smiled, gently touching the trembling man upon the shoulder. Then he hugged the driver's head against him as he whispered, 'You need not fear the Grand Master's wrath, my good man. I will make sure he never knows of this little incident.'

The driver pulled away from the knight and looked with suspicion at the black faceplate. He opened his mouth to express his gratitude. But before he had a chance to speak, d'Alville summoned two of his warriors with a wave of his hand.

'Dispose of him,' the knight commanded coldly. The Hospitallers grabbed the man roughly by the arms. In seconds they had dragged him struggling and begging for mercy off into the forest to a place far from the road where his body would not be discovered for a long time.

Satisfied that the driver would not have an opportunity to report this incident to his superiors, the Hospitaller lifted the heavy helm from his head. Once free of the dead weight, he breathed deeply. But a frown spread across d'Alville's brow as he stared into the distance. The black knight realised then that the Templars had arranged this whole episode as a diversion.

At last, with resignation, he replaced his headgear and went to his horse. D'Alville was mounted by the time his men returned but he did not wait for them. Before they had found their stirrups he was already galloping down the road, eager to return to the stronghold of the Hospital.

Four men, poor native Gaelic cattle herders, carefully made their way noiselessly into the little wood, their sharp boar spears held chest high at the ready. Though the hunters were elated at successfully cornering their quarry, none among them so much as made a sound. Nor did they dare exhibit any outward sign of excitement.

The slightest provocation, they all knew too well, could be disastrous when dealing with a wild boar. And this particular beast was more dangerous and more powerful than most. It had led them on a wild chase for the better part of the day. Now they were all determined it would not escape their net.

In the thicket the four hunters stood as still as a circle of standing stones. Then, prompted by their leader, they each gently dropped their cloaks to free their hunting arms. In the confusion of a fight a cloak could easily become entangled with a branch or snagged in the underbrush. Any precious seconds lost could bring disaster on a hunter.

The dark-haired bright-eyed young man who was their leader caught the eye of each man in turn. Then he let out a low trilling whistle from a gap between his teeth. The noise was like the call of a tiny bird. His comrades recognised the signal meant they should keep perfectly still.

Nothing stirred. The lonely grove on the hillside was perfectly tranquil. But there was a subtle scent on the breeze. It was the mingled aroma of the sweat of man and beast. The delicate, unmistakable odour of fear.

The tallest among the four hunters raised a shaking hand to his comrades. The others took it to mean he reckoned their quarry was skulking off in the bushes to his left. The leader frowned, then shook his head with confident certainty. Lifting the point of his spear to the right, he indicated he was sure the beast had retreated deeper into the cover of the woods where the underbrush was much thicker.

The tall man opened his mouth in frustration, barely able

to contain his protest. The fair curls of his hair fell around his face as he shook his head. He knelt down, placing his spear on the ground in front of him while he pulled his locks back off his face. As he tied his hair with a piece of leather so it would not obstruct his vision, he caught his leader's eye again.

The two men glared at each other for a few tense seconds, then they broke into smiles as all rivalry melted away and they turned their attention back to the task at hand.

It was not a moment too soon.

The great black boar, enraged and frightened, chose that very instant to launch an attack on the hunters in a desperate attempt to drive them off and away from his woodland home. With a frenzied screech the animal leapt up from its hiding place and hurled its full fury at the fair-headed man still kneeling on the ground.

'Braonin!' cried the dark-haired hunter. 'He's coming at you from the right!'

The leader raised his spear, but before he could hurl it at the fearsome beast, he was knocked off his feet by another animal of comparable size and weight. The cunning old boar had drawn them right into his nest. Now his mate had joined in the defence of their home and was embarking on an ambush of her own.

Four men armed only with spears and short knives might have run down the boar if he were alone. But they were no match for two of these aggressive animals. The sow grunted a deep ferocious roar, stamped her feet and threw herself at the winded leader. This was no diversion to gain time, this was a savage last stand for her life.

At precisely the same moment Braonin managed to pick up the spear which lay at his feet. He dodged nimbly around, remaining just out of reach of the enraged boar, all the while keeping him at bay with the point of his weapon.

'Donal!' he cried, panting more from shock than exertion.

'Where are you, for God's sake? Donal!' But the leader of the hunters was nowhere in sight.

The very moment Braonin was distracted, the black boar launched a frenzied screaming assault. Braonin slashed at the beast with the leaf-shaped edge of his spear, tearing at the beast's front leg as he did so. But he could not compete with the animal for weight and sheer strength. He was quickly thrown over onto his back by the force of the attack. In the fall he lost his grip on the spear and it landed with a clatter against the trunk of an old yew tree.

The hunter turned as still as stone. His enemy withdrew slightly and stood breathing hard and heavy. Legs askew, shoulders forward, the great creature surveyed his now defenceless foe.

Braonin was in deadly danger. Now there was nothing between him and the wrath of a vicious injured boar. At any moment the animal would come charging again to gorge at him with its ugly tusks. The hunter had heard stories of men who had been killed by creatures half the size of this beast. And this monstrous boar was larger than any animal Braonin had ever seen.

'Oh Jesus,' he whispered, not daring to speak too loudly, 'have pity on me.'

As if in prompt answer to the prayer, the boar squinted his heavy eyelids and breathed out with a great tumultuous gush of wind, stamping his bloodied foot, kicking up the dust in a show of rage. Then all of a sudden his eyes opened wide again. The animal hissed loudly with a hideous rasp that ended in a low menacing growl.

Braonin knew instantly that his only hope lay in being on his feet when the creature made his charge. With that one thought in mind, he gently moved to sit up, taking great care that he make no sudden jerking moves which might prompt the boar to attack. But as the hunter got to his haunches and squatted, something entirely unexpected happened. Braonin's eye caught the fearful gaze of the boar.

The hairy beast snorted, defiantly returning the hunter's stare. And there they stood, monster and man, unmoved by the shouts going on about them or the screams of the sow as she battled the other hunters.

Braonin concentrated all his being on remaining quiet and not making any move which might provoke the animal. Then all other activity in the little wood seemed to cease as if a magic veil had been drawn around the hunter and the black boar. The only noise was that of two frightened animals; one four-legged, the other two-legged. They both breathed hard as they faced each other down.

Braonin calmed himself as much as he could, realising the boar was losing a lot of blood. The beast was weakening by the minute. The hunter felt a trickle of sweat at the back of his neck, and then he noticed something that in all his years of tracking boar and deer he had never previously experienced.

As his gaze sank into the animal's shining black eyes he began to sense a deep and enlightening kinship with this awesome creature. This, he realised, was a familiar spirit.

The hunter looked upon the hunted. And for the first time in his life Braonin discovered a real compassion for his quarry.

'I asked God for pity and this is how he gave it to me,' he whispered. The boar cocked his ears forward to listen and Braonin was certain he understood him.

'Are you going to kill me?' he muttered carelessly and was immediately answered with a growl that shook the ground.

Braonin froze, fighting back the urge to speak again, forced to squat quietly. He was waiting for some sign from the wounded animal that his strength was finally failing.

Just such a move was not long in coming. Some distance away the sow gave a trailing cry which ended in abrupt silence. The boar was obviously disturbed by the ensuing quiet. Thick dark blood had gathered in a pool at the animal's feet and he was swaying slightly from the loss of life fluid.

Once or twice the boar took a chance and broke eye contact with the hunter, just long enough to glance into the woods for a sign from his mate. Each time the animal did so, Braonin glanced at his spear, trying to gauge whether it would be too dangerous to make a dive for the weapon. As an outward sign to his adversary that he was no longer of any threat, the hunter began sighing deeply as he let out his breath. The boar seemed to acknowledge this gesture by dropping his guard enough to turn around and scan the bushes.

Eyes no longer fixed on Braonin, the beast took in a deep breath. Then, much to the hunter's surprise, the black boar let out a long, exasperated howl. Braonin knew the animal was singing a strange lament for the sow.

When he had used up his breath, the boar swayed a little on his feet again. Then unexpectedly kneeled down on his front legs as if he were giving a sign of surrender.

In that instant the other hunters struck.

Braonin's comrades launched their ambush masterfully. All the squatting hunter saw was the body of the boar jolting as two long spears thumped hard into the beast's belly and shoulder. The animal nearly lost his balance with the sudden impact of the weapons, but somehow he managed to remain on his feet. Then the creature coughed a splash of blood from the back of his throat and fell to his knees, turning to stare towards Braonin as he did so. This time there was hatred in the animal's eyes. Hatred, loathing and revenge.

The boar concentrated all his remaining energy on the defenceless man in front of him. There were flames of malice in the centre of each dark beastly eye. The creature was defeated but the hunter could see the animal had no intention of giving up the fight.

Before he took in another breath, the boar gave out a loud snort then staggered onto all fours again. He lurched forward like a man who has drunk too much ale. And then began a stumbling headlong charge at the defenceless hunter who still squatted helplessly on the ground.

Braonin saw the attack coming. If he had wanted to he could have rolled out of the way in plenty of time. He could have wrestled with the weakened boar and brought him to submission. He might even have been able to reach for his spear in time to thrust it at the stricken animal's chest. But he could not find the will to do any of these things.

He closed his eyes in readiness for death, believing the time of reckoning had come upon him. Barely moving his lips, he began to utter a prayer he had recited endlessly since childhood. He was astonished to find the words suddenly contained a real meaning for him.

Engrossed in his invocation, eyes shut tight, Braonin did not witness the spear which pierced the boar's heart, bringing the beast down within a few paces of his target. The hunter heard the squeal of the boar as the weapon hit its mark. But he dared not open his eyes until all noise had ceased and the heaving body had come to rest at his side.

As the animal breathed his last, Braonin reached out a trembling hand to caress the hairy snout. 'I am sorry,' he whispered gently.

'Cousin, are you injured?' cried Donal.

The hunter did not answer.

'Braonin!' the dark-haired hunter barked, waking Braonin out of his trance.

'I'll be fine after I've had a good long draught of your wife's ale,' Braonin mumbled, instinctively hiding his feelings about the boar as best he could. 'He nearly had me.'

'Conor has been hurt by the sow,' Donal informed him.

'We'll have to get him home. We'll come back for the carcasses later.'

'Someone should stay with the bodies to guard them,' Braonin snapped. 'We shouldn't leave them unattended.'

'Who's going to make off with them?' Donal asked, surprised at his cousin's suggestion. 'There's no-one for miles about. And there is no beast in the forest that could drag such a weight very far.'

'What about the Normans?' the fair-haired hunter demanded, still in shock.

'They never come up here,' the other man laughed. 'Are you sure you're not injured?' he added, looking his cousin over quickly to make sure he was not hurt.

'I'm fine.'

Braonin did not have a chance to say anything else for just then the sound of approaching horses caught his attention. The same thought immediately struck both men. They had just been speaking of the Normans. And they were hunting on the lord's lands. Lord William had a reputation for even-handedness, but he often imposed harsh penalties on tenants of the estate who wantonly broke the law. Both men knew they risked a flogging or a large fine for poaching Norman boar.

'It's William's men,' Braonin whispered in panic. 'We'll have to make a run for it!'

'Be quiet, you fool!' Donal shot back as he knelt down beside his cousin. 'Don't make a sound.'

The hunters strained their ears and all their senses in an effort to discover who could be out on the hills on horseback at this time of day. Then, unexpectedly and to their utter relief, they heard a familiar word. A word in their own language.

'I never met a Norman who spoke Irish that well,' Donal pointed out. As he stood up, his own name was carried across to him on the breeze.

'Donal O'Regan!' the voice beckoned urgently. 'Are you there among the bushes?'

The dark-haired hunter cupped his hands to his mouth and called, 'It is Donal who answers you. Who are you and what do you want?'

'Thank God I've found you!' the messenger cried, neglecting to identify himself in his hurry to pass on his news. 'It's your father, Mathúin,' the man yelled. 'He was struck down by a convulsion this morning. Now he lays deathly ill and your kinfolk have sent for the priest to attend him. He's saying it's all over with him. He's calling for you. You must make haste if you are to have any chance of making it home before he passes away.'

In an instant Donal had dragged Braonin to his feet and muttered his apologies. 'I must go. Can you look after Conor?'

'Leave him with me,' Braonin assured his friend. 'I'll take care of him. Go quickly while your father still has some life left in him.'

Donal leapt through the bushes and out into the open, making for the messenger who held a spare horse by the reins ready for him. Before Braonin had finished dusting himself off, the two horses were galloping off towards the clachan of Cúil Ghréine.

Braonin watched after his friend until the two horsemen had passed out of sight. Then he turned to look at the gruesome bloodied body of the boar again. He thought he saw a twitch, just a hint of life in the glazed empty eyes. But Braonin told himself not to be so foolish for without a doubt this black boar was truly dead.

Chapter Two

t the gentle plodding sound of iron-shod hooves the young woman looked up from her work at the enclosed well. A horse was tramping across the cobbled stone path that led to the well-house.

In one hand the woman held the rope which was used to draw the large wooden bucket from the well. Quickly she secured the rope to a post, then brushed her clothes down before venturing outside.

The small stone structure built to cover the communal well looked exactly like any other house, except that the roof was made of stone instead of thatch. Five stairs cut out of the rock led down from the doorway into the water, which at this time of year lapped against the bottom step.

The girl brushed the strands of black shining hair out of her eyes. Then she leaned out of the entrance to the well-house, trying to catch a glimpse of the horse. But, to her surprise, she could not see any rider passing by. The horse must not have yet rounded the bend in the path. The young woman quickly unbound the rope again, threw the bucket down into the water and hauled it in to finish her chore. There was only one more water skin to be filled and she was eager to return home to her family before sunset.

By the time she had retrieved the bucket and filled the skin, the hoofbeats had ceased. The girl had not heard any greeting and this puzzled her a little. The clachan of Clonough was a small settlement. Everyone knew each other. If one of her kinfolk rode up to the well, they would surely shout out to see if anyone was working inside.

Her curiosity aroused, the girl pulled up her long skirt, tucked the decorated hem into her belt and hastily tied her hair back with a strip of leather. Then, once more, she leaned out from the stone enclosure of the well. A horse neighed nearby as it ambled riderless across the road, its reins dragging in the grass at the side of the path.

'That's a strange thing,' the girl said half to herself as she put the bucket down, climbing out of the well-house to see if anyone was about.

The horse, a stout broad-shouldered animal with a shiny jet-black coat, approached her as soon as he heard her footsteps. When he reached the girl he began pushing gently against her body in a wordless plea for a morsel of food. The young woman smiled as she cradled the mount's head, stroking his nose. At this he nuzzled himself closer and whinnied softly to express his pleasure.

'What is your name, my pretty one?' she cooed as the animal nudged persistently at her. She traced her fingers over the intricate hand-beaten design which edged the finely worked red leather saddle. This was Norman handiwork and it was of the highest quality. The bridle and straps alone would have cost a fortune. The whole saddle was many times more valuable than the horse it was made for.

Behind her the girl heard the sound of footsteps and as she turned to see who it was, a man spoke.

'And what is *your* name, my pretty one?' the heavily accented voice sighed in answer, mimicking the young woman's tone.

The girl put a hand to her throat and gasped in surprise at the sight of the warrior leaning casually against the side of the well enclosure. He had a broad smile on his freckled face. His red hair was cropped short at the back and sides and his chin was smooth in the Norman fashion from the daily routine of shaving. A long yellow tunic, quilted and padded thickly, covered his upper body down to his thigh. The hose he wore were made of elegant black cloth with garters of golden cord tied just below the knees to keep the garment from sagging around his ankles. A long shield was slung over his left shoulder and he rested one hand on the steel pommel of a sheathed sword.

There was no doubt about it, he was a Norman.

'I am called Neesh,' the girl said meekly as she moved to go back to her work, 'and my mother told me not to waste time talking to soldiers.'

But the man manoeuvred easily to cut her off. In seconds he stood with folded arms in front of the well, effectively blocking the doorway. As she got closer to him the stranger put out his arms as if he expected she would walk straight into his embrace.

'Surely, Neesh, you've got time to talk to me?' the man teased. 'There's nothing a soldier likes more than to spend a little while chatting to a beautiful maid. And I have a particular weakness for dark-haired beauties. I see you have met my warhorse. Until now he was the most beautiful creature I had ever seen.'

'I have to get on home,' the young woman answered, blushing nervously and hoping her mother would not suddenly appear to berate her. But secretly she found herself enjoying this young man's flattering attention. 'I have lots more work to do before sunset,' Neesh muttered unconvincingly. 'I am sorry but I must leave. My mother is waiting for these water skins.'

The warrior smiled again. And as the young woman looked into his pale green-grey eyes she could not help but wish her mother was not always looking over her shoulder. Suddenly Neesh found herself blushing again. To avoid further embarrassment, the girl pushed the soldier's arm out of the way to get past him.

The Norman relented as her hand touched his sleeve. He gently fell back to let her by. 'If that is your wish,' he half sang, half whispered. 'What Christian knight in all the world could refuse the desires of a fair lady such as yourself?'

Neesh quickly gathered her water skins, feeling her face burning red with excitement. She tidied up the well rope and made sure the water bucket was turned upside down to drain. Then she untucked her skirt again so it covered her legs. When that was done she made her way once more out into the open. But when the girl emerged outside into the sunlight, the warrior was nowhere to be seen. He had vanished.

Her heart sank a little in disappointment as she looked around her, hoping he might simply be hiding. But there was no sign of him at all. Then Neesh noticed the horse still contentedly chewing on moist grass at the side of the road. She could not help smiling.

'I wonder where he disappeared to?' she asked herself aloud. Then, with a shrug of her shoulders, the girl turned around to make off towards her home, a short distance away on the other side of the hill.

Neesh had taken five or six steps toward the horse when she heard the sound of a man's laughter behind her. She spun around, but the soldier had already slipped off out of sight. It was then she spotted his long shield lying in the grass near his horse. Beside the shield was his sword still in its leather scabbard.

The girl thought it strange that the weapons had been abandoned and it suddenly made her feel very uneasy. Neesh could not immediately discern what it was that frightened her, but instinct told her it was definitely time to go home.

She had just tied the straps on the water skins and slung them over her shoulder when there was another noise nearby. Footsteps. Running.

Before the young woman had a chance to turn around, she was pushed hard on the shoulder from behind and sent tumbling onto the ground. Her water skins were scattered and a few of the vessels lost their leather stoppers.

Neesh ignored the pain in her shoulder for the moment, quickly moving to prevent the contents of the skins spilling all over the ground. Angry, she glanced up from her task. 'You bloody fool,' she shouted, furious at the warrior's stupid act. 'What do think you're doing?'

Behind her the Norman soldier stood with his hands on his hips. He had a smile on his face different from the one he had worn earlier, and there was a look in his eyes which made her feel threatened and helpless.

Neesh turned on her knees as she tried to rise to her feet, at the same time hitching her skirt up to allow her to run without being hindered by the long garment. She did not have a chance to get up before the soldier landed a heavy slap on the side of her face, which sent her sprawling on the roadside into the long grass. The girl let out a scream as she fell, to which the warrior instantly and effectively responded.

Before she knew what was happening, the Norman had drawn a knife from his belt and leapt on top of her. In an instant he threw her flat onto her back in the grass. Once she was pinned down securely, the Norman held the weapon to her throat with one hand and grabbed at her hair with the other.

'Do not think to make a noise, my pretty one,' he sniggered, 'or I'll slit this lovely neck of yours and leave you for the crows to fight over.'

Now it was clear what the soldier wanted from her. Neesh began to shake with fear. She sobbed desperately from the shock of the fall and the great weight of the soldier's body squashing her. Hardly able to breathe, she felt as though the warrior was pressing the life out of her. He must have had some fighting experience, Neesh realised, for he knew how to hold her perfectly immobile.

Without warning, her attacker pricked his blade against the skin of her throat hard enough so she could feel the sharpened edge biting into her skin.

'Don't hurt me,' she pleaded in a voice weakened by apprehension and shortness of breath. 'Please let me go.'

To her surprise the Norman pulled back a little so his weight was not too overbearing. Her hopes rose that he might, after all, release her relatively unharmed.

'Is Neesh really your name, my pretty?' he growled. It was obvious from the stench of his breath that he had been drinking ale.

The girl turned her head away from him in disgust as he spoke. 'Yes,' she stuttered, sobbing.

'Neesh,' he repeated. 'It has a lovely sound to it. And you've beautiful green eyes to match the name. Like a pair of emeralds they are. I have always had a fancy to own a couple of emeralds like those.' He laughed again quietly but it was not a reassuring sound and it made the girl squirm under him with renewed fear.

'Please let me go,' Neesh repeated. 'You're hurting me.'

'I will let you go, my dear,' the Norman answered. 'After you have done me a service,' he whispered. As he spoke he brushed at her hair lightly with his fingers.

Neesh caught the man's meaning straightaway and desperately took in a shuddering breath so she could scream for help. But she had no sooner filled her lungs when the warrior slapped his rough palm hard against her jaw. The shock of the blow forced her into silence.

'You will not tell anyone about this, my dear,' he ordered. 'This roll in the long grass will be our little secret. Just between you and me. And if you're good, I'll come back again by and by and we will get ourselves even better acquainted.'

'If you hurt me, I'll tell my father and my brothers,' Neesh hissed from behind his hand. 'And they'll come after you and kill you with their own hands.'

'And I'll tell them you came to me willingly,' the man sniggered. 'Who is going to take the word of a water girl before that of a Norman knight?'

'You'll hang,' Neesh added despairingly. 'Lord William is not afraid to string up men who take what isn't theirs. And not just Irish folk. He just as readily punishes his own kind for their crimes.'

The Norman stopped dead, making no sound for a moment. The threat of punishment seemed to have a profound effect on him. The resolve melted out of his expression.

'Do you know Lord William?' the soldier demanded. 'Where have you met him?'

'I have seen him at Cúil Ghréine a hundred times,' Neesh answered, but her tone was unconvincing.

'But you are not from Cúil Ghréine, are you, my darling?' the Norman smiled. 'You come from that little collection of houses just over the hill near the River Clonough. I'm willing to bet you haven't so much as seen the lord since he came back from Jerusalem, have you? You probably don't even know what he looks like.'

'I live with my sister in Cúil Ghréine,' the girl lied. 'I am visiting my old father at Clonough.' Suddenly she thrashed out violently at her assailant, but she was no match for him, despite her terror.

The Norman smiled again, certain he had successfully called her bluff. With a deep-throated laugh he shifted his weight just enough so Neesh managed to get a hand free. At the first opportunity she grabbed at the top of the man's tunic and began to pull it tightly around his neck.

The warrior grabbed her hand in his and crushed it, but in the struggle his knife was knocked to the ground out of reach of both of them. When the Norman released the girl's grip on his tunic, he grasped the front of her long dress and tore at it, exposing her breasts to his view. Delighted with what he saw, he promptly pinned Neesh down again as she tried vainly to cover herself with her hands.

'That's enough struggling now, girl,' he barked. 'You put up an honourable fight and it was a fine show. No-one will ever accuse you of being a willing bedmate to the enemy.'

Neesh was sure her heart had stopped beating from fear. She struggled once more to scream but the Norman struck her hard across the cheek with the back of his hand. She felt her head spin and saw bright flashes of light in the corner of her eyes.

Now she was so terrified that even the full weight of the warrior pressed down on her could not prevent her squirming an arm free. Her dread gave Neesh new strength. The girl grabbed at the man's ear, tearing at the fleshy part of it with her fingers in one last urgent attack, all the more vicious for its desperation. In unexpected pain the warrior pulled back as far out of her reach as possible. Blood streamed down the right side of his face from a tear at the side of his head.

Enraged and surprised, the Norman grabbed both the girl's wrists above her head with his right hand so she could not attack him again. Then he dabbed at the wound carefully with his fingers. The warrior winced slightly when he realised how bad the tear was.

'How dare you raise a hand to me!' he yelped in genuine shock that she had put up so much resistance. 'I am your landlord!'

'Lord William is my landlord!' she screamed back at him, wide-eyed.

'And I am his son!' the man yelled, so close to her ear that it hurt. 'So you will obey me.'

Neesh stopped breathing for a moment as she realised exactly what the warrior had admitted. In deepening horror she comprehended the grave danger her life was now in. The reputation of the Lord of Bally Raine for the harsh punishment of any wrongdoers was almost legendary. Neesh knew any man who disciplined his soldiers severely for minor breaches of custom very likely kept his own sons in even closer check. The young woman looked into the warrior's face, and it seemed as if he had heard her thoughts.

'My father must never find out about this, my pretty one,' the Norman said softly. 'And one way or another you will keep quiet about this little meeting of ours. No-one will ever know of what has taken place at this well.'

Neesh did not wait for him to explain any further. It was clear that the warrior meant her deadly harm. With another twist she freed her hand and grasped his ear again. This time she tore at it with even greater viciousness.

The sound of a weapon scraping against a leather scabbard rang out as the Norman drew his body back slightly to get out of her reach. In a flash of steel he pulled out another knife from a scabbard hanging at his waist.

Neesh screamed at the top of her lungs but the warrior pushed the long knife close up to her throat. She was instantly silent when she felt the cold iron against her skin.

'Now you are going to stand up,' the soldier instructed her, 'and we are going to take a walk over to the well. It will be dark soon enough and no-one will be returning here till morning. If I am lucky, your body will not be discovered until long after dawn.'

Neesh had no choice but to do as the Norman said, but she lay on her back shaking slightly as he got to his feet. In the end he had to drag her up by the wrists. Once she was standing, her captor held her from behind, the knife to her chin, forcing her to lift her head back towards him. With his other hand the warrior twisted one of her arms around to her back. Neesh tried to wrap her torn dress around her to cover her breasts, but each time she did so the Norman twisted her arm and she shrieked with pain.

'Why are you taking me to the well-house?' she gasped, frightened out of her wits.

'Because a knife like this spills too much blood,' he explained, 'and such a sharp weapon is too obviously Norman. When your family find you tomorrow you will have no wound upon you except a few bruises about the head. Everyone will think you were knocked unconscious when you fell into the water. No-one will question that your drowning was purely accidental.'

Neesh exhaled loudly as she understood what he meant to do her. But she could not escape—the soldier's grip on her arm was too firm and each time she struggled, he twisted it further. It felt to her as if the bone could easily break. She soon gave up the struggle in order to save her energy. They covered the last few steps to the well-house with Neesh offering token resistance and the warrior kicking her along with his leather-soled riding boots.

At the entrance to the building the Norman shoved Neesh hard towards the door. But the young woman pushed back against the soldier so he would have to struggle with all his might to throw her down into the water.

At the top step there was a little pool of spilled water from the bucket. Neesh felt her feet slide across the slippery stone stair as she tried in vain to push against her attacker. Suddenly she slipped and fell heavily onto her backside. Before she knew what had happened, Neesh was sitting on the step with her feet braced against the next stone stair.

Realising the warrior had not expected this any more

than she had, Neesh abruptly stopped resisting him and slid sideways on the stair. The Norman teetered forward, surprised the girl had abruptly ceased her struggle. Despite his best efforts he could not brace himself against the wall with the hand that held the knife. He was forced to let go of the girl's arm. In that brief second Neesh saw her opportunity.

With all her remaining strength, she pulled her attacker forward by the arm. He lost his balance immediately and she dragged him past her and into the well-house. Neesh heard the splash as the Norman hit the water headfirst. Then there was a clatter as his knife fell on the stones, but that was all the young girl waited to witness.

In a blink of an eye Neesh was up and out of the well-house, running for the safety of home. Without a second thought she left the precious water skins on the road and headed for the fields. She scaled a low stone wall and was off toward the houses of the Gioll Martin where her father and family lived before her attacker had clambered out of the well dripping wet and cursing his ill-fortune.

Neesh sprinted through the fields without even glancing behind her to see if she was being followed. The young woman was almost home when she realised she had made a terrible mistake.

'I should have driven his horse off!' Neesh berated herself. 'He'll be back in the saddle by now and riding along the road in search of me.'

With that she stopped perfectly still in the middle of the field and strained her senses. Neesh could not hear a horse, nor could she see any movement on the road, but her heart was beating so loudly in her ears all other sounds were muffled. She did not want to take the risk of being caught again.

'I'll hide until after dark,' she told herself. 'If I go straight home to the Gioll Martin he might come looking for me. The next time he sees me he will not hesitate to use his knife.' She was certain the Norman would do everything in his power to silence her.

Neesh tried to slow her frantic breathing so she could think clearly. Where could she hide? Suddenly she remembered the little stone chapel at the foot of the hill near a bend in the River Clonough. No-one visited this small stone building any more and Neesh was certain the Norman would not search so far afield, so she decided to hide there until the shadows of evening covered her journey home. Still shaking terribly, the girl approached the chapel, scanning each of the fields before she crossed it for any sign of the Norman warrior.

When she reached the oak grove that grew around the long-deserted chapel, Neesh found the doors bolted shut. But she felt a lot safer here than she had in the open fields, so she sat down on the moss-covered steps to take a few deep breaths. She thanked God for watching over her and fought back her tears.

'I'll move on when I've calmed down,' she snivelled to herself, wiping her nose on her torn dress. All her senses remained focused on the sounds about her and it was a long time before she even dared to lie back and rest on her elbows.

Chapter Three

William FitzWilliam, grandson of the acclaimed Reynard of that name, Lord of Bally Raine, leaned forward in his carved oak chair. The firelight flickered across the grey stone walls in the great hall of his castle as flames consumed the dry timber in the hearth.

Slowly and painfully the old knight opened his hands, spreading his fingers wide. A well-fed and contented ginger cat, woken by the movement, stretched himself on the Old Man's lap, clawing at his knees. The animal looked up at the lord and purred as William ran a hand along his undulating back.

The Old Man smiled at his sleeping feline companion. 'The years have flown by, Angus,' he sighed. 'Here I sit at home in Ireland, once more safe in my stone fortress, and all I do is go over in my mind everything that happened to me since I set out for the Holy Land.'

William moved his toes in his boots to get the blood circulating into his feet. His eyes fixed on the generous crackling fire. The Lord of Bally Raine wondered how he could have possibly spent five whole years of his life on a journey that should have taken only two at the very most.

'I only desired,' he explained to the sleepy-eyed cat, 'to light a candle for my late wife at the altar of the Church of the Holy Sepulchre in the greatest city on earth. The city at the centre of the universe. Jerusalem.'

Angus purred more loudly but showed no sign that he was listening to his master's words. The lord ran a hand over his greying beard as his thoughts drifted on.

'Somehow I became overawed by the enchanted Holy City,' William's voice was full of weariness, 'and stayed on much longer than I had intended.'

William thought to himself that, for many years, he had been searching for some deeper purpose to his life. But for so long he had not been able to discover what that mysterious purpose might be. His first glimpse of a different life came one evening as he was leaving his apartments in the old city of Jerusalem to attend midnight mass at the Church of the Holy Sepulchre. Just outside the door of the building he met a Scottish knight who wore a spotless white tunic and sported a long flowing beard. The two knights sat together during the mass and afterwards shared a meal and a few jars of ale.

'Henry St Clair was his name,' William told his cat. 'He was a gallant knight and a fearless warrior.'

Suddenly the old man was disturbed from his thoughts by the cook pulling a blanket up over his knees. William looked around him at the great blocks of cold stone that lined the hall of his home. He was a world away from the bustling markets and dusty streets of Jerusalem, yet it was as if he had never left that sacred city.

'Do go on, my lord,' the old cook chimed in enthusiastically, her eyes sparkling with anticipation. In the orange firelight the lord's hair no longer seemed so grey but shone red as it had in his younger days.

William half turned in his seat and noticed Lonan the chamberlain and Colm the game-keeper seated nearby, listening intently to his every word.

'Yes, my lord,' Lonan agreed, leaning forward, 'tell us more about this knight St Clair.'

'When we got to talking,' the lord went on, glad that

someone other than his faithful cat was listening to him, 'we both realised that we had once been bitter enemies. We had fought each other hand to hand during the Breton wars. But this half-Scots, half-Norman knight turned out to be more than just another adventurer. He was a warrior and a monk, a member of a holy military order sanctioned by the Pope to protect pilgrims and preserve the city of Jerusalem from the scourge of the infidel. If it were not for the Knights of the Temple, the Christian kingdom of Outremer would have been swallowed up by the heathen long ago.'

The cook handed William a wooden cup filled with sweet aromatic ale seasoned with wild herbs and heather from the fields. The lord took it with a smile and went on with his tale.

'Within a very short while of meeting St Clair, I came to an understanding that my life's duty lay in utter devotion to God. My new friend turned out to be an influential man who arranged for me to be admitted to the Order of the Temple as a postulant without any delay.'

'We are indeed fortunate to have such a pious master,' the game-keeper noted. The other two servants nodded agreement as William sipped his ale.

'Everyone gives back to God,' the old man observed as he rested the cup on the arm of his chair, 'the talent that God has gifted them with. St Clair taught me that,' he added.

William smiled to himself, stroking Angus across the side of his furry face as more of the servants gathered around to hear what he had to say. They never tired of stories of his exploits in a far-off exotic land. The ginger cat purred loudly, curling into a tighter ball, not caring for a story just now.

'A man with a talent for language may become a priest or a theologian,' old William continued, speaking up a little to make sure that he was heard. 'A stonemason builds churches to the glory of heaven. A peasant who has nothing pays his tithe to the Church just as a king must also do. Even a fishmonger ensures that we all keep the meatless days in each week according to God's will and the rites of the Mother Church. And a knight, a warrior, must give to God what service he can. I have been fortunate enough to have been allowed to fight for my God against the heathen and He has accepted me as a brother of the Holy Order of the Temple of Solomon.'

'Your place in heaven is assured,' the chamberlain intoned, 'and we are blessed to have you as our lord.'

'And I am blessed to be among you all again,' William added quickly. 'Mathúin and I sorely missed our home all those years we were away.'

'And sad it is,' the chamberlain retorted, 'that so good a man as Mathúin will not likely live through this night.'

'What's that?' William demanded, shaken from his reminiscences. 'Has he been taken ill? Has he been injured?' The cat grumbled and stretched, letting William know that he was moving about too much.

'I believe a messenger came to him at noon,' Lonan stammered nervously, 'and Mathúin took to his bed soon after. His family has had a priest by his side all day. But he is an old man . . .'

'He is not a day older than me!' William bellowed as Angus stood up, arching his back in protest at the disturbance. The servants were dumbfounded. Not one of them dared speak.

'Fetch my horse,' the lord commanded. 'I will go to Mathúin's house to be by his side.'

'My lord,' the chamberlain appealed, 'the night is wet and Cúil Ghréine is a difficult journey, over the fields and along mud-soaked roads. You should take better care of your health until you have grown used to the cold and damp again.'

'Be quiet!' William snapped. 'Do you think a little spot of rain would stop me coming to the aid of a friend? There were times in the midst of the heat and dust of Outremer when I would have welcomed a good soaking. Fetch my horse. And it had better be waiting by the time I am dressed or I will see that it is you who is getting used to the cold and damp. You will be sleeping with the cows.'

William's tone was still good-natured enough that Lonan was able to laugh a little at his lord's amiable rebuke. The master of Bally Raine did not laugh, however. He simply stood up, placing the cat back down upon the seat as he did so. Then he turned around before the fire, enjoying the warmth for just a few seconds longer while the cat cried, unimpressed at all the noise on so cold a night.

'I really do wish you would reconsider this action,' Lonan gently begged, expecting a stubborn reply but determined to be heard. 'You have only just recovered from a terrible sickness yourself. You may recall that it was caused by persistent phlegm on your lungs from riding in the rain.'

'Mathúin saved my life!' the lord barked, unexpectedly losing his temper. 'Do you understand? Now get my horse ready or find yourself a ditch to sleep in.'

'Yes, my lord,' the chamberlain bowed, his cheeks burning with embarrassment at this unusual tirade, then he rushed out of the room to perform his errand as quickly as possible.

'Does anyone know,' William asked the other servants, 'what this messenger had to say to Mathúin that could have upset him so and sent him to his bed?'

'It was a letter,' the cook confidently replied. 'They say it came from the Holy Land.' The other servants immediately tried to hush her but it was too late, she was in full flight. 'A great disaster has befallen the kingdom of Outremer.'

'Disaster?' the lord inquired. 'What disaster?'

'I do not rightly know,' the cook admitted.

William looked hard and long at each of his attendants,

certain that they were already aware of the contents of the letter. For some reason they had chosen to keep the news a secret from him. Now he was truly furious.

'What was in the letter,' the lord began, speaking slowly and deliberately, 'that upset Mathúin so? What disaster has befallen the kingdom of Outremer?'

No-one answered. An uncomfortable silence followed until, at last, the cook spoke up again. 'I will have to get your cloak ready for you if you are riding out in this weather.' William dismissed the woman curtly with a nod.

'I'll fetch two soldiers to accompany you on the road,' offered the game-keeper as he made for the door. 'And you'll be wanting master Robert along, I don't doubt.'

Each of the others came up with some excuse to leave the hall until William was left standing alone by the fire. He sat back down in his seat, placing the cat upon his lap again as he awaited the return of his chamberlain.

'Can you tell me, Angus,' the lord quizzed his cat, 'what was in the letter?'

At that moment Lonan came back into the room and approached the fire, spreading his thin wiry hands out before the flames.

'Why will you not tell me what you know?' William demanded, eying his chief servant with suspicion.

'I have told you all that I can be sure of,' Lonan replied.

'There is no-one left to tell but me!' the lord shouted.

'Your horse will be waiting when you are dressed, lord,' the chamberlain reported, changing the subject. 'I have seen to it.'

'What was in the letter?' William repeated, his voice booming.

Lonan coughed uncomfortably. 'We have a saying,' he began. 'There is nothing so satisfying as the solution to a riddle. With respect, my lord, it is better that you find out from Mathúin yourself. All I know is that the news concerns the Holy Land. I have no knowledge of the contents of the letter, I promise you. I have only the gossip of the other servants to go by and I hold very little store in that.'

'Even the cat knows more about what happens on this estate than I do,' the lord stormed. As if to confirm this assertion, Angus gave a cry and rubbed his jaw against the old knight's hand.

William turned so that he was facing the chamberlain. Lonan managed a half-hearted smile, hoping that his master might calm down and reconsider this rash midnight journey. Instead William stood, handed the cat to his chamberlain in silence and then strode off to his private chambers to don his riding clothes.

Some miles away in a roundhouse set in the middle of a collection of other modest dwellings, old Mathúin, friend of Lord William, lay staring at the roofbeams of his home. His mouth was wide open. His blank eyes twitched at the sound of a bird settling somewhere high up in the thatch. His skin was a pallid waxy colour and the shuddery outpouring of breath from his lungs was irregular. He was semiconscious, unblinking and, to the casual observer, almost completely lifeless.

The hearth of this house, unlike the dwellings of the Normans, was set in the centre of the building and there was no chimney to guide the smoke up and out into the night. The single room was filled with the choking misty aroma of turf, for timber was too precious to burn. The thick smoke seeped out through the thatch so that from a distance the roof seemed to be engulfed in a thin layer of mystical steam.

A woman came to throw the covers over the old man but Mathúin came to life suddenly. He pushed the blanket away as quickly as she set it neatly about his shoulders. The woman pulled the covers up once again, ignoring his protests. This occasioned a grunt from her chieftain.

'Do not be so,' she chided, 'I am only trying to relieve your suffering a little.'

The greying woman put her hand on Mathúin's forehead. Then she brushed the few dishevelled strands of hair that grew at the back of his head around so that she could tie them into a knot.

'I know well enough how bald I am, woman,' Mathúin grumbled slowly. 'I don't need the likes of you reminding me of it.'

At any other time she might have laughed at this comment for the old man was prone to pointing out his own shortcomings. But now, with him looking so ill and with the light of life gone from his eyes, the words struck her as having an air of resignation about them.

'Get up off of that bed,' she chided. 'No brother of mine ever lay in bed when there was work to be done. You're not leaving this earth just yet. Not with all the debts you owe.'

'Go away,' Mathúin muttered, 'and let me be. I know well enough that debts incurred in this life are paid for in the next. Now keep silent and allow me pass on in peace.'

At that moment the door to the cottage opened and Donal strode over to the fire, throwing off his brown cloak as he knelt down beside his father. The hunter could see immediately that some terrible sickness had come suddenly upon the old man, changing him into an almost unrecognisable withered creature. Mathúin's sister withdrew a little to give the two men some privacy.

'What's happened to you, Father?' Donal asked urgently. 'Are you taken ill?'

'I've had a shock, that's all,' the reclining man replied. 'I'm just in need of some rest.'

'What sort of a shock?' the son pressed.

'The kind of a shock that brings down a weight on your chest like the whole world has ended,' Mathúin replied, mumbling. 'So great a shock that I cannot speak of it with you for I know that you would not understand. You could not know.'

'Lord William is on his way, I've heard,' Donal offered. 'One of your kinsmen sent for him. Where's Eilish?'

'Off at her father's house, the Gioll Martin of Clonough,' the old woman cut in tersely, betraying the fact that she was listening in after all. 'Your wife is helping with the birthing of Eileen's child up there, when she should be at home with the chieftain in his time of need.'

'Ah yes,' Donal recalled, ignoring his aunt's gentle scold. 'She will be back tomorrow or the day after, I guess.' He looked about the cottage and swiftly reckoned what yet needed to be done to properly welcome the lord into their house. 'Would you gather everyone to help with the preparations for the lord's arrival and have the men throw some timber on the fire?' he asked the old woman. 'The Normans are accustomed to burning wood in their homes. Braonin will be back shortly with a boar's head for boiling and the flesh of a sow for the roast. William is fond of a good feast.'

'Put me in the corner,' Mathúin whispered. 'I wish to sleep until the lord arrives. He must not see me looking so ill.'

Donal nodded and put his arms around his father's body to lift him. As he raised his father gently he was astonished to discover that the old man barely had any weight to him at all. He asked himself how Mathúin could have become so thin without anyone in his family noticing. The hunter also noted with concern that his father's skin was cold and clammy, even though he had been sitting close by the fire for most of the day.

When Donal had placed his ailing father among the straw at the far end of the room, he covered Mathúin with a blanket and a fur. The old man tersely threw them off again.

'I am afraid for you, Father,' Donal stammered. 'You are not yourself.'

'I am dying,' Mathúin stated simply, and hoarsely. 'I will be gone by daybreak and I have a task for you to complete once I am gone.'

'You're not going to die yet, Father,' Donal scoffed, unwilling to believe for a moment that the old man was at death's door. 'You've just got a chill, that's all. It's the time of year.'

'I have had a letter,' Mathúin explained, 'and it carried such news as I never dreamed I would hear.'

'What news, Father?'

The old man looked deeply into his son's eyes and sighed. 'I will speak of it to none but Lord William.'

'I don't understand,' Donal pleaded. 'What tidings could have brought such a sickness upon you?'

Mathúin took his son's hand and spoke slowly. 'I'm not long for this world. It is a chill in my heart that has struck me down. It is my spirit that is suffering,' he answered with genuine pain in his voice. 'And such a hurt cannot be healed save by the release of death.' The old man coughed a little and then went on before Donal had a chance to reply, 'The laying out of the chapel of Saint Mary Magdalene on the lord's estate is nearly finished, is it not?'

'I have not been there for a few weeks but I would guess that the foundations are near to completion,' Donal answered.

'Then this is what I ask of you,' the old man breathed. 'I wish to be buried under the floor of the chapel at Bally Raine and I want all the walls of the building decorated with scenes of the Holy Land, especially of Jerusalem. There is more than enough gold left from what I brought back with me. Lord William has it in his safekeeping.'

Mathúin coughed again, a dry rasping gag that rattled in his chest and made him sit up a little with the pain of it. Even so, Donal still could not accept that his father was dying. Mathúin was a strong man who did not usually succumb to sickness of any kind.

'One of the men FitzWilliam brought back with him is a mosaic worker, a master tiler from the city of Acre,' Mathúin continued after a while. 'My gold will pay for the necessary materials and keep him well fed and lodged while he sets about his task. William will approve of funds being given to the building of his chapel, I am sure, so there is no problem there. Mind that you watch the craftsman well. Do not let him squander his time. If you can keep a tight rein on the tiler, there will be enough gold left over for you and Eilish to make some repairs to this house and ensure that, even if the crops fail and the cattle die, the whole family will be provided for in the future.'

'I cannot believe that you are talking this way, Father,' Donal exclaimed under his breath so that none of the other kinfolk would hear. 'You who survived the rigours of the sea voyage to the Outremer and then battled the hordes of the Saracen armies.'

'I was not alone then,' the old man pointed out, 'but I soon enough will be and I would appreciate it if you would give me an assurance that the needs of my soul are going to be met just as the needs of my body have been.'

Donal nodded his assent with a blank, expressionless face. 'We'll talk about it tomorrow, Father. For now you should rest. Lord William will likely want to speak with you when he arrives, so close your eyes until then.'

'William will want to speak with me, no doubt. And I have sorry news for him. Would that I had none at all to give, or that the messenger had passed the letter on to him instead of me.'

Before his son could question him any further, Mathúin rolled over to face the wall. The old man gently closed his eyes and groaned. Then he drew his arm over his head so that it blocked out all the noise of the room and he would not be disturbed by the flickering light of the hearth fire.

Donal withdrew to sit by the fire but he did not take his eyes off his father for a second. For a long while the room was silent save for the old man's strained wheezing. Once or twice Mathúin's breathing seemed to cease altogether but each time, after a long pause, the old man's body heaved and drew in air once again.

Donal felt helpless without his wife. It was times like this when her strength and wisdom rallied those around her. The young O'Regan prayed that she would return soon and for a while even considered riding off to Clonough to fetch her. Eilish was renowned throughout the estates for her healing ways and her accurate reading of any illness. If she were here, Donal told himself, she would know what to do and what to say to brighten the old man up. But she could not be everywhere at once, he conceded, and decided it was best not to leave his father's side.

Some hours later, after most of Donal's kinfolk had left to return to their own houses for the night, Braonin returned with Conor, the wounded hunter. The men had with them the choicest cuts of the sow and the black boar's head wrapped in an old sack. Mathúin's sister took the meat and busied herself to prepare a fitting feast for their overlord, racing against time to make all ready before the knight arrived on their doorstep.

'A fitting thing it is,' she sang, laying the bloody head down on the board to be cleaned, 'for the lord to feast on one of his own boars.'

'Whether it belonged to William or the King of the Saracens himself,' Braonin declared, 'it all tastes the same. And best he not know where it came from,' he added.

As soon as Braonin had settled Conor and seen to the wrapping of his wounds, the fair-haired hunter came and sat beside Donal.

'How is the old man?' Braonin asked under his breath so as not to disturb Mathúin.

'He says that he is dying,' Donal answered with a little laugh but Braonin could see that his cousin was worried. He raised his eyebrows in surprise at the comment but did not ask any more questions. He was exhausted from the journey home and still reeling from his encounter with the boar. After a few more moments both men withdrew into their private silences and for a long while each was lost in his own troubled thoughts.

A light dry breeze that had crossed the desert of Outremer from the sea blew in through the window of the abbot's chamber high in the fortification known to the crusading knights as the Krak. The wind was almost imperceptible yet it spread a thin film of dust across the sandstone room and cooled the air noticeably.

A young man dressed in the white but unwashed clothing of a novice monk stood motionless at the great oak table in the middle of the room. Here he patiently waited for his master's return. The novice was grateful for the breeze. It brought meagre relief from the terrible heat that had soaked his body in sweat.

His black hair hung lank over his eyes and his head bowed slightly so that it looked as if he was praying silently as he waited. But he was not praying. He was struggling against sleep.

'I must stay alert,' he rebuked himself. 'I cannot let the old man catch me yawning. He will use any excuse to punish me.' The young man's words were full of contempt for the abbot, who was a fat, arrogant man renowned for his cruelty to the younger members of his community.

The stifling heat dragged the minutes into hours until the hours seemed to melt away. Even as the afternoon sun began to stream into the room through the fine latticework windows, the young man remained standing before the solid desk where the abbot usually received visitors.

The novice ran a thin bony hand through his hair, brushing the strands out of his eyes. He stretched his arms high in the air with a yawn and then squatted on his knees to relieve the nagging pain in his legs. A fly buzzed around his head and he watched it, too listless to swat the insect away. His thighs and calves were in agony from waiting in one spot for so long. His body longed for a little rest and perhaps some food. He had missed breakfast that morning and, unless the abbot returned shortly, would likely go without the evening meal as well.

The young man ventured to reach under his patched habit to rub at the aching joints of his legs, no longer caring if his master should catch him acting in such an unseemly manner. His black hair fell about his face once more as he bent over, and then he noticed that he was feeling slightly nauseous. He forced himself to stand again. As he did so the sweat rolled down his spine into the small of his back.

'Why did Godfrey send me to this hell on earth?' he whispered. 'Why did he not want me to be with him, defending the land against the Saracens? I am no use to the cause of the Cross stuck here far from any of the fighting.'

The oak desk stood within his reach so the young man steadied himself against it. Dizzy from exhaustion, his gaze fell on the abbot's chair and he found the attraction of its soft leather covering almost too great to refuse.

'Careful, Brother Geoffrey,' the novice told himself, 'you are giving in to temptation.'

He looked longingly at the chair with its supple inviting folds and cool surface. Then his resolve melted away completely.

'Forgive me, Lord,' he prayed earnestly, 'but the laws of the Cistercian order clearly state, rest not till thou feelest the desire.' He knew that he was probably misinterpreting the true meaning of the commandment, but his body would not be denied a reprieve from this torture.

Quietly he moved across the room to take a seat on the opulent throne which the abbot had brought to the Outremer with him from Venice. In this isolated fortress there were few luxuries, but this beautiful chair was certainly the chief one among them.

In the distance the young man could hear the constant heavy pounding of the Saracen siege engines hurling rocks at the defensive walls. But he was confident in the certain knowledge that no force on earth would ever bring down the ramparts of this castle.

'Why did my brother not send me to Acre where his knights are stabled?' Geoffrey asked himself. 'What use am I here, besieged and enslaved by a fat abbot? And why assign me to a house owned by the Knights of the Hospital? Godfrey is a Templar and I know there is little love lost between the two orders.'

Succumbing at last to drowsiness, he lay back in the chair, savouring the comfort. Then the rhythmic noise of the enemy's battering rams slowly lulled Geoffrey's senses. Not for the first time in all these months he noticed the low rumble which flowed through the entire fortification after each thundering hammer found its mark. He felt the pounding noise travel through every stone until it shook the meagre contents of his gut and unsettled the dust on the desk before him.

Still listening to the steady hammering, he closed his weary eyes. Within minutes he was beginning to move into a trancelike state that was halfway between sleep and waking. He did not want to be soothed into slumber but the heat, the exhaustion and lack of any food that day meant that his body was weakened. Finally the young novice curled his legs up on the throne, made himself as comfortable as possible and vowed that he would only rest for a few minutes at the very most. And then he promptly fell into a deep and troubled sleep.

It was one of those slumbers that was filled with vivid dreams. Geoffrey rarely took short rests in the afternoon heat of this land as was the local custom, even though the climate in the Outremer could strain the bodies and minds of men more used to colder weather. The abbot of this monastery frowned upon his monks taking any rest at all during the daylight hours for he sincerely believed that such respite encouraged indolence. For that reason, new brothers were sent out into the scorching sun to tend the vegetable gardens, mend the monastery fences or even to minister to the pilgrims.

There were, however, not many pilgrims these days. The flocks of travellers who had once made their way to Jerusalem and the other holy places had disappeared like desert dust scattered in a sandstorm. There were only soldiers and monks now at the Krak and most of them were Knights of the Order of Saint John of the Hospital.

The men of this order were known as Hospitallers because their brotherhood had once been purely devoted to healing the wounded and sick. It was only after the establishment of other military orders that they evolved into a fighting force. There were still physicians among them but only a few. Most Hospitallers were warriors who dressed themselves in black armour and clothing.

The young man shifted on the leather and saw in his mind the siege taking place all around him outside the walls of the mighty Krak. After six months of constant battling it was difficult to escape the conflict even in one's dreams. The earthworks all around the castle seemed constantly to be crawling with hundreds of Saracens. Geoffrey saw himself looking down at the enemy from the battlements. The thought crossed his dreaming mind that they looked rather like ants swarming around the entrance to their nest.

Abruptly his reverie took on an aspect that was unfamiliar to him, and even in sleep the sudden change brought a frown to his youthful face. Inexplicably the noise of the battle ceased completely for the first time in half a year. A troop of knights wearing flowing beards and dressed in long white tunics rode through the enemy lines unscathed. The Saracens retreated before them, falling to their knees as this gallant shining company rode past.

Up to the gates of the castle the band of warriors came to demand entry from the fortress commander. The gatekeeper obeyed their orders without hesitation, throwing the defences open to them so that the white knights could pass by unhindered.

This marvellous troop then rode triumphantly into the castle with their black and white banners waving. Every Christian knight within the battlements raised a chorus of adulation in their honour.

Borne on a cart behind the knights the young man could see a great box covered in a pure white cloth that shone in the sun like silver. The warriors entered the monastery gate and formed lines, as their whole company assembled. Once every man was within the courtyard, the knights gathered around the cart to unpack their treasure.

The novice looked with wonder on this object as it was unloaded, asking himself what it could possibly be. Geoffrey suspected that anything that could fill the infidels with so much fear that they retreated completely from the siege must be a gift from God himself.

'It is the Ark,' a voice informed him and in his dream the young man turned to see a beautiful woman, dressed in the poor clothing of the local people, standing close beside him. A blue veil fell around her face in the afternoon breeze. Geoffrey thought for a second that she was very much like the statues he had seen in Venice of the Mother of God, the Virgin Mary. Her face shone like the cloth of silver which covered the loaded wagon.

'The Ark of the Covenant,' she went on, 'that was given to my people in the ancient days. Now, Geoffrey, your folk have it and mine will suffer for the loss and mourn it bitterly forever.'

The beautiful woman turned to the novice now and smiled warmly. Geoffrey returned the gesture, filled with an inexplicable joy. Then the woman spoke again, but now her voice was much more serene, full of the wisdom of age.

'You will be the guardian of all the treasures, my son,' she informed him. 'Especially the Holy Cup of Life. The black ones are seeking for it even now. Keep the few remaining treasures from the hands of the enemy at all costs.'

'What enemy?' he asked. 'The Saracens?'

The woman laughed. 'No, my son, not the Saracens. They are not the enemy. The evil ones are the enemy. You must keep it safe from the servants of darkness. You must not fail for everything depends on you. The world will fall into a thousand years of war if the black knights should gain possession of these sacred objects.'

'What knights?' he begged her. 'Do you mean the Hospitallers? Who is it I must guard against?'

'You will know when the time comes, my son. You will know.'

'I am not a knight or a soldier,' he protested. 'What can I do?'

'When the time comes,' she repeated. 'For now you must tell me the deepest wish that is in your heart.'

'To be free of the Krak and the rule of the Father Abbot,' the novice replied without needing to consider his answer.

'Then you shall have your wish,' she replied. 'Farewell.'

Before the young man could ask the woman who she was, she had turned and walked briskly down the battlements. She paused for a moment before the door of a tower which was topped with a bright red rose carved from stone. Geoffrey wanted to call out to her to ask her what she meant but, as is the way with dreams, his tongue would not do his bidding.

The woman disappeared into the tower, the door slammed shut and the light that had illuminated the air all about her was abruptly snuffed out. The novice looked over the wall again, hoping to get another glimpse of the legendary ark.

In that instant a hand clasped down heavily on his shoulder and he heard his name being called.

'Geoffrey!' the gruff and ugly voice shouted. 'Geoffrey d'Acre!'

The young man moved in his sleep, suddenly uncomfortable.

'If you do not stand up immediately,' the man bellowed, 'I will have you flogged for your insolence!'

The novice opened his eyes in alarm, immediately wide awake. At first he did not discern the presence of anyone else in the abbot's chamber, but as his sight focused a shape took form before his eyes which almost stopped his heart with fright. It was the form of a large overweight man with a greying shock of hair which grew long at the sides to cover a pair of ears that stuck out at a strange angle.

'Lord Abbot!' Geoffrey stuttered, falling out of the chair and sprawling across the floor. 'I did not hear you come in.'

'Stand up!' the older monk screeched, his face reddening. 'How dare you be seated in my presence . . . in my chair!'

'I am sorry, Lord Abbot. I had been waiting all day and—'

'Be still,' the abbot snapped. 'You will do penance for this,' he promised, 'but first you will go and attend to the knights who have arrived at the gate. The siege is lifted and tonight we will thank God for his protection.'

The young novice could not believe his ears. It was as if his dream had been unfolding in reality all along or as if he had somehow drifted beyond the confines of his body to witness events as they happened.

'Forgive me, lord,' Geoffrey ventured, 'but have the white knights brought the Ark of the Covenant with them?'

The abbot's jaw dropped in astonishment. 'You foolish boy,' came the reply. 'Have you lost your wits? Where did you hear such a fanciful tale? Have you been listening to the troubadours again? On second thoughts, go to the kitchens at once. I cannot risk you giving offence to our guests. They are here to aid us in our need and I don't want to feed the old animosity between the Hospitallers and the Templars.'

The young novice bowed dutifully. He was about to retreat from the chamber when he remembered why he had come there in the first place.

'Lord Abbot,' he muttered, genuinely frightened at the response he was likely to receive.

'What is it now?' the elder monk screeched, his voice cracking.

'You summoned me here,' Geoffrey went on, 'but you have not told me why.'

The abbot grunted, remembering that he had indeed sent for Geoffrey. The old man lowered himself down into his chair, picked up one of the papers scattered about his desk and read it to himself quickly. Then he reported the contents with callous disinterest. 'Your brother was killed two months ago at the siege of Acre. I have received a letter confirming that he had no heir. You are to return to that city. You will take over his household and duties as soon as possible.'

Geoffrey coughed loudly in shock, and his hand instinctively found, tucked into his robe, the last letter he had received from his brother.

'My brother is dead?' the lad repeated but was given no response. 'I hardly knew him,' he added, half to himself, realising that the news had not really touched him. Then another thought crossed his mind.

'I could not possibly undertake to run my brother's household . . .' Geoffrey began but the abbot cut him off before he could say another word.

'It is clear to me that you are not suitable for the duties and observances of this order. You don't have the stuff that makes a good brother in Christ,' the older monk announced. 'Go to your kinfolk and settle this matter. If you are still determined to take your vows as a monk, then I suggest that you travel to Tyre where there is a fine Cistercian house. If you should wish to follow in your brother's footsteps, you might be admitted into the Templar order. But the Hospital of Saint John has no place for you.'

'Would the Knights of the Temple take one such as me?' the novice blurted.

'If they take the lowest scum from the streets of Paris, Marseilles and Lyon,' the abbot replied, 'I do not see why they would refuse you. At least you wash regularly and have no immediately discernible perversions about you.'

'Are those Templar knights going to Acre?' the novice ventured.

'They are.'

'Will you send me with them?'

'Gladly, but for the fact that they are engaged in clandestine work for King Baldwin,' the abbot informed him.

'It will be a month or two at least before you will be able to travel on. I will send you with the next caravan.'

The abbot put a hand inside his cloak and felt the weight of a small bag of gold which hung at his waist. The old monk did not care why the Templar knights would pay so handsomely for such a troublemaker. Overjoyed to be rid of the lad and to have his purse weighted down, the abbot could hardly restrain himself from smiling.

'I will even go so far as to find an errand for you to perform for me in that city,' the abbot added as an afterthought, 'as an excuse for the Templars to escort you there. Now go to the kitchens and help the cooks with their tasks before I change my mind and have you flogged for wasting my precious time.'

Geoffrey spun around in excitement, making for the door and slamming it loudly behind him, much to the abbot's annoyance. The young novice did not know it then, but far from being released from an existence of endless boredom and punishment, his whole life was about to take a most disturbing turn.

When Neesh awoke it was very dark and she was a little confused. There was no moon in the sky and the shadows of the surrounding trees engulfed the whole area of the chapel in utter darkness.

She had not intended to fall asleep when she sat down on the steps of the chapel but she had been totally exhausted from her ordeal. Though she was aware of the danger she had put herself in succumbing to slumber. Now cold and hungry, the only thought on her mind was to make her way quickly home to the safety of the Gioll Martin of Clonough.

She got to her feet, mindful of just how dangerous it was to be abroad at night. Even if the Norman had given up searching for her, there were still the demons of the other world to contend with. She knew too well from the stories of her childhood that faeries and other spirits haunted hills. Deserted chapels such as this one were their favourite domains.

At that Neesh caught a whiff of something on the breeze. At first she thought it was the aroma of broth simmering gently on a fire. Then she was certain she smelled wood-smoke. She shook her head when she realised how hungry she was and told herself not to imagine such things.

'What was I thinking,' she rebuked herself, 'to imagine I would escape harm by hiding in this place?'

The wind picked up then and as it moved through the branches of the trees every leaf shook. All the boughs creaked, groaned and sighed as they bent to the breeze. Neesh felt her spine freeze in dread at the sound. It struck her as disturbingly similar to a chorus of monks chanting their evening office.

She rubbed her legs to warm her flesh and get her blood moving, but as she did so she caught sight of something out of the corner of her eye. A shadow moved swiftly along the ground behind the trees. The girl had only glimpsed the movement, which startled her all the more.

Not waiting for her fears to be confirmed, Neesh pulled the hem of her dress up, ready to run. But just as she was about to flee, a man dressed in dark flowing robes appeared from among the tree trunks as if he had stepped from out of the air itself.

'Faerie,' Neesh whispered in terror, certain that she was in deadly danger now.

Frozen with fear, convinced that she was destined to be a captive of some faerie king, Neesh took a step backwards and stumbled on the steps of the chapel. This took her by surprise and she began to feel faint. Frightened, she fought off the sensation and suddenly her fear was replaced by a determination to stand as tall as she could in defiance of any threat.

'You will not have me,' she whispered to herself. 'You will not be the first I have fought off today.'

The figure did not move, nor did it make any sign that it meant her any harm. Feeling slightly more confident, Neesh took a step forward, trying to see the stranger's face, but it was hidden by the shadows.

The head turned slowly under the hood. Neesh got the impression that the stranger was making sure she was alone. After a few moments the figure confidently sauntered into the centre of the path that led to the chapel, blocking her only means of escape.

'Who are you?' Neesh blurted. 'What are you doing here?'

'I might ask you the same question,' a deep male voice replied.

Neesh heaved a huge sigh of relief. This was no faerie. And he spoke her own language without an accent, so he was not a Norman soldier either.

'What is your business at the chapel of Saint Finnian?' the stranger demanded. 'Have you come to offer prayers in the manner of the Culdees?'

'There are no Culdees in this part of the country,' Neesh replied. 'The Normans drove all those heretics away.'

'Are you a friend of the Normans,' the man hissed in the next breath, 'that you call the Culdees heretics?'

'I am no friend to any of those heathen bastards!' Neesh exclaimed. Then she bit her tongue, suddenly unsure whether she should reveal too much about herself to this stranger. 'One of their soldiers threatened me at the well,' she went on carefully. 'I decided this would be a good place to hide from him until dark. Now it is time I made my way home.'

'He threatened you?' the stranger inquired, gesturing for her to wait a few moments.

'I think he would have robbed me if he had been able to hold me still,' Neesh added, taking a couple of steps forward to indicate that she wished to leave.

'What would an unwashed girl like you have that was worth stealing?' the stranger laughed.

Neesh frowned. 'He tried to force his will upon me,' she hissed, indignant at being referred to as unwashed. Now she was sure she did not wish to waste any time explaining what had happened.

The man stepped forward slowly and deliberately, approaching the girl as he might a horse that had slipped its bridle and run off.

'How did you manage to escape this Norman?' the man asked as he got closer to her.

'He slipped his footing at the entrance to the well and I pushed him in.'

'Do you know this man?' the stranger pressed, standing still again.

'He claimed to be the son of Lord William,' Neesh admitted, 'but I have never seen him before.'

The stranger whistled through his teeth. 'Congratulations, my dear. A fine enemy to make indeed. But you should understand that if this fellow truly is the son of a Norman lord, then your life will likely be in great danger. Since you are no friend of the Normans, you will be a friend of the Culdees.'

The man in the cloak was now only a few paces away from Neesh. She could clearly see that his hair was dark and unkempt. His beard was long, his eyes deep set and mysterious. Tattered clothes hung from his body. They were dirty and too large for his short, wiry frame.

As she looked closely at his features the man suddenly produced a large iron key from a fold in his robes. 'You are welcome to spend the night inside the chapel with my wife and myself. The Normans will not think to look for you here.'

In the next instant he pushed past her and put the key firmly into the lock hole. 'My name is Cinneach. I belong to the community of the Culdees. I am a priest and a seanachie,' he explained. As he spoke the chapel door swung open and a small woman with long red hair came out bearing a lighted candle.

'Where have you been?' she asked the man in a scolding tone. 'I was beginning to get worried for you.'

'I cannot speak to you of that now,' he replied tersely, hushing the woman's questions as he hugged her close. 'We have a guest who shares our distaste for the invaders.' Cinneach ushered the girl past him toward his wife. 'This is Fidach, my wife,' the man explained.

'I am called Neesh,' the girl answered politely.

'Bless you, child,' Fidach said. 'You will be safe here with us. Now come inside before this light attracts every Norman sentry from here to the Isles of the Blest.'

As the heavy door swung shut behind them Neesh looked in wonder at the interior of the tiny church gently illumined by a small fire. There were no windows at all, just thick stone walls grey and moss covered. She noticed, to her surprise, that the massive stone altar was placed in the centre of the building. Neesh had never seen a church laid out in such a fashion.

The walls were covered in tapestries embroidered in rich colours of deep blue and dark red. The finest details were worked with fine gold thread that sparkled in the firelight. Neesh wondered quietly that the Normans had not plundered this finery for themselves.

At the far end of the chapel there was a fireplace and on the little fire was a pot of broth. Neesh recalled that she had caught the sweet scent of food on the breeze earlier and she remembered how hungry she was. Without hesitation she went straight towards the cooking hearth. She sat down near the pot in the hope that she would be offered some of the food.

'We have not much to share with you, child,' Fidach explained, reading well what was on the girl's mind, 'but you are welcome to partake of what little there is.'

'I must go now,' Cinneach stated, embracing his wife again. 'I only came by to make sure all was well. Neesh, you will be safe here with my wife. I will return before the dawn. Remember, only dry wood on the fire so there is very little smoke. It would not be well to draw too much attention to our little chapel.'

'Where are you going?' Neesh cut in, worried that it might be more dangerous for her to remain here than to head for Clonough.

'It is better that you don't ask too many questions,' Fidach cut in. 'Cinneach has work to do tonight.'

'If you know too much about us, your life could well be in danger,' Cinneach explained. 'The Normans would surely torture you if they suspected you were involved with us. So you must forgive us for this breach of hospitality in keeping secrets from you, but it is absolutely necessary.'

With that he disappeared through the door into the night. Neesh heard the huge key turn as Fidach handed her a small bowl of broth.

After she had eaten, Neesh curled up beside the fire, unwilling to talk too much about all that had happened to her today. Fidach propped herself against the wall, listening intently to the sounds of the night.

'I thought there were no more Culdees in Ireland,' Neesh said, hoping the woman would tell her something about herself and her husband.

'Well, we have proved you wrong,' Fidach answered sharply. Then she softened her tone, realising that the girl was simply making conversation. 'There are many of our folk still in the western lands. And in Alba, the land of the Scots. The King of Scotland is one of our strongest supporters.'

'I have never known any of your people,' Neesh went on. 'I have only heard stories of how the Normans drove the Culdees out of Ireland.'

'You heard that tale from a Norman, no doubt,' the other woman laughed. 'There are still more of our people than there are followers of the Catholic faith. You live on a Norman estate, run by a lord who is a zealous follower of the Pope. I am not surprised that you have not met any of our kind. Lord William and his kind murdered our people in the hundreds.'

'Why do the Normans hate your folk so much?'

'Because our ways are older than those of the priests and abbots,' Fidach explained. 'The Culdee traditions can be traced back to the earliest Christians in Ireland. And also because we keep the most ancient doctrines as sacred. Customs that originated in the times before Christ.'

'Father Lucius says that the Culdees are evil pagans,' Neesh recalled, speaking her thoughts aloud. 'He says that they perform lewd rites of fertility and worship the spirits of wells. He reckons that the Culdees pray to the old gods and bestow gifts on stone heads that the devil has carved for them.'

'Father Lucius sounds like a learned gentleman,' Fidach smiled, barely able to contain her mirth, 'who would probably not recognise his own arse if he sat on it.'

Neesh blushed, unused to such language.

'We have a reverence for the land,' Fidach went on. 'We do not pray to any old gods. What is the use of begging any god for intervention? We each make our own destiny. If anyone is ever going to map out our lives for us, it will not be some god with a grey beard sitting in heaven.'

Fidach tucked her elbows into her sides and opened her palms to the ceiling. 'This is one of our prayers,' she explained. 'Our Father who rules in heaven. Our Mother who rules the earth.'

Neesh gasped, recognising the prayer but disturbed that it mentioned a mother. The girl cast her gaze around the chapel and realised that there was not a cross or statue to be seen. 'Are you not frightened of the Normans?' she asked.

'Frightened?' Fidach replied. 'The only fear my husband and I have is that with our deaths the truth of what we know will be forgotten. If the Normans capture us, they will not waste time torturing us. We will be quickly hanged and forgotten. I do not fear death because I do not believe there is any such thing.'

'If there is no death,' Neesh exclaimed, 'what becomes of the soul after it passes away?'

'The soul takes on another form,' the other woman explained. 'When a soul has had enough of this life, it may take the form of another human and be born into a new body. In this way we accumulate knowledge and wisdom through many lifetimes.'

'How is it that you know so much about theology?' Neesh asked, clearly impressed.

'My husband is a priest,' Fidach answered as if that were obvious. 'And I am studying for the priesthood myself.'

'You are a woman!'

'There has always been a tradition in the Culdee faith of women becoming the leaders of their community. That is one reason why the Normans would like to eradicate us. To the Normans, women have only one use and that is to provide them with sons. They do not want their own women to get the idea that they would be able to rule as equals to the menfolk.'

'I have never heard anyone speak so,' Neesh admitted, unsure what to think of this woman.

'There was a time,' Fidach told her, 'when this little chapel heard the words of the old gospels every day of the week. This building was here five generations before the Norman invasion.'

Neesh finished her bowl of broth and placed it down by the fire again. Despite wanting to hear more of Fidach's tales, she found that she was very sleepy again. She lay her head down while the other woman told the story of Saint Maelruan who was one of the founding members of the Culdee Church. Neesh drifted off during the tale of Maelruan's magic staff.

In her half-conscious state she heard Fidach chanting a prayer and then she woke with a start. The other woman was shaking Neesh lightly. The girl opened her eyes to see the fire had died down. It was still dark but Fidach beckoned her to the unlocked door and wished her a safe journey home.

'My husband was here a short while ago,' Fidach explained. 'The Normans are not looking for you tonight. They have other things on their minds. Go quickly home and do not tell anyone about us,' the Culdee woman warned. 'If you keep our secret, you will be welcome to stay here whenever you wish.'

Neesh thanked the woman and assured her she would not say anything about the chapel to anyone. Then, still sleepy eyed, the girl headed off over the fields in the dark, making for Clonough. It was not yet day when Neesh glimpsed the houses of Gioll Martin. She checked the road for horsemen. Sure that the road was quiet, she crossed it quickly and headed towards her family's house.

Chapter Four

William FitzWilliam rode off into the light rain, followed by two men-at-arms and accompanied by his eldest son, Robert. They had been riding for about an hour and a half when a fifth rider mounted on a black steed sprang out from the bushes to join the party. The two guards raised their lanterns high in the night air. But neither the lord nor his eldest son so much as lifted an eyelid at the appearance of this horseman. It was as if they half expected him to appear unannounced from out of the fields. Undistracted, the party pressed on to the south-west. As soon as he noticed the unidentified rider, William gave his horse a taste of the spurs, determined to make it to Mathúin's bedside before the old man passed away.

Half a mile before the settlement, the road deteriorated into a mud-soaked mire which the local people called the bohreen. This word literally meant a cow path, but it was more than a track down which the cows were led each day to pasture. This path was a churned mixture of cattle dung, urine and softened soil and it smelled of the sweetness of the earth.

So slippery was the surface of this track that William and his men were forced to rein in and dismount for fear of injury to their precious warhorses. They were leading their animals across this patch of muddy ground when the rider who had joined them on the road walked his horse briskly up to stride proudly alongside Lord William.

With a cough the man announced his presence and threw his short riding cloak back over his shoulder. Then he pulled off the skull cap which he usually wore when he had no need of a helm. Even in the dark of night his red hair shone as bright as polished copper. His features echoed those of the lord. It was obvious that they were father and son.

'Where have you been?' William demanded without taking his gaze off the road. He did not offer any other greeting to the rider whose horse trotted along beside his.

'I was out along the forest edge scouting for poachers, Father,' the other man replied, noticing that his father's beard seemed to have grown much greyer in the last few weeks.

The lord stopped in his tracks and turned his head slowly to look at his son from head to foot. 'Your clothes are soaking wet, my lad, and there is blood on your collar from a wound. I'll wager it was you doing the poaching and the young women of the estate were your quarry,' William snarled. 'Why were you not in attendance at my side this morning when the peasants from Shelton brought in their taxes?'

'Robert was with you,' the man pointed out. 'I did not think you would be needing my services.'

'I am obviously not the only person on this estate who does not require your services,' William remarked, referring to his son's dishevelled state. 'What did she do? Did she pick you up and dunk you in the River Clonough, my boy?'

The lord managed to laugh half-heartedly, but then his tone turned darkly serious again. 'When I am gone, Robert will need your assistance with the running of this landhold. The peasants must be used to seeing you as holding authority and responsibility on the estate. Without some effort on your part they will never learn to respect you. If they do not respect you, they will try to cheat you. It is about time that you curbed your insatiable appetite for peasant girls, don't you think?'

'I do not care what the common folk think of me,' the young man with the red hair blurted. 'If any of them ever tried to cheat me, I would punish them. I would hang a few of them. The Gaels respect a heavy hand. After a few untimely deaths the peasants would be compliant enough.'

'Hang them?' William exclaimed bitterly, not caring if the common soldiers heard his rebuke. 'You may wear the mail-coat of a knight, but you are nothing more than a foolish lad who abuses those he should be protecting. Who will bring in the harvest if you start hanging the peasants for every misdemeanour they commit? Who will rush to defend the estate if it is ever attacked by one of the lords from the north? Not men and women who have been brutalised and starved by an impulsive petty tyrant, a man who regularly rapes their daughters. They will shun you and leave you to your fate. Then they will thank God that disaster has come upon you. Or one night you may be woken by a crowd of noisy tenants gathered together with a hanging of their own in mind.'

'They would not dare!' the young man spat. 'The soldiers would butcher the bloody lot of them.'

William's eldest son Robert handed the reins of his horse to one of the men-at-arms and walked toward a stand of trees to relieve himself. He could not bear to be near these two when they fell to arguing, which they did all the time.

'If the warriors cared enough about their lord, they might come to his rescue,' laughed William, but the smile fell away from his face as quickly as it had formed. 'I wish I had not lived to say this to you, Rufus, but the fact is you are a lazy, talentless drunkard. Your tastes are self-indulgent and more expensive than I am willing to tolerate.'

'How dare you berate me in front of my brother and men of the common soldiery!' Rufus spat back under his breath. 'Is it not bad enough that you give me nothing useful to do on the estates? Are you not content that I have to sit with the servants below the salt cellar at table while my halfwit brother has your right hand? The warriors mock me behind my back and say that you treat me like the bastard you never had! Now you openly sneer at me without thought for my reputation.'

'Silence!' his father ordered. 'You have said enough. From now on you will be perfectly quiet in my presence. You will speak only when and if you are addressed. You will do my bidding without complaint or you will be sent to Normandy to earn your spurs in battle as I and my father and grandfather did before you. If I thought for a moment that you had any hope of one day becoming a competent warrior, I would send you off to the Holy Land. But your skills with sword and lance are so deplorable that even the cowherds boast they could knock you off your horse with a blackthorn stick.'

'That is not true!' Rufus exclaimed, his grey-green eyes flashing.

'I told you to be quiet!' William barked, and his flashing eyes mirrored those of his son. 'I have watched you at the jousting lists. You haven't the will to ride against anyone these days. You conveniently disappear whenever there is a tourney to be fought. I could understand it if it was just a matter of you preferring the company of women to that of your fellow knights. But I know that there is not one woman on this estate who would willingly go to your bed. Take my advice, beware of your desire for the female sex, my boy. They will sap your strength and distract you from the more important things in life.'

'What more important things?'

'Honour, duty and the love of God,' the lord explained

impatiently as he glanced toward the little hamlet of Cúil Ghréine. 'Service to Christ is a higher love than the love one might feel for any mere woman. That is why I travelled to the kingdom of Outremer and gave my body in service to the Order of the Knights of the Temple. In guarding the Temple Mount, the Church of the Holy Sepulchre and the lives of the pilgrims who travelled there, I surrendered myself to the will of God. There is no greater purpose in life than this. There is no greater joy to be had than to wear the cross in the service of Christ.' William dropped his eyes to the ground and breathed hard, trying to calm his temper. He sighed loudly, wishing his youngest son had proven worthy of the FitzWilliam name. He was about to speak again when he noticed that Robert had disappeared and was now out of earshot.

Robert was as different from Rufus as it was possible to be. His hair was black like coal and his eyes were dark brown. He was tall, broad shouldered and distinctly comfortable in the garb of a warrior. Rufus, on the other hand, shared his father's red hair but he did not share the old man's passion for all things military and religious.

It was clear to William that Robert would never be a great warrior. At least, he consoled himself, his heir was proficient with lance and sword. Seeing his eldest son returning to the party the lord sighed, 'If only you were more like your brother.' Then he tugged at the reins to lead his horse on.

Rufus felt his stomach turn with disgust and would have protested had his father given him the chance.

'We are about to come into the house of a loyal and trusted servant,' William declared, raising his voice for the others to hear. 'He was my sergeant-at-arms and he still holds that rank by virtue of his deeds in battle. Besides that, he is one of my greatest friends. He will be treated with the respect due to him.' The lord emphasised this last point, making no attempt to disguise the fact that his words were directed specifically at Rufus.

The two men-at-arms saw to the horses as William and his sons came to the door of the little dwelling where Mathúin and his kinfolk lived. The inhabitants of the hamlet of Cúil Ghréine were not wealthy when judged by Norman standards, but their ancestors had been the traditional chieftains of all the people in the valley long before the coming of William and his knights. For this reason they held a position of high respect among the lord's subjects. Mathúin was particularly revered as a wise and experienced leader in the community and was addressed by his kinfolk as they would a great chieftain.

The three Normans did not have to stand long at the door of the dwelling before it swung open. Donal stepped out into the night to greet them.

'Welcome to our home, FitzWilliam,' Mathúin's son declared, 'and welcome to your offspring. You do us great honour by this visit.'

'As you do to me with such a courteous welcoming,' Lord William replied. 'I have come because I have been told of the illness of Mathúin O'Regan, my honoured companion in the wars against the infidel. How is he faring?'

Donal stepped up close to the Norman so that only he and his two sons would hear what was said. 'He says that he is dying, my lord,' he replied simply.

'How can this be?' William asked under his breath. 'I spoke with him less than a week ago and he was in fine spirits. I thought at the time he'd outlive us all!'

'There was a letter, my lord,' Donal explained and William noticed the concern in the young man's eyes. 'I have not seen the parchment, but my kinfolk say that when he received the message he fainted, clutching at his breast in agony.'

'You have no idea what news was contained in this letter?' William inquired.

'My father will tell no-one, not even me. And he will not let the parchment out of his grasp.'

'Let us go and speak to Mathúin, then,' William sighed. 'Perhaps I will be able to learn what is ailing him. Lead on, Donal.'

The younger O'Regan ushered them inside, William first, followed by Robert and then a sullen Rufus. The fire was burning fiercely in the central hearth and around it were cuts of the boar roasting on skewers. There were also pots filled with bubbling broths and infusing herbs.

Rufus smelled the food and realised that he was very hungry. The aroma of cooking meats was so overpowering that he felt weakened with every breath. Without a word to his host he strode over to the fire and began inspecting the feast, eager to begin his meal.

In the corner, against the wall, lay a dark shape dressed in a long brown surcoat and surrounded by discarded blankets and skins. William pointed silently to the form. Donal nodded to confirm that this was indeed his father. The lord coughed loudly to get the old sergeant's attention. When this did not elicit any response, William finally spoke.

'Fine it is,' he said, formally complimenting the household, 'to come into a warm dwelling on a cold night and to find such an abundance of foods in preparation. Truly this does your name honour, Donal O'Regan, and it honours the hospitality of your father also.'

Mathúin recognised the voice immediately and rolled over on the straw, clearly startled that his master had appeared in his house and that he had not been at the door to greet him. Years of military habit had the old man struggling to his feet to pay his respects, but William quickly crossed the floor to stop Mathúin from rising.

'Stay where you are, my friend,' William urged. 'Take

your ease. You have paid me enough honour for one lifetime. You do not need to further prove your worth to me.'

Mathúin's face reflected his obvious gratitude and he sat back down on the bedding with William's help. The lord grabbed a blanket and threw it about the old man's shoulders. 'Have you eaten?' the lord asked and Mathúin shook his head.

'Then you must. I still have a great need of your help and I will not release you from your duties willingly.' With that William turned around on his knees and looked over toward the cooking hearth to see how the preparations were going.

The sight that met his eyes, however, was unexpected and infuriating. While he had been seeing to the comfort of Mathúin, Rufus had helped himself to a bowl of broth from the largest cauldron at the fireside. He was at that moment dipping his bread into the bowl to clean out the remnants of his first helping. That done he reached for the ladle to fill his bowl again.

Braonin was hovering around the lord's son, unsure of what to say and obviously very put out by this affront to the hospitality of the house. William could see clearly that Donal had decided to ignore the breach of politeness, but Braonin, his friend and cousin, was becoming more and more agitated.

'Is the boar's head to your liking, Master Rufus?' Braonin inquired coldly, unable to restrain himself from comment.

'Well seasoned,' the Norman answered as he held the bowl to his lips and gulped down another mouthful of the broth. When he had drained the contents, everyone relaxed a little in the hope that the insult would not be carried any further. But Rufus was still hungry. Straightaway he took the iron ladle and spooned out yet another generous serving for himself as his father watched on, incredulous and deeply humiliated.

'I faced that animal down myself,' Braonin stated, 'and Donal here dispatched it with a single thrust of his boar spear.'

Rufus murmured approval through a mouthful of food, raised his eyebrows but did not look up. Then a thought suddenly crossed his mind and he swallowed the contents of his mouth so that he could speak. 'It was not caught on my father's land, I trust,' Rufus sneered in as threatening a tone as he could muster.

'That boar nearly killed me,' Braonin went on but the Norman did not acknowledge the comment. 'And when we found its nest we discovered the dismembered half-eaten bodies of several small children inside.'

Rufus stopped chewing. His eyes widened and he spat the contents of his mouth into the fire in horror. He was still gagging when both Donal and Braonin broke out into subdued fits of laughter at the joke. Even William had to struggle not to smile. When Rufus realised that they were having a joke at his expense, his face turned bright red with a rage that he only just managed to control.

'How dare you mock me?' he hissed. 'Bloody thieving poachers!'

'You will be silent!' William demanded angrily. 'You have caused offence to our hosts. You have brought shame to me and I will deal with you later.' Then the lord turned to Donal. 'Where is your wife?'

'Eilish is attending her sister, Eileen, who has reached her term and is ready for birthing,' Donal answered.

'One more O'Regan to deal with,' William smiled, shaking his head. 'Where does the sister live?'

'At the ford of Clonough.'

'Very well,' the lord nodded and then turned to Rufus again. 'As recompense for your rudeness you will ride to Clonough with a spare horse and, if Eileen is well and can be left in the care of her own womenfolk, you will bring

Eilish back here. I believe that she may be able to comfort Mathúin if all I have heard about her skill is true.'

Rufus did not answer. He looked around the room from man to man and then twisted his mouth in a futile gesture of defiance. But he did not move.

'You will leave immediately!' William restated and for a moment it seemed as if he was talking to one of his lower ranking soldiers rather than to his own son. 'If you have not returned here by sunrise, I will be even more disappointed with you than I am at present. And I think you know what it means to incur my displeasure.'

'My horse needs rest,' Rufus replied. 'I have been riding all day long. If I push the animal any more it will drop dead under me.'

'If that happens,' the lord said sternly, 'you will have to walk. But walk briskly, one of my loyal servants is relying on you for his comfort.'

'But Father—' Rufus began.

'Go outside, swing your lazy arse into the saddle and do as your lord and father bids you!' William barked, finally losing his temper. 'Or, by heaven, you will be aboard the next ship that sails for Jerusalem and the captain will have orders to set you ashore in the lands of the Saracens.'

Mathúin groaned loudly and clutched his chest when William mentioned Jerusalem. Suddenly he was up, half sitting, desperately trying to speak. The lord turned his attention away from his son, immediately throwing an arm about his old friend's shoulders to support him.

'Get him some water,' the lord pleaded. 'He is having another seizure.'

Mathúin was convulsing in pain by the time the cup was brought to him, but after a few sips of water he seemed to settle again. Finally, after many long minutes, the old sergeant reached up to touch his lord's hand and tried again to speak.

'Rest yourself,' William soothed. 'It is no use to try and talk. You are only draining your strength.'

'The letter,' Mathúin gasped. 'Read the letter.' And with that he reached into his surcoat and produced a stained and folded piece of parchment with a red seal and ribbon of black silk attached to it. Everyone in the room knew that black silk was the universal sign of mourning. Used in this manner it signified the untimely death of a person of great importance.

'How did this come to you?' the lord asked.

'My brother, Braonin's father,' Mathúin replied, 'is in the service of Reynard d'Harcourt in Acre. He wrote this letter and it came by the hand of one of our kinsmen.'

With shaking fingers William took the parchment from his friend and thoughtfully turned the letter over in his hand. The seal was broken but the lord instantly recognised the design as that of the Master of the Knights Templar in the Holy Land. William stood up and went to the fire where there was better light to read by. Full of apprehension he unbound the black silk and slowly unfolded the dry document until he could see all that was written there.

The room was perfectly silent as the lord read the letter to himself. It seemed a long while before William closed his eyes and let his hand drop to his side, still clutching the dispatch.

'What does it say, Father?' Robert asked gently. 'Is it some famous knight who has been killed in battle?'

William slowly lifted his eyes to meet those of his eldest son. 'It is not a person who has died,' the lord began, his voice cracking with emotion. 'It is a dream that has passed away. A dream that many of us sought to preserve and thought would last until Judgment Day.'

'What do you mean?' Robert stuttered, confused by his father's answer.

'Jerusalem has fallen to the infidel Saracens. The Church

of the Holy Sepulchre and the relics of the True Cross are in the hands of the Vizier, Saladin. And the city of Acre is engulfed in a siege. Almost the whole country of Outremer, from Egypt in the west to Syria in the east, has fallen into the hands of the godless heathen.' William let his words trail off as he turned to face his old sergeant. In that moment he knew that all was over for his friend. 'Mathúin?' the lord whispered.

It was then Donal noticed his father was no longer shivering. The old man had become completely still, his open eyes were glazed, staring toward the door, and his lips were blue.

Donal O'Regan, abruptly elevated to the rank of chieftain of his clan, solemnly signed the cross and approached his father's side. Robert and William followed the example, and then those of the servants who were present also made the sign of blessing.

'Call for Father Conlan,' Donal said under his breath. 'There is a priest's work to be done here.'

Lord William came to stand beside Donal. Then he leaned forward and gently brushed the old man's eyes shut, realising now that there was no point in Rufus riding off to Clonough to fetch Eilish. The lord's eyes searched the room for his younger son but it was already too late to stop Rufus from leaving. The angry youth had impetuously stormed off into the night, taking his father's horse with him.

Eilish stood at the low wall of the cattle enclosure near her father's house at Clonough, the home of her family, the Gioll Martins. Eileen, her sister, had just given birth to her first boy after a long and difficult labour. As soon as the new mother was sleeping peacefully, Eilish had left the house to take in the night air.

She wrapped her shawl tightly around her head to keep out the chill of the cool breeze. The brown woollen garment covered her long fair hair completely so that she was almost invisible in the dark. After standing at the wall for a few minutes, Eilish sat down on a large rock by the water's edge and stared into the sky.

The healer was still lost in thought when she heard the sound of someone walking close by. Instinctively she froze and concentrated all her attention on the noise. After a few moments Eilish was certain she heard the footsteps again. Her heart beat a little faster as she pulled the shawl away from her ears.

But there was no further sound for a long time and finally Eilish decided she might have imagined the noise. After all, she had not slept for a day and a half and now the sunrise was only an hour away.

'I should not wander from the house,' she reminded herself, 'not after dark.'

Suddenly feeling the full effect of her exhaustion and ready for bed, Eilish stood up to make her way back to the house. She had trod no more than four steps up the path when she heard another sound. This time she was sure it was the sobs of a woman crying.

The healer remembered then that one of her cousins, a girl of no more than seventeen years, had gone missing earlier in the day. Eilish wondered if it might be this young woman she could hear.

'Neesh,' Eilish whispered, hoping not to wake anyone in the nearby houses. 'Is that you?'

The crying abruptly ceased.

'Neesh?' the woman repeated. 'It's me, Eilish from Cúil Ghréine. Is that you there?'

Before long the healer heard the unmistakable sound of

someone trudging slowly through the mud. In a few moments Eilish caught a glimpse of the girl's shadow as she approached the hamlet from the ford.

'Neesh?' Eilish said again, nervous that she had received no answer. She had been warned as a child that the faerie people prey on the foolish and the unwary. Often these otherworldly folk would steal their victims away and none would know what had become of them.

'Eilish?' a young woman's voice trembled. 'Where are you?'

'I am here by the stone wall,' the midwife replied, relieved that she recognised the voice. In moments the girl called Neesh was standing with her arms tightly wrapped around her cousin in a crushing hug.

'What's the matter, child?' Eilish asked. 'Were you lost?'

'I was not,' Neesh replied indignantly.

'Then what's come over you, wandering about in the dead of night, attracting the attention of every demon in the district?'

'I can't speak of it,' the girl replied, drying her eyes. 'I was lost,' she contradicted herself nervously.

The healer brushed the strands of hair away from the younger woman's face and regarded her with suspicion. There was a look in her cousin's dark brown eyes which told Eilish straightaway that a man was the cause of these tears.

'Is he from this valley?' the healer asked, smiling. 'What is his name?'

Neesh opened her eyes wide in fear and darted a look over her shoulder. Eilish noticed that her cousin was shivering.

'Don't worry,' the midwife cooed, hugging the young woman closer and rubbing her palm along Neesh's spine to soothe her. 'I won't tell a soul.'

'I don't know what you mean,' Neesh said, resisting the

healer's supportive gesture. Neesh was beginning to think it would be better if no-one knew the shame of her secret. 'I was out wandering alone. I became lost and got a little scared. That's all there is to it.'

'Come now, girl,' Eilish laughed, catching the terseness of the reply. Neesh looked up at her cousin's face and noticed a flash of blue from the healer's sparkling eyes. It crossed her mind that she would not be able to keep a secret from this perceptive woman.

'I smell a man about you,' Eilish pressed. 'So you might as well tell me everything that happened.'

The girl coughed and started to sob as she put her head on the older woman's breast. Neesh wanted to tell Eilish all about the Norman and his rough attack on her, but somehow she was too ashamed, as if it were her fault.

'Come along, child, out with it,' the healer insisted. 'It is best to talk about these things. And who better to share them with than a midwife, a healer, your cousin?'

Neesh looked up into Eilish's face again and knew she had to say something. She opened her mouth to speak, struggling to concoct a tale, but before she had spoken a word, both women heard another sound on the road at the far side of the ford.

'Two horsemen,' Eilish declared, 'judging from the clatter of their hooves. We had best get inside and call on the watchmen to find out who is approaching Gioll Martin at this time of night.'

Neesh nodded in agreement, relieved that these horsemen had provided a distraction. Then she realised one of the men might be the lord's son out looking for her. Frightened, she grabbed Eilish by the arm and dragged her toward the houses, seeking the safety of her family.

'I'll tell you all about it later,' Neesh promised under her breath as they came to the door of the main building. 'After everyone else is asleep.'

'I will wait up for you,' Eilish agreed, despite being exhausted and feeling very weak from a lack of sleep. 'I have not eaten well today, so come to the fire after the riders have stabled their horses.'

With a yawn Eilish went inside the small cottage to sit beside her sister for a while and warm herself again. Neesh pushed past her urgently to make for the main house where she could hide among the guests who were sleeping near the large fire.

It was much later, after sunrise, just as Eilish was finally beginning to doze, when Neesh came to her. The girl seemed very much more upset than she had been earlier and Eilish put her arms around her to comfort her. 'What is it, child? What has upset you so?'

'There is a soldier here,' Neesh stammered nervously. 'A Norman. The son of FitzWilliam. I heard him say that you are to go with him to Cúil Ghréine. He says that Mathúin is dying and that Lord William has sent for you.'

'Good God!' Eilish exclaimed, shocked at this unexpected news. She let go of her cousin and grabbed her shawl, wrapping it around her shoulders. 'When did this happen?'

Neesh shrugged her shoulders, unable to answer the question.

'Would you help me gather my things?' Eilish asked. 'I must give instructions to the women for Eileen's care.'

Neesh grabbed the healing woman by the arm and squeezed hard. 'You must not go with him,' she insisted. 'He is . . .' She paused, choosing her words carefully. 'Anything could happen to you on the way. It is too dangerous. Wait here until one of the watchmen can escort you.'

'I cannot wait. Mathúin is ill and he must need me. Hush now child,' Eilish soothed, patting the younger woman's head, 'I'll be all right. There's nothing to worry about. Show me what this soldier looks like.'

Neesh opened the door just enough for her cousin to poke

her head out and see a red-haired warrior standing beside a black horse. Nearby was another animal which was instantly recognisable as Lord William's mount. When Eilish had got a good look at the soldier, she moved back and stood close to Neesh.

'There's no reason to fear,' the midwife said in the calmest tone she could muster. 'That man is Rufus, the son of William FitzWilliam. I have nothing to fear from that one. He wouldn't dare harm a hair on my head. If he so much as spoke to me harshly, his father would flog him senseless. To say nothing of what Donal would do if he offered me insult. I think it's time you got yourself a good stretch of sleep. You are obviously overtired. Lie down here by the fire and rest. When my sister wakes, tell her what became of me.'

Neesh still grasped at the older woman's arm. 'But I haven't told you what upset me,' she sulked, holding back the tears again.

'I'll be back in a day or two to check on the baby,' Eilish said. 'We'll sit and have a long talk then, I promise.'

With the realisation that she would not be able to change the healer's mind, Neesh sighed deeply and blurted, 'If he hurts you, I'll kill him myself.'

Eilish grabbed her cousin by the shoulders and looked into her eyes. 'Has he harmed you?' the healer suddenly asked.

Neesh swallowed hard searching for the right words.

'If he has done anything to upset you,' Eilish advised, 'it would be best you went to Lord William with the complaint. He will make certain the lad is punished. But if it is a lover's quarrel you are suffering, then do not expect old William to be sympathetic.'

'I was only concerned for your safety,' Neesh lied, realising that the Norman lord would probably not believe her story.

'If Rufus FitzWilliam does not behave himself,' Eilish assured her young kinswoman, 'I will relieve him of something more precious to him than his life.' She made a gesture as if she were holding a knife. With a smile on her face she drew the imaginary blade up between her legs, illustrating exactly how she would deal with such an attack.

'If there's one thing the Normans value above anything else,' Eilish commented, 'it's their ability to erect a strong tower in a strategic position.'

Neesh caught the meaning of the euphemism immediately but she did not smile. She turned away and began to pack the midwife's herb bags, and Eilish did not notice that the girl shuddered with revulsion.

By the time the healing woman was ready to go, Neesh had readied the bags. Then she handed a small bowl of soup to Eilish to help her on the journey.

'Thank you, my dear,' Eilish said as she took the bowl. 'This is just what I needed.' As the healer drank her broth she noticed that her cousin's face was pale and the girl was obviously still very upset.

'I don't know what the matter is,' Eilish said when she had drained the soup, 'but I would think the best thing you could do is try to talk to the boy. He has really upset you, hasn't he?'

Neesh coldly nodded assent.

'Did he hurt you?'

In that moment Neesh decided to tell Eilish everything, but right now she did not want to keep the healer from Mathúin's bedside. So once again she bit her tongue. 'I will tell you about it when you return,' she murmured, reassuring herself that nothing untoward would happen to Eilish.

The healer took her hand. 'I am sorry that we have not had a chance to talk, but we will when I return.'

'Take care!' the girl exclaimed as Eilish left the house.

The very moment the midwife closed the door, Neesh

went to the fireside to curl up in a tiny ball. Though she did not sob again nor make any sign that she was upset, she felt her stomach churning with fright.

When she heard the sound of two horses galloping off down the road and over the stream, she prayed with all her might that Eilish would be safe. And she prayed also that God would visit his revenge on Rufus FitzWilliam.

Chapter Five

Donal and Braonin laid out all the food and drink they could find in the house while William sat by the fire and drank ale. Among the Gaels the passing of a relative was always marked as an event of great importance. Vigorous feasting and drunken celebration would precede the funeral and might last for days, depending on the rank and importance of the individual.

Death was not considered a sad occasion calling for much mourning. It was, more importantly, a time to give thanks for the gift of life and to rejoice in the departure of a soul beyond the pain of this existence.

When a loved one crossed over to the realm of the afterlife, all other concerns were put aside until the family could be certain that their departed relative was resting easy. It was considered very dangerous to leave the corpse alone in the room until everyone was sure the spirit had moved on to its next adventure.

Donal's ancestors had marked death in much the same manner since long before the coming of the Christians. For generations untold they had sat watches on the departed to keep their souls safe from the thieving faeries. Most Normans flinched at this heathen practice, believing that no Christian should be involved in vigils over dead bodies. However, Lord William, though a pious man, was well aware of the importance of this tradition to his hosts and

Mathúin had been a friend. So he made no protest at this celebration and joined the kinfolk of the O'Regan household in swilling large quantities of ale.

Encouraged by Donal and Braonin, the two Normans ate their fill of a great feast that had been prepared for their welcoming but now served a more fitting purpose. Then more ale, mead and barley spirit was brought out in jugs to be passed around the company.

Old Father Conlan returned just as the last of the ale was being finished. Dressed all in pure white he was immediately out of place among the hard-working farm folk in their grubby clothes. Lord William, suffering the effects of too much drink, got to his feet as the clergyman entered.

'This is the priest,' he loudly explained, 'who has come down from Shelton Abbey to oversee the consecration of the chapel of Saint Mary Magdalene.'

Grey-haired Conlan was polite to his hosts, but it was plain from the expression on his weathered face that he was less than impressed with the behaviour of the O'Regan household.

'I am known to these folk, my lord,' Conlan replied tersely. 'I was here most of the day watching over their chieftain.'

'May he rest in peace,' William added and the priest realised then that Mathúin was dead.

At that several neighbours entered the house, pushing past the priest to make for the food and drink. Conlan could not hide his disgust that these folk were feasting so soon after the death of their chieftain and before prayers had been properly said over the body. As a Gael himself, Conlan understood the ceremony but he had been educated in the traditions of the Latin Church. In his view, such rites were inspired by the Devil. However, the priest did not want to risk offence to Lord William so he resolved not to rebuke the O'Regans. Father Conlan knelt beside Mathúin's corpse to pray, struggling to ignore the drunken revelries at the other end of the house. Throughout the rest of the night he chanted his prayers, stopping every once in a while to listen to what was being said and to take a bite to eat. He was certainly not disgusted enough with the O'Regans' behaviour to deny himself a good meal when it was offered.

As soon as Conlan was facing the corpse, William removed his short riding boots and unbuttoned the sleeves of his tunic, not out of disrespect for the offices of the clergy but simply to dry his aching feet by the fire. His son, Robert, however, did not relax at all, nor did he share any of the strong liquor offered to him. This was a particularly Norman practice. One among their company always remained sober and on guard while the others were given licence to drink their fill and relax. The gathered O'Regans could not believe someone would refuse a drink on such an occasion and so they continually passed the jug to Robert. Only Donal had some inkling of why Robert was abstaining.

When the lord had finished eating he drew up some furs and leaned on them as he spread his body out on the warm stone floor close to the fire. He was fairly drunk by this stage and Robert was determined to keep an eye on his father. He trusted his hosts without question but it was his nature to be careful.

'He saved my life, Donal,' the lord declared mournfully. 'Your father saved my life,' and the entire household ceased their talking to hear William's words.

'Was there a great battle?' Braonin asked excitedly. 'Did he save you on the field in some fight against the Saracen hordes?'

'No, no. None of that,' the lord scoffed, shaking his head and chuckling to himself. The barley spirit had relaxed him considerably. 'We never saw a real battle. The enemy we fought struck hard and then disappeared into the very air.'

William gestured dramatically with his hands, swirling them about to add emphasis to his words. 'The heathen are cunning and swift. You have no idea of the dangers lurking in every street of every city in that land.'

'Mathúin spoke of Jerusalem many times,' Braonin cut in. 'He said that he had never seen any place on earth like it.'

'It was not Jerusalem where he saved my life,' William went on solemnly. 'We were in the marketplace in the city of Acre, the main port in the kingdom of Outremer. I was there to buy dried foods for the men under my command. The Master of the Temple gave me that task as a test of my obedience.'

The lord stopped speaking for a moment to recall exactly what had happened. 'It was not long after I had taken the vows of a postulant. But I was not in the front line of the defences of the city. I was ordered to command a guard over some supposedly precious storehouse. Ridiculous. A man of my experience watching over a shed full of spice goods. But one has to follow orders. That is what being a Knight of the Temple is all about.'

'What happened?' Robert piped up, surprised that he had not heard this tale.

'Well, of course I was wearing my white robe and mantle and the cross of the order on my chest. Fool that I was to mark myself so openly as a Templar. I should have dressed more soberly.' Donal silently offered the jug again and William filled his cup with a smile at the young man's impeccable sense of timing.

'Many folk think that the whole kingdom of the Outremer is peopled by knights from the western lands and their families. But most of the inhabitants are natives of that country and a good number are not Christians but infidels who venerate Mohammed.'

A few of the gathered folk hissed at the mention of

that heathen name and one or two crossed themselves in fear.

'Generally,' the lord continued, 'there is an unwritten agreement between Moslem and Christian. Each respects the rights of the other as much as possible and most people on both sides are happy with the arrangement. And I must say that the infidels place a higher value on their word than most high-born knights of the west would do.'

'You said that you were in the market,' Robert reminded his father, trying to keep him to his story.

'Ah yes,' William remembered, 'the market. Have you ever heard of the fanatical Hashishim?' He looked around the room to see if anyone had.

By this time most folk from the nearby cottages had arrived to pay their respects to Mathúin. Many of them stayed to share food and drink, so the room was beginning to crowd with people. Even Father Conlan turned around from his devotions to give the old knight his undivided attention.

'The French knights call these zealots the assassins, because they cannot pronounce the Arabic tongue,' the lord went on but realised that no-one present recognised the term so he launched into a description of the men who inspired so much fear in the people of Outremer. 'The assassins claim to be a holy order, much the same as the Templars or the Hospitallers, but they are, of course, followers of the Prophet Mohammed.'

At the second mention of this name most of his audience crossed themselves and a few murmured the opening lines of the 'Ave'. William was not too drunk to notice. He smiled indulgently, realising that they had no idea what they were frightened of.

'The Hashishim are mostly noblemen,' the knight continued. 'They value learning above all else. In this they are brothers to the Templars. But the speciality of their order is the way in which they fight. They do not engage in open battle, unless forced to by circumstance. Their methods are more clandestine, infinitely more subtle and far more effective. Their warriors train in the arts of concealment and subterfuge. They often live as Christians among Christian folk for many years without attracting any suspicion whatsoever. Then one day when no-one expects it, they move into action. Sometimes they work in groups of two or three, but mostly these men operate entirely alone.'

'But how can one or two men, no matter how skilled, hope to defeat an entire Christian army?' Braonin asked, dis- believing.

'Murder,' William answered. 'They murder the leading knights of the army or strike down the princes and dukes of the kingdom. Without leaders a Christian army is no better than a pack of hungry children who dream of ransacking a bakery.'

'So how did you encounter these assassins?' Robert pressed, very interested now. 'Did they send someone to murder you?'

William laughed, genuinely amused at his son's naivety. 'No, I would not have been worth the effort to these men. They strike at the real leaders, the men who make decisions. My encounter with the assassins was purely accidental.'

With a swift movement the old knight swallowed another draught of barley spirit and held out his cup for Donal to refill.

'A group of Templar knights, none of whom I knew, were passing through the market at the same time as Mathúin and myself. Four of them bore a large box on long poles which they carried high on their shoulders. I never found out what was inside the box for it was covered with a white mantle that concealed its exact size and shape. It was obviously a receptacle for some precious cargo. Loot, no doubt.

Perhaps the plunder from some recent engagement or a payment of ransom for the return of some wealthy infidel prisoner.'

William stopped speaking for a second to take another gulp of his drink, and everyone in the room leaned forward in anticipation of the next part of the tale.

'All of a sudden,' the lord went on, 'from out of nowhere, half-a-dozen infidel knights appeared as if they had been conjured up by some heathen sorcery. As swift as the wind they drew their long curved blades. They cut down the four Templars who carried the box and were hacking into the five remaining knights before I even had a chance to put a hand on the hilt of my steel.'

The lord coughed a little and then took another sip to settle his throat.

'The ferocity of the attack surprised me,' William recalled. 'It was obvious these men were determined to kill every Templar who stood in their way and to get their hands on whatever was in that box. Mathúin and I looked at each other and without a word or any hesitation rushed to the aid of our embattled brothers. All the rest of the people who had been thronging the marketplace fled for safety, leaving the street completely deserted. Four infidels fell and four more Templars until there were just two of the enemy facing Mathúin, myself and another knight whose name I only learned later.'

'And how did my father save your life?' Donal asked in a subdued, respectful tone which barely covered his excitement.

William turned to look the young man in the eye. 'The other Templar knight was sorely wounded and fighting for his life. I was knocked to the ground. My sword was just out of reach of my grasp. I had no shield with which to parry an attack. I was defenceless. One of the infidels stepped forward to strike at me with his blade. As I awaited the blow I commended my spirit to God, sure that I was drawing my last breath.'

The house was perfectly still. Everyone was silent, straining to hear the tale.

'But by some miracle,' William sighed, 'Mathúin was there. He dispatched the Saracen and then moments later rushed to the aid of the other Templar. Single-handed, after a brief but bitter struggle, he drove off the last enemy knight. I have never been in such an ugly brawl and I hope I never find myself in such a situation again. I was sure that I was a dead man when that heathen lifted his fearsome blade against me. I was certain that I heard the voice of God calling to me from the gates of heaven.'

'And what of the box?' Robert interrupted. 'And the other Templar?'

'The other Templar was a knight called Godfrey d'Acre, one of the priors of my order and perhaps the most respected Knight of the Cross in the whole Kingdom of Outremer. He died in my arms, pierced through the heart by an assassin's knife. But before he breathed his last he entrusted the safekeeping of his treasure to me and made me vow to return it safely to his own stronghold. I took the box under my protection and escorted it to France where the prior of the order relieved me of it. Shortly thereafter I was ordered to return home with a goodly reward for my deeds.'

'And you never discovered what the box contained?' Robert inquired persistently. 'You never opened it?'

'I did not,' William replied regretfully. 'Out of respect for the man who had entrusted it to me. But I heard a tale on my way through France which made me wish I had taken a look. A Cistercian brother told me a story he had heard about Godfrey d'Acre. He believed that Godfrey was entrusted with a great treasure from the Temple of Solomon and that he was murdered in a failed attempt to steal the precious goods. When I told the monk that Godfrey had passed away in my arms, the poor brother nearly fell over himself with joy that the story was true.'

'And did the monk know what that great treasure consisted of?' Robert begged, frustrated at the way his father had answered the question but managed to leave so much unsaid.

'It was rumoured that Godfrey had been involved in building works on the site of the Temple of Solomon where the headquarters of the order was situated. It was said that while he was supervising the work a cup was discovered. This monk claimed that Godfrey had uncovered the vessel from which Christ drank the wine of the Last Supper. I was told that this cup was also the container in which Joseph of Arimathea caught the blood of the Saviour as the Son of God hung upon the Cross. It is reputed to be one of the most miraculous relics in all of Christendom. I have heard some men refer to it as the Cup of the Holy Grail, though I do not know where the name originates.'

All the way back to Cúil Ghréine Rufus rode several horse lengths ahead of Eilish. On occasion he spurred his warhorse so that she had to trot to keep him in her sights. This amused him somewhat and relieved the tedium of his task. It was a short ride, a little under an hour, but Eilish could not wait for the journey to be over with.

She rarely had anything to do with the Normans at all and she only knew Rufus by reputation. She quickly judged, however, that he was an unpleasant fellow. Her husband had pointed the man out at a fair once as being one of the more difficult Normans to get along with. Donal had called him a gruff boaster more full of wind than wisdom. To

Eilish this comment summed up most of the Normans pretty accurately. She considered them to be generally insincere, dishonest, somewhat childish. They also seemed to labour under the mistaken view that women were created to be subservient to their menfolk.

Eilish had only ever known one Norman woman and that was William's wife, Eleanor. She had been a kind and generous soul and was mourned by all the Gaelic folk on the estates when she passed away. But, the healer conceded, Eleanor was only half Norman, being a Breton on her father's side. Eilish could not remember any of the men among the Normans being grieved over when they died. If this young Rufus was anything to judge by, that was hardly surprising.

Finally, as they reached the place where the bohreen widened into a broad muddy track, the Norman dismounted to lead his horse up towards the hamlet. Eilish caught up with him at this point and jumped down from her animal, landing in the muck. Now that she was on her home territory she was determined not to be left behind. The healer caught up the hem of her skirts and tucked them into her wide brown belt as she took in the familiar scent of her own hearth fire.

Then, with a strong, purposeful stride, Eilish set off up the rise toward the buildings, her borrowed horse following dutifully behind. She let the reins of her mount fall as she approached Rufus and the animal followed after her as if it had known her all its life and was coming home to its own stable. The Norman trod carefully so as not to get his feet and legs dirty and this slowed his pace. As she overtook Rufus, Eilish noticed the care he was taking. It was unbelievable to her that anyone would bother trying to keep clean on such a filthy bit of track. The healer could not help but laugh incredulously at this behaviour.

'You can wash your pretty clothes up at the house,' she

chided, pulling the shawl back from around her hair. 'Wouldn't we be in trouble if the Saracens swept down out of the hills now! How would you fight them off and keep your lovely boots from getting muddied?'

Rufus made a show of ignoring her, but the woman had injured his pride. He refused to be outdone, so he picked up his pace in an effort to catch up with her again. The ground was very slippery, however, and his long military-style tunic hampered the free and quick movement of his legs. So it was that he had not tramped but five paces when he slipped his footing and landed heavily on his backside in the oozing mud.

In an effort to save face, Rufus tried to regain his feet immediately but only managed to slide onto his side instead as he struggled to get up. Eilish did not look back at him but by the time she had reached the waiting men-at-arms, Rufus was only just standing again. The healer could hear him cursing loudly in his own tongue.

For once Eilish was glad she could not understand the Norman speech. The two men-at-arms knew what he was saying though. They looked at each other and smiled broadly, but they did not go to the assistance of their lord's son.

When no-one came out of the house to greet Eilish and she heard the sound of many voices inside, the healer knew that Mathúin was already dead. She paused for a few moments to allow the realisation to touch her heart. Once inside, all her thoughts would be taken with seeing that folk were fed and watered, and she would have little opportunity to grieve. Eilish conjured up a picture of her father-in-law in her mind. The memory that came to her was of the strong man who set out for the Holy Land in the entourage of Lord William. A man of wit, she recalled, cutting and often self-deprecating in his humour. He was a loyal friend and an extremely open-handed chieftain to his clan.

Then the realisation struck Eilish that her husband was now chieftain of the O'Regans of Cúil Ghréine. From this moment on all the responsibility for the people of the estate would rest on his shoulders. Donal would have the job of ensuring smooth relations with their Norman overlords. If there was any shortfall in taxes from one part of the estate, he would have to see that it could be made up for in another part of Lord William's lands.

Eilish knew her husband was up to the task as he was a man very much like his father. Mathúin had been well respected and admired by everyone on the landholdings. It was largely due to his efforts that the family had managed to retain ownership of their fields. This was despite strong pressure, and on occasion heavy-handed force, from William who had originally demanded that the titles be handed to him. The lord was wise enough, however, to realise that in the long term he would get more grain in taxes from people who owned most of their own land than from downtrodden slaves who worked for a pittance.

Mathúin's friendship with Lord William had saved his clan much of the trouble that had plagued the northern folk. FitzWilliam was not a greedy man, Eilish reflected, nor was he as godless as most of his people.

The healer carefully arranged the shawl over her shoulders before opening the door to the house she and her husband had shared with Mathúin for so long. All those in the room fell silent as she entered, and she was grateful for that show of respect. Without stopping to greet her guests she walked straight over to where the old man's body lay. She felt a tear come to her eye but knelt down beside the body in silent prayer before anyone had noticed. The assembled neighbours remained as still as the corpse itself until she stood up again and turned to face them. Only when she rose did they breathe a little easier. Eilish, as the woman of the house, had the duty of beginning the eulogy for Donal's father.

'Mathúin O'Regan lies here in this house. Ochone!' she cried and William felt a chill rush through his body as she wailed. 'His soul has surely gone to heaven for he was as good a father to me as my own.' She directed her speech to her husband as if no-one else were there with them.

'And the best father I could have hoped for,' Donal replied.

'He was a wise judge in all things and a keeper of the truth,' she rejoined straightaway.

'All the folk hereabouts respected his wisdom,' her husband agreed and the crowd hummed, nodding their heads to show they shared that opinion.

'He was a brave man in war and a gentle man in love,' she continued.

'His compassion was like a signal fire burning brightly in the night. And his fury was like the wind on the high mountains, relentless and unquenchable,' Donal added.

'His humour would ease the pain of the sick,' Eilish ended.

'And his passing to the next world has brought an end to humour in this house for a while,' her husband rounded off.

Just as Donal finished speaking the door flew open again and there stood Rufus, muddied from head to foot and dripping wet. He had an expression on his face that could have turned milk sour and his complexion was redder than usual from the humiliating circumstances of his arrival.

The fresh earthy odour of cow dung preceded him into the room, and before he could cross the doorstep, his brother Robert had ushered him back outside. Most folk present could not understand exactly what was said between the two brothers, but it was obvious Robert was demanding that Rufus wash in the horse trough before returning.

William, now quite drunk, saw his younger son at the door and put his head in his hands to hide his shame, at least that was what everyone thought. But, to the utter surprise of all those gathered in the house, he started to laugh, quietly at first and then a little louder until he could restrain his amusement no longer.

'Humour has not died with Mathúin,' William giggled, 'for I have a feeling he still has one or two jokes to share with us.'

The lord pointed at the door, indicating that he thought his younger son's predicament may have been occasioned by the still present spirit of his old sergeant-at-arms. There were nervous smiles in the house as the lord tried to get to his feet.

'Let us drink to our departed friend,' William urged, raising his wooden cup and slurring his speech, 'and to the health of the new O'Regan. When we've done that, Donal and I will agree on the decorations which will adorn Mathúin's tomb in the chapel of Saint Mary Magdalene.'

In the three months following Mathúin's passing, many more letters arrived from the Holy Land. The news painted a disastrous picture for the Christian Kingdom of the Outremer. All but a few isolated fortresses had fallen to the Saracen Arabs or to the Turks.

Jerusalem was completely overrun. And as if to add insult to the disaster, the infidel commander, Saladin, the Vizier of Egypt, began allowing Christian pilgrims to return to the Holy City on one condition. A humiliating toll had to be paid upon entering the gates and a further tax submitted to to visit the church where Christ's tomb was believed to have been. Saladin was not the first potentate to demand such a fee: the Christian knights had always done so. Nevertheless, it was an affront to the crusaders that this heathen had the gall to demand an entry toll to Christian shrines. It was, to many, like rubbing salt into the wounded pride of Christendom.

King Saladin's revenge on the Christians was both effective and well-reasoned. He did not allow the merciless killing of any of the inhabitants of Jerusalem as the Christians had done when they had first conquered the city. Indeed, the great Moslem commander was most eager for the people of the Holy City to go on with their lives as soon as possible after his conquest. Christian landholders were generally allowed to continue farming the country. Merchants went on trading in exotic spices and rare gems. The Venetians sent a delegation to Saladin to congratulate him on his victory and to ensure that they were allowed to use the trading ports just as they had done before. The Hospitallers, too, brokered a deal with the infidel which allowed their order to oversee all trade and not be harried any further by the Saracen forces. So it was that peace returned to the Holy Land and life went on as if nothing had really changed at all.

It was said, however, that the conqueror of Jerusalem would not countenance any negotiations with the Templars. The order had upset the King of the Saracens by refusing to negotiate the surrender of the city when it was besieged. Or so it was claimed by some. Whatever the truth, Saladin would not accept the Templar envoys. He began pressuring the other military orders to have them removed from the Holy Land altogether.

When the Grand Master of the Temple and his council realised that their rivals, the Hospitallers, were probably as much behind this development as anyone, they began a campaign to win support for a third crusade. The Templars had the ear of the Pope, who spoke of restoring the kingdom of Outremer and ridding the Holy Land of the heathens once and for all.

Thus the old feud between the Knights of Saint John of the Hospital and the Knights of the Temple of Solomon took a new twist. Both orders were now doing their best to grab a larger share of the Holy Land for themselves and to claim the crusades as their own.

William, in his outpost far away from Jerusalem, received this news from his comrades in the east and none of it eased his mind. When he had been sworn as a postulant of the Temple, he believed that all the knights he served with were honourable men and trustworthy. It seemed incredible to him that the two greatest holy military orders in Christendom could have come almost to the point of war with one another. And all because of a lust for earthly power.

It was not entirely clear to William, either, why the Pope did not intervene and unite both factions against the real enemy, the infidel Saracens. As the days drew on into the new year and the mornings became warmer with the approach of spring, the lord began to suffer a bout of sullen depression.

The winter had been even harder on him than he had expected. Sickness had confined him to his bed for much of the time and melancholy for most of what remained. No-one but the old knight understood that he was suffering a crisis of his fâith for he never spoke of his illness and ignored all inquiries after his health.

When word came of the short-lived but bloody crusade against the heretic Cathars in the south of France, William retreated from everyone to contemplate the meaning of this new war. The Cathars, he reasoned to himself, were Christians. Though they had been declared heretics and their lands forfeited to the Crown of France and to any knight who joined this new crusade, at least they were not Saracens. The Cathars still worshipped Christ and followed the teachings of his wisdom.

Now William found himself questioning the definition of a heretic. He began to believe that this world was coming to an end just as the scriptures predicted. Or at least, he reasoned, it had been turned upside down as a prelude to the Last Days.

All his old friends were either dead, serving in far-off lands or living miserable lives as captives of the Saracens. A few of his comrades had broken their vows rather than return to certain death in the Holy Land and thus had been forced to travel beyond the vengeful jurisdiction of the Grand Master.

One frosty spring morning William rose early to attend chapel. For the first time in months the servants noticed that he had a broad smile on his face and they whispered nervously to each other behind his back. After prayers the lord cheerfully inspected the progress on the roofless chapel dedicated to Mary Magdalene. He said a benediction at Mathúin's tomb, lit a candle for his friend and then questioned Balek, the Master Craftsman who was working on the mosaic walls. Satisfied that everything was going well, he returned to his chamber in the upper part of the keep and immediately called for his two sons.

When he was informed that Rufus was still asleep and that Robert was out riding, the smile fell away from his face again. But William was determined that this minor setback was not going to ruin his changed mood.

As he ran a hand gently along the back of his faithful ginger cat, the lord issued orders to his chamberlain. 'When the lazy one is awake,' he hissed, 'bring him to me to break his fast. And when the pious one returns, bring him straight to this chamber to await my pleasure.'

Then William went up onto the battlements to take in the

air and survey the lands all about. The servants murmured uneasy words about how the strain of the last few months showed on their master's face. Most of them suspected that old William had gone a little mad during the long confinement of winter. A few were openly mourning his steady decline into old age and dementia.

Upon returning to his room William called again for Lonan to bring pen, ink and parchment. When the old chamberlain arrived, the lord had him draw up one charter in the name of his elder son and one for the younger. By the time the task was finished, Robert and Rufus were both waiting to be admitted to the chamber.

Lonan ushered them into the room with a bright merry grin on his face and a spring in his step which the brothers both noted with apprehension. Their father rarely summoned them together into the same room at the same time. And the chamberlain had not smiled at either of them since they were children.

When Robert's eyes adjusted to the gloomy chamber, he noticed that his father was perched on the broad stone sill of the only window. His wife, their mother, used to sit in that spot and read during the day. The cat, curled up on the desk, gave a spitting snarl as Rufus crossed the room. The old knight looked up from the papers he was reading when he heard the fuss. But not until the door was shut did Lord William of Bally Raine address his sons.

'It warms my heart that you could manage to be with me today,' he began sarcastically. 'You could have at least bothered to brush your hair or to wash, Rufus,' he added. 'But never mind, what do such vanities really matter?'

'What is it you want of us, Father?' Robert stuttered. He feared his father, for when the old knight slipped into these moods he could be unpredictable. At times William barely restrained his temper and could strike out violently at his sons in unbridled rage.

'I have come to a decision,' the old lord announced, his voice subdued and pleasant. 'The rule of William FitzWilliam Lord of Bally Raine is ended. Tomorrow I will take my full vows to the Order of the Temple. I am no longer a postulant.'

He waited to see the reaction. Rufus's slack jaw said it all. 'That means, of course, that one of you must inherit the estate before I enter the abbey. It is the rule of the Temple that I must give all I own to the order. This matter must, therefore, be settled today so that the Temple does not appropriate this land from our family. The papers have all been drawn up.'

Rufus rolled his eyes in exasperation and huffed to show disdain for his father's words. Robert could not manage to speak or move at all. He had long known that this day would come. He feared the result would be a long drawn-out argument between himself and Rufus over who should run the estates.

'This charter,' William said as he held up the first parchment, 'endows Robert FitzWilliam as lord over the castle and demesne of Bally Raine. He will be protector of the inhabitants of Cúil Ghréine and commander of all the soldiers on these lands. My last act as lord is to free all those who are bound in debt to me. I also grant each of my servants a piece of their own land so long as they remain loyal to my successors forever. A copy of this testament is to be sent to King Henry in Normandy for his approval, but I cannot foresee there will be any problem. This is a family matter and the King rarely intervenes in the private affairs of his subjects. There is your seal and my sword,' William went on, pointing to the table in front of him where the objects had been carefully laid out. 'God grant you wisdom, Robert, for up till now you have shown yourself to have had rather a deficiency in that area.'

'And what is contained in the other charter?' Rufus

asked, noticing that his father still had another piece of parchment in his hand.

The chamberlain smiled broadly again, clearly pleased that he had been granted a small holding but obviously also aware of what the other charter contained.

'Ah yes, this,' William hummed, holding up the paper. 'This charter concerns you, Rufus. My son, you have been a deep disappointment to me ever since the day you were old enough to don riding breeches. Your grandfather and great-grandfather would doubtless have disowned you for your stupidity, your boorish contempt for the people we rule, and of course for your immeasurable and ingenious laziness. I am not sure whether they would have believed that one of their own bloodline could have turned out to be such a clumsy, ineffectual soldier so disliked and ridiculed by his peers that his very name has become synonymous with stupidity.'

Rufus lowered his eyes and looked down at the floor. But it was not out of shame. He had heard all of this many times before and was not willing to hear it again.

'If you had devoted yourself to learning the art of war,' William continued, 'as diligently as your brother has to his overpious prayer vigils, you might have received something of value from me on my passing into the abbey. As it stands, I find I can summon no respect for you whatsoever. I cannot think of one redeeming feature that might show you to have any skill or aptitude in any pursuit other than sleeping late in the morning. You ill-treat the servants and squander my fortune as if it were your own. You steal from the treasury and spend large sums of money on horses. Apparently you have been unconcerned that one day I might wake up to your thieving ways. I have tolerated your habits long enough, my son, and now that I am leaving for the life of a monk, you will begin to pay back your debt to this landholding.'

The young man's face paled at this last comment and he opened his mouth to protest, but William did not give him the chance to speak.

'Detailed in this letter is an account of all the gold, spices and other treasures that you have stolen from my coffers in the time since I returned from Outremer. My loyal servants have been watching you carefully ever since I departed.'

Rufus shot a malicious glance at Lonan.

'But,' the lord went on, 'I can find it in my heart to excuse you for your petty thievery while I was away in the Holy Land. It was by no means certain that I would ever return and there was no-one here truly capable of keeping you in check.' William looked at Robert to let him know that he held him responsible for his brother's thieving.

'It is for all that you stole after my return that I will hold you accountable,' William announced with contempt. 'In future you will own nothing but the clothes you stand up in. The rest of your lavish wardrobe is being cleared out at this moment. It will be sold to recover part of your debt. If the account is not settled by this measure, then you will have to sell one or two of your horses and a few of those pretty saddles you have collected.'

'You can't do this to me,' Rufus protested, his voice full of anger. 'I am your son. How will I eat? How will I survive without your patronage?'

'I am not withdrawing my patronage, Rufus. I am withdrawing myself.' William looked at the young man sternly now. The strained smile disappeared from his face. 'You are in your brother's hands now. He will decide whether you are worth feeding, clothing and nurturing. I would not blame him if he threw you out of the door on your fat lazy arse to let you fend for yourself. But I have a feeling that your brother is a better man than that. At least for your sake, I hope he is.' William smiled again. 'Certainly Robert is a good Christian and a compassionate man. He probably would not dream of doing that to you. More's the pity.'

William held the parchment up again. 'This charter excludes you and your descendants from lordship over these lands forever. It is law, or will be when the King of England adds his seal to the document. There is nothing you can do about it except to change your ways and pray that your brother remains as charitable as he has always been.'

'I will write to the King!' Rufus bellowed. 'He is a man of honour. He will not see me treated this way.'

'Henry is a dear friend of mine,' William countered. 'And you may remember that he crowned his own eldest son as joint king in recognition of his piety and readiness for responsibility. But Henry disowned his younger son, Richard, who spent too much time at the French court. If there is one thing that Henry cannot stand it is a son who deviates from his father's wishes. I suggest that you may not just be risking your reputation by stating your case to the King, you may also be risking your life.'

'I will not stand for this!' Rufus cried. 'I have worked hard for you and your damned estate. The soldiers would have revolted but for my firm hand. And the peasants would have sat back in the hay and watched the stronghold fall to ruin without lifting a finger. I will not be disenfranchised by an effeminate, book-bound cleric lover.'

William raised an eyebrow. 'You may be right. Robert may spend too much of his time at prayer and too little of it chasing young women, but he is an honourable man who can look after himself in a fight. And after all, I only have the two of you to choose from. Which one would you hand everything over to?'

Again Rufus was about to speak but William cut him short. 'Let's ask Robert that question first, shall we?' The lord turned to his eldest son who was frowning at being involved in this ongoing dispute between his father and brother. 'Robert, if you were in my position, which brother would you give everything to?'

The elder brother put a hand to his forehead and closed his eyes tightly as if he could avoid the question by not being able to see his father. When he opened them again he scratched the back of his head and finally spoke.

'I would remember the story of the prodigal son,' he began, 'and grant each an equal portion of the wealth which I had amassed in the hope that they would use it wisely. And if they did not, I would not berate them for their actions but would love them both just the same as I always had.'

'I hope that you grow in wisdom before you have sons of your own,' William admonished curtly, 'or only God will be able to help this estate.'

'Robert would need to show some interest in bedding a woman before there was any hope of him having a son,' Rufus cut in. 'That one would rather spend an hour with Father Conlan than ten minutes alone with one of the serving girls.'

'I don't even need to ask you,' William snapped, 'what your decision would be if you could choose.' The lord laughed and then his expression changed to one of utter seriousness. 'There it is, my sons. The decision has been made and now your lives have been changed for good or ill. The future will be what you make it. I am going to spend my remaining days in peace and repentance until the Lord my God calls me to his side.'

With that William turned his attention to the world outside of his window and, without looking at either son, said, 'You may go now. This audience is ended.'

Angus, the ginger cat, jumped up onto William's lap and started to knead at the lord's surcoat before finally settling down. The old knight stroked the animal softly and spoke under his breath, 'I wish I could have left all this to you,

Angus my friend. At least then I could be certain that the rats would be kept at bay.'

After a few moments William looked up and noticed that neither of his sons had moved. 'Why are you still here?' he bellowed. The two young men flinched slightly, then turned obediently to leave as the chamberlain swung the door open for them.

Robert went straight to his own rooms where he had a small private chapel. He was shocked by his father's sudden decision and wished only to be alone for a while to contemplate how all of this conflicted with his own plans.

Rufus stormed outside onto the green which led down to the moat. He was furious and determined that this rash act on the part of his father would not see the end of his hunting, his drinking or his womanising.

'What else is there to do in this damned country?' he screamed to the sky and heard the wooden shutters of his father's apartment slam loudly.

'I'll have what is rightfully mine, one way or another,' Rufus vowed under his breath. 'Robert is a weakling. He is too spineless to be an effective ruler. And too feeble to stand up to me. I'll find a way to claim the lordship of this land. Then that old man will be sorry he insulted me. He will rue the day that he humiliated me. When I'm Lord of Bally Raine old William will regret he chose that halfwit Robert to rule in his place when he could have placed me at the reins of this estate.'

Rufus paced up and down the green, swearing, cursing and avowing his vengeance until the fire of his anger finally began to subside. As soon as he was thinking clearly again, he started to plan his next moves more carefully.

'The first thing I need to do,' he said to himself, 'is prevent the letter that disenfranchises me from ever reaching King Henry. If the King does not ratify it, then its contents can never be enforced. Yet the charter announcing Father's withdrawal from the running of the estates and the handing over of the lordship to Robert must get through to Normandy.'

A solution to that minor problem came to him quickly. Then his devious mind moved on to tackle the next obstacle standing in the way of his rise to power.

Robert.

Chapter Six

The journey from the isolated fortress of Krak in the north of the Christian Kingdom of Outremer to the city of Acre in the west was an arduous and dangerous one at the best of times.

Arduous because of the dry, draining heat which sapped even the strongest men and beasts of their stamina. Dangerous because it was necessary for any caravan or convoy to pass directly through lands held by the armies of Saladin. To make matters worse, this barren territory was patrolled by bands of brigands who held no allegiances and answered to no-one for their actions.

Four and a half months after he had learned of his brother's death, Geoffrey, astride a donkey, was riding among the wagons at the rear of a Templar caravan. He was far behind the knights in their bright armour and white robes, but he contrived to be close enough to the cargo they were transporting that he could always keep it within sight.

Another box, much like the one he had seen in his vision, was tied down on the back of a flat cart. And the strange cargo gnawed at Geoffrey's curiosity so that he was drawn toward it. At every opportunity he edged his way closer to the cart. But each time he came within twenty paces, a knight would come silently between him and the mysterious object. Many times he was forced to withdraw. Eventually he had to be content with merely riding along at the back of the column, speculating as to what it could be that warranted such a heavy guard of armed knights.

The woman bathed in ethereal light returned to his mind as he rode. He had only once before experienced anything comparable. On the evening of his father's death Geoffrey had had a disconcerting experience. He had been looking out over the castle grounds at home in Marseilles when he noticed a ghostly figure crossing the lawn. The man turned to wave at him and Geoffrey recognised his father immediately.

'At the very moment of his passing,' Geoffrey muttered to himself, 'I saw his spirit departing on its journey to the afterlife.' Suddenly the young monk understood that his vision of the Holy Mother had been real. He knew too well that few men were granted these unearthly gifts and he was humbled that two such blessed experiences had been conferred upon him in this life. He covered his face in his white monk's cowl to keep the full force of the sun from scorching his pale skin. His donkey ambled along, jolting him back and forth so roughly that even though he was desperately tired he could not sleep a wink nor rest at all.

He wrapped the cowl more tightly around his head as the wind picked up and fine dust filled the air, choking horse, camel, donkey and man alike. Geoffrey ignored the discomfort as he endeavoured to recall everything he had ever been told about the Ark of the Covenant.

He had heard many stories about the sacred object. But he had had very little opportunity to practise reading and he had never read the tale as it was written in the holy books.

The wind storm blew into a driving gale that spread tiny grains of sand high into the air, making it difficult to see the road ahead. But Geoffrey hardly noticed. His mind was focused on other matters.

Abruptly the caravan came to a halt, and before Geoffrey

knew what was happening, he could hear shouts above the noise of the wind. Soon several knights came galloping back down the line to bark orders at the travellers. One Templar, face wrapped in a long white scarf to keep the dust out of his nose and mouth, rode up to Geoffrey and grabbed the young man by the shoulder. The knight dismounted and roughly snatched the reins of the novice's donkey. He hauled the protesting animal to the side of the road as he unbound the scarf from his face.

'We are going to seek shelter in among these caves,' the knight yelled.

'What caves?' Geoffrey answered, concerned that he could not see anything but windblown sand.

'Follow me,' came the reply. 'Get out of the saddle and lead your mount.'

Geoffrey did as he was told without hesitation, though it took a few moments for him to find the knight in the swirling dust. After they had struggled a few hundred paces they reached the entrance to a great hole in the side of a rocky hill.

The wind disappeared as the two men and their mounts passed under the natural stone arch of the cave entrance. Inside the massive fissure Geoffrey was surprised to see the rest of the caravan regrouped and preparing camp. Horses, camels and men were congregating around a wide, dark, inviting pool of clear water. Many of the travellers were drinking their fill from the revitalising spring. The young man suddenly realised just how thirsty he was and immediately led his donkey down to the pool so they could both partake of its life-giving water.

Face down on the cold stone near to where the spring emerged from its underground source, Geoffrey sucked up the cool clear liquid until he could take in no more. He thought that he had never tasted anything so sweet as this cleansing water bubbling up from within the earth.

Suddenly Geoffrey became aware of a strange and overpowering smell. It reminded him of the scent of rotting fruit mingled with that of horse dung. The odour steadily grew stronger and for a moment the novice thought that he must have rolled in animal urine.

'You are Godfrey's little brother?' a deep voice inquired from behind him.

Geoffrey rolled over onto his side to get a look at the man who had addressed him. 'I am Godfrey's brother, Geoffrey d'Acre,' he confirmed as soon as he laid eyes on the stranger. Then he realised that this knight was the source of the terrible stench.

'My name is Henry St Clair,' the stranger declared. 'I was honoured to count myself a good friend of your brother. He was one of the great pillars of our knightly order.'

Geoffrey scrambled to his feet and looked into piercing blue eyes set in a tanned face. Fine locks of grey hair and a beard framed the features and the young man found himself strangely drawn to this knight.

With one hand held up to his nose to allay the stench, Geoffrey reached out to take Henry's hand in greeting. The older man grasped it firmly. As he did so the novice noticed that the knight pressed his hand tighter and tighter until it began to hurt. Henry was looking the young man directly in the eye as if he were expecting some sort of recognition from him.

Taken aback at this, Geoffrey answered with the greeting his brother always used when meeting a knight for the first time. 'Blessed are the meek for they shall inherit the earth.'

'And blessed are they that hunger and thirst after righteousness for they shall be satisfied,' came the immediate reply.

Henry was still staring straight into Geoffrey's eyes, searching for something, though the young novice had no idea what it might be. Finally, after a few moments of silence, the older man released his hold on Geoffrey's hand and smiled. By this time the young man was gagging slightly from the foul stench.

'Forgive me,' St Clair began. 'Knights of the order are forbidden to wash. Do not fear, you will quickly grow accustomed to the sweet scent of our vows. Drink your fill,' Henry directed, 'and then come to my fire to speak with me. We will not be travelling any further today for fear of attracting more attention. Thank God the sandstorm came upon us when it did or we would surely have had to fight off that small army of brigands who have been following us most of the day. They will wonder what happened to us when the wind dies down,' he laughed.

'I will come over as soon as I have watered my donkey,' Geoffrey promised.

'A well-watered steed will carry you through any catastrophe,' Henry added and then turned on his heel to pick his way through the crowd of knights, servants and camel drivers.

The young man saw to his animal as quickly as possible. Once he had garnered some hay for it to eat from the stores, he made his way across the great cave, searching among the campfires for the place where Henry St Clair waited. This man, Geoffrey hoped, might be able to answer some of the questions that had plagued him over the last few months.

The novice wanted to know exactly how his brother Godfrey had died. What affairs he was to look after in the city of Acre that were so important. But most of all he wanted to know the secret of the great box that was being transported across the desert by a small army of Templar Knights.

After his father's death Donal spent as much time at the chapel of Bally Raine as he could spare. He liked nothing better than to watch the craftsmen at work assembling the vast mosaic that would one day cover each wall. Most of all he was intrigued by the master craftsman who was addressed by everyone respectfully as 'tilecutter'.

It took Donal a long while to feel comfortable with this stranger. The two men were forced to communicate in a language that was foreign to both of them: Latin, the universal language of Christian diplomacy. Each man had only a smattering of the language, enough to be understood.

The simple struggle to communicate quickly cemented their friendship in a way that would have likely been impossible had they shared a common mother tongue. Every idea was a challenge; every word an effort. So they valued their time together and grew close from tackling the mutual hurdle of discussing simple concepts.

In a few short weeks they both worked at their Latin until each became proficient beyond his expectations. Soon enough they found communication to be less of a struggle and more of a joy. It was not long before they could chat to one another with only the occasional break in conversation to search for a particularly difficult word.

Balek of Acre, master mason, artist and, in his own opinion at least, philosopher, was a short man of dark complexion, fine black hair and a full beard. His eyes sparkled constantly with a sense of wonder and the light of a mischievous intelligence. He wore the clothes that William had provided for him: a Norman-style tunic and hose and a soldier's cap that had once served as the padding for a war helm.

The garments did not suit him. They were too large and he was obviously not comfortable wearing them. But what else was he to do? He was a long way from the marketplace in Acre. And the clothes he had brought with him were hardly suited to this climate. His sandals were the only piece of his old apparel that he wore, but in the winter he had packed them away in favour of leather shoes and woollen hose that completely covered his legs and feet.

Balek was a man possessed of a very happy disposition, at least as far as Donal could ascertain. The master mason was always smiling and quick to laugh. And he knew many stories which, once the two men had overcome their initial awkwardness, he began to share willingly.

On the day that William summoned his sons into his chamber to tell them what fate he had settled for them both, Donal visited Balek to arrange payment of the master's monthly wage. The chieftain also brought a present of some fresh meat for the tilecutter's dinner. Balek had just completed laying out the edges of some of his work, intricate and exotic designs made up of hundreds of tiny tiles each no bigger than the tip of a finger.

When Donal looked carefully at the motifs he was deeply impressed by the beauty of the handiwork. Mosaic tile work was fairly common in the Norman households but Donal had never seen any that approached the standard of this fellow's craftsmanship. The look of awe on the chieftain's face prompted Balek to invite his patron to inspect the drawings for the next stage of the chapel.

The master took out a large rolled parchment made from the skin of a single cow. On it were sketched the patterns for the walls, worked in colourful pigments the tilecutter had ground himself and then painstakingly applied to the design.

Donal sighed with pleasure when he saw the border all around the edge. 'I have seen these patterns before,' he declared.

'A priest showed me a book of the Gospels,' Balek explained, 'that was full of these designs. They are called knots.'

'Old Father Lucius who was our priest before Conlan had a Gospel with these patterns in it,' Donal remembered. 'It was very beautiful. Do the knots come from your country?'

'I have seen similar designs in Egypt,' the tilecutter recalled, 'but I was under the impression they originated in this land. The monks produce them in their monasteries. These knots symbolise the eternity of creation,' he explained, tracing a finger along one of the designs. 'They swirl and twirl around the edge of the page but they always come back neatly to where they started.'

Then, with a flourish, Balek put a finger on one part of the parchment and said in his heavily accented Latin, 'This is Jerusalem, the jewel of the east. This is where the Church of the Holy Sepulchre stands.'

'I have heard Lord Robert speak of that place,' Donal murmured with excitement.

'Under the domed roof of that sacred building,' Balek told him, warming to the tale, 'is the entrance to the tiny chapel encasing what was the tomb of our Blessed Lord. Sometimes it is difficult to believe that I have not looked upon that shrine in over thirty years for I have visited it countless times in my dreams. Lit by the glow of a hundred candles, the Tabernacle of the Sepulchre might have been crafted by a tribe of radiant angels. Gleaming gold and sparkling gems adorn the niches of this sanctuary. A thousand jewels glitter in the flickering yellow half-light that plays upon the splendid mosaic walls.'

The chieftain gasped in wonder as a clear picture formed itself in his mind. He could not contain his amazement at Balek's eloquence.

'The low hum of chanting monks forever fills this hallowed vault,' the tilecutter continued. 'A hundred voices rise and fall, peaking in passionate crescendos, to trail away into whispered prayers and droning hymns. Holy brothers from Greece, Byzantium, Alexandria, Ethiopia, or the Christian communities in the Frankish kingdoms, sing, give praise, offer thanks, seek guidance. At every moment they are attentive to their God. Pilgrims file in at all hours of the day and night. Men, women and children come from the four corners of the earth to worship at the entrance to this monument, entreating the benevolence of the Creator. Under this dome they search for salvation and plead for the remission of all their sins.'

'Truly, you speak as though you had never left that place,' Donal observed.

'Jerusalem lives in my heart,' Balek explained as he moved his hand slowly along the edge of the drawing to a place marked on the eastern edge of a sea. 'This is Acre. My home.'

Donal nodded to show he understood the design was a map of the Holy Land. 'I have heard that Acre is a very beautiful city.'

'You speak the truth. And it is a sadness to me that I cannot see my home,' Balek said but the smile did not leave his face, not even for a second. 'One day I will go back.' Then he pointed to another part of the design. 'This is the battle of Kerak. I was there at the wedding feast of Humphrey d'Toron and the Princess Isabella when Saladin and his army arrived to lay siege on the castle.'

Donal's eyes widened with wonder. 'You were besieged by the King of the Saracens?'

'Oh yes,' Balek beamed. 'And the lady of the castle sent the Saracen a gift from the feast table. But the infidels ran away when King Baldwin of the Outremer came to our rescue. See here,' he pointed, 'here is King Saladin riding off towards the east.'

'Have you witnessed any other great battles?'

'No,' the tilecutter answered quickly, 'and I thank God that I have not. Now come, I will show you my apprentices at work. They have been learning to cut the ceramic ready for it to be placed on the wall. This is a skilled task which I would not normally allow them to do, but this chapel is a very large undertaking. If I cut all the tiles myself, it would take many years to complete the decoration of the entire building.'

The two assistants sat outside in the sunshine, each with a smooth flat stone in front of them. One of the men wore a large white head covering which wrapped around his forehead to keep his long hair from falling over his face as he worked. The other had a headband which served the same purpose. Both men sported thick black beards and work-toughened hands exactly like those of the tilecutter.

Slowly, steadily each apprentice placed a square of coloured ceramic on the stone before him. Then they took up their mallets and a strange instrument shaped like an axe head. The blade of this tool was carefully placed across the ceramic where the cut was to be made.

Donal got the impression that the assistants were rather nervous about being watched intently, so he restrained himself from asking the master mason any questions for the time being. The first man raised his mallet but did not even get a chance to strike before Balek caught the shaft of the tool and corrected the man's posture.

'If I teach them this skill,' he explained to Donal, 'I must do it well because a teacher is known by the hand of his student. If they smash tiles and cut badly, men will say that Balek taught them. Balek's name will no longer be respected. Balek will not be allowed to work and he will starve.'

He broke off from his explanation to encourage his apprentice again. The student lifted the mallet and when it came down squarely on the head of the tile-axe, the ceramic split into two neat pieces. Balek slapped the man on the back to congratulate him.

'I will leave them for a month or so to cut the tiles which will be used for the background arrangements. It is not so important for these tiles to be perfectly shaped and this frees me to prepare the walls completely and refine the patterns that I will use. By the time they have cut four or five thousand pieces, they will be on the road to becoming tilecutters.'

'Where did all these tiles come from?' Donal asked, knowing they could not have been produced locally.

'Lord William sailed through the straits that are called the Pillars of Hercules on his journey home. In the Moorish kingdom of the north live the best ceramic craftsmen in the world. There is peace and tolerance between Christian, Jew and Moslem in that land, so William was able to negotiate a very good price for these tiles.'

Balek swept his hand through the air, indicating the collection of tiles which lay stacked by the wall of the chapel. 'Alas, there are not enough here for me to complete the task. I will have to build ovens and begin sampling the local clay. I will have to make many more tiles before this chapel is finished.'

'You will make the tiles yourself?' Donal asked, puzzled. 'I had no idea that you had such skill.'

The tilecutter shook his head and laughed as he explained that all master tilecutters could do such work. Then he went on to describe the magnificent mosque in Acre which had so impressed the crusaders that they had spared it from destruction and converted it into a church. The tilecutter spoke also of the exotic customs of the Jews and Moslems of that country. 'Every devout follower of Mohammed kneels to pray five times a day,' he told the chieftain.

Donal listened intently to every word the man had to say, fascinated by such exotic tales. He got the impression that Balek considered the Saracens to be a very pious people, despite their heathen ways. The chieftain found himself wishing that he could travel to the distant land of Outremer and witness the marvels for himself.

That afternoon passed quickly. Donal had not intended to stay so long at Bally Raine but the day slipped by without him noticing. It was dark before he managed to drag himself away from the chapel and the tilecutter's magnificent stories, though he promised to return soon to hear more about the world beyond the shores of Ireland.

By the time Donal made his way back to Cúil Ghréine, Eilish was already rugged up in their bed in the loft. The turf had been stacked on the fire for the night and all was silent. The chieftain did not wish to disturb his wife so he tried to make as little noise as possible, but Eilish was not asleep. She rolled over in bed and looked up at her husband, her golden locks falling about her shoulders.

'Out with the tilecutter again?' she asked and Donal stopped in his tracks, hoping she was not too annoyed with him.

'He is doing a fine job,' he answered, removing his boots and placing them carefully by the door.

'He is doing a fine job of distracting you from your work,' Eilish noted wryly. 'I would be surprised if he has the time to concentrate on his own chores after bending your ear all day long.'

'Now, now!' Donal laughed, seeing his wife was only half serious in her rebuke. 'It is my duty to develop a strong relationship with him. Balek is going to decorate my father's tomb.'

'He will be decorating yours,' Eilish quipped, 'if I am left to bring in all the cows by myself once more this month.'

Donal hung up his cloak and removed his tunic. On his way to bed he picked up a few morsels of food from the fireside and ate hungrily.

'Did you not eat today?' Eilish asked.

'I did not have much time,' the chieftain began. 'I worked very hard all day.'

'Since when is it work to sit and listen to travellers' tales?'

'We reviewed the plans for the chapel,' Donal protested. 'There is still much to be done.'

Then the chieftain took a cup of ale and climbed up the ladder into bed with his wife. She pulled the covers around them both and took a sip of the brew, then settled back as her husband drained the cup.

'Tell me one of his stories,' she begged gently. 'I want to hear of the lands in the east.'

'What tale would you like?' Donal smiled as he put his cup down and placed an arm around his wife. She nuzzled into his body but did not state a preference. 'He told me about the siege of Kerak,' the chieftain offered.

'What else do men ever talk about but war?' Eilish sighed. 'Tell me about the people of Outremer and their customs.'

Donal settled down to relate all that Balek had told him. Eilish listened intently, asking questions here and there. When Donal finished telling her of the general low standing of women throughout the kingdom of Outremer, she could not resist commenting on the absurdity of treating women as possessions to be bought and sold in the marketplace.

'Why do the women stand for this?' Eilish asked, incredulous. 'Why do they not rise up and do away with their chieftains and kings?'

'They have lived in this manner for so long that it has become natural for them. It is their custom, though Balek assures me that it is not really men who are in charge of everything. He says that the women of his country have subtle powers of coercion which they exert on the menfolk to get their way.'

'Perhaps I could learn from the women of Outremer,' Eilish said with glee. 'Does Balek know any recipes for subduing a man?'

'You have already mastered that art,' the chieftain laughed. 'I am sure you could teach your sisters in the Holy Land a thing or two.'

'Perhaps I could,' Eilish conceded. 'But I hope you do not suspect that I have worked a charm on you.'

'Of course you have,' Donal replied. 'I have known it since the first day I laid eyes upon you.'

'A love charm works two ways,' his wife smiled. 'If I had cast a spell on you, then I would have been as besotted with you as you were with me when we were courting.'

'Were you not besotted?' Donal cried.

'A little,' she laughed, then she rolled away from him and closed her eyes. 'Good night, Donal.'

The chieftain grinned. 'You cannot be just a little besotted. That is like saying a sheep is a little bit hairy.' He pulled Eilish closer to him, stroking her arm with the tip of his fingers as she pretended to sleep. Finally he leaned forward, kissed her gently on the back of the neck and let his own eyes shut.

'I'll leave the cows to you in the morning then,' Eilish said after a few moments and Donal's smile widened.

After darkness fell and the FitzWilliam household began settling for the night, Robert remained on his knees, immersed in prayer in the little chapel in his chamber. His aching legs did not distract him from his devotions.

All his attention was focused on a beautiful painted wooden statue of the Virgin dressed in a long white robe and blue head scarf. Robert meditated upon this image for at least an hour every day.

The Mother of God.

Mary was his guardian and his guide. Robert was certain that she spoke to him in whispers at times, advising him on what to do and how to behave. He had told Father Conlan all about his special relationship with the Virgin, but the priest did not entirely approve of this type of veneration. Instead he advised Robert that the true object of prayer should be Christ, for it was His sacrifice that had saved humankind from the slavery of sin. Mary, Conlan argued, was merely a woman, just the vessel which God had chosen for the task of bearing His Son, and therefore insignificant.

Robert was not swayed by this argument. If Mary was the holy vessel which carried Christ, then she herself must be a queen in heaven. She was the ideal woman, unstained by sin, faithful to her lord and the wishes of God.

As the moon rose Robert ceased his prayers for a while to rise from his altar and light some candles in the darkened room. The heir of Bally Raine had lost track of how long he had been at prayer. When he was meditating he never really took too much notice of the hours flying by. Being in that state of quiet bliss was, to him, like spending the hours in the company of an earthly beloved. Time ran differently when he was in the presence of the Blessed Virgin.

Once the candles were lit, Robert laid another cushion on the ground on top of the first and prepared to return to his devotions. This night, of all nights, he had much to pray about and a great deal to contemplate.

As he settled himself a servant came to call him to supper. He curtly informed the woman he would take his meal alone in his chamber. As she was leaving he changed his mind, inspired by the thought of sitting through the night at a vigil of thanksgiving.

'Never mind,' he called to her. 'Bring me some water. Tonight I will sit in fasting and prayer, thanking God for the gifts he has given me.'

The servant rolled her eyes, shook her head then left

quickly to inform Lord William of his son's decision. She knew what the old knight would say. William was a pious man but he did not approve of Robert's zealous vigils. In the old lord's opinion these religious outpourings took place too often and lasted too long. He was sure that the strenuous devotions had resulted in his son's thin face and pallid complexion. The servants, on the other hand, were convinced that the whole family was odd and so were rarely surprised by anything that any of them did.

Robert did not care what the gossiping servants or his father said. What need had he of mere food? Bread could only feed the body. But bathing in the presence of the Virgin satisfied a deeper need. It nourished his soul.

Before returning to prayer, Robert thought over the events of the day. With the rising sun he would become the lord of the estates, even though he did not really wish to. He had, after all, been running Bally Raine for quite a while in the absence of his father. One part of Robert was excited at the prospect of being able to order things entirely in his own way. But another part of him was devastated that he would be tied to this land for the rest of his life.

Through great effort of will he blocked out all fear of the future to lose himself in the ecstasy of the soul. 'I offer my life to you, Queen of Heaven,' he chanted gently under his breath as if he were speaking to his lover. 'Take me and let me do thy works as you will.'

Robert had repeated these words a thousand times but only now did the true meaning of them strike him. His mind was drawn back to the night of Mathúin's death. He remembered the awe he had experienced when his father spoke of the legend of the Grail Cup, the holy vessel which, according to legend, had been the sacramental cup at the Last Supper. The Grail was believed by many to be the chalice by which God offered eternal life in the Kingdom of Heaven.

'The holy vessel,' he said aloud, 'which held the blood of Christ. Just as the Virgin was the holy vessel which bore Christ into the world. The Holy Cup of Life which grants an eternity without death.'

Suddenly the realisation came to him that such a cup, if it existed, belonged rightfully to Mary, the Mother of God.

'What became of it?' he asked the statue as he looked up at the ever-smiling face. 'Where is the Grail Cup? When Outremer was overrun, did the chalice fall into the hands of the infidel?'

The wooden effigy did not answer, she merely continued smiling blankly and Robert understood then that he would have to find out the answers to these questions for himself. He could not bear the thought of such a sacred relic being in the possession of some rude Saracen who had no idea of its true value or significance to the world.

'I will ask Father,' he decided, and with that he kissed the feet of the statue, crossed himself and rose from his knees. When he had slipped on his house shoes and found a large candle to light his way, he started down the stairs to the feasting hall.

He stopped short, however, before he reached the bottom of the steps. There was no sign of William but the servants were seated around the fire telling stories and swapping news of the district.

'Where is my father?' Robert asked, trying to sound as if he had some authority.

'Gone to his bed, my lord,' answered the old woman who was in charge of household duties in the manor and castle. 'And he begged not to be disturbed on his last night in his old home,' she added as an afterthought.

Robert nearly jumped when she addressed him as her lord, but found himself not altogether comfortable with the appellation.

'Congratulations, my lord,' the chamberlain said merrily.

'I am sure you will be as kind and good a master as William was. Will you join us in a drink?'

'No,' Robert stammered without thinking and then realised that this was now a duty expected of him; once in a while he would have to accept the goodwill and company of his servants. He well understood that this was how his father had engendered such loyalty in everyone who worked on the estates.

Robert looked at their faces across the hall and then his eyes were drawn to the roaring fire where a spare seat had been set. He decided that it would not hurt to spend a while with them. 'I do not want to intrude on your conversation. It is a kind offer that you have extended.'

'You would be most welcome, my lord, to sup with us,' Lonan answered with sincerity. 'Do come and join us.'

Robert smiled and quickly crossed the hall, making for the chair closest to the fire. Before he had a chance to sit down, however, the old victualler stopped him.

'That chair is for Cinneach. You must not sit there,' she exclaimed. 'Here is a stool for you.'

With a laugh to himself at the strange ways of these folk, Robert took his place and the conversation turned to the day-to-day running of the estates. These half-a-dozen folk were the real lords of the land, Robert thought. Around him were gathered the game-keeper who controlled all the hunting, the grain warden who kept a tally of the oats and barley, the victualler who ensured every household had sufficient food, the cook who also brewed the ale that was a staple of their diet, and the husbandman whose duty was to the animals on the estate. The chamberlain, who kept the accounts, managed the others and implemented the lord's wishes.

Not long after Robert took his place, the priest, Father Conlan, arrived to listen in on the gossip. Ale tinged with sweet and aromatic herbs was passed around. After only two cups Robert felt his head begin to spin from the potency of the brew.

'Careful, my lord,' the old victualler laughed, 'that keg was more than double strength and it is not Norman ale. Drink it slowly or you'll have two heads in the morning and you'll wish they'd both drop off.'

Everyone laughed heartily and knowingly. Robert, despite being embarrassed at his inability to keep up with his servants' drinking, had a laugh also. Then, before he knew what was happening, the room fell silent and a short man with a long cloak entered the chamber from the rear door. There was a flurry of activity as a cushion was found and placed carefully on the empty chair closest to the fire. An especially large wooden cup was brought out brimming with ale. This was shortly followed by breads and meats on a large tray which were passed around the company.

The stranger threw off his cloak and Robert was surprised at the man's youth. He could have only been twenty-five years old at the most, the same age as he. Beneath the unfashionable weather-worn cloak, he was wearing the strange attire of the western clans, a people who had little contact with the Normans of the north and east.

Robert felt a chill run down his spine. Folk of the western tribes were reportedly savage in the extreme. Their warriors were said to collect the heads of their enemies as trophies. Indeed, there was a story that, when Dermot MacDermot the last high king of all Ireland was slain in an ambush, the westerners dismembered his body and cut off his head. Then they battled among themselves for possession of the gruesome trophy with heavy sticks until it was no more than a soggy mess of smashed bone and brains.

The stranger's tunic was short and made of wool; his hose were not tight fitting and he wore no garters, so the garment sagged around the knees and ankles. His feet were bare and toughened from walking. Around his waist he wore a dark brown woollen length of cloth that was long enough for him to throw over his shoulder and wide enough to be spread over his chest. This garment hung to just above his knees.

His long black hair was tucked up under a large wool cap that bulged at the back with the mass of locks. His beard had not been trimmed in a long, long time and it was matted and dirty. The young lord's eyes widened at the sight of a small parasite in among the hairs.

It had always struck Robert as strange that the Irish rarely shaved their beards entirely. William had told stories about the first Normans to arrive in Ireland who had made a sport of pulling at the beards of the Gaelic chieftains in mockery. His father had explained to him that it was this behaviour more than anything else that had caused the five years of war that followed. The Irish were a proud race. Now Robert thought it ironic that William wore his own beard long in the fashion of the Templars.

'My lord,' the old victualler spoke up, to get Robert's attention, 'this is Cinneach O'Hare, a famous seanachie from the kingdom of Connaught. He is travelling in this land at the behest of his king. Among our people he is accorded the same honours as one of royal blood.'

Robert sat absolutely entranced by the strange-looking creature before him. He decided that Latin would be the best language to try on this fellow. His own command of the Irish tongue was good but he knew that no westerners spoke the Norman language. Robert stood up and bowed slightly.

'I am Robert FitzWilliam, Lord of Bally Raine,' he declared, rising from his chair.

'It is a pleasure to serve you, my lord,' Cinneach answered in perfect Latin and in a voice that was both soothing and sonorous. 'I am a storyteller and a musician.'

Robert sat down, surprised at the man's manner and

grasp of the language. He had expected that the stranger might have had a few words of Latin, but in fact he spoke it better than anyone Robert knew.

The seanachie pulled a bag from his back and produced a three-stringed instrument. Robert immediately recognised it as a rebec, a simple fiddle common in France.

'I hope you will forgive me,' Cinneach said, 'I have left my harp in the safe keeping of my wife for the night. I have this to play and it is a sweet instrument.'

'Where did you learn to play the rebec?' Robert asked. 'I have never seen such an instrument in Ireland. I did not know your folk played it.'

'I learned the art of the rebec from a court musician in the retinue of King Louis of France,' Cinneach explained. 'I went there with my king when he was hoping to obtain assistance from the French.' He began tuning the instrument as he spoke. When the three strings were humming in harmony, he set the rebec down by the chair. 'It will take a while for this one to get used to the warmth of the room so in the meantime I will tell a tale.' Then Cinneach sat down and took the great cup of ale that was offered to him.

'Do you know any stories of the Grail?' Robert blurted out and the seanachie raised an eyebrow at this.

'I know a few tales,' he answered. 'Which one would you like to hear?'

'I have only heard that Godfrey d'Acre found the Holy Cup in Jerusalem and that he died whilst returning to France with it.'

'Then you know a part of the tale that I have not heard,' Cinneach admitted. 'But I can tell you something of its origins and of its reputed power. Stories of the Grail are common in the Frankish kingdoms.'

Cinneach looked about the room and realised it would be best if he spoke in the Irish tongue. Few of the servants would understand if he told the story in Latin.

He turned to Robert and said slowly in his own language, 'How well do you speak Irish?'

'Well enough to answer you,' Robert replied carefully, not wishing to seem unlearned in this man's presence.

'Would you be offended if I related the tale in my own language for the benefit of these people?'

'I will let you know if I miss any of your meaning,' Robert replied quickly. He was proud that he had managed the answer with very little trace of his accent and surprised at himself that he was so proficient at the foreign tongue.

'This is the story of the Holy Cup of Christ,' Cinneach began, 'which, like the Cauldron of Plenty from the tales of the ancient days, is said to be able to provide any company with the food of their desire and to pour out enough drink to quench any thirst.' At that the seanachie smiled and took a long draught of the cup in his hand. Then he set it down on the floor beside his chair.

'I heard this story from a man who had travelled with his lord to the Holy Land in search of the cup. Sad to say, the knight was not worthy of the Grail. He returned to France empty-handed and broken-hearted.' Cinneach paused for a second, staring into the fire.

'Some say that the cup is made of olive wood from the garden of Gethsemane where Adam was conceived and Christ betrayed,' he continued after a moment. 'Others claim that it was fashioned out of the pure gold of the sacred treasures of Solomon's temple after the Romans destroyed the great building. I have also heard that no-one living really knows for certain what the cup looks like. At the Last Supper Christ served the wine from this cup and then gave it to his uncle, Joseph of Arimathea.'

Cinneach looked around the room, satisfied that everyone was giving him their full attention. As soon as he stopped speaking each listener returned his gaze, eager for more.

'Later, when Christ was dying on the Cross,' the seanachie went on, 'Joseph collected drops of Our Lord's blood in the cup. After the Lord had risen, Joseph distributed the healing liquid to the sick and needy. When Christ's blood touched the cup, the vessel was transformed into the magical Grail.'

Cinneach glanced at Robert to make sure the Norman was keeping up with the tale. Sure he was, he went on. 'Joseph fled the Holy Land in fear of his life when the Romans began to persecute the early Christians. In time, he and his followers came in their wanderings to the Isle of Glass in Britain where they established their church on the hill. The Saxons call this place Glastonbury in the midst of the Summer Land. Joseph brought the Grail Cup with him, built a shrine for it and, when the little chapel was finished, a magical spring erupted from beneath the floor of the building. The water that poured forth from this spring was the same colour as Christ's blood and may still be seen to this day.'

All the servants gasped in appreciation at this twist for they recognised a common thread that ran through many of the ancient tales. The magical death of the hero and the mystical transformation that took place at his passing were well-worn themes. Even the concept of the sacred power of healing blood was a familiar idea to any who knew the old legends.

'I, myself,' Cinneach announced, 'have visited the Holy Well at Glastonbury and bathed my brow in its blood-red waters. I have seen the staff which Joseph struck into the ground and which bloomed at his command into a thorn-bush. The bush still flowers in the midst of winter on the sixth day of January which the Culdees celebrate as the day of Christ's birth. But the Grail Cup was stolen and fell into many hands before one known as the Fisher-King retrieved it. He returned it to the Holy Land and built a castle to house the sacred vessel. But in a war against the Saracens the Fisher-King was wounded in the thigh by the same lance that had punctured Christ's lung and he was ever after rendered impotent.'

Cinneach looked over at Robert and noticed that the young lord's eyes were wide and his mouth had dropped open.

'Have you spent time among the Culdees?' Robert asked.

Cinneach glanced at the servants one by one before he replied. 'I have known men and women who followed that path,' he admitted carefully.

'Are they as evil as I have been told?'

'They are worse,' Father Conlan answered before Cinneach had the opportunity. 'They are bloody pagans and servants of the Devil himself.'

'Simply because they keep the old ways?' the seanachie snapped. 'The old customs were good enough for our ancestors and many of them were Christians. Saint Columcille, the founder of the Church in this land, was a druid!'

'I don't understand that word,' Robert cut in.

'Druid is a term for a law-keeper and a poet,' Cinneach explained, 'or a very learned person.'

'Culdees are heathens who do not recognise the Church of Rome or the Pope,' the priest argued. 'Columcille was one of their kind, that is certain. He was an evil old sorcerer. Saint Patrick is the true founder of the Church in Ireland.'

'Patrick was a Roman!' the seanachie laughed. 'At least Columcille was one of our own. The Romans are the worst pagans of all.'

'Watch your tongue,' the priest spat, 'or you may regret your foolish words!'

Robert raised an eyebrow. Cinneach, realising there was no use trying to change Father Conlan's mind, went on with his story, to the relief of all the servants.

'The thigh wound not only rendered the Fisher-King unfit

to rule, it also brought a plague upon his land. When the plague ended the desert started to encroach upon Jerusalem as it does even in these times. But it is said that one day a knight who is chaste, poor and who follows strictly the word of God will come to dine at table with the Fisher-King. If he asks the correct question of the king, the waste-land will retreat, the king will be healed and the Grail will grant that knight everlasting life in the Kingdom of Heaven.'

'And where is the Fisher-King's Castle?' Robert interrupted.

'No-one knows for certain,' the storyteller replied. 'I have heard a rumour that the Fisher-King dwells in the maze of caves under the great Temple of Solomon. The man who told me this story also claimed the Order of the Poor Knights of Christ were established specifically to search the Temple Mount from top to bottom in the quest for the Grail Cup. That is why they take the vows of chastity, obedience and the sharing of all property in common, so one of them will be worthy to ask the question of the Fisher-King. And that is why, before the fall of the city, their headquarters was within the Temple itself. It is well known to any who have visited the Outremer that the Temple Knights were always digging passages beneath the ancient ruin.'

'So the Knights Templar seek the Grail?' the lord confirmed.

'That is what I have been told,' Cinneach replied. 'Though I cannot be certain. Is your father not a postulant of that order? You might ask him. There is one other tale I have heard,' the storyteller added. 'The Grail is capable of granting an eternal life full of bliss, but that is a common thread in my people's stories also. We mortals always yearn for what we cannot have.'

'Have you been to the Holy Land?' Robert asked.

'I have not,' Cinneach answered politely.

'Would you ever travel there yourself?'

'I might consider it,' the seanachie stated carefully, unsure of what was being asked of him. 'I might. But I have a family here and cannot disregard my duties as a seanachie.'

'Tell us the tale of the Mare of Macha,' the victualler cut in. 'It is a much better story.'

'You always ask for that story,' the chamberlain complained. 'I would like to hear the tale of Da Derga's Hostel or the Cattle Raid of Cuilgne.'

'The Hound of Cullen,' the sergeant-at-arms begged, 'or the story of the Knights of the Red Branch.'

Cinneach put up his hands to quiet them all. 'I will tell you the tale of the Battle of the Trees,' he offered and that seemed to satisfy everyone.

Robert did not hear a word of the following story. Nor did he listen very intently when Cinneach later began to bow his rebec and strike up a merry tune. It may have been the strong ale or the seanachie's talent for tale-telling that had distracted him, but the young lord was already imagining himself dressed in the white robes of the Templars, riding off to Outremer in search of the Holy Cup of the Grail.

Rufus had to pay the soldier much more than he had originally intended. Ten gold marks was certainly more than the sentry would have earned in five years of standing guard, watching the safety of his lord. But the task of intercepting his father's rider was delicate and essential to his plans. So, Rufus reasoned to himself, the eventual benefits well justified the expense.

William's messenger to Henry's court prepared to leave on his errand the same morning that the lord made ready for his departure to the abbey at Shelton. It was no more than a short ride from the abbey to his old estates, indeed the monastery fell within the bounds of his land. But William would be so removed from the day-to-day life of the estate that he might as well have been in Jerusalem, for the abbey was closed to all outsiders. The brothers received no news from beyond its walls.

The soldier Rufus hired had often travelled to the court of the English king and had kinfolk there, so no eyebrows would be raised when he arrived with a letter from William. And Rufus promised to give the fellow even more gold upon his return, so it was unlikely that the soldier would betray him.

To pay a man to murder a messenger with letters for the King was treason, and a charge of treason, if proved, would put an end to all the young FitzWilliam's ambitions. In truth, the conniving mind of Rufus had already decided that this hired killer would have to be somehow silenced upon his return. This would not just save Rufus an immense amount of money but also eliminate the only witness to his wrongdoing. He sent the soldier off hard on the heels of the messenger, with four marks in gold in a purse at his belt, in lieu of the remainder, and the warrior was well pleased with the sum.

Now Rufus prepared to farewell his father and to set in motion the next part of his strategy. At the door to Robert's chamber he waited until he thought he could hear his brother on the other side putting on his cloak ready to leave. At that moment he knocked loudly. Robert opened the door immediately.

'Ah, brother,' Rufus began, brightly, 'I was hoping we might have a chat about the future.'

'Father has not left yet,' Robert scowled. 'Do you think we might wait until the hearth in his chamber is cold?'

'It is your chamber now, brother,' Rufus pointed out.

Robert touched his brow with his fingertips. 'I could not sleep there. I am happy with my own chamber. You may have Father's room if you wish. I have no objection.'

Rufus felt his heart beat for joy in his throat. This might be far easier than he had expected. 'I was thinking,' he went on, not missing a beat, 'we should make a show of unity for Father before he leaves. Let us reconcile before him and all the household. Let us openly pledge our support for one another.'

Robert eyed his brother with suspicion.

'It would be fitting, I believe,' Rufus continued, 'if I were to swear an oath of fealty to you and you to swear your obligation to me in return. That way Father need never worry in future about our feelings for one another. And you may rest easy that I wish nothing but to work with you for the good of the estate.'

'Have no fear, brother,' Robert replied. 'Father may have toyed with the idea of disenfranchising you but he judged me correctly. I would not dream of doing such a thing. I know that I could not rule this estate alone. I will be depending on your help to keep everything running smoothly. I have been seriously considering raising the taxes slightly to pay for . . .' He stopped himself and consciously reworded the rest of the sentence. '. . . certain improvements that I have long had in mind.'

'An excellent idea!' Rufus agreed, impressed with his brother for the first time ever. 'I have been trying to convince Father to raise the taxes for years. The peasants on this land pay less for our protection than any in the whole of Ireland. It is expensive keeping an estate like this going. What with fortifications, training and feeding the men-at-arms, purchasing seed grain, repairing the roads, feeding the poor, there is much to pay for.'

'We are agreed then,' Robert interrupted, getting to the point. 'You will pledge fealty to me and I will see that you are well looked after in the future. We will work as a team but I will remain in control. I will make all the decisions. And you will repay your debt to the estates as quickly as possible.'

'As you wish it,' Rufus agreed, slightly put out that his brother had chosen to emphasise that aspect of the arrangement. 'I place myself in your hands.' He could hardly believe that things were going so much better than he had expected. Rufus smiled at his brother in genuine gratitude.

'So,' Robert continued, 'the first task you can complete for me is to provide me with a full list of the accounts for the past five years. When Father is gone we will meet with the chamberlain in your new room. We will review every expense and income, from the amount of grain in the storehouse to the number of cows in the fields. We will cut costs where appropriate and raise the level of revenue wherever possible. It will distress old Lonan but it must be done if we are going to live the kind of lives we aspire to. Now it is time to farewell William. Let us speak no more of this.'

Rufus watched his brother set off down the stairs and could hardly believe the change that had come over him. He had always considered Robert to be a weakling without any will of his own, but now he found that he had some grudging respect for his older sibling. He even found himself regretting somewhat that he had set in motion a plan to destroy entirely his brother's claim to the title of this land.

But that was a fleeting moment of weakness that soon passed away completely. Rufus knew in the heart of his heart that it was he, not Robert, who deserved to be Lord of Bally Raine. And he was not going to settle for anything less.

Chapter Seven

When Balek had seen to the cutting of the many tiles for the mosaics inside the chapel, he began to plan the most difficult part of the project. Certain that his two apprentices would be able to work unsupervised for a time, the tilecutter concentrated on a task that would prove to be his greatest challenge.

The overall construction of the chapel was not his responsibility, for that had been left to the skilled craftsmanship of the stonemasons. The great long windows would be coloured and fitted together by glass blowers, so this was not his concern either. The task he had to consider was the crafting of two thousand new tiles for the roof of the chapel and a further thousand for the floors of the interior.

Each day he rode out, a man-at-arms as escort, to the hills and valleys all around the estates, looking for suitable clay from which to fashion his tiles. Balek was a lucky man. Within a few weeks he located two excellent sources of clay, both of which were fine and fairly free of stones or foreign matter. Once he had tested out his samples back at his workshop, he was satisfied that he would be able to make both the white tiles for the interior of the chapel and the brown tiles for the roof.

Lord Robert arranged for some of the tenants to help Balek excavate the clay and lay it aside. Two great piles of earth less than five hundred paces apart were built above a stream half a day's walk from Bally Raine. Throughout the winter the clay would be left in these heaps to be broken up by the frost and cleaned by the rains.

While the clay was settling in its stacks Balek went about constructing the first of two kilns for the firing and glazing of his tiles. Back at the castle he had the men-at-arms dig two holes, each large enough to fire as many tiles at once as possible. Once that was done, Balek called on Donal and his kinsmen to help build the ovens. They used stones that had been cut for that very purpose by the stonemasons.

It was hard dirty work and it took a month of trial and error before Donal and his men, unused to working with stone, managed to complete the first kiln. Their job was made harder by the fact that they could not use any mortar to hold the stones together as this would likely crack with the heat of the furnace. Every stone had to fit perfectly into place with its neighbours so that the whole structure was secure. If the roof collapsed after the furnace had been loaded, all of Balek's work would be wasted and most of the tiles shattered.

By the time the spring festival came around, Balek was ready to start forming his tiles from the cleaned clay. He requisitioned as many wagons as he could to bring it up from the valley where it had been sitting for three months. After two weeks of toiling at this task, his team had brought the precious earth to a specially constructed wooden shed. Here Balek intended to begin the long process of pressing the tiles and forming their shapes.

His apprentices had mostly completed their tilecutting by this time. One was put in charge of seeing to the white clay and the other made sure that the dark clay was ready for forming. Throughout this whole process Donal spent as much time as possible at Bally Raine, watching the tilecutter at work and lending a hand wherever he could.

Lord Robert put his men-at-arms at Balek's disposal to help get the job done in time for the kilns to be fired in the summer.

When the earth had been shifted, twenty men sat around a long wide table sorting the clay, removing stones, twigs and other impurities. Another five men, watched over by Balek and his apprentices, had small wooden boxes into which they pressed the damp clay to form the shape of each tile. After the excess clay was scraped off the top of this mould, the tile was tipped out onto the table.

If the tile was intended for the chapel roof, the sides were pressed together to form little raised ridges. These ridges would channel the water down the middle of the tile and away from the edges so that the roof would not leak. Then the top of the tile had two holes stabbed in it so that it could be fixed securely to the roof beams with wooden nails. If the tile was destined for the interior of the chapel, it was left flat and set aside to be taken directly to the drying shed.

As the spring was usually wet and the rains this year showed no sign of abating, the drying shed was built without any windows for ventilation. A central hearth was kept burning day and night to keep the house at an even temperature. It was essential that the tiles be dried out slowly and evenly. For this reason Balek regularly visited the drying house to make sure that the man tending the fire had not fallen asleep or built the flames too high so that the clay dried out too quickly and cracked.

Donal helped Balek carve designs into blocks of wood which were then used to make impressions in some of the tiles. Once they were painted with a special pigment, these tiles would be used to cover the floor around the altar of the chapel.

Even the process of making the colours for the tiles was painstaking. The pigments were produced by taking lead and burning it in a furnace until it turned to powder. This powder was then mixed with soured ale and painted onto the tiles before they were placed in the kiln.

The result, Balek assured Donal, would be a cream-coloured glassy surface over the tile which was waterproof and, just as importantly, fireproof. Copper filings were added to the mixture if a green glaze was required.

By the approach of the midsummer festival, the kilns had been finished and most of the tiles were ready for firing. Lord Robert agreed that precious timber, which would usually be burned in a great bonfire to celebrate the festival, would be used to feed the kilns instead.

By tradition, as chieftains of the estate, the O'Regans were responsible for ensuring that everyone attending the festival was well fed and watered. So Donal and his kinfolk travelled to the castle a few days beforehand to help with the preparations. This year they had the extra responsibility of making certain that all was in readiness for the firing of the kilns, for Donal's father had helped pay for the chapel decorations. Eilish sent word to her family at Clonough that she would appreciate whatever help they could give in the running of the kitchens and the doling out of the ale.

There was always plenty of strong ale brewed especially for the occasion, which was traditionally supplied by the lord of the castle.

The fair at Bally Raine had been held every year on midsummer's day since Donal's ancestors had crossed the River Clonough in ancient times. Folk from far and near gathered at the festival to buy and sell cattle. And to spend the evenings drinking with kinfolk or dancing with strangers. At the end of all the festivities men and women were usually apportioned their responsibilities in the coming harvest. It was also the time when rents and taxes were set down for the coming year.

As this was his first festival as lord of the estates, Robert made sure that he surpassed his father in generosity to the folk who worked the lands and paid rents to the castle. As the preparations advanced, the word quickly passed around the tenants that the Lord of Bally Raine was going to provide a fine feast, so everyone on the estate was in high spirits. That is to say, almost everyone.

Three nights before the great market was to be held, Rufus went to his brother's chambers to protest bitterly that so much money was being wasted on the common folk. But Robert shrugged the objections off, explaining that he wanted all the tenants to realise he meant them well and regarded them highly.

'They will grow lazy if you spoil them too much!' Rufus bellowed.

'They will work harder when the harvest comes in if they know they are going to be rewarded for their toil,' Robert replied quietly.

'I will not allow you to waste so much gold on these folk. They are not our people. Our father's generation conquered them. We owe them nothing.'

'Our father's generation may have invaded most of this land but our father did not rule this estate by force. He won the people's trust by treating them with respect and not allowing the kind of famine that was induced elsewhere in this country by greedier lords.'

'I will not permit this flagrant waste of money!' Rufus repeated, his grey-green eyes flashing. 'I will inform Father of your intentions.'

Robert stood up, unintentionally knocking his chair over as he did so. The cat ran from the room screeching. 'I am Lord of Bally Raine!' he stormed, his usually soft voice cracking slightly with pent-up anger. 'And you are in my debt no less than any of the tenants. Try to remember your place, little brother, or I will be forced to reconsider the arrangement that we have between us.'

'The men of the garrison need new horses,' Rufus pleaded, trying a different approach to get his brother to see reason. 'The soldiers need repairs to their weapons and armour. If we are going to continue expanding the production of oats and other grain, we will need more men-at-arms to guard the stores and better defences for the castle itself.'

'By the end of the harvest, dear brother, I will have assembled the largest fighting force this part of the country has ever seen. There will be more soldiers, blacksmiths, horses and weapons than even one such as yourself could be content with.'

Rufus's jaw dropped. 'What are you talking about?'

'I am thinking of going on a journey. I cannot tell you all the details now. There are still some arrangements to be finalised. I will reveal my plans to you in a day or two. In the meantime I want you to know that I will be counting on you to run this estate alone for a time. That is, without my consultation.'

Rufus gasped, staring at his brother in shock. Not for the first time he was reminded of their mother. When she was determined to get her own way, she had the same look in her dark eyes.

'There is more to be done than just the harvest being brought in,' Robert continued. 'Mills have to be maintained, taxes gathered, law-breakers brought to justice, the defences to be seen to and,' the lord paused, making sure that his brother caught the emphasis of what he was about to say, 'the chapel that Father started is to be completed.'

'Where are you going?' the younger FitzWilliam sputtered, convinced now that destiny was delivering the estates into his hands. But before he got an answer, the solution struck him.

'A crusade,' Rufus cried mockingly. 'You are going off on crusade.'

'Do not get too excited, brother. You might discover that you are ploughing a fallow field. I will tell you everything in good time,' Robert insisted. 'But I would ask that you mention this conversation to no-one for the moment. Now I wish to be left alone. I would like you to inspect the chapel tonight before you take your rest and report to me tomorrow on its progress. I will need to know how much more must be spent on its completion.'

Rufus bowed as he withdrew. Outside the door he grabbed the chamberlain by the sleeve and dragged the man after him. 'What is he up to?' he whispered hoarsely as soon as they were both on the stairs.

'He will not tell anyone!' Lonan answered. 'I have no idea what is going on. I have spent the last few weeks gathering all the gold that I can and counting it over and over. But it never seems to be enough for him. He has sold cattle and leased part of the forest to farmers for them to clear. And he has had me write to all his father's debtors insisting that they pay their outstanding obligations immediately.'

'What is going on here?' Rufus wondered aloud. 'Has my brother suddenly become a miser? He is not the sort to travel off to the other side of the world to fight someone else's battles. Is he looking to build something bigger than a chapel?' The young FitzWilliam slapped his thigh, sure that this must be the answer.

'There is certainly more than enough money coming in for him to consider that possibility,' the chamberlain admitted.

'That is just like him,' Rufus hissed, 'to waste a fortune on a useless monument to his own piety.' He grabbed at the chamberlain's arm. 'We cannot let him do it!' he snarled. 'It is our duty for the good of the estates to stop him wasting our resources.'

'Master Rufus,' Lonan interjected, nervous that he was being included in this conspiracy, 'is that wise? Hadn't we better wait and find out exactly what Lord Robert has planned?'

'Tomorrow may be too late!' Rufus declared. 'Tonight, after he has gone to sleep, you will bring the accounts to my chamber and we will go through them together. I will speak with the soldiers myself first thing in the morning. We must put a stop to this madness.'

'I am sorry, my lord,' the chamberlain stammered, certain that this was not a wise course of action, 'your brother is perusing the books this evening. And Donal O'Regan has been waiting in the hall for an audience with Lord Robert since after dinner. I believe the lord will go to bed after they have spoken.'

'What does O'Regan want?' Rufus snarled, angered that he would have to wait to inspect the accounts.

'Lord Robert sent for him,' Lonan explained. 'He did not tell me the reason for the summons.'

'I will wait until tomorrow then,' Rufus conceded. 'But I must see how much has been gathered.'

Lonan bowed nervously, not wishing to side with this man in any dispute.

Rufus saw the look of concern on the chamberlain's face but misread it. 'If you exhibit loyalty to me in this,' Rufus whispered, 'I will not forget you when I am Lord of Bally Raine.' Then the young FitzWilliam turned to make his way to the chapel.

As soon as Rufus was out of earshot the chamberlain crossed himself and muttered under his breath. He would sooner see the Devil as lord of all the estates than Rufus FitzWilliam. But Lonan told himself that this young upstart had no chance of ever becoming lord. Not so long as William's wishes were respected.

Rufus stepped out into the night air and felt a heavy hand on his shoulder. He turned around to face his assailant, at the same time placing a hand to his side to grasp the hilt of his dagger. But before the Norman had time to draw his weapon, he recognised the warrior who stood before him.

'What have you to report?' the young FitzWilliam snarled under his breath, annoyed that he had been approached in this familiar manner.

'The messenger broke his neck in a fall from his horse,' the soldier replied. 'I have the letters here.'

The warrior thrust his huge arm out toward Rufus. There were two parchment rolls in the massive hand. These were Lord William's letters to King Henry. The young FitzWilliam glared at the warrior and then smiled to show his approval.

'A good job cleanly done,' Rufus stated, taking hold of the letters. But the warrior did not let the parchments go.

'Clean work is expensive,' the soldier hissed in a low whisper.

Rufus raised an eybrow at the warrior's tone.

'You have been paid four marks already, Quicktoe,' the young FitzWilliam replied, 'but you have done well. I will have much more work for you in the coming months. As of this moment you will join the garrison as my personal assistant. Now I am going to inspect the chapel. You will accompany me.'

The warrior grinned and bowed respectfully, pleased with this reward. Then he fell into step behind his master as the Norman strode off toward the chapel.

Certain that Rufus had left the castle, Lonan ushered Donal into Lord Robert's room. The faithful old servant knew his lord would not want Rufus knowing the details of his discussion with the chieftain of Cúil Ghréine.

As the door closed and Lonan left, Robert rose from his seat at the fireside. The young lord held his hand out to Donal in greeting.

'Welcome, O'Regan,' Robert said sincerely. 'I am very grateful that you could spare the time to speak with me. How are the preparations going?'

'Very well, my lord,' answered the chieftain, taking Robert's hand and grasping it tightly. 'Very well indeed. We had to bring in ale from the monastery but I am sure we will have enough for the first day at least. I just hope that folk aren't as thirsty as last year or there may not be enough drink in the whole kingdom to satisfy them!'

'I want to make sure that everyone has a good time,' Robert smiled. 'And I want to show my gratitude for all the hard work everyone has done since my father passed the lands on to me. How goes the tiler's work?'

'If the weather holds dry, we'll be ready to fire the tiles the day after tomorrow. That will free the workmen and their families for the market day.'

'Excellent!' Robert enthused. 'It is all going to plan.'

'The chapel is certainly going to be grand,' Donal said. 'A monument to both our fathers and their heroic adventures in the Holy Land.'

'And a fitting tomb for them both,' Robert agreed.

'Is William ill?'

'No,' the lord replied quickly. 'My father is well. I just want to make sure that everything is settled before . . .' Robert looked over toward the door to make sure that it was shut. 'Come and sit by the fire, Donal,' he said. 'I have something to ask of you which I don't want to be repeated beyond this room for the moment.'

'You know that you can trust me with any information. I won't breathe a word of it to any man.'

'I do know that,' Robert agreed, 'but the walls of this

castle are not thick enough to discourage my brother's spies.'

'Spies?' Donal gasped, and then quickly moved to take up a seat beside Robert.

'I am about to tell you a great secret,' Robert began. 'Though within a few days it will no longer be a mystery. In the meantime you must not discuss this with anyone, not even your wife Eilish.'

'Eilish has her ways of finding things out,' Donal laughed but before he could say another word, Robert frowned and spoke in a lower voice.

'Then you must do your utmost to prevent her from discovering this secret. Do you understand?'

'Yes, my lord,' Donal answered, taken aback by Robert's strange tone.

'Years ago my father, William FitzWilliam, and your father, Mathúin O'Regan, went off to the Holy Land together to fight for the Cross. Their places in heaven are assured. But Jerusalem was in the hands of the Christian armies then and the threat to Christendom was not so great. Now the Infidel has wrested the Holy City from the hands of our brethren and I have a duty to lend my fighting arm to the struggle. I have decided to follow in my father's footsteps. I intend to raise a fighting force and travel to Outremer to help rescue the Holy City from the hands of Saladin.'

Donal sat quietly for a few moments, looking at his lord's face, trying to discern whether he was serious or not. When Robert did not lift his gaze from the fire, the chieftain decided that the young lord must be speaking from his heart.

'There is much to be done here on the estates,' Donal began, 'before you can think of going off on such a journey.'

Robert turned to face the chieftain, a look of disbelief on his face. 'What has to be done that isn't done every year?

The planting, the reaping, the ploughing and stocking up for winter. These things always need to be finished.'

'The chapel needs to be completed,' Donal pointed out with apprehension. 'If you spend money on this adventure, then your contribution to the building will likely have to be cut.'

'I have set aside money for the chapel,' the lord assured his guest. 'It will be finished whether I return or not.' Robert took a jug of ale and offered a cup to the chieftain. 'The cost of my journey will place some burden on the estates, that is certain,' he admitted, 'but I am sure that we can all work together to make sure the chapel is completed. That is why I have asked you here.'

'Yes, my lord. Go on.'

'You are a skilled hunter and a proficient warrior, trained by no less a man than your own father. Mathúin was sergeant-at-arms to my father. Lord William did not hold many men in such high regard as he did your father.' Robert fell silent for a moment, staring at the fire once more. Then he lifted his eyes to look directly at Donal. 'Come with me to Outremer.'

'My lord,' Donal protested, shaking his head, 'is this wise? Did you not listen to all the tales our fathers told of the wars in that country? Of the terrible hardships of which we can only imagine? Did Lord William not tell us both of the hazardous journey by land and sea just to reach Outremer? Look at this country, my lord. Do you think there is anything in this world that could drag me away from my home, my family and the safe life I have here?'

'And what of your soul, Donal?'

'My soul will be none the worse for remaining in Ireland than it would be for sailing halfway round the world. I have no desire to end up dead of thirst in some lonely outpost at the edge of the earth. Or to perish at the hand of a savage heathen far from my wife and kinfolk.'

'Donal, I need your help,' Robert pleaded. 'Without your support I cannot hope that the other tenants will agree to the increase in taxes or the sending of their sons to the crusade.'

'With my help or without it you will have a difficult task in that regard,' the chieftain retorted. 'Is that why you are putting on a such a fine festival this year? To soften the blow of this news? We are hard pressed as it is to pay the taxes set down for us, though I know there are many in Ireland since the coming of the Normans who are worse off than the people of Bally Raine.'

'My father was more than fair in his dealings with the tenants,' Robert cut in, 'but he also made do with the barest essentials on campaign and he did not have more than a few men with him. I will keep the costs of this journey to a minimum wherever I can, but I intend to fit out a hundred men-at-arms and twenty crossbowmen. Ten other knights will join the retinue. Every man is needed if we are to have any chance of winning back Jerusalem for the Christian world.'

The chieftain looked at his lord in utter disbelief. 'Your father levied taxes fairly because he understood that surpluses of grain and food have to be laid aside in case the crops fail or some other disaster befalls our estate. If you take every sack of oats from us, what will the people do if the rains come early next year? Have you thought of that?'

'Of course I have thought about that!' Robert insisted. 'And I have thought about how your father would feel, if he were alive, to know that his son had no regard for this cause. The Holy Crusade was always close to his heart. Indeed, it was the shock of the news of the fall of Jerusalem that killed him.'

'I do not feel as strongly about a far-off city in a foreign land as I do about my own kinfolk and their continued wellbeing,' Donal stated coldly. 'I will not speak against your plan, but I cannot in all conscience encourage folk to support it either.'

'I was afraid that you might say that,' the lord said softly, 'but I have not exhausted all my arguments. Your father left an amount of gold in the keeping of this estate. If you resist the tax increases or oppose me in my intention to raise an armed company, you will forfeit that gold to me.'

'I can hardly believe my ears!' Donal roared. 'My father intended that gold to be spent on the chapel, not on some wild adventure that will surely end in disaster.'

'Govern your tongue, chieftain,' Robert asserted, 'I am still your lord. You have sworn an oath of loyalty to me, just as your father swore loyalty to my father.'

'You are abusing the position you hold within this community.'

'I am offering you a compromise.'

'What are you talking about?' Donal scoffed. 'It doesn't sound like you are willing to give any ground at all on this. First you tell me you intend to squander the incomes of this estate on some foolish escapade to the furthest end of the earth. Then you inform me that the tenants will have to pay for your expedition out of their own pockets. And in the end you warn that if I don't support this incredible scheme, you will resume my father's hard-earned treasure which was left in your care. Where is the compromise in that?'

'I am your lord!' Robert shouted and immediately regretted this hasty expression of frustration. After a few moments he sighed, leaning toward his guest as he did so.

'Come with me to Outremer, Donal. Be my sergeant-at-arms. I want you to oversee my journey in the Holy Land as you oversee expenditure here. I have watched you working alongside the tilecutter. Don't you think I know that you are keeping a close eye on the purse strings? You are very talented at such tasks. Come with me and I will charge you with supplying my troops and with balancing all the expenses. You will have absolute control over the payment of all costs.'

'What do you mean?' Donal asked sceptically.

'Taxes will not be raised unless the expenses of the journey prove to be more than I have planned. If you are in control of the expenditure, you will be able to make sure that every golden mark is well spent and that not one penny is wasted.' Robert paused to allow his words to sink in.

'The journey will go ahead with or without you,' he continued after a moment. 'With your cooperation I am sure there will be no great burden on the tenants of the estate. Without your cooperation I will have to appoint another chancellor. That may mean your father's fortune will have to be laid aside against the possibility of some accident or turn of chance.'

Donal sank back down in his chair and put one hand over his eyes, but he said nothing. After a long while he lifted his wooden cup in Robert's direction and the lord poured out some more ale. But the chieftain did not meet his lord's eye. He looked directly into the fire instead, searching for an answer to this terrible ultimatum.

'If I agree to do as you suggest,' Donal breathed finally, 'what assurances have I that the chapel will be finished while we are away?'

'Work will not cease on the chapel,' Robert answered. 'The craftsmen will all be paid their wages for one year in advance. And there will be enough to cover their next instalment after the settlement of the new year's taxes. Your father's gold pays for their board and lodging and it may be drawn on to help pay costs for materials should the need arise.'

'And what of my kinfolk?' the chieftain inquired. 'How do I know that you won't raise the taxes to a level that causes hardship or even famine among my people?'

'If I were to appoint you as chancellor,' Robert began,

'you would conduct a review of the taxes before we left for the Holy Land. I will leave it to you to set the level of tax as long as the safety of the expedition is not compromised in any way whatsoever. You will instruct my brother Rufus on the intricacies of the taxes and he will collect them.'

'Rufus,' Donal spat, 'that stupid oafish layabout! You would leave the estates to his hand?' The chieftain shook his head. 'There is nothing more to be said between us. If Rufus is to be our de facto lord, then you will find the people of Bally Raine reluctant to support your crusade.' Donal put the wooden cup down and made to rise, but Robert reached out to grab his arm in desperation.

'You may appoint a man of your own kin to be chancellor of the estate in your absence if you really think that the tenants will not accept Rufus.'

Donal sat back. 'And that man will have the power of veto over your brother's excesses?'

'Believe me, Donal, I am not happy about leaving him behind in complete control of the lands either. I know him much better than you do, so if the prospect of Rufus becoming lord frightens you, imagine how it makes me feel.'

'And what if you lose your life on this crusade?' the chieftain asked. 'Will Rufus have a free hand then? Will he inherit the estates?'

'My father saw to that possibility. Letters were sent to King Henry stating that under no circumstances was Rufus to be elevated to lordship over the lands of Bally Raine. To make sure, I have amended my will to that effect. If I die in the Holy Land, the entire property will be handed over to those who work the land—your kinfolk—apart from the castle which will go to the Cistercian order and the Temple.'

'I can appoint any man I wish to the post?' Donal asked again, just to make sure that he fully understood the proposal.

'Any man you have confidence in to carry out the responsibility.'

'And when do you plan to leave on this crusade? Have you thought about that yet?'

'It is my intention to sail for Normandy before the winter and to wait there until the roads are fit to travel. We will ride to Venice, take ship and arrive in the Holy Land within six months.'

'Six months!' Donal exclaimed. 'You hope to walk your horses to the gates of Venice from the shores of Normandy? From the tales my father told, it would cost much less time and money to travel directly to the southern ports of the Languedoc and take ship from there.' Donal reckoned quickly in his head. 'Three months at the most, so long as we do not stop in any place more than a day or two.'

Robert's face lit up with admiration. 'You see, you are already saving me money, Donal. What a great service you would do to me, to the people of this estate and to God, if you were to accompany me on this crusade. I am told that King Henry himself has decided to take part in the glorious recapture of Jerusalem.'

'Kings and infidels,' Donal muttered, 'holy cities and knights in bright mail. You have an answer for everything, but neither you nor I will have the last word. I must talk to my wife about it. If she thinks that your plan is worth pursuing, then we will speak earnestly about the measures to be put in place.'

'I would prefer you did not repeat any of this to her . . .' Robert began but Donal smiled as if to say there really was no question of that. 'I can hardly wait to hear what your wife has to say,' the lord conceded as he shrugged his shoulders. 'But no matter what she says, I want you to know that there is nothing that will keep me from my quest.'

'Your quest?' the chieftain asked. 'What do you mean?'

'I have been given a great gift, Donal,' the lord replied enigmatically. 'A gift of secret and sublime knowledge. I'll speak no more of it now until you let me know your answer.'

Donal O'Regan drained his cup and stood up to leave. 'We will talk again within the next few days, my lord.'

'I'll meet you on market eve before the lighting of the kilns. In the meantime you may go to my chamberlain and peruse the accounts of the estate at your leisure. I have instructed him to show you everything. And remember, not a word to anyone apart from your wife, do you understand?'

'I do, my lord. Goodnight.'

'Goodnight, Donal,' Robert replied. 'Rest easy.'

'And the same to you, my lord.'

Donal left the chamber and went straight to see Lonan. The chamberlain was ready to show Donal the accounts but even so he had his reservations. 'Life under this lord is becoming more and more uncomfortable by the day,' he muttered to himself, wishing he knew exactly what Robert was planning.

For a long time Geoffrey could not find Henry's fireplace among the many within the deep grotto. Finally he found himself at the back of the cave where the leading knights' standards had been planted in front of the rock wall. Geoffrey walked up to one of the guards to ask where he could find Henry St Clair.

The soldier grunted, pointing to a pile of baggage that

had been arranged in such a way as to conceal any activity behind it. Geoffrey frowned, not sure whether the soldier had understood him, but he shrugged his shoulders and pushed past the guard impatiently.

Before he knew what had hit him, the young man was lying on his back on the ground with a spear point pressed hard against his chest. Geoffrey heard a menacing growl. He looked up at the guard who was glaring wildly back at him. The soldier increased the pressure of the spear point. Geoffrey tried desperately to back away, certain that he was about to be killed. The razor-sharp weapon pierced his cloak. Were it not for his thick monk's robe, the spear would have cut into his ribcage.

Then, as suddenly as he had leapt upon him, his attacker withdrew, pulling the weapon up to his side to snap a salute.

'Let him pass,' a voice commanded quietly. 'I summoned him here.'

'Yes, my lord.'

The guard lowered the spear onto the ground. Then he held a hand out to the novice who was too dazed to comprehend exactly what had happened. It was not until Geoffrey was on his feet that he realised it was the old knight Henry St Clair who had intervened on his behalf.

'You act as though you are the commander of this caravan,' the young novice quipped, still surprised that such a noble knight would be interested in speaking with him.

'I am the commander of these troops,' St Clair admitted humbly. 'And you are a holy brother?'

'I was a novice,' Geoffrey answered in as polite a tone as he could muster, considering how shaken he was. 'The abbot of my community released me from my vows.'

'I believe that he considered you unsuitable for the vocation of the clergy,' Henry added, stroking his greying beard as he looked at the young man. 'The abbot told me as much when I asked for you to be given into my care.'

'You requested that I be given into your care?' Geoffrey stuttered. 'I don't understand.'

'Your brother Godfrey requested me to take you under my wing should anything happen to him. I am now fulfilling my promise to him.'

'You were a good friend of Godfrey's?'

'He and I were the closest of friends,' Henry answered. 'And I would like you to consider me in the same way. Surely he spoke of me.'

'Forgive me, my lord,' Geoffrey stammered nervously, 'I do not wish to offend you, but my brother never mentioned your name to me. But we had an arranged signal which we agreed to pass on to each other if either of us came into any danger.'

'Do you mean the gold ring that I have been wearing all these months?' came the reply. The knight slipped a small object from his finger and tossed it to the young man.

Geoffrey caught it deftly and immediately examined the jewel. In the centre of the pure gold setting was a black stone darker than any he had ever seen. There was no doubt in his mind now that this ring had been his brother's. The novice's heart sank as he realised that Godfrey truly had come to some horrible end. It was almost as if he had doubted it until this moment.

'How did my brother die?' Geoffrey asked, keeping a tight rein on his emotions. He did not want this knight to see how upset he was.

'He was escorting . . .' Henry paused for a moment, consciously lowering his voice, 'a certain treasure to Acre where it was to be loaded on a ship for transportation back to France. His caravan was ambushed within the city walls and every man was slaughtered.'

'When was this?'

'Nearly one year ago.'

'So he did not die as recently as I was led to believe,' Geoffrey noted bitterly. 'Why was I not informed sooner?'

'I had a great deal of trouble finding you,' Henry explained. 'Your brother was very careful to conceal your whereabouts. He was obviously concerned that you not fall into the hands of the enemy. By the time I did eventually track you down, the Saracens were on the move. I thought it best to let you stay in the Krak until I could come to you. The Krak is impregnable.'

'Why did you not send me word when you discovered where I was lodged?'

'As I said,' Henry explained, 'your brother went to a lot of trouble to conceal you from the enemy.'

'And thc treasure that my brother was escorting,' Geoffrey asked, 'what happened to it?'

'The treasure was . . .' Henry paused, smiling. 'You have your brother's sharp wit. I can see that I will have to be careful what I tell you. Godfrey was one of the most senior members of our order. He was my most trusted friend and he was a great soldier. For this reason he was entrusted with a caravan loaded with gold and jewels belonging to the treasury of the Templar order.'

'If you will forgive me, my lord,' the young man ventured, 'you do not seem to be too distraught by the loss of so great a treasure.'

'How can I compare the loss of my precious friend Godfrey to that of mere gold and jewels?' came the reply. 'Besides which, as I am sure you have guessed, though much Templar gold has been seized by the enemy in this war, the real treasure had not been lost at all.'

'My brother's caravan was a diversion to make the infidel think all the Templar treasures had been captured. It was your hope that the enemy would then concentrate their attention elsewhere.'

'You are wise beyond your years,' Henry stated, raising

an eyebrow, clearly impressed, 'but the real enemy of the Templars in this land is not Saladin. The treasure we guard is of no value whatsoever to him or his followers. Our real foe is the Order of Saint John. It was Hospitallers posing as assassins who murdered your brother.'

Geoffrey gasped in horror.

'Your brother set a trap for the black knights,' St Clair explained. 'But he did not expect his men to be outnumbered. If it had not been for the intervention of a Templar postulant, the Hospitallers would have taken what gold they found in the caravan and been satisfied. The real treasure was already on its way to France.'

'But the Hospitallers are Christian!' Geoffrey exclaimed. 'How could they be enemies of the Temple order?'

'Some treasures will make enemies out of the best of friends. I myself have seen two gentle deacons fight to the death over the affections of a woman.' The old knight looked about him and then led Geoffrey towards his fire. 'We should not speak so openly of this matter. Every man here is hand-picked for his loyalty to the order, but any man may be bought if the price is high enough. The Hospitallers would go to any lengths to obtain the precious items in my care.'

'The real treasure is here!' Geoffrey gasped. 'I knew it! It is just as my dream predicted.'

'You are very much like your brother,' Henry observed, smiling, and his eyes sparkled at the memory of Godfrey. 'He also listened to his dreams. Part of the treasure is here but I will need your help in finding the rest of it. Your brother left something for you which I believe holds a clue to the whereabouts of the great treasure.'

Henry stopped speaking and Geoffrey realised that the knight was already volunteering more information than he had originally intended.

'Have you ever held a sword?' St Clair inquired, changing

the subject before Geoffrey could ask what his brother had left him.

'I was taught to fight as a young lad but I will never be as great a warrior as my brother. Our father sold a large part of the family freehold to pay for Godfrey to be outfitted, so my training was put off indefinitely.'

'And when your father died,' Henry finished the tale, 'you were sent to the Holy Land to find your brother.'

'For reasons that were never explained to me, I ended up in the Hospitaller stronghold at Krak,' Geoffrey went on. 'I know my brother had little time for the Order of Saint John. I must admit I was surprised that he left me in their care. I was most unhappy to be billeted among them.'

'Your brother was wise enough to understand it was safer to have you lodged among the enemy, right under their noses,' Henry explained. 'Godfrey was very clever to realise the Hospitallers would not search for you among their own people.'

Geoffrey frowned. He had no idea why the Order of Saint John would be searching for him.

'I cannot answer that question for the moment,' St Clair cut in, guessing what was on the novice's mind. 'All I will say for the time being is that we have known for a long time that Saladin was preparing to recapture these lands. And many of us guessed that he would be successful, for he had help from within the kingdom. Krak is one of the most impenetrable fortresses in the land. If we had billeted you with the Templars, you would almost certainly be dead by now.'

'I am grateful,' Geoffrey replied, trying to sound as if he meant it, 'but the lord abbot was a hard master and he treated his brothers with contempt. He was universally hated. I would have rather taken my chances with the infidel.'

'You should not say such things,' Henry admonished, 'for

it may yet happen that despite all my best efforts you will fall into the hands of the heathen. If you do, you will pray to be back with your beloved abbot, scrubbing the stone floors at midnight. Or, worse still, you may find yourself a guest of the Hospital of Saint John. I would not wish that on any man who held information which the Master of the Hospital desired.'

'You said that Saladin had help from within the Christian camp,' Geoffrey flashed. 'Did the Knights of Saint John aid the infidel?'

'I must be more careful,' the older knight laughed. 'You are extremely perceptive for one so young. I believe that the Grand Master of the Hospital may have had clandestine contact with Saladin. Many towns garrisoned by the Knights of Saint John fell to the Saracens without too much of a fight. Yet no Hospitallers were taken prisoner. Saladin allowed every man among them to return to their homes without the payment of ransoms.' Henry paused for a moment and summoned a guard with a wave of his hand. 'Are you hungry?' he asked his guest.

Geoffrey nodded and the knight ordered the guard to bring a meal to them.

'What will I do when we arrive in Acre?' the young man asked, eager to discover what task his brother had intended him to complete.

'We are not going to Acre,' Henry stated. 'The city fell months ago to the Saracens. Did you not hear the news? Ah, but of course, the Hospitallers would have kept such tidings a secret from their followers. It would not do for the defenders of the Krak to know that the great port city was no more.'

'Acre has fallen?' Geoffrey stammered. 'Then where are we going?'

'We are not going anywhere for a few days. We will bide our time in this sanctuary, then we will make for the safety of my castle. I am expecting a messenger today or tomorrow to make the arrangements. When we have located the Temple treasure, you and I will return to France . . .' He paused, realising he was revealing too much too soon.

'The real treasure,' Geoffrey stated. 'Whatever is loaded on that cart is simply another decoy meant to confound the enemy. You have no idea where my brother concealed the treasure of the Temple and you hope I will be able to help you find it.'

'Speak of this to no-one,' Henry snapped. 'We must not risk the Hospitallers discovering our strategy. To no-one,' he emphasised again, 'whether they wear Templar garb or not.'

'What is the Templar treasure?' Geoffrey asked eagerly. 'What could possibly inspire the two most holy military orders in Christendom to come close to war with one another?'

'It would not be the first time that these two societies came into conflict,' St Clair informed him. 'There has been a bitter rivalry between them since the earliest days of the Temple. But I cannot tell you any more for the moment. I believe you are entitled to know the truth since your brother gave his life in the defence of this wonder, but I must be careful.'

'If my brother was trusted with the secret, then why do you not trust me?'

'Because you have not yet made your vows as a Knight of the Temple,' Henry explained. 'Unless you commit yourself fully to our cause, I am bound to withhold the truth from you, even if that means I will never discover the whereabouts of the treasure.'

'Would you accept me into the order?' Geoffrey asked immediately.

'I believe that it is your destiny to join us in our quest,' the older knight answered. 'Yes, I would gladly initiate you into the order and sponsor you as a knight as your brother would have wished. Are you ready to take the oaths?'

'There is nothing I wish for more than to take up the sword in my brother's place and carry on his work for the greater glory of God.'

'Then I will tell you the tale of the Poor Knights of Christ, also known as the Order of the Temple,' Henry went on. 'In the days after Jerusalem was freed by the first Christian crusaders, nearly eighty years ago, nine knights from the noblest houses in France came to the Holy City on a mission.'

'To guard the roads and protect Christian pilgrims in the Holy Land,' Geoffrey cut in.

'Yes,' St Clair agreed, 'that is the tale they told folk. That is what most people believe was their motive.'

'What other purpose could they have had?'

'Almost immediately after their arrival in the Holy City the knights, led by the great chevalier Hugues de Payen, entered the ruined Temple of Solomon. There they established their headquarters in the stables beneath the great rock. For nine years they remained within the confines of their new home, rarely emerging for any reason. They certainly never once went to the aid of any pilgrim, nor did they ever patrol the roads.'

'Nine years!' Geoffrey exclaimed. 'What on earth were they up to, locked away for so long?'

'Under the patronage of King Baldwin the Second, the Christian king of Outremer at the time, they were exploring the great labyrinth which lies under the Temple Mount. In particular they were searching for a chamber that is said to lie directly beneath the most sacred part of the Temple. Before the Romans destroyed the building there was a special room set aside at the epicentre of the structure where God was believed to reside. The Jews named this place the Holy of Holies. In the days of the ancient Temple only the highest priests were ever allowed within this sacred place for it was said that the famed Ark of the Covenant was stored there.'

Geoffrey's face turned pale. 'In my dream the Blessed Virgin told me that the treasure on the back of your cart was the Ark of the Covenant.'

Henry looked at the young man for a moment, trying to discern whether this was a clever trick to extract more information. But Geoffrey could not possibly have known anything about the Ark, so the knight went on.

'I believe,' St Clair stated, 'there were once many sacred objects and texts hidden beneath the Temple Mount. The Ark was only one which, according to tradition, was stored there for the use of future generations. And it may be true that it was the Ark which de Payen originally hoped to find. In the end, however, he discovered much more than he had expected. He and his brother knights came upon a secret that still has the potential to shake the Christian world to its very roots. A secret more powerful and devastating than anything the nine knights could have imagined.'

Geoffrey was just about to ask what this secret was when the guard returned with three servants bearing platters of bread and two earthenware jugs of wine. Henry thanked them, waited until they were out of earshot, then continued on before Geoffrey could question him.

'This secret was at the root of the foundation of our order as it exists today. Our founder, de Payen, returned to France when he realised the full weight of his discovery. There he gained a Papal blessing to form his nine friends into an organisation based on the Cistercian rule. Bernard of Clairvaux composed the law of the Temple order and brought many more knights into our ranks by preaching the holy crusade. Within two years the Order of the Temple was a company of three hundred knights with an immense amount of wealth at its command.'

'Where did that wealth originate?'

'Much of it,' Henry explained, 'I believe was discovered within the labyrinth of the Temple in the form of sacred golden objects and coin. But each new recruit to the Templar order signed over his estates and property to the organisation upon taking final vows. A great deal of gold was accumulated in that manner.'

Henry paused to see if the young man had any further questions, but Geoffrey sat silent and motionless, a look of shock on his face.

'Your brother and I were appointed guardians of the treasury four years ago. In our time as overseers of the secret, several Hospitallers have infiltrated our order. This desperate search for the rumoured storehouse of de Payen and the Temple of Solomon has already led to many deaths. The Knights of Saint John have always been jealous of the power and wealth of our order. They have tried time and time again to have the Templar knighthood disbanded or discredited. The Grand Master of the Temple is very wise, however, and by tradition no knight may hold the position of guardian of the treasury unless he can prove his descent from Hugues de Payen.'

'So you are de Payen's grandson?' Geoffrey interrupted.

'He was my great-uncle,' Henry replied quickly. 'He is your great-grandfather.'

'Don't be ridiculous!' Geoffrey exclaimed as he worked the cork from a wine jug. 'My father's name was de Montbard, not de Payen. If I were descended from such a famous knight, I'd know about it, don't you think?'

'Your father took the name Montbard in order to conceal the identity of his two sons. Your brother assumed the name d'Acre to hide his ancestry further. The Hospitallers spent many years picking up the thread of the secret, but in the last thirty they have come very close to discovering it. Anyone with the name de Payen would have been marked as involved with the treasure.'

'I am the direct descendant of Hugues de Payen, founder of the Temple?' the novice muttered, quite unable to believe the assertion. 'I assume you can prove this story.'

'You are his only direct living descendant,' St Clair confirmed, 'and the only man eligible since your brother's death to act as guardian of the treasure. I have seen the parish records of your birth. Your brother went to great pains to ensure you would be properly informed at the appropriate time. When we have returned to my castle, I will show you the proof you ask for.'

'I am the last of the de Payen line?' the novice asked, incredulous.

'Indeed,' St Clair affirmed. 'You are the last male of the bloodline of Hugues de Payen. That is why I am sure your brother would have left some clues for you as to the location of the Temple treasure.'

'If I understand you correctly,' Geoffrey stuttered as another realisation dawned on him, 'then I am also entitled, by virtue of my bloodline, to one day become Grand Master of the Order?'

'There is much for you to learn,' St Clair stated coldly, seeing that the conversation had come to a subject he was not ready to discuss. 'But one day, with God's help, you will first be elevated to the role of guardian of the treasury. I must tell you now that most of the minor treasures have been smuggled out of the Holy Land. What remains is the most precious of all. It therefore must be guarded with the greatest vigilance.'

Geoffrey smiled when he realised Henry had not answered his question. Then he noticed the old knight was staring at him intensely.

'If you take the vows of a Templar,' St Clair continued, 'and accept the guardianship, you may never have an uninterrupted night of peaceful sleep again. Your every move will be watched by ally and foe alike. In order to survive, you will forever be suspicious of even your closest friends. Godfrey would have been Grand Master in his time. You may yet walk in his footsteps if you live long enough to grow in wisdom.'

'But if I choose to walk away from this quest, my brother's death will have been in vain?'

'And many men will die as a result if the Hospitallers discover the true nature of the great secret,' Henry added.

'Then I have very little choice, it would seem,' Geoffrey noted, wondering what this great secret could be but realising St Clair would not tell him yet. 'Little choice but to follow the example of my illustrious ancestors.'

Chapter Eight

onal lay back on the bed he shared with Eilish high among the rafters of their house. As he stretched his arms above his head he laughed uncontrollably until he was short of breath.

'If I were to say that to the lord,' Donal declared, 'he'd have me flogged for inciting our kinfolk to rebellion or insulting his parentage.'

'If your father were alive, things would be very different,' Eilish answered sharply, her bright blue eyes flashing. 'He would have told young Robert exactly what he thought about the matter. He certainly would not have allowed the little upstart to threaten what was rightfully his!'

'Mathúin happily accompanied old Lord William to the Holy Land without a word of complaint. My father didn't even know in which direction Outremer lay! I suppose that's what you'd call standing up to the lord and giving him a piece of your mind?'

'Your father would never have allowed himself to be trapped in this situation in the first place, you know that,' Eilish commented. 'He was wise enough to bend the Normans to his will in order to get his own way.'

'And that is how he came to be the only other survivor of William's expedition after the lord himself. And William only came home at all because Mathúin saved his life! All these Normans are foolish braggarts who think they are a people chosen by God to rule over the rest of us. Most of them wouldn't know which end of the pig faces the trough and which end is its arse.'

'Who looked after the estates while they were gone?' Eilish asked, changing the course of the conversation.

'It was that surly old chamberlain,' Donal replied, 'who couldn't see a mountain if it was growing on his nose. Of course, William would have had us believe it was his son Robert who was left in charge. But everyone knew that Lonan held the purse strings.'

'Just like old William, Robert dare not leave the estate in the hands of a servant,' she added, 'in case the steward gets ideas above his station. One of the FitzWilliam family has to be put in charge. That means Rufus,' she shuddered.

'Rufus will not be given any authority,' Donal informed her. 'Robert gave me his word on that.'

'But Rufus will run the estates in name,' his wife asserted. 'Mathúin could see trouble brewing like other men can see storm clouds gathering. He would never have agreed to let a fool like Rufus run the estates in his absence.'

'It won't be Rufus alone,' Donal said slowly and deliberately, letting his wife know that he was tiring of this discussion. 'Robert has asked me to appoint one of our folk to be in charge of all the financial matters on the estate.'

'Who will you choose?'

'Braonin,' Donal replied sheepishly.

'Braonin!' Eilish laughed. 'He couldn't tell you how many cows make a dozen! He never learned to count.'

'That's nonsense, Eilish, and you know it,' Donal snapped, but the chieftain had to admit to himself that Braonin was not all that good with numbers.

Eilish saw the uncertainty in her husband's face, and she took the opportunity to drive her argument on. 'And what about your family?' she demanded. 'What about me? Would you leave me behind for one year, or two, or three?

Or would you be gone longer, stretched out in some foreign grave with no headstone to mark your last bed?'

'I don't have any choice in this, Eilish,' the chieftain tried to explain. 'Robert has said that Mathúin's gold will be forfeit if I do not aid him. If we lose my father's gold, the chapel will never be finished and our kinfolk will have no reserves against a bad harvest. On the other hand, if I go on this crusade to serve Robert, the gold will be administered by one of our own people—Braonin—and the building will surely be completed within a year. And when you send me word that the work is done, I will return to you immediately. Even if it means deserting Lord Robert on the field of battle. In some respects, my father probably would have wanted me to follow in his footsteps.'

'Follow in his footsteps?' Eilish stammered. 'Are you serious? He was back in his home little more than three months when some devilish hand reached out from that faraway city to strangle the life out of him. Can you guarantee the same thing won't happen to you?'

'Eilish,' Donal breathed, wishing they did not have to discuss this any further for the moment, 'I am the only man who will really be able to make certain that every expense of Robert's is legitimate. I will ensure every purchase is wise and well bartered. Put one of the Normans in charge of the purse strings and the whole lot of them will be drinking the finest ale there is, all the way to Byzantium and back.'

'And why would you be any better at such a task than some grovelling Norman servant who was born to fill in the lines of a ledger?' Eilish hissed.

'Because,' the chieftain answered, struggling to control his temper now, 'my kinfolk will be paying for this stupid adventure out of their crops and their cattle. If I do not watch the gold carefully, there will be hunger in the home of my family. Without my guiding hand I fear that our people will lose more than Father's gold. We will be asked to pay higher and higher taxes to cover the lavish tastes and misguided follies of an inexperienced knight. What is more, Rufus will have a free hand over the entire estate. I would not like to see such a vain man have so much power thrust upon him. He has the eyes of a tyrant, that one. Within a few short months he would have all the tenants in arms at his gate, ready to burn the castle to the ground.'

'Donal,' his wife sighed, 'you cannot leave Braonin in charge of the estates.'

'And I suppose you think you would do a better job?'

'Of course I would,' Eilish replied without hesitation.

'Then so be it!' the chieftain snapped. 'Though I am sure Robert would never agree to it. I've never heard of a Norman who allowed himself to be ruled by a woman.'

'That is why they so often resort to bitter fighting,' his wife countered. 'It takes the wisdom of a woman to avoid warfare.'

'He would never agree,' Donal repeated, 'but you could keep a close watch on Braonin without the Normans realising you were giving him advice.'

'Then Braonin will be the chancellor in name and I will oversee his duties,' Eilish suggested, warming to this possibility.

Donal lifted his eyes to meet those of his wife. 'Now I remember why I married you! You can find an answer to any riddle. But do you suppose you could think of some way I could stay in Bally Raine, or perhaps something to distract Robert so he might forget his crusade altogether? And that the chapel would be finished and all the taxes paid?'

'Give me a few days to consider the problem,' she teased, 'and I'm sure I could come up with something.'

The chieftain laughed and, taking his wife's hands gently in his, said, 'I've thought this through a hundred times and all I got was a headache. There's no way out of it. I will have to go to the Holy Land as Lord Robert's sergeant-at-arms and fulfil my duty as controller of his expenses.'

'But you'll be gone not one day more than a year,' Eilish insisted, 'for that is how long you said it would take for the chapel to be built.'

'Not one day more than a year,' Donal repeated. 'By then the building will be done and it won't matter how Robert spends the remainder of Mathúin's gold.'

On market day at the midsummer festival at Bally Raine there were merchants from all over Ireland plying their wares and tempting customers. Lord Robert opened the first barrel of ale himself before the midday meal. An hour before sunset there were a hundred tenants gathered on the lawns outside his castle, gossiping and eagerly awaiting the lord's speech.

Eilish was placed in charge of the kitchens of the castle. It was her duty, as wife of the chieftain, to ensure everyone who was hungry had food in their belly. Four or five times a year the lord of the estate provided a feast for all the tenants as a show of goodwill. It was an effective way of enticing the common folk into the castle to settle disputes, conduct their business with the lord's approval and pay outstanding debts.

The castle cook was given the day to herself on these occasions, as were several of the other servants. Here lay the secret of old Lord William's popularity. No matter what his own personal financial position or the pressing worries of the estate, the lord always rewarded those who exhibited loyalty to him.

The black-haired Neesh presented herself at the kitchen

door as the last of the bread was being removed from the long stone baking oven. She had been very reluctant to come to the festival this year but Eileen, Eilish's sister, had convinced her they would need her help. Assigned to oversee preparation of all the roasted food for the evening feast, Neesh waited patiently for instructions from Eilish.

Four fire pits were dug within a few paces of each other outside the kitchen door. Over these shallow holes men were already erecting iron spits on which they would mount two large boars, a calf and a sheep. The meat would take six or seven hours to cook slowly over the coals.

The entire Norman garrison had been called in from their duties for the day. It was, after all, highly unlikely that any of the tenants would be out poaching from the lord's stock of game. Especially as there was so much food being given out at the castle.

Rufus tagged along with the off-duty soldiers, drinking, laughing, and letting off steam with his comrades-at-arms. The soldiers accepted him as they would any man of rank, showing him the respect due his birthright. Some of the men-at-arms concluded that Rufus had been responsible for the free-flowing ale. And Rufus was happy for them to go on believing that.

When William had been lord he had established a practice of announcing the taxes and rents for the coming year just before the feast was served. It was also a time when the lord would call on his landholders to help with the maintenance of the castle, the moat, all the holy shrines in the district and the few roads. The lord's sheep also had to be sheared each year and everyone lent a hand to that task.

No-one from Bally Raine, Cúil Ghréine or the Gioll Martin at Clonough had ever begrudged their lord a few days out of each year to help with such projects. Indeed such instances of communal toil were a chance for everyone to meet and socialise beyond the normal round of festivals and feasts.

But this year there was an air of uncertainty about how Robert would discharge his duties as lord. Rumours abounded. Some folk who had family ties with the castle servants claimed they knew Robert was about to hand everything over to his younger brother and enter a monastery. Others were certain that the rents would be substantially increased and the taxes raised. The abundant strong ale doubtless inspired one or two people to theorise Robert might be planning to evict those tenants who were late with their rents. A few folk were already saying that such action would lead to open rebellion.

While all the gossiping, preparation and merry-making was taking place, Donal managed to slip away unnoticed. He made his way down to where the chapel, which his father and Lord William had founded, was slowly taking shape. Since the scaffolding had recently been removed, the walls were free-standing. The floor had been filled with fine soil, rammed flat ready to take the ceramic covering. But the roof timbers were still bare and open to the sky, awaiting their tiles.

The altar stone was an ancient slab of granite that had stood upright for generations on the spot where the chapel was begun. This great rock had been laid on its side to form a rough table. The chieftain walked straight up to the altar, ran his hand over the pitted surface and tried to imagine what the building would look like when it was finished.

He had not thought about it before, but now he realised he had never seen a church altar placed in the exact centre of the building. Every church he had seen had this feature either in the eastern wing of the structure or exactly opposite the main doors.

The plan of this chapel, he suddenly understood, was such that the worshippers would have to sit in two groups facing each other and the central altar. In that moment Donal glimpsed just how clever his father and Lord William had been in devising such an arrangement. In this chapel the Normans and their kin would always have to look directly at the tenants and their families over the top of God's holy altar.

'It is an old idea,' a voice said quietly and Donal turned to see a man dressed in shabby clothes, sporting a long matted beard. The chieftain immediately recognised Cinneach the Culdee, though he had not seen him for a long time.

'Greetings to you, father,' Donal respectfully offered.

'And the blessings of this day upon you, Donal O'Regan,' came the reply. 'In the first churches that were built in Ireland, the altar was always placed in the middle of the building. All of the churches of my folk are constructed in that manner.'

The man turned his attention to the stone altar itself. 'And it is an ancient practice to use these stones as the focal point of the structure. Our ancestors, in the days before Saint Columcille, venerated these stones as marking the holiest places in the land.'

'Then this spot was sacred even in the old days,' Donal asked, 'for this stone stood here before the chapel was ever dreamed of.'

'In the times even before the Gaels came to Ireland,' Cinneach went on, 'it was the old ones, the children of the Goddess Danu, who placed these stones where they stand.'

'Do you mean the faeries?' the chieftain asked.

Cinneach nodded, smiling.

'Do we not risk offending the faerie kind,' the chieftain blurted, 'by using their stones as Christian altars?'

'Do not fear, my friend. The Doaine Sidhe, whom you call the faeries, are not all that concerned with the goings-on in our world. They have shifted themselves beyond the confines of this earth since the coming of the Gael. All that is important to them is that the stone is still regarded as holy and treated with respect. They would be overjoyed that this place is still considered sacred even though they have not visited it in a long while.'

'You have not visited this district for some years either,' Donal ventured, changing the subject. He never felt comfortable talking about the faerie people. He had been brought up to believe that they were an evil race banished by God to a living hell. The chieftain feared to speak about them in case their tortured spirits were invoked. The Culdees, on the other hand, believed the faeries to be akin to God's angels.

'I have been away in the north aiding the rebellion against Strongbow's son,' Cinneach explained. 'Last summer the chieftains of Ulster gathered at the old fortress of Emain Macha to plan their revolt but were ambushed by the Norman lords of the north. Thanks be to God that my wife and I escaped injury, but many other folk were captured or slaughtered. The gathering of our people to discuss war gave the Normans a perfect excuse to attack us. Now most of the north belongs exclusively to them and many Gaelic families are without chieftains.'

'I thank God that old Lord William came to us,' Donal replied sincerely. 'My kinfolk have been spared much misery by his rule.'

'All the Normans smell of the same manure,' the Culdee retorted sharply. 'Lord William was unusual among his kind. Be careful that young Robert does not follow in the footsteps of the northern lords.'

'Robert is a pious man,' Donal protested. 'The thought of betraying my people would not cross his mind.'

'And yet he intends to raise the taxes and build himself a small army,' Cinneach said lowly, stepping closer to the chieftain. 'Why would he need over a hundred soldiers to govern such a small, law-abiding estate as this?'

'The soldiers will not be staying here . . .' Donal began but then thought better of letting Cinneach know too much.

'Ah yes,' the Culdee sighed knowingly, 'the great crusade.'

Donal shot a startled glare at the man. 'What do you know of the lord's plans?'

'Only what I have heard from his own mouth,' Cinneach admitted. 'I believe that he is sincere in his wish to join in the recapture of Jerusalem. I am not so sure, however, that young Rufus will honour the assurances of Lord Robert.'

'Is it safe for you to be here?' the chieftain asked, not wishing to pursue this conversation any further for fear that he might be accused of talking rebellion. 'What if you are recognised?'

'I was introduced to the lord at his own fireside as a seanachie. He believes that I am merely a wandering storyteller. He has no idea that I am a priest of the Culdee church or that I was saying mass with the chieftain of the O'Niall clan only a few weeks ago.'

'You are welcome here,' Donal cut in, 'as long as you do not bring danger to my kinfolk with your ways. There have been no Culdees here since William first drove the monks out as heretics.'

'But the common folk of this estate are still Culdees at heart. I have been speaking with them. I believe they would support the return of a small community to Saint Finnian's.'

'Robert is even more pious than his father!' the chieftain exclaimed. 'He would not tolerate the return of an order which is condemned by Rome and under sentence of immediate execution throughout the Norman lands.'

'You might be surprised,' Cinneach smiled. 'I have known many fanatics who changed their views through some chance encounter with the very thing they feared most. It may be some years in coming, but perhaps even Robert is capable of learning tolerance.'

'I beg you not to mention your true vocation in front of any of the Normans,' Donal whispered. 'If they should even suspect that we were harbouring outlaws, the delicate relationship between us might be shattered. My father and I have laboured long to keep the peace between our two peoples. It would be a great disaster if Lord Robert were to become as heavy-handed as his northern cousins.'

'I will be discreet,' the Culdee laughed. 'My neck is in no need of stretching. And although I have an unshakeable faith in the afterlife, I am in no immediate hurry to discover its mysteries.' Cinneach reached out and put a hand on Donal's shoulder. 'One more word of advice,' he added.

'Yes?' Donal replied.

'If you are going to sup with the Devil, it is wise to use a long spoon. Do not become so involved with Robert's dreams that you forget your own kinfolk.'

The chieftain nodded and laughed. 'Thank you, father. Remember that you are always welcome in my house.'

'I will remember and I will watch over Eilish while you are away,' Cinneach added. 'You need not worry too much.'

'How did you know I was intending to go with Robert on his crusade?'

'I didn't,' the Culdee smiled, 'but I do now. Don't worry, the secret is safe with me.' With that, the man turned around and made for the doorway, obviously very pleased with himself. In a few moments Cinneach was gone, leaving Donal to curse his own stupidity at allowing that information out before the lord had officially announced it.

The chieftain waited a few minutes before he also left the chapel. He did not want anyone to notice that he had been alone with a well-known rebel like Cinneach. When he judged the Culdee would already be a good distance from the chapel, Donal strode outside and headed for the place where Balek the tilecutter was stacking the last few tiles into the kiln. He had promised to help with the final preparations before the load was set on fire and he wanted to ask the advice of his well-travelled friend.

Henry St Clair received a messenger three days after his caravan took refuge in the great cave. The old knight immediately sent out orders that his convoy was to be on the road within the hour. The campsite, which had been a sheltered resting place for hundreds of men, immediately erupted into activity at the command. And before the hour was passed the first knights set off to scout the road ahead for enemy troops.

Geoffrey was invited to ride alongside Henry in the main retinue of knights. In place of his slow plodding donkey, he was given a white horse to ride.

'We will be within our new stronghold by evening,' St Clair assured his young guest. 'Just to the north of these mountains there is an ancient fortress which the Order of the Temple has refurbished. It is reputedly invulnerable and, more importantly, it is a very well-kept secret. It will be a simple matter for us to pass safely from here to the main gates now that the brigands have given up their search. I have gathered enough supplies of food and water within the walls to keep a large army going for many months. So we will all be able to sit out this latest trouble with Saladin for some time.'

Henry smiled at the novice, trying to read what the lad

might be thinking, but Geoffrey was careful not to reveal his surprise.

'I have been told,' St Clair went on, 'that your brother's will has been sent to my castle for safekeeping. When we arrive I will arrange for the contents to be revealed to you.'

Geoffrey nodded politely but he was beginning to understand the dangerous position he was in. If it had been necessary, he reasoned to himself, for the caravan to hide inside a mountain for three days to avoid contact with the enemy, the enemy must be strong and determined. Templars rarely, if ever, avoided battle. The rules of the order stated that they must not shy away from a fight unless the odds were greater than three to one. These warriors had a reputation for stubbornly facing almost any conflict. And reputations must be upheld.

It was also Temple policy that ransoms would not be paid for the return of captured knights. Before the crusades there was an unwritten rule among Christian knights. In battle a warrior would only kill another of his class in the most dire situation. Common soldiers were slaughtered in great numbers, but knights captured one another, thus preserving life and bloodlines. This practice also encouraged the fluid shifting of allegiances. An enemy today could be pursuaded into becoming an ally tomorrow if his family could not raise sufficient funds to secure his release.

When a captive knight was successfully ransomed, the fighting could begin all over again. This led to wars which were little more than attempts by one lord to kidnap as many wealthy knights as possible. The Saracens soon learned the value of such a policy.

A mounted man and his warhorse were highly trained. It was expensive and difficult to replace such a warrior. Far less costly to pay a ransom demand than to risk the death of the captured knight. If a warrior was killed in battle, it might take many years and a great deal more expenditure before another man was trained to replace him.

The Temple paid no ransoms because they had more than enough willing recruits who were eager to sign over all their possessions to the order. Most of them only desired a chance to fight in the Holy Land under the banner of the Temple.

When the Saracens realised that Templars were worthless prisoners, they began to murder their captives as a matter of course. This merely drove the Knights of the Temple to fight to the death and to endure greater hardship than the other Christian orders.

A great animosity grew between the Saracens and Templars. But this was also tinged with a great respect. Each side studied the other with interest. During those rare times of peace when Muslim and Christian were able to communicate freely, many surprising friendships developed between the men of each camp.

There was another thing about the Templars that inspired the respect of the Saracens. Their beards. Knights of the Order of the Temple were required by their rules to cut their locks short but not their facial hair. Among the Moslems a long flowing beard was considered a sign of great virility and warlike temperament. Other Christian knights shaved their faces as was the fashion in Europe, which earned them the ridicule of the Saracens.

Geoffrey noted that Henry St Clair had a long beard, marking him as having taken his vows many years earlier. All of the knights under his command were obviously new recruits to the order for they had shorter beards.

As the caravan approached the northern shores of that great salty lake, known to crusader and Saracen alike as the Dead Sea, it turned to head east. Before dusk the company had come to the edge of the mountains which framed the salty waters. After nightfall the soldiers continued riding until they came to a steep track which wound its way into the foothills. No torches were lit anywhere along the column for fear of attracting the attention of enemy scouts. Henry ordered the column to halt and they silently waited at the foot of the track until riders galloped down the line with word that all was well ahead.

The caravan set off again climbing into the mountains. They had not gone far when Henry reined in his warhorse so that he was riding close beside young Geoffrey.

'This will be your home for the next few months while you learn the rules of the order and prepare to take your place as one of the leading members of the Temple,' the old knight explained.

'I have not seen the castle walls!' Geoffrey exclaimed. 'Have we passed within the defences?'

'We have,' Henry laughed. 'This castle is fortified by a great ring of mountains. An attacker must gain the passes before having any hope of assaulting the fortress itself. But as it stands the enemy does not yet know of this place. Many scouts have entered this pass but none has ever left it alive. When warriors regularly disappear without trace, superstition becomes yet another line of defence.'

'And I suppose that same defence against attackers makes this the perfect prison,' Geoffrey noted.

'The more we talk,' Henry declared, 'the more convinced I am that your sharp mind was sent to us as a gift from God. You are, of course, correct. No-one leaves this valley except with the blessing of the master of the castle.'

'And who is the master of this place?' the young man asked.

Henry St Clair smiled and then proudly answered, 'I am.'

Geoffrey caught his breath. He could not help but feel he should trust this knight, yet there was something in the tone of what Henry had said that did not ring true. Geoffrey shrugged off his doubts, unable to pinpoint exactly what had made him so uneasy.

The young man peered out into the darkness, hoping to discern some sign of his whereabouts. If he was in danger from Henry St Clair, he told himself, there was very little he could do about it for the moment.

Ahead of them a trumpet call sounded, muffled and thin in the night air. Henry spurred his horse on to the front of the column and Geoffrey followed along behind him. Within twenty paces the two men halted before a great wooden drawbridge which had been laid across a deep chasm. Four rows of Templar knights mounted on black chargers and dressed in bright mail armour blocked any further progress.

'What is your business here?' one of the knights declared as his horse stepped forward.

'I have come to rebuild the Temple of Solomon,' Henry replied.

'Where are you going?' the first knight shot back at him.

'To the west,' Henry answered.

'And why do you forsake the east to travel to the west?'

'In search of that which was lost, brother.'

'*Nil nisi clavis de est*,' the first knight pronounced in Latin.

'All that is needed is the key,' Geoffrey translated under his breath.

'*Si tatlia iungere possis sit tibi scire posse*,' St Clair intoned.

'If you understand this, then that is enough,' Geoffrey muttered.

In that instant the rows of warriors fell back, allowing Henry to pass through. Geoffrey spurred his horse on to keep up with the old knight. As they passed under the arch which supported a great drawbridge, the knights of the castle garrison turned their mounts around and followed as a guard of honour. The remainder of the caravan followed on after that.

Geoffrey counted three further moats with drawbridges before they came at last to the door of an enormous keep, larger than any he had ever seen in France. Here Henry St Clair dismounted, and as he did so the doors to the keep opened inwards. A great party of men dressed in the white robes of the Temple emerged from the darkness within the building to stand on the steps.

From among this group one stepped forward, an old man with a flowing beard and deep-set grey eyes. He stood out from all the others for he was dressed in a long dark green tunic. On his hands were gloves of the purest white. Geoffrey wondered how such an item of apparel could possibly be kept so clean.

'Welcome, my brother,' the old man declared, addressing Henry. 'I was beginning to despair of your return.'

'Much has happened in the world beyond since I last feasted in this hall,' Henry answered.

As the two men approached each other, they performed a curious ritual which Geoffrey had never witnessed before. While they were still a few paces away from each other both men bowed to touch the earth with the very tips of the fingers of their right hands. In one smooth movement they both then reached for the other's hand in a clasp of friendship followed by a warm embrace. The old man dressed in green did not, however, remove his gloves to greet the other knight.

'Father,' Henry began, 'may I present Geoffrey d'Acre, brother of my dear friend Godfrey.' Then he turned to Geoffrey. 'This is Father Thomas, the Chaplain Commander of the Temple.'

Geoffrey bowed low, extending his hand to the priest. The novice expected to be offered a ring of office to kiss. Instead the old priest took Geoffrey's hand in a firm grasp just as Henry had done.

'Welcome to Mont Salvasch. We do not indulge in idle

vanities here,' Father Thomas explained, indicating that it would not be necessary to kiss his hand. 'In this place you are among equals.'

Outside the moat of Bally Raine, Balek the tilecutter put the finishing touches to his two stone kilns. Late that afternoon the tilecutter planned to light his first fire under the stacks of tiles within one of the kilns. This slow-burning blaze was intended to dry out the clay without allowing it to become too hot. If the tiles heated up too quickly, any water in the clay would rapidly turn to steam. The slightest miscalculation in temperature could lead to tiles exploding. This would almost certainly damage everything in the tightly packed kiln. The whole operation had to be watched carefully to ensure that the fire did not get out of control. For this reason a series of vents was built into the structure so Balek would be able to cut off the supply of air to the fire to bring it under control.

The steady heat would have to be fed and maintained for two days. When the first stage of the firing was complete, specially bound bundles of dry bracken would be pushed into the opened vent holes. The apprentices would stack fuel all day long, raising the kiln temperature dramatically so the tiles hardened into a weatherproof ceramic. After that the ovens could be left to cool for three days or more before they were unpacked.

Donal arrived at the kilns just as Balek was supervising the arrangement of flat stones over the roof to seal the interior from above. The tilecutter was sweaty and tired and his voice was hoarse from shouting instructions in Latin to his helpers. The chieftain waited patiently for him to climb down from the roof and as the tilecutter headed for the water barrel to cool down, the chieftain greeted him.

'The work is done,' Donal observed.

Balek doused his head and shoulders with a small bucket of water. 'The work is just beginning, my friend,' he laughed. 'From now until three days from today I must be here by my kilns on constant watch. I cannot trust my apprentices to tend the fire alone and alas no-one else but me knows what must be done.'

'I will come and keep you company,' the chieftain promised, 'and we will tell each other stories to shorten the watch.'

'Thank you, my friend,' the tilecutter remarked gleefully. 'It will be good to have you here. I have appreciated your help in the last few weeks. I have learned much from you.'

'You have learned from me?' Donal exclaimed. 'What could I possibly teach someone like you?'

'I have learned that a great work such as this chapel can be more valuable to a community than all the gold of the east,' Balek replied. 'I have observed your deep interest in my labour and it has warmed my heart. You are the first patron I have ever known who got his hands dirty with me and was so interested in my craft that his questions never ceased to end.'

Donal blushed. 'I did not mean to be a nuisance,' he apologised. 'I am genuinely interested in your work and your stories.'

'So interested that you must have heard my tales of Acre a hundred times!'

The chieftain covered his eyes with his hands to show his embarrassment.

'Anyone would imagine,' the tilecutter laughed, 'that you were intending to travel to my homeland yourself and set up trade as a maker of fine ceramic tiles.'

Donal dragged his hands gently over his face as he lifted

his eyes to meet Balek's. The tilecutter realised in that moment that he had spoken very close to the truth.

'Are you intending to travel to the kingdom of Outremer?' the tilecutter asked, tripping over his words in his agitation. 'Are you going to join the great crusade?'

'It is possible,' the chieftain admitted, 'that I might be making that journey soon.'

'Do not go,' Balek advised, and for the first time that Donal could remember the smile dropped from the craftsman's face. 'Why would you leave this paradise of green grass and plentiful food? The cool fresh water here is as sweet as honey and as abundant as the ocean. The winter is cold and damp but the discomfort is nothing compared to the heat of the sun in my country. You will not like it there!'

'I must accompany my lord,' Donal explained.

'And who will look after your wife while you are away?'

'Her family will take care of her. It is only for a year.'

Balek looked at the chieftain and laughed. 'A year? You will be gone for longer than that, I fear. The journey there alone could take you up to a year. That is, if you are lucky enough to find passage on a ship. All the merchant ships going to Outremer are laden with goods to be sold in the markets of that land. And the Templar navy does not take passengers.'

'How did you come to be here then?' Donal asked. 'How long was the journey?'

'Lord William was travelling on business of the Knights of the Temple. A ship was provided for him to France. Once he had unloaded his cargo there, he was free to fill the ship with whatever goods he wished to bring home. He was rewarded for his work in guarding the treasures of the Temple; that is why he had such a fine ship to bring him home. There are no such vessels available to young knights such as Robert who have not earned their swords in any battle.'

'I have promised my wife I will return within a year,' the chieftain informed his friend.

'It is most unwise to promise that which you cannot guarantee,' Balek jibed. 'You have turned yourself into a dishonourable man before you have even had a chance to break your promise. The journey will take you many months, my friend. And even then there are brigands and thieves; folk who would think nothing of slitting your throat if they could see a profit in it. And that is just the Christians.'

'What of the Saracens?'

'Should you ever meet any of the Vizier Saladin's followers, you will probably be surprised,' Balek declared. 'They are steadfast friends and honourable people, but they make bitter enemies. If you survive the Christian merchants, the robbers and the renegade warriors, you may be unfortunate enough to meet the Saracens in battle.'

'You speak as if they were people just like us!' Donal exclaimed. 'But how could that be? Are they not servants of the Devil?'

'They hold a different religion to us,' the tilecutter explained, 'but they are men and women just like any Christians. They have the same fears and dreams. And they believe in the same God.'

'They do?' the chieftain frowned, for he had heard a very different tale.

'What does it matter if they call their God Allah?' Balek asked. 'And what matter that we name our God with another title? There is only one God. That is what we all believe, is it not? We all follow the same basic guiding laws. We all have faith that God is good. We all pray we may one day gain the keys to paradise. We all bow down to His wisdom.'

'What you are saying is heresy,' Donal stammered, utterly shocked by the tilecutter's words.

'In the Holy Land you will discover many things that will unnerve you. Some will certainly be far more distressing than this doctrine. Are we not all descended from the same Adam and Eve that were created by God in His sacred garden?'

Donal dropped his gaze, thoroughly ashamed that Balek should be speaking in this manner to him.

'Am I so different to you?' Balek reasoned. 'Do you think I am not also made in God's image?'

'You are a Christian,' the chieftain murmured. 'Of course you were made in God's image.'

'If you are a true believer in the teachings of Christ, then you would know Jesus taught that everyone was created by the same God,' the tilecutter went on. 'Even those men who do not believe in our God were, in Christian belief, created by the Heavenly Father. Christ commands us to honour all men and women and for that reason even our enemies should be respected as brothers and sisters.'

'But the Devil leads men astray,' Donal pointed out, 'and then bends them to the worship of his evil ways by showing them the path of wrongdoing.'

'Yet God created all of us and we each make a decision to take whichever road we choose. The Lord God gives us that choice, and even if we turn against Him, the perfect love which created us all is not diminished so much as the weight of one tiny speck of dust.'

'Father Conlan says,' the chieftain argued, 'that any man who does not take the sacrament of the one true Church is a servant of Satan. Such folk are condemned to the fires of hell.'

'Father Conlan does not know,' Balek countered, 'or he would not tell you if he did know, that there are older Christian communities than the Church of Rome. In my country there has been an unbroken succession of Christian teaching since the time of the apostles. The Romans only came to believe in Christ many hundreds of years after they crucified Him. My people have venerated His teaching since the earliest days. Which of us is the better Christian?'

Donal shook his head, confused.

'The answer is,' the tilecutter declared triumphantly, 'that we are all equals in God's sight. Christian, Muslim, Jew and pagan are all the same. Faith is a strange thing. It is not defined in any sacred book. Every man has his own faith and his own battles to fight in defence of his faith. Often we are blinded to the fact that one's man's adherence to his faith is as virtuous as another's. Even though they may believe different things.'

'I don't understand.'

'We have a saying in my country,' Balek smiled. 'The grain of sand that is in your brother's eye, you can see; but the rock which covers your own eye, you cannot see. When you have removed the rock from your eye, then you may be able to cast out the grain of sand from your brother's eye.'

'Do not criticise others,' Donal rejoined, 'unless you, yourself, behave in a manner beyond reproach.'

'Yes,' Balek smiled, 'that is one way of interpreting the verse.'

The chieftain looked at his friend with a new respect, believing that he was beginning to understand the wisdom of the tilecutter's words.

'Do not judge a man,' Balek went on, 'by the God he worships or the language he speaks. Do not judge his philosophy by the lineage he claims to be descended from. In the Holy Land there are as many religious teachers as there are trees in the forest. The Pope of Rome claims Saint Paul founded his authority, but the Patriarch of Jerusalem says his jurisdiction came from the apostle Saint James who was the brother of Christ. Which man is right?'

The tilecutter shrugged his shoulders, indicating that he did not know the answer, and then went on. 'The best strategy is to judge men by how well they keep their promises and how well other men trust their word.'

'I am afraid if I go to Outremer I may never return,' Donal admitted, looking at the ground again. 'What will become of Eilish if I go off on this adventure only to die in battle?'

'If it is God's will that you die fighting for the cause of Christendom, then you shall. You should be glad to be placing your life in God's hands. Few men ever have the courage to do that. For He offers us lessons no priest can teach and answers questions not found in any book of wisdom. For what is goodness but learning to work together and accept one another? Is that not the most difficult, the most rewarding and the most holy path of all? When we learn acceptance, we learn the true value of what God has given us. It is extremely difficult to learn acceptance of others when campaigns are fought over minute points of ideology.'

The tilecutter reached into the leather pouch which hung around his waist and produced a small coin which he pushed into Donal's hand. 'This is a bronze dinar from the kingdom of Outremer and I wish to pass it on to you as a gift.'

The chieftain shook his head, overwhelmed by the gesture, but the tilecutter insisted he take it.

'This coin,' Balek explained, 'has been with me since I left my homeland. Every once in a while I take it out, look upon it and am reminded of my wife and family who are living still in the city of Acre.'

'I cannot accept such a gift,' Donal protested.

'It is not for you alone,' he said. Then he snatched the coin from Donal's open hand. He strode over to where the flat stone and tilecutting tools were laid out. Carefully the tilecutter placed the coin on the stone and then laid the wide blade of the tile-axe across it. Then, before the chieftain had worked out what was going on, Balek struck the tile-axe with his hammer and the coin split neatly into two pieces.

The tilecutter picked the two halves up and handed them back to Donal.

'Keep this half with you at all times,' Balek advised, 'but give this other half to your wife. For we have another saying in my country, that no force on earth but God can keep two pieces of a penny apart for long. Protect it and, if it is God's will, you may see your wife again one day.'

'You are full of wisdom,' the chieftain smiled, accepting the gift at last. 'You and I have grown to know each other very well through our work and I believe that we will always be close friends. It is strange to think that if it had not been for us sharing a common goal, we might never have even spoken to one another.'

'Christ said,' Balek intoned, 'where two men are in the same house and at peace with each other, they will command the mountain to move and it will move.'

'Where did you learn that?' the chieftain asked. 'I have never heard that saying.'

'It is from the Gospel of Thomas,' Balek explained. 'A very old text which the Romans discarded long ago as being of little value.'

'And how do you know it so well?'

'I was a priest, once,' the tilecutter laughed. 'A priest of the eastern church.'

As the day came to a close and folk gathered for the feast, Robert summoned his brother to his private chamber. But just as the lord expected, Rufus did not answer the call before Robert was ready to leave for the lighting of the kiln fires. The chamberlain made a quick search of the castle, but when he returned he had not found Rufus anywhere within the building.

'Very well,' Robert sighed, accepting the inevitable. 'I did not want to surprise him with what I have to say, but he leaves me no choice in the matter.' Then the lord turned to face Lonan. 'Send word to Donal that I will meet him at the kilns before the firing.'

'He is already waiting for you, my lord,' came the reply.

'Of course he is. Donal is more loyal to me than my own brother. I should not have expected too much from Rufus really,' Robert noted with sadness. 'After all, I did present him with a temptation too great to resist when I ordered ale laid out for the tenants. Is that what he is doing?' the lord snapped. 'Supping ale when he should have his mind on the business of the estate?'

'I believe Rufus has been at the barrel all day long, my lord,' Lonan ventured. 'Perhaps he has fallen asleep.'

'Fallen asleep,' Robert repeated, 'on this of all days. He must have guessed my intentions and yet he could not stay sober until the announcement was made. Donal is right. I cannot leave Rufus in sole charge of the estates when I am gone.'

'Your servants would be eternally grateful if you chose another steward,' the chamberlain agreed. 'If you will excuse my saying so, your brother does not have half the skill with his tenants that your father had.'

'And neither do I?' Robert retorted. 'Oh, do not fear to say what is on your mind,' he insisted. 'I am well aware of my shortcomings. My father was one of the most esteemed lords in this land simply because he respected everyone he knew. Unless, of course, they earned his contempt through some selfish act. Even then he was a forgiving master. That is a rare quality in a leader and it is why his servants, soldiers and friends were all so loyal to him. Unfortunately he did not pass the skill of his wisdom on to me nor to my drunken brother.'

'Leadership is a craft you must learn for yourself,' Lonan admonished, 'and in your own time.'

'I wish Father had not retired to the monastery,' Robert murmured, 'without teaching me something of his skills.'

'My lord, you are learning a great deal now,' the chamberlain soothed, 'and I believe you will not so easily forget these lessons as you might if your father sat you down and drummed them into you. You must give yourself time. Even the great King Henry was a prince once. Each of us must struggle through our apprenticeship. Be patient.'

'Come with me to the kilns,' Robert sighed, feeling a little better. 'I will need you to witness the agreement between Donal and myself. And send someone to wake my brother. I would like him to hear what I have to say at the lighting of the fires.'

'Yes, my lord.'

The chamberlain bowed low and withdrew, rushing off to see his master's orders were carried out. By the time Robert had walked down the staircase into the great hall of the keep, old Lonan was waiting for him with the lord's cloak over his arm.

Robert allowed his servant to wrap the garment around him. Then he went to the door and stepped out into the cool evening air. The scent of roasting meats tempted his nostrils immediately. Robert realised he had been so preoccupied with other matters that he had not eaten all day long.

Many folk were milling around the spits in anticipation of the feasting to come, but it seemed only his own warriors had gathered around the ale barrels. Then the lord noticed the slumped form of his brother propped up against a half-empty keg. Robert cast a questioning glance at his chamberlain.

'Your brother seems reluctant to rise, my lord,' Lonan observed nervously.

Robert smiled at his servant to reassure him it was not his fault. Then he strode purposefully over to where the soldiers were drinking.

'I am glad that you are all enjoying my hospitality,' Robert declared, addressing the warriors. But his tone indicated that he was not impressed at all. 'Tell me,' he went on, 'why are none of the tenants drinking with you?'

The soldiers parted ranks, falling back before their lord until all but one of them had stepped away from the barrels. This warrior was a large man with a long ugly scar across his face from an old wound that must have split his left nostril. The man downed the jug he was holding before he answered.

'They don't seem to like drinking with us,' he said in as innocent a tone as he could muster. 'Do you think it has something to do with the fact that we are the conquerors and they are our pitiful subjects?'

'How dare you address me like that!' Robert bellowed.

The man defiantly stood to his full height, turning his head to spit over his shoulder.

'What is your name?' the lord demanded.

The warrior smiled but it was a gesture full of malice. Then he put his massive hand on the hilt of his sword and drew it quickly. None of the other warriors made a move to stop him. It was obvious they were all a little afraid of what he might do if any of them interfered. The sound of the blade being drawn brought all the people nearby to complete silence. All eyes fell on Lord Robert and this warrior.

Carefully and slowly, without taking his eyes off the lord, the soldier turned the blade around. He placed the point at his feet, then knelt down behind the weapon, his hand resting on the hilt.

'I am called Jon Quicktoe, my lord,' he said with mocking respect in his voice, 'and I am at your service.'

'Give me your sword, Quicktoe,' Robert replied, 'and I will dub you.'

The man's eyes brightened in surprise and he lifted the weapon into Robert's hand. As soon as the lord had a hold of the hilt, he handed the sword to his chamberlain. Then Robert looked into the eyes of each of the warriors gathered around. 'Arrest him,' he ordered.

There was a moment of hesitation before the soldiers responded, but once they realised Quicktoe had been disarmed, two of them grabbed his shoulders to restrain him. The warrior did not struggle as they lifted him to his feet.

'You said you were going to dub me,' the man complained, struggling slightly against the hands that held him.

'I shall see you dubbed,' Robert assured him, 'with the lash.' The lord turned to Lonan. 'See that he receives forty strokes, then disarm him, confiscate his armour and send him on his way. I will not employ brigands and I will not see them drink the gifts intended for my tenants.'

'I am not in your employ,' Jon Quicktoe stormed, 'so you have no right to treat me this way.'

'Who is your lord?' Robert asked, shocked at the man's impudence.

The warrior indicated the body of the still unconscious Rufus.

'He cannot master himself,' Robert remarked dryly, 'let alone an ugly oaf like you. You are released from his service.' The lord ordered his chamberlain, 'See that the punishment is carried out tomorrow at first light. In the meantime, lodge this animal in the strongroom of the castle.

And see he has no more to eat or drink. He has already had his fill, I suspect.'

The warrior was dragged away cursing and vowing that he would seek retribution as soon as Rufus had awakened. The moment the warrior was gone, Robert went over to the ale barrel. He dipped a cup into the dark brown liquid and sniffed at the contents.

'A fine brew!' he proclaimed it and then slowly and deliberately tipped the cup over his brother's head. Robert was smiling all the while, obviously enjoying the experience.

Rufus shook himself. His eyes snapped open as the ale ran down his face and over his clothes. He coughed hoarsely before he managed to focus on Robert.

'Hello,' he said merrily through a thick fog of drunkenness. 'I think you've spilled your ale, brother.'

'Take him to the moat and throw him in,' the lord hissed. 'But mind you don't let him drown. He owes me money.'

Two warriors picked Rufus up and carried him toward the water.

'When you've washed the stench of strong drink out of his clothes,' Robert called after them, 'bring my brother to the kilns. I wish to speak with him.' Then the lord turned his attention to the fifteen or so soldiers still standing around near the ale barrels. 'If you wish to remain in my employ,' he began, 'you will clear this area immediately. Go and put on your armour and come to the kilns. And bring the rest of the ale barrels with you.'

For a brief moment not one of the warriors moved and the thought struck Robert that if he was not careful he might well have a bloody mutiny on his hands.

'I warn you,' he snarled in the most menacing tone he could muster, 'the next man who dares to insult me will end up as crow food hanging from a gibbet at the crossroads. Do you understand?'

No-one moved.

'If you do not do as I say immediately,' Robert went on, 'I will call on my loyal tenants to see that you are dealt with.'

All of a sudden, in a show of support, the crowd closed in around the warriors. The soldiers stood eye to eye with the people of the estate and they were heavily outnumbered. Recognising the odds as overwhelming, each of the warriors backed down and pushed through the crowd to get dressed in their war gear. It was clear that the lord was serious and he was capable of enforcing his will with the aid of his tenants.

Robert signalled to the chamberlain to follow him and the two men walked briskly down to the kilns.

'You will have to keep a close eye on Rufus,' the lord said under his breath, barely concealing the relief in his voice, 'or he and his friends will steal the hair off your very head.'

'Perhaps that is where my hair has been going all these years, my lord,' the chamberlain jibed, but then his tone became more serious. 'I fear there may be no stopping your brother if he decides to take matters into his own hands.'

'Then you'd best keep him so drunk that he hasn't the energy for mischief,' Robert suggested, only half joking.

'I think I could arrange that, my lord. The cook knows an old recipe for a wondrous spirit made from barley, oats and kitchen leavings.'

Robert screwed up his nose. 'I've tasted it,' the lord recalled. 'Two years ago, when I had the cough.'

'It cured you,' the chamberlain noted, a little put out that the lord was speaking so disparagingly about the cook's poteen.

'That brew made me forget how bad the sickness was,' Robert quipped. 'I kept no food down for a week. What my stomach did not reject, passed through me like a hot spear through new butter.' The lord shivered at the memory.

'Alas for your brother,' the chamberlain lamented in a mocking tone, 'but there are two sicknesses which even a drop of the poteen cannot cure.'

'What are they?'

'Death and stupidity,' Lonan smiled.

'Then no amount of the cook's brew will have any positive effect on my poor old brother Rufus,' the lord added. 'Though his stupidity might one day prove to be the death of him.'

Chapter Nine

Geoffrey spent his first night at the castle of Mont Salvasch in a fit of sleepless tossing and turning. The chamber set aside for him was the grandest he had ever occupied in all his life. The bed, made for some high-ranking official, was extremely comfortable, but the young man could not quiet his mind enough to rest.

Whether it was the growing sense of unease he felt about Henry or just that so much had happened to him in the last few weeks, he could not tell. In the end he contented himself with lying awake in the dark, trying with all his might to imagine what it could be that his brother had left for him in his will.

Just before sunrise Geoffrey got out of bed and dressed in his simple monk's habit. After he had slipped his worn-out sandals onto his feet, he stepped out into the corridor. It took him a few seconds to remember which staircase he had come up the previous evening. Eventually, however, he made his way silently out into the courtyard.

The morning sun was beginning to make its influence felt, shading the sky a light grey that hinted of the dawn to come. Geoffrey closed the door to the building quietly behind him, taking note that it was a beautiful shade of green such as he had never seen before.

As he surveyed the empty courtyard the young man was deeply relieved to see there was no-one about. The yard was set out in four blocks like the equal arms of a large cross. The novice walked into the centre of the cobbled pathway to get a better look around. Within each arm of the cross there was a patch of grass with a path running through it leading up to a door.

The young monk looked at the four doors, each of them a wondrous hue of green. But he could not remember which one led to the outer parts of the castle. Indeed he could not recall passing this way at all on the previous evening.

'I must have come down the wrong stairs after all,' Geoffrey told himself. He turned around, deciding to return the way he had come. The door closed heavily behind him and he felt it thud as its weight slammed into the door joists.

But what the young monk saw as the door shut confused him slightly, then startled him. Instead of stepping into the corridor where his room was situated, he had opened a door that led directly to the outer yards. Just across the way, not thirty paces on, was a large gate which led into the stables.

Geoffrey stood for a few moments, trying to take in the scene, still dazed that he had made such a simple mistake as to open the wrong door. But as the stables was the place he had been looking for, he shrugged his shoulders Then he walked across the straw toward a groom who was brushing one of the fine warhorses.

The groom heard the approaching footsteps and turned around, showing obvious surprise. 'Where did you come from?' he demanded of Geoffrey.

'I just came from the courtyard,' he pointed back over his shoulder, 'through that door.'

The young monk saw the groom frown but did not understand why until he looked back in the direction he had come from. Instead of a door there was a blank moss-covered stone wall ten paces wide and as tall as a fully mature oak tree.

'What door?' the groom finally asked, looking at the young monk with disbelief.

'That door,' Geoffrey answered, still struggling to see where it might have been.

'There is no door in that ancient wall,' the servant pointed out.

'How do I get to the chapel?' Geoffrey asked, trying to avoid any further questions and quickly deciding that this mystery would have to be solved later.

'Through the stables and into the keep, my lord,' the groom answered, still perplexed.

After Geoffrey found his way across the main courtyard to the keep, he noticed the sun was rising, for the light was steadily growing stronger. Great torches burned at the entrance to the building, throwing shadows across the cobblestones.

He edged the great wooden doors apart and slipped through into the keep. Inside there were more torches spread at regular intervals to ensure every corner of the lower floor was well lit. This was the largest central fortification Geoffrey had ever seen and by far the most complex.

To the left and right of the main hall there were several passages which were blocked by gates with iron bars. Two staircases spiralled up the walls on either side of the chamber to the upper floors.

Geoffrey decided to explore these upper levels first. Halfway up the left-hand staircase Geoffrey came across three doors in the supporting wall. They were scarcely large enough for a child to pass through. But to his disappointment every one of them was locked.

He was about to climb down to ground level again when the lad heard a familiar sound echoing through the passages. It was the soothing notes of the morning offices sung by a choir of the most excellent male voices. Geoffrey stopped still for a few moments to take in the beauty of the sound.

It was then he heard a shuffling sound coming from somewhere out of sight on the ground floor. He turned around and realised that two men were speaking. Instinctively he flattened himself against the wall so he would not be seen.

With his back to the stones Geoffrey could just see the tiles of the floor below him and hear the booted footsteps of two men pacing slowly across the chamber. A pair of shadows flickered in the lamplight as Geoffrey took a sharp intake of breath, frightened at being discovered.

'I must have it as soon as possible!' one of the men insisted. 'I have orders from the Grand Prior of Outremer. It is to be given into my care, immediately!'

'That may not be possible,' the other man answered and Geoffrey recognised the voice as that of the knight and commander of the castle, Henry St Clair.

'You had better make sure that it is possible,' the first man hissed, 'or you may find yourself guarding one of those lovely but lonely islands in the middle of the Great Ice Sea.'

'I cannot promise anything because I simply do not know what is in the will,' Henry explained.

'Then why did you not open the document and read it?'

'What would we have learned from that?' St Clair stormed. 'Godfrey d'Acre was hardly likely to make a detailed map of the exact spot where he concealed the treasure.'

'Enough!' the stranger screamed, losing his temper. Geoffrey heard the sound of a blade being withdrawn from its scabbard. He leaned forward to try and see what was going on. The two men stood opposite each other in the hall below. The stranger held a long hunting knife threateningly towards St Clair.

'I should have let you die at the hands of my soldiers,' the man holding the knife declared.

'I agreed to do your bidding,' St Clair admitted, 'because my order would never have paid a ransom for my life. I am paying my own ransom in serving you. But what is the point of all my hard work if you cannot be patient?'

'You are already a traitor to your own brothers,' the other man hissed. 'It would not be a challenge to your morals to betray me.' There was a moment of tense silence before he went on. 'You had better do as I command, Lord St Clair, or you will find yourself praying for the release of death.'

'And you had better keep your end of the bargain,' Henry replied in a low voice. 'I am your key to the treasure. Without me you have no hope of finding the prize you seek.'

'I have been searching for these treasures for ten years,' the stranger snapped, 'ever since I realised the Templars had discovered them. I have taken a ridiculous personal risk in going along with this scheme of yours. I have invested a great amount of trust in you. It is your duty to repay my mercy with results. Find out what was written in the will.'

'We can't be sure whether Godfrey ever even mentioned the treasure to his younger brother,' Henry whispered, the frustration clearly showing in his voice.

'If he did mention it,' the other man spelled out, 'then I must know before anyone else. Do you understand?'

'If it is so well hidden that you and I cannot find it,' Henry went on, 'and after all it has been given into our keeping . . .'

'The treasure was given into *my* charge,' the other man corrected him.

'If you and I cannot locate these treasures,' Henry repeated, ignoring his companion's interjection, 'then no-one else is going to find them either. There is no rush. We can take our time about locating the treasure.'

'You are wrong,' the other man commented sternly,

moving a step closer to St Clair. 'Every day that goes by we risk discovery. Every day we risk the treasures falling into the wrong hands. I must have that treasure. I must.'

'Why?' St Clair ventured. 'What is it about these trinkets that has so maddened you?'

The other man laughed, sheathing his blade again. 'The treasure I seek is not made of gold or silver. I have learned of a sacred vessel which restores life to the old, brings health to the sick and lengthens the years of any who drinks its contents.'

'The Grail Cup?' St Clair asked, raising his eyebrows.

'Some call it that,' the stranger confirmed, 'though I have heard the same properties attributed to the Ark of the Covenant.'

Geoffrey's ears pricked up and he leaned forward a little at the mention of the Ark, anxious not to miss a word of this intriguing conversation.

'What makes you think these items are part of the Templar treasure?' St Clair scoffed.

'I know they are,' the stranger insisted. 'And I believe you know of them also.'

'Rumours,' Henry replied quickly. 'Troubadours' tales. Exaggerated voyages of the imagination.'

'Yet who bothers to guard mere gold and jewels to such an elaborate degree?' the stranger smugly inquired. 'There is much more to this treasure than precious metal. And you know much more than you are telling me.'

'I am a sworn knight of the order,' St Clair protested. 'I beg you not to ask me to dishonour my oaths.'

'Yet you will help me find the true treasure of the Temple?'

'I am bound to you for saving my life,' Henry conceded.

'I have explicit orders from the highest office of our order,' the other man went on. 'The Grand Master himself has been consulted on this issue. And I must leave for the south next week to organise treaties with Saladin. If this ruse has not borne fruit by then . . .'

'We will be sure whether Geoffrey has any knowledge of the concealed vaults after he has read the will,' St Clair interrupted in as soothing a voice as he could muster.

'Very well, but if he claims to know nothing, then you will hand him over to me immediately.'

'What are you suggesting?' Henry asked.

'You'd be amazed what a good long look at the instruments of torture will do for the memory,' came the reply.

When Geoffrey heard this comment, he gasped and pressed his back harder against the wall.

'There will be none of that,' Henry spat. 'You are not in France now! As long as I am master of this castle there will be no use of the branding iron and the rack.'

'Do not overstep your authority, Master Henry,' the man snarled, and there was a hint of mockery in his tone. 'We both know you are little more than a traitor. It is my soldiers who garrison this castle now. I advise you to remember where you came from and to meditate on how easy it would be for me to destroy you. I will do what is necessary to carry out the commands that have been given to me.'

'And you would squander an asset that could prove extremely valuable to us in the future,' Henry reasoned.

'You spent too many years among the Templars,' the stranger sniped. 'What is the life of one boy compared to the glory of the Order of the Hospital?'

'The Hospital?' Geoffrey whispered, hardly able to believe his ears.

'This lad may prove to be as indispensable as his brother,' Henry reasoned.

'Godfrey?' the other man laughed. 'He was of no more value than one leaf upon a tree. His passing was not even commented upon in the central enclave of the Hospital.'

'And yet he was among the upper echelons of the Temple. It was he who led us to this great treasure,' St Clair retorted. 'Perhaps the lad will also serve us in some way. What a triumph it would be to have one such as him inducted into the Order of Saint John.'

'If you think,' the other man said slowly, 'just because his grandfather was the first master of the Temple he is entitled to special treatment, let me assure you that you are wrong. I will give you one week to extract the information from him. Then I will take over this inquiry. If you want to preserve your new status in the Order of the Hospital, you had better work swiftly. But I cannot guarantee the life of the boy in any case. His fate is in the hands of the Grand Master.'

As Geoffrey listened he could feel the sweat breaking out across his brow and trailing down his face in streams. His back was soaked with perspiration, his knees shaking so much he was sure he would collapse with fear. He put a sweaty palm inside his habit, clutching the last letter his brother had sent him, and with all his might prayed for deliverance from this prison.

The two men passed on across the hall below, their voices becoming half-understood mumbles. Geoffrey knew that he would have little chance of escape if he did not act immediately. It seemed his earlier suspicions of Henry had been confirmed.

Geoffrey tried to reason why the stranger would have mentioned the Order of Saint John. And the only answer he could come up with was that Henry and this stranger had infiltrated the Templar order to steal its precious treasures. They were, in reality, members of the black-garbed Hospital.

Geoffrey knew he had to get as far away from Mont Salvasch as possible. Escape would be extremely difficult, but he had a better chance now than he would ever have again for Henry and his guest did not know he had overheard them.

Cautiously and quietly the novice edged his way down the stairs, keeping his body as close to the wall as possible in case anyone entered the hall unexpectedly. Once he was on the ground level again, he made straight for the door through which he had entered, slipping silently across the cold stones as he did so.

When he reached the door he paused, panting not from exertion but from a nervous premonition that he was about to be discovered. He shrugged the feeling off and grasped the iron handle of the door, pulling the great wooden weight back towards him. The door swung silently on its hinges and through the widening gap Geoffrey could see the reflected light of many candles.

The familiar stench of the unwashed knights drifted out to meet his nostrils. He had once again opened the wrong door. There were many voices in the chamber beyond and laughter also. He was sure that his heart had stopped beating from fear and he pushed with all his strength against the door to close it again. But its great mass refused to do his bidding. As if it had a will of its own, the door slid wide open.

As it thudded against the wall the sound caught the attention of all the knights gathered in the chamber beyond. Before he had a chance to turn and run, all eyes were on him. Geoffrey's throat was dry or he would have called out in shock. And his legs felt like they were about to collapse under his weight.

Then a familiar form stepped forward from the crowd of thirty or forty knights and addressed him. 'Young Geoffrey! How did you find your way here?'

It was Henry St Clair.

'Come in, lad,' Henry called. 'I have someone here that I would like you to meet. After devotions we will be handing you your brother's will and passing his possessions over to you.'

Geoffrey somehow found the strength to put one foot in front of the other and walk slowly and reluctantly into the chamber. He berated himself for his foolishness and prayed that he would be able to keep his wits about him. It would be very dangerous if the stranger suspected he had overheard his conversation.

Geoffrey had not walked ten paces when his gaze was drawn upwards toward the ceiling of the chamber. High above, almost out of reach of the candlelight, there were intricate treelike designs carved into the stone ceiling. These beautiful patterns flowed all along the stonework, cascading down the walls and filling every space within the chamber except for the floor beneath his feet.

Geoffrey looked carefully at the slabs of polished marble covering the floor. The ground was laid out in a design made up of massive stones which alternated black and white in a chequered design. As he was observing these marble blocks Henry stepped forward and clapped a hand on the young man's shoulder.

'I have never known anyone to look on this chamber for the first time and keep their composure,' he laughed. 'But you are the first to have come here without any previous training. At least those who came before had some idea of what to expect.'

A man about the same age as Henry, dressed in a long white Templar robe and wearing a small red Templar cross on the left shoulder of his garment, stepped forward to stand in front of Geoffrey. The young novice forced himself to look at the stranger, certain that this was the very fellow who had suggested he be tortured.

Though Geoffrey feared what might meet his gaze, he stared into the stranger's face. And he was surprised by the gentleness of expression he saw there. Two deep-green eyes, set in a face framed by a short pointed black beard, looked back at him steadily. The stranger's reddened skin was obviously unaccustomed to the harsh sun of Outremer.

'Geoffrey d'Acre,' Henry began, 'I would like to introduce you to Guy d'Alville, newly appointed to serve the Prior of Outremer.'

'Please forgive my appearance,' the stranger begged. 'This is my first journey to the Holy Land. I have been less than careful in the burning midday sun.'

Geoffrey recognised the voice immediately, but somehow managed to control himself enough to hold out his hand in greeting. He had no choice but to treat this stranger with the respect due his rank and give no clue of what he knew.

But the thought struck him that d'Alville's beard was too short for him to have been a Templar for more than a few months. Geoffrey could not believe that one so new to the order could have been promoted so quickly. In fact, he was now convinced many of the warriors of the garrison dressed in white were in fact Hospitallers posing as Templars.

'Henry has told me much about you,' Guy went on, glancing sideways at the other assembled knights, who had by this time returned to their various conversations. 'I am glad that you could join us at devotions. I always admired the stories of your brother's exploits. I feel honoured that, though I did not have the opportunity to meet him, I now have the chance to know his sibling.'

Geoffrey barely heard a word the knight was saying. He was too distracted by his surroundings. At the other end of the chamber, set apart by no more than a half-a-dozen paces, there were two massive pillars cast from pure bronze. Like two great polished metallic tree trunks they stood close to the opposite wall. But there was something more curious about them than their beautiful decoration or their unimaginable bulk.

Though easily capable of holding up the whole building,

neither of these pillars actually reached the ceiling. Geoffrey realised in wonder that these columns had no purpose in the structure whatsoever. They were both purely decorative.

Guy coughed to get Geoffrey's full attention. 'It is time to take our places,' he informed him.

A low battle horn sounded through the chamber as all the knights in the room moved towards the walls. When they had reached their allotted positions, the warriors stood facing the centre in a great circle.

Geoffrey followed Henry, staying as close as possible to the old knight. Between the two great pillars there was a throne carved from a solid block of white marble flanked on either side by two candelabra, each holding twenty wax candles. In some other part of the building Geoffrey heard the booming of a great deep drum. Three times it rang out, slow and sonorous. As the sound died away it seemed to Geoffrey that the air was suddenly alive from the energy of the vibrations.

Then, much to his surprise, the young man noticed that the wall opposite him was moving, swinging open like a great door. In the flash of an eyelid there was an opening where seconds earlier there had been only flat, featureless stone. Geoffrey immediately thought of the door through which he had emerged into the stables earlier that morning. He realised then there were probably many such concealed portals in this castle.

'What is happening?' he asked Henry in a low whisper.

'We are to be graced with the presence of the Master of the Order in Outremer,' came the reply.

The knights moved back to allow a solitary figure to enter the chamber. Then they returned to their positions as he passed by. The great door swung shut once again after this figure had entered. Geoffrey looked on with wonder, noticing that indeed there was no trace of an opening at all once the wall had closed.

The Master of the Order, dressed in a long mail-coat under the flowing white robes of the Templars, limped to the throne, leaning heavily on a walking stick. As he reached the throne he turned carefully to take his seat, stretching his right leg out in front of him. To either side of the master, near each candelabra, incense wafted from an unseen source in great clouds that engulfed the throne in thick smoke.

It was Henry who stepped forward then, motioning for Geoffrey to remain in his place until summoned. The knight approached the throne and, when only a few paces away, declared in a powerful voice that all could hear, 'The garrison of Mont Salvasch welcomes the Sublime Prince of the Royal Secret.'

The voice that answered was thin and weak. 'I, Bertrand Guesclin, Supreme Master of the Knighthood Order of the Temple in the Holy Lands of Outremer, thank you, Henry St Clair, Commander of the Temple, Guardian of the Royal Secret and Knight Elect of the fortress of Mont Salvasch. I bear letters for you from the Grand Master of the Temple and the confirmation of your elevation to the rank of Knight of the Sun.'

Every warrior in the hall suddenly gave three cheers in unison, as if this had been rehearsed many times or they were following some signal indiscernible to an outsider. When the echoes of their voices had faded, Henry bowed his head to the master and knelt down before him on both knees.

'Answer me this,' the master intoned, 'before you are admitted into the higher orders. Which is stronger,' he went on, 'a draught of wine, a king or women?'

Henry answered immediately, without pausing to think of the answer. 'Wine is strong but not as strong as a king. Women are stronger still. But truth will conquer all of them.'

'Rise,' Guesclin commanded, 'and tell me of your work.'

Geoffrey had not expected to witness the ceremony that was taking place before him. When Henry had mentioned the devotions to be carried out, the young man had thought there would be a formal mass celebrated by the old chaplain Thomas. It was then he looked around the room and realised he could not see the old man anywhere. There were no green robes such as a priest of the order would wear, only the white robes of the knights.

The other thing that hit him was that if Henry and Guy were really Hospitaller infiltrators, they had clandestinely risen very high in the ranks of the Temple. Geoffrey was confused as to how they would have managed such a feat without being discovered. Unless of course every knight in the chamber truly was a Hospitaller in disguise. In which case he would have to be extremely careful in dealing with all of them. Men who would go to so much trouble to obtain what they desired would not value the life of a novice.

'There is one among you,' Henry declared, 'who is known to many by his brother's deeds. He has come to this place seeking the path to the Temple.'

'Let him step forward,' came the answer from the gathered knights.

Henry turned to face Geoffrey, summoning him with a hand gesture. The lad stepped forward and instantly felt all eyes upon him once again. He made his way as quickly as possible to Henry's side.

'*Theca ubi res pretiosa deponitur*,' the master intoned. Geoffrey struggled to translate the words before the man continued speaking. He thought that the master had said, 'A place where the precious thing is hidden,' but he could not be certain if his interpretation was strictly correct as Bertrand Guesclin had spoken quickly.

'I am told that you seek admission to the Temple,' Bertrand stated and Henry prodded the young man with his elbow, indicating that he should answer.

'I have come here at the wish of my late brother who commended me to the care of the order. He wanted me to carry on his work.'

'Then you will spend the next few months in earnest study to that end,' the master informed him, 'under the tutelage of Henry St Clair.'

'I will strive to live as my brother would have wished,' Geoffrey answered.

'When this assembly has dispersed,' Bertrand went on, 'you will come to my chambers, receive your brother's possessions and witness his last will.'

Geoffrey bowed his head. 'As you wish, my lord.'

'Now you must leave this chamber, for there will be ceremonies performed here which no man may witness unless he wears the robe of our order.' The master smiled at the young man. 'Father Thomas will show you around the castle and return you to me after we have completed our devotions. Go now.'

Once again Henry gently prodded the young man in the ribs. Geoffrey stepped back a few paces before he found the door from which he should exit. The knights made a path for him to pass through. In moments he was standing in the great hall where he had overheard Henry speaking to Guy. The door slammed shut and Geoffrey felt his knees begin to buckle at last.

As soon as the great door shut, Guy d'Alville wrenched open his white tunic to reveal a black surcoat beneath.

'I will not wear these rags one moment more than is necessary,' he declared.

'Fear not,' Henry replied, 'he is the one we have been waiting for. You will not have to wait long.'

'How can you be sure he will find the treasure for us?'

'He found his way here to this chapel without a guide,' St Clair reasoned. 'His intelligence is like a beacon in the night. We were lucky he stumbled on our little ceremony—I think he was fooled, don't you?—but we will have to watch him carefully or he will soon discover our true intent.'

Then Henry's eyes narrowed. 'You, my dear Guy, will have to hide the dark tunic a while longer and guard your tongue lest all our work be wasted.'

'For now we will worship as Hospitallers!' d'Alville shouted defiantly and the gathered knights began to remove their white surcoats also. 'We may have to pose as Templars,' Guy added, 'but in the sight of God we are still Knights of the Order of Saint John.'

Outside the chamber, oblivious to all that was going on inside, Geoffrey leaned against a pillar and breathed deeply. He had no idea what was happening or what these men intended to do with him. But he was frightened, all the more because he knew matters were now entirely out of his hands.

'What would they have said if I had asked to be allowed to leave the castle?' he mused aloud. 'What if I did not want to be accepted into their order?'

There was a shuffle to his right as Father Thomas stepped out of the shadows, 'Every knight doubts the path at some time in his life,' the old priest said kindly. 'Even I have wondered if I was making a mistake once or twice. But do not fear. You are among friends, and after all, the rest of your family are dead. Where else would you go? What other plans do you have?'

Geoffrey caught his breath and was about to answer but the old man cut him off.

'Come,' the priest said cheerfully, 'and I will show you the wonders of Castle Mont Salvasch.'

Robert sat on a large flat stone near to the place where the kilns had been built. He wiped his forehead in frustration. The lord looked away from the chieftain of Cúil Ghréine as he spoke.

'I agree with you, Donal,' he said, trying to conceal his mounting anger. 'I do not believe Rufus can be trusted either. But I cannot allow a woman to take the office of chancellor.'

'Why not?' the chieftain inquired. 'My wife is perfectly capable. She has a good head on her shoulders. She will be the chieftain of my clan while I am away.'

'She is a woman!' Robert exclaimed, still finding it difficult to understand why that was not enough of a reason in itself. 'The King would never recognise such an appointment. Under the law it would allow Rufus too much room to manoeuvre. He could challenge her position in the royal court and he would surely win the case.'

'Women act as chieftains throughout this land,' Donal objected.

'But not in the Norman lands,' the lord insisted. 'That is simply not our way.'

'If Braonin is appointed,' the chieftain suggested, 'then perhaps my wife could act as an adviser to him.'

'That would not do either,' Robert said, holding the palm of his hand up as a gesture of the futility of the suggestion. 'Women do not hold any official duties at court, nor anywhere in the Norman kingdoms.'

'But you understand that the tenants respect her and will follow her lead?'

'I understand,' the lord admitted, 'but my hands are tied. The chance of rebellion from my own brother would be too great if a woman were left to control the expenditure. No,

Donal, it must be a man. He must be of your clan and he must be seen to work alone without consultation from any woman.'

Donal shook his head, staring at the ground in defeat. Robert could see that there would have to be some compromise between them but he was reluctant to initiate it.

'If, however,' the young lord finally relented, 'Braonin were to casually mention the accounts to Eilish every once in a while, in the strictest confidence, mind you, then I could see no harm in her passing on advice to him. On the understanding that he would not necessarily have to take her words to heart and he would always remain independent.'

Donal smiled. 'You will not regret this,' he beamed.

'I will if my brother gets wind of it,' the lord frowned. 'I have heard the cook say there are three kinds of men who fail to understand women,' Robert smiled wryly. 'Young men, middle-aged men and old men. I imagine Rufus could fit into a fourth category all of his own. He is a proud man and his pride has been injured a great deal already. I am not sure how he will react if he discovers Eilish has more influence over the running of the estates than he does.'

'But you can rest assured,' Donal added, 'that while we are both away, Bally Raine will be managed well. And your brother's appetites will be curbed somewhat.'

'My brother's appetites would not be diminished if he were laid in his grave,' Robert sighed. 'I can only pray your cousin and your wife may distract him from his pleasure-seeking. With luck they will restrain him long enough that he can do no real damage to the estate.'

'Why don't you bring him with us?' Donal suggested.

'He hasn't the stomach for a sea voyage,' the lord answered, 'nor any activity which requires that he put the welfare of others before his own. When he has a sword or axe in his hand he is more of a danger to himself than his enemies. The life of a warrior would not suit him.'

'Then you will announce the appointment of Braonin when you make the news of your crusade public?'

'I will,' Robert confirmed.

As they finished speaking, Robert's warriors arrived dressed in their mail and bearing six ale barrels between them. The lord excused himself to oversee the soldiers. As soon as Robert was gone, Balek the tilecutter touched Donal on the arm to get his attention.

'I am ready for the firing,' he announced. 'I beg your pardon, my friend, but the lord does not seem happy with you.'

'He is content enough with me,' Donal laughed. 'It is his brother that troubles him so.'

At the mention of Robert's brother, two warriors appeared with the semi-conscious form of Rufus draped between them. The proud younger FitzWilliam broke away from the soldiers, though, and insisted on walking without their aid.

Balek raised an eyebrow and shot a worried glance at Donal when he noticed the Norman staggering towards the kilns. The younger FitzWilliam was soaking wet from his dunking in the moat but blissfully unaware of just how ridiculous he looked.

Other folk were now gathering around the kilns, hoping to hear Robert's first summer speech as Lord of Bally Raine. An air of expectation hung about the crowd as many folk debated whether the rents and taxes would increase in the coming year.

Rufus sat down on the grass near the tile ovens and struggled to sober himself up. It may have been the cold moat water or the brisk march down to the kilns, but whatever the reason he was now becoming aware of his surroundings. Robert approached his younger brother, squatting down in front of him to speak.

'I suppose you have a good explanation for your disgraceful behaviour,' the lord began, speaking under his breath so none of the tenants would hear what he had to say.

Rufus faced his brother with a contemptuous sneer. All of a sudden he took in a loud breath and spoke. 'My God!' he exclaimed with a slur to his speech. 'For a moment there I thought it was my father berating me for my drinking. You are so much like him, you know,' he added with venom. 'Same eyes. Same neat clothes. Same holy-as-a-martyr pronouncements. Same petty bloody outrage.'

'Please, brother, for your own sake do not make a scene,' Robert pleaded. 'I wish to let you know beforehand what I intend to announce to everyone else very soon.'

'You and he are so much alike,' Rufus went on, bitterly. 'More like a pair of bloody-minded priests than father and son. Tell me, Father Robert,' he said sarcastically, 'why have you not followed in the footsteps of your illustrious sire and taken ship for the Holy Land? What's stopping you? Wasting your inheritance on building chapels you are. And what will it be next? A great cathedral? Or a bloody basilica?'

Robert stood up, enraged. 'Get up off your arse and move yourself over to the kilns,' he commanded in a low, threatening voice, 'or I swear by the Holy Mother of God I will throw you out on it to fend for yourself. I have witnessed you and Father fighting for years. I always wondered why he lost his temper with you so quickly and so easily. Well, now I know.'

Rufus giggled a little but he was beginning to glimpse the precariousness of his situation.

'Get up,' Robert said again, 'before I have you dragged to the edge of the estate and dumped on the road where you will be left with only the soaking clothes you have on to cover you and whatever gold is in your purse to keep you.'

Rufus rose slowly, not wishing to push his brother any further. As he got to his knees a man reached out a hand to him. It was Father Conlan.

'Come along, my son,' the priest appealed. 'Do as your lord and brother asks.'

Robert looked at Father Conlan with surprise. 'Leave him, father,' the lord commanded. 'He has spread manure in his bed straw, let him lie in it.'

The priest hissed back under his breath, 'It is obvious that he cannot rise without a helping hand, my lord. In the spirit of true Christian charity you should be more caring for your sibling. Would you really cast him out upon the road to fend for himself? I know your father spoke of it many times, but he never would have done such a thing, would he?'

Robert turned his face away, suddenly ashamed that he had considered washing his hands of Rufus once and for all. The priest was right, there was nothing to be gained from punishing Rufus so crudely. What was the point, Robert asked himself, of travelling halfway across the world to fight for the cause of the Cross if he could not find it in his heart to forgive his own brother?

'I give him into your care, father,' the lord finally said with a sigh. 'Bring him close by the kilns so he can hear my speech.'

The priest helped Rufus to his feet as Robert strode over to stand by Donal at the kilns. All the tenants and freeholders had gathered by this time and many were casting dark glances at the ruddy-faced Rufus. Among them, standing with Eilish and her family, was Neesh.

An empty ale barrel was turned on end and Robert climbed up on it to speak. As soon as he was ready he raised a hand to bring the assembly to silence. Donal moved in behind his lord, waiting for his role to be announced. Braonin stood to the chieftain's right hand, also waiting.

'My friends,' the lord began. Everyone immediately ceased their talking and speculation, eager to discover what great changes were about to take place.

'My friends, tenants, freeholders and warriors.' Robert

took a deep breath before he launched into his announcement. 'Today marks an occasion of which we should all be very proud. Today the roof and floor tiles of the Chapel of Saint Mary Magdalene will be hardened in the flames. This is the culmination of many months of work. The results will still be with us many years from now.'

The lord coughed nervously, clearing his throat.

'I am sure you have all heard rumours that the taxes are about to rise, but I would like to reassure you that I wish to avoid doing that if at all possible. I know many of you work very hard to provide for your families. I would not ask more of you than it was fitting for you to give.'

Robert took another deep breath and relaxed a little, beginning to feel that standing in front of the assembly was not such a frightening task.

'There is a great city at the centre of the world,' Robert went on, 'where the people, good Christians like yourselves, are starving. Many have been injured in the wars against the infidels. Many have lost their homes and their families. Many cannot even imagine what our peaceful land is like. The rain rarely falls on that country. It is as if God has abandoned these folk to their fate. The churches have been desecrated so there is nowhere for the people to pray. Their holy relics have been stolen and dispersed amongst the heathen. A cruel tyrant rules them with a heavy hand and it must seem to them as if they are living through the last days before the coming of the judgment of God.'

Everyone was silent, deeply moved by the vivid scenes Robert conjured in their minds. At the back of the crowd Cinneach stood with his arms folded and a smile on his face, silently congratulating the lord on such masterful words.

'It seems to me,' Robert went on, 'that I have a duty to these people, though they live far away. For if the wealthy knights of our country do not answer the call to arms, then what hope do the Christian folk of Outremer have? In order to lend my assistance to them, I have decided to leave this place which I call home and travel to the Holy Land to win it back from the Saracens. There has been no other time such as this. If indeed we are living through the last days leading to the final battle of Armageddon, I wish to stand up and fight on the side of Christ.'

The crowd raised a cheer for Robert the very moment he stopped speaking, proud of the man they now called lord. Here was a knight so devout he would willingly offer up his life in service to the Cross.

The lord raised his hand again to quieten his people. As he did so he caught a glimpse of Rufus in the crowd. It seemed that his brother had finally sobered up somewhat. Rufus was standing tall and smiling proudly.

'But I find I cannot achieve this high goal on my own,' Robert went on once he had silence again. 'I will need the help of each and every one of you. I am not asking any man to join me on this quest to free the city of Jerusalem. I am asking those who stay behind to work hard and maintain the estates in my absence. Your hands will ensure I have enough resources to carry on this crusade for as long as necessary. I will need your loyalty, your sweat and your prayers if we are to free the Holy City.'

The crowd was quiet as everyone waited to hear how much the rents would rise. They all expected some levy on the tenants for the keeping of Lord Robert's retinue while he was abroad.

'First, let me repeat, I do not wish to raise the level of taxes. To that end I will be appointing two trusted men from the estates to act as my chancellors during this campaign. One of these men will be in charge of my expenditure on the voyage to Outremer and for costs during the time I am in the Holy Land. The other man will oversee the running of the estates with the help of my chamberlain, Lonan Feeney.'

Robert paused again, trying to discern whether his brother was showing any signs of anger, but he could see none so he went on.

'On campaign, Donal O'Regan will act as my chancellor and sergeant-at-arms as his father did before him for Lord William.'

Donal stepped forward to stand in front of the ale barrel on which Robert stood.

'Here on the estates I have chosen as my representative a man in whom I know you would all willingly place your trust. He is Donal's cousin and kinsman. Braonin O'Regan will be the chancellor of Bally Raine in my absence.'

Braonin stepped forward to take up his position next to Donal.

'These two men are my trusted servants,' Robert added. 'I am sure they will perform their tasks diligently. To aid Braonin in keeping the accounts in order, I have asked Lonan to give his advice wherever possible. Of course, my brother Rufus will also lend a hand where appropriate.'

People were nodding their heads in agreement with their lord. If he had to undertake such an expensive and dangerous journey, this seemed the wisest way to be going about it, though he had already given them enough information to keep the arguments going on throughout the night.

'As to the recruiting of men-at-arms,' the lord said, raising his voice to get everyone's attention again, 'those landholders who provide me with two able-bodied men to accompany me on the crusade will have their taxes halved for the coming year. Those who provide one man skilled at arms will have their taxes or rents reduced by a quarter. Any family providing me with one skilled archer will have their taxes annulled for the coming year. A landholder who can provide a horse will have his taxes reduced by one-tenth for every draught animal and halved for any horse capable of being used for war.'

There was a general muttering among all those present, some pronouncing the terms generous, others still suspicious of bad news to come. At the back of the crowd Robert saw his brother standing perfectly still, as if turned to stone. The lord told himself this was a good sign. At least Rufus was not ranting and raving.

'Any man who wishes to join me on this crusade,' Robert continued, 'should come forward after the fires have been lit. The terms of his service will be explained to him then and his name written down. I encourage all the strong men of the estates to join me.' He paused for a moment, then turned to the tilecutter. 'And so we come to the lighting of the fires.'

Balek held up a lighted torch and handed it to Robert as the lord got down from the empty barrel. Robert put the flame to the tinder and as the first flame flickered the crowd cheered again. The assembly closed in around the stone ovens, ready to partake in the ale before returning to the castle to begin the feast.

Rufus, however, stayed where he was and for the first time in many years offered up a heartfelt prayer to the God he thought had long ago forsaken him.

'It has pleased you to deliver this prize into my keeping, Lord,' he whispered, 'and I will cherish it forever more.'

Rufus FitzWilliam solemnly made the sign of the cross over his chest. Then he turned around to head back to his chambers to plan his next moves.

Before he was led into Henry's private chambers, Geoffrey stood before a rare and expensive glass-paned window to look with wonder at his reflection. After the chaplain had shown him some of the features of the Castle Mont Salvasch, Geoffrey had been presented with new white military-style garments.

He had been told by the servants that the master of the castle had provided these clothes for him. There were white woollen hose, soft brown leather shoes with soles of wood, a fine white shirt made of a light material the servant told him was called damask, and a tunic with a long slit in the front which was made to be worn over the top of the shirt. On his head he wore a white coif to keep his hair in place and a black cap with decorated edges.

These new clothes would have cost a small fortune in France and certainly would have been beyond his means even a few short months ago. He was still admiring his reflection when the servant opened the door to St Clair's chamber. The man coughed to get Geoffrey's attention, then stood back to allow the young novice to pass.

'Now you are beginning to look like a postulant to the Temple,' Henry exclaimed as he looked up from his desk. 'Later we will have your hair cut in the common style of all our knights. That should complete the picture. I have consulted with Bertrand Guesclin, the Master of the Order. And I have spoken at length with Guy d'Alville. Together we have decided to elevate you through the ranks as quickly as possible.'

'You do me great honour,' Geoffrey began as he gazed around the interior of the chamber in awe. 'I hope I will measure up to the tasks you set me.'

The room was large, windowless and lit entirely by candlelight. There were strange spherical devices, which Geoffrey guessed were seaman's instruments, stacked haphazardly in one corner. Small tables all around the room were covered in parchments and various colourful drawings. The walls were hung entirely with rich tapestries depicting the stations of the cross, interspersed with other scenes which the young man did not recognise as biblical.

As Geoffrey took in the many decorations and different items of furniture he felt inside his tunic for the rough parchment he always carried with him: his brother's last letter. His hand brushed over his stomach where the parchment was tucked into his breeches. Reassured it had not been lost, he pretended to smooth his tunic flat.

'Don't think it is going to be easy, my boy,' Henry confided. 'I will make sure you earn every one of your promotions and all your fine clothes. The Temple has great plans for you but you will have to prove yourself worthy of the work first. Do you have any armour or war gear of your own?'

'No, my lord. My brother was fully outfitted but my father did not have the resources to equip me also.'

'I will have to see what I can do about that,' the knight mused aloud. 'Your brother's mail-coat, helm, sword and shield are here in the castle in storage. Perhaps it would be best if you used those for the time being until we can have some fitted to you.'

'Thank you, my lord,' Geoffrey replied respectfully. 'I would be more than happy to wear my brother's armour.'

'So be it,' Henry decided and clapped his hands loudly. A servant opened the door and bowed to the lord of the castle.

'Fetch me the armour of Godfrey d'Acre,' St Clair commanded, 'and when you return wait outside where you cannot hear me clap. If you can hear me slap my hands together, you can also hear all the secrets of the Temple and I would not like you to listen to those.'

'Yes, my lord,' the servant answered, trembling. The man backed out of the chamber, bowing low.

'I am perhaps being a little overcautious,' Henry explained, 'but only recently one of the servants was caught listening a little too intently to a conversation between

Father Thomas and Bertrand Guesclin. He turned out to be a knight of the ...' Henry paused, rewording the phrase, '... enemy order, playing the part of a serving man. He hoped to learn what he could about this place. I have no idea how he came to be here but one thing is certain. No-one leaves this place unless I approve it.'

'You had him executed?'

'Naturally,' the knight laughed. 'He had forfeited the right to live because of his carelessness. It was no less than what he expected, I am sure.'

Just then Henry realised his guest was still standing and he ushered Geoffrey into a seat not unlike the one which the Bishop of the Krak had brought from Venice. Several of these beautiful chairs were spread around the room. Each one of them was covered in designs beaten into the leather and then highlighted with gold leaf. The young postulant looked about him, overawed by all the finery of the decorations and furniture.

'This room is very beautiful, isn't it?' Henry commented.

'This is the most wonderful chamber I have ever sat in,' the young man answered. 'I have never seen so many books.' He pointed to the shelf stacked with leather-bound volumes.

'I have works here that deal with every subject,' Henry boasted proudly, 'from medicine to map-making, from botanical essays to a treatise on the black arts of magic. Over here is a manuscript describing the original treasures of the Temple of Solomon which I would particularly like you to have a look at.'

The old knight went to the shelf and thumbed his way through the covers until he found the volume he was searching for.

'At last!' he exclaimed. 'Always hiding in amongst the others is this one.' And he pulled the great book out from the shelf by a long piece of braided leather attached to the spine. St Clair carried the manuscript over to Geoffrey and laid it open on his lap.

'The detail in this work is really astonishing,' Henry enthused. 'I must find you a glass so you can see it more clearly.'

The knight opened a cabinet propped against the wall in a corner and weighted down with piles of parchments. As he opened the door of the cabinet a large object rolled out onto the floor. When Geoffrey saw the human skull tumbling across the chamber, he gasped loudly. But Henry picked the gruesome article up again and placed it back on the shelf without a second thought.

'Here it is!' he exclaimed. 'I knew I had left it here.' And with that he brought a seeing-glass to Geoffrey. The knight rubbed the glass against his surcoat and held it up to the light to see if it was clean. Satisfied, he handed it to his guest.

'You will see the detail better with this,' St Clair assured the young man.

Geoffrey held the piece of glass over the first page, astonished that he could indeed see every detail in the illustration much more clearly.

'I will finish the work I have to do while we wait for Guy and Bertrand to arrive,' Henry announced. 'You should sit back and look carefully at the illustrations in that book.'

Geoffrey turned another leaf and saw, to his surprise, a drawing of the Ark of the Covenant sketched in the most beautiful colours. On the opposite page there were many words written but, as they were not in Latin, he could not discern the meaning of the strange letters.

Eagerly he turned the page. Before him was the plan of a large building with parts of the drawing designated in a script that, again, he did not recognise. On the next page there was a picture of a golden cup and on the next a drawing of two pillars exactly like the ones Geoffrey had seen the previous morning in the keep of the castle. This book was a list of all the marvels the young man had ever dreamed about.

When the other two knights finally arrived, Henry took the volume from Geoffrey and produced a small but heavy chest bound with iron. The strongbox was built out of sturdy oak. It was unlocked but tied all around with wide black silk ribbons. The silks were joined in three places with massive circular red wax seals to ensure no-one tampered with the contents. Each seal had the weight of a large candle in its wax.

Guy and Bertrand took their places, each in one of the beautiful leather chairs. As soon as the two men were comfortable a servant brought in a polished brass bottle decorated with fine red enamel. Several pipes protruded from the bottle at different angles. Geoffrey had never seen such a device before and had no idea what it might be.

Bertrand put one of the pipes to his mouth and drew in a deep breath through it. To the young postulant's surprise there was a low sound like bubbles being blown in water. But then smoke erupted from the master's nose and Geoffrey gasped aloud.

Henry noticed the look on his guest's face. Unable to conceal his amusement, the commander explained that this was a Saracen habit. 'The smoke of the burning herbs is said to be very good for the relief of pain.'

'I was speared through the thigh,' Bertrand took up the story, 'eight months ago during a skirmish near Jaffa. A Saracen physician advised me to partake of the smoke from these herbs every day as long as the pain was still unbearable. I will never have the full use of my leg again, but this concoction certainly eases the agony of the injury.'

'I would not advise you to try any of the Saracen medicines,' Henry interrupted, 'unless they are specifically recommended to you. While these herbs may dull physical pain, they also impair the faculties of the mind. I have watched many men forsake their God-given ability to reason sensibly once they have inhaled that smoke.' The knight tapped his forehead with the tip of his fingers and rolled his eyes to show what he meant.

'I have never noticed that particular property,' Bertrand retorted indignantly. 'The Saracens may be a heathen race but they are the best physicians in the world. I knew a man once who was blinded by ugly growths over his eyes. He was given back his sight by a learned Saracen with no more than a sharp knife and a book describing the procedure.'

'Is it not time we presented Geoffrey with his brother's will?' Guy cut in, his impatience getting the better of him.

'You are right,' Henry agreed and he clapped his hands loudly.

The servant waiting at Bertrand's side scurried from the room, closing the door to the chamber behind him. No-one spoke again until they were all absolutely sure the attendant would not hear anything they were about to discuss.

'It is extremely unusual for a Templar knight to be permitted to indulge himself in the splendour of writing a last will,' Guy commented as Henry St Clair placed the small box in Geoffrey's hands. 'But your brother was an unusual man.'

Geoffrey noticed Guy had an unnerving habit of touching his tongue to his bottom lip after he finished each sentence. This involuntary twitch only served to reinforce the young man's distrust of him.

'A man who is the direct descendant of the founder of the order,' Guy went on, 'and a guardian of the treasury may have the rules relaxed in his favour occasionally. Your brother prepared this box for you in the event that he fell in battle or was taken captive by the enemy. Bertrand and myself are interested in this matter simply because there are a few unsolved aspects about your brother's death which we hope to have explained for us when you have read the letter he has left for you.'

'I did not realise there were still some unanswered questions regarding my brother's passing,' Geoffrey stated, quite sure that something was being kept from him. 'I have been told he died in the defence of the Templar treasure.'

'That is true.' Guy smiled insincerely and then took a breath as he carefully considered his next statement. 'The treasure which your brother was escorting at the time of his death was rescued by a fellow Templar knight and then taken to a safe place far from the wars in Outremer. However, there were other valuable items in Godfrey's safe-keeping which have not been recovered. We believe your brother concealed them in some safe place, intending to collect them later. We know he was transporting the treasure in lots. His reasoning was that if one consignment were to be captured by the enemy, the remaining treasure would still be in safe hands.'

'And my brother did not leave any clues,' the young man asked, 'as to where this cache of valuables might be?'

'He may have done,' Guy conceded, once again touching his lip with his tongue. 'But he did not trust many people. It was the nature of his task. That is why we are hopeful there is some clue in the box which he left for you. As a blood relative and the only other direct descendant of the founder of our order, it is possible Godfrey felt you were the one person he could trust with such information.'

'Well,' Henry chimed in, obviously eager to get on with the business at hand, 'are you going to open the chest?'

'Yes, of course,' Geoffrey answered nervously as he began breaking the three wax seals. Once the black ribbon was unwrapped there was only an iron catch holding the box closed. Geoffrey flipped this open and lifted the heavy lid.

There were several items inside the box but the first to catch his eye was a piece of parchment as long and wide as his hand. This thick card had been carefully laid flat on top of everything else packed into the box. Geoffrey picked the parchment up to examine it more closely. There was a colourful drawing on it which depicted a blindfolded man carrying a staff. The blinded man seemed about to step over the edge of a cliff.

'What is it?' Henry asked excitedly. Geoffrey dutifully handed him the parchment. In the meanwhile he went on to investigate the other contents of the chest.

'The fool,' St Clair declared triumphantly. Both Guy and Bertrand nodded their heads. Clearly this sign was of great significance to them.

'What does it mean?' the postulant asked.

'It signifies the journey of the novice,' Henry explained. 'This card is one of many that we use as a system to communicate certain ideas between members of the order without the risk of any outsider understanding what is really being said. This card clearly represents you in your coming journey into the Order of the Temple. The fool trusts he is on the correct path. There may be pitfalls along the way but it is as important to make mistakes as it is to celebrate triumphs.'

As Henry was speaking Geoffrey removed a larger rolled section of parchment and broke the single wax seal that held it shut. Then he carefully unfurled the letter and examined the contents.

'Would you read it to us?' Guy asked.

Geoffrey nodded, knowing he could not really refuse. He held the document up to the light and began to decipher the thin letters of scrawled handwriting.

'"To my dear brother, Geoffrey d'Acre,"' he began, '"this letter, in my own hand. It is time for you to decide the true path of your life, whether to remain in the Holy Land or return to France to claim the titles our father left to us. I have entrusted your education to St Clair who is my dearest friend and confidant. Trust no man but him and your troubles will be few."' Geoffrey stopped reading for a moment, trying to make out the next few words.

'There is a poem after that,' he explained. 'It says:

'"Here begins the tale of your descent.
Here begins the story of the Holy Grail.
Here begin the terrors.
Here begin the marvels.
A sword length from the east, another from the west,
Hold the pommel a measured distance from the floor,
Lift the hanged guardian high upon the Three,
Look to the throne,
Wherein lies the secret realm, the lance that wounds,
The dish that feeds the multitude, the cup that heals the maimed king,
And above all others the scroll on which is writ the book of ages."'

The young man read the words to himself again, perplexed as to their meaning. When he realised he could not make any sense of the poem at all, he raised his eyes to meet Henry's. Geoffrey was surprised to note the old knight was just as confused as he was.

Bertrand drew in the smoke from his water pipe and for the moment the sound of its bubbling was the only noise in the room. Guy stared directly at the young man seated opposite him, studying his face and touching his bottom lip with the tip of his tongue.

'What else does it say?' Henry queried.

'The letter goes on,' Geoffrey continued, woken from his thoughts, '"If you stay to the path I set down for you in my last letter, my dear brother, your quest will be fruitful. As long as you do not stray from those rules I have given you, then your success is assured. Beware the enemy for he wears many guises. Beware the black wolf who pretends he is a white sheep. I pray to God that He may pardon my sins as He did those of Saint Mary Magdalene."' The young man paused again for a moment and then added, 'It is signed "Godfrey d'Acre".'

Geoffrey turned the parchment over in his hands to examine the other side. 'There is nothing more written here,' he stated. Then he put the letter down and once more looked inside the box. In a moment he had pulled out two more thick parchment rectangles exactly the same shape and size as the first card. One of them featured the design of a man hanging upside down from one foot on a strange cross that resembled a tree. Geoffrey handed this card to Henry and looked at the second parchment.

This card had a drawing of a woman seated on a chair set between two pillars in much the same way as Bertrand had been enthroned the previous morning at devotions. Scrawled across the bottom of the card were the words: 'I am black and I am beautiful. O daughters of Jerusalem.' This card Geoffrey also handed to Henry.

'The hanged man,' the knight gasped, 'is the symbol of one who has died for the cause and is lying in his tomb awaiting the Last Judgment.' He turned to the other card. 'The high priestess signifies many things. A mystery or a quest for truth or ancient wisdom. Its presence implies that the answer to these riddles is within your grasp.'

'I have no idea what all this means,' the young man muttered in confusion. 'There is no bequest in this will at all as far as I can see. There is only a collection of strange riddles which have no discernible answer.'

'Do you still have your brother's last letter?' Guy cut in tersely.

Geoffrey felt a shudder of fear run through his body. 'Why do you ask?'

'Your brother mentions that you should hold fast to the rules he laid down for you in that document. I rather thought this letter, if it still exists, might hold some clues to the conundrum. May I see it?'

'The abbot held all of my letters,' Geoffrey lied. 'I was allowed to read the letter but I was forced to surrender it to him afterwards. It was his opinion that public reading was unseemly for brother novices. He considered correspondence from outside the monastery walls to be bad for the spirit of the community.'

'I see,' Guy grunted, flicking his tongue. 'And, by any chance, do you remember what rules your brother advised you to keep in that letter?'

'To obey my superiors,' Geoffrey shrugged, pretending he had not taken too much notice of the contents. 'Keep the fast days. Pray for the soul of our dead father.'

'I believe Guy would like to know,' Bertrand spoke up, 'whether there was anything unusual you remember about the rules Godfrey set out for you? Was there anything you did not fully understand? Anything that might give us any clues as to where he might have concealed the remaining treasure?'

'What sort of clues?' Geoffrey asked innocently.

'Clues about the hundred hidden meanings in this confounded will!' Guy stormed.

Geoffrey cast his eyes down to the floor to show his embarrassment. 'I don't remember anything specific,' he mumbled.

Guy stood up briskly, clearly agitated by this unconvincing answer. For a brief moment Geoffrey feared Guy was going to cross the room and strike him down. But Henry stood up and held out a hand to calm his comrade.

Guy d'Alville grunted but relaxed somewhat. 'Would you mind if I had a look at the contents of that chest?' Guy asked, his voice barely concealing his frustration.

'Not at all,' the young man replied as the knight crossed the room.

Guy brushed past Henry to take the parchments from the young postulant. He spent a long time examining the letter, holding it up to the candlelight, running his fingers back and forth across the surface. Certain there was a message to be found here, he took each of the three cards and looked closely at them in turn. He kept this up until it was clear to him there were no further clues to be discovered.

'Have you any idea what your brother meant to say to you in this will?' Guy asked finally.

'I am sorry to say I do not, my lord,' Geoffrey answered. 'I only wish I understood his words. I would like nothing more than to help you recover the treasure.'

'And you remember well the last letter that your brother sent to you? You are sure it contained only mundane advice for the future?'

'I am certain, my lord, that I remember exactly what was contained in the last letter I received from my brother,' the young man stuttered. 'But it is always possible the abbot did not pass all my brother's letters on to me.'

'What do you mean?' snapped Guy.

'The abbot may have withheld some correspondence from me,' Geoffrey explained. 'I know that he commonly did this when he wished to punish the brothers in the community. I was not, after all, one of his favourites. Perhaps he still has this letter in his possession. Perhaps he forgot it ever arrived.'

The three knights looked from one to another with deepening frowns. Not one of them liked the sound of this answer but it obviously made a great deal of sense to them.

'It is possible,' Henry agreed. 'We should have checked more thoroughly before we returned here.'

'Damn that fat little blowfly!' Guy strained through gritted teeth. 'He lied to us! I will ride to the Krak tomorrow and question the man. If he has this letter we will soon know.' Then the knight turned to Bertrand. 'Master, it is time I saw to my horse. Will you join me?'

Bertrand got up from his seat slowly and nodded. 'I will accompany you, my son,' he agreed. And Geoffrey could not help feeling that, despite their stated ranks, it was really Guy who was the senior knight in this room.

'Good day to you, my son,' Guy said politely to Geoffrey, and his tongue touched his lip. 'May this morning prove to be the beginning of a fruitful education. If you remember anything at all about your brother's letter, you must tell me immediately. Do you understand?'

'I do. Thank you, my lord, for your well wishes,' the postulant answered, 'and good day to you.'

Guy turned to Henry. 'I will meet with you again later in the day before I leave . . .'

At that very moment Guy was interrupted by a loud knocking at the door to the chamber, and before Henry had a chance to berate his servants, a stranger came barging into the chamber.

'How dare you burst in on us like this?' screamed Guy, turning to face the man who had disturbed them. 'Can you not see we are speaking privately?'

'I have an urgent message for the master of the castle,' the man gasped. 'I have come a full day on horseback without any rest to bring the news here.'

'What can be so important it encroaches on the time of the Master of the Temple?'

'It is the Krak,' the man sobbed, clearly distraught. By this time the messenger was on his knees and panting. 'The Krak has fallen to the Saracens.'

All expression left Guy's face as the full meaning of the news hit him. Suddenly his complexion changed from a sunburnt red to pale then to a ruddy hue much redder than he had been before. The knight drew his sword to hold it high above his head in a rage. Geoffrey was sure he was going to strike the exhausted messenger down.

Guy's sword hovered in the air for a few seconds. 'Bloody heathen bastards!' he screamed as he slammed the flat of the weapon down upon Henry's table. The blade shattered as it struck the oak desk and the knight petulantly flung the useless hilt aside. It landed in the corner of the room with a clatter.

'I will enter into negotiations with the Saracen commander immediately to have that letter returned,' Guy stated. Then the Templar Prior of Outremer stormed past the messenger and out of the chamber. Bertrand, obviously benefiting from the painkilling herbs, followed after d'Alville, attempting to look as dignified as possible.

When the messenger had withdrawn, Geoffrey turned to Henry. 'Was there anything else that my brother left me?' he asked.

'Nothing much aside from his sword, his mail-coat, and some other items of clothing,' Henry replied. 'There were some writing implements, a few bottles of ink and a bundle of unused parchment, but nothing else I know of. I will send for the armour so that you may inspect it. I cannot allow you to wear it, though, or to bear a sword until you have passed into knighthood. That may take some months, perhaps up to a year.'

'It will give me a goal to aim for,' Geoffrey declared, 'to one day carry my brother's sword. May I have the writing tools?'

'Of course,' Henry agreed. 'I will have them sent to you.'

'Would the old abbot have been murdered by the Saracens?' Geoffrey inquired.

'That is very likely, I am afraid,' the knight answered, a defeated tone in his voice. 'Your abbot was not renowned for his charity to the infidel. And I have heard Saladin takes the view that the cruel should be cruelly dealt with.'

'So we may never know what my brother meant to say in his will?' Geoffrey said, realising he may have been saved from the rack by the news of this defeat.

'We may never know,' Henry confirmed. 'We may never know.'

Under his shirt Geoffrey could feel the dry parchment against his skin. He had originally kept the letter on his person just to stop the old abbot from confiscating it. But he had gradually come to like having it close to him; it was a reminder of the only family he had left in the world.

Now he could not wait to get back to his little cell so that he could examine the parchment again in the hope of unravelling at least part of this mystery. Geoffrey guessed from what he had read of the will that he would need his brother's sword to solve the entire puzzle.

'If I have your leave, my lord,' he said respectfully, 'I will go to my midday prayers.'

'Yes, of course, my son,' the old knight replied, woken from his thoughts. 'And this afternoon we will begin your education in earnest. I have a sword master in mind who will teach you the art of the warrior. After we have seen what you can do with a wooden weapon in your hand, I will begin to teach you more about the Order of the Temple.'

Geoffrey left St Clair's chamber clutching the heavy chest close to his body. He prayed ceaselessly all the while that Guy had not seen through any of his lies. In a few minutes the young man had arrived at the door of his little cell. Now he was a postulant Templar he would no longer sleep in the great chamber he had been given on his first night in Castle Mont Salvasch. He had been assigned a humbler room. Geoffrey breathed a sigh of relief as the hinges on the door to his cell creaked shut. The iron bolt slipped into place behind him and he whispered a few words into the air.

'Now I will try to unravel the threads of your mystery, brother,' he promised.

After all the servants had gone to their own houses for the evening, Eilish piled turf up on the fire so it would burn steadily throughout the night. Donal came in shortly afterwards when he had finished seeing to a sick cow. Unlike all their neighbours, the chieftain of the O'Regan family and his wife did not share their home with the cattle. The O'Regan cows spent their nights in the care of close kinfolk of the chieftain. This kept the bond of obligation strong between the leader of the community and those he was elected to lead.

Donal seated himself before the fire on a block of wood he liked to use for a stool. As the night was warm he dropped the cloak from around his shoulders, letting it fall onto the earthen floor. Eilish instinctively picked it up as she walked past. She was about to hang the garment on one of the many wooden pegs set at intervals around the walls of the cottage, but her husband caught her around the waist and dragged her onto his lap before she had the chance to do so. At first she protested that she had many more chores to finish before she could sleep, but Donal would not let her go. Eventually Eilish relaxed and put her arms around her husband's neck.

They sat there together for a long while, watching the glowing coals of the burning turf. Not a single word passed between them as they held each other close. The festival was ended, there were no pressing chores to be done, no kinfolk to entertain, no sickly tenants seeking healing. For the first time in many weeks they could simply rest contentedly in each other's arms.

'Jerusalem is on the far side of the earth,' Eilish said, no longer able to keep herself from expressing her fear a moment longer.

'So they tell me,' Donal answered.

'You'll be gone a lot longer than one year, won't you?'

'I'll come back as soon as you send me word the chapel is finished,' the chieftain assured her. 'I'll not wait a day longer in that land than I have to.'

'And what if you are captured by the Saracens?' Eilish replied, pushing herself up in his lap so she could look into his eyes. 'Or besieged in a castle? How will you come home to me if you are trapped in some terrible place with no escape?'

'I promise you I will return to my hearth and home,' Donal declared. 'There is nothing could keep me from fulfilling my promise to you. No Saracen will hold me prisoner against my will. There is no siege I would not break in order to come home to you.'

'And what if you fall in battle?' Eilish flashed. 'What if you are killed?'

'I will not fall in battle,' he stated firmly. 'I will take the greatest care. I am more worried about how you will get by here on the estates without my help.'

'I will get by as I always do.' Eilish placed her hand flat against her husband's chest. 'It is not your help I'll miss so much as your presence in my bed and the smell of you about the house.'

'What smell?' Donal said, picking up on the jibe.

She poked a finger into his shoulder. 'The smell of that tired old mare that you insist on calling a workhorse,' she teased. 'The smell of the cows on your boots. The smell of ale on your breath.'

'It truly doesn't sound like you'll miss me at all,' the chieftain replied in mock hurt as she twisted the strands of his dark hair around her fingers. 'I'll have to find myself some wild eastern woman who doesn't mind the odour of a man's work about him.'

'You've been talking to that tilecutter again, have you not?' she laughed, letting go of his hair. 'It is him that's been filling your head with stories of the far-off lands of Outremer. I should have kept you away from him from the start.'

'He gave me a gift,' Donal told her.

'Did he now?' Eilish exclaimed. 'That was grand of him!'

'It is only a trinket but he says it will guarantee I return to you.'

'What are you babbling about, you poor mad fool?' she giggled. 'Supping too much of the magic brew again, have you? Thank God the tilecutter is not a horse dealer or we'd have a hundred tired old mares to look after.'

'Be quiet with you,' the chieftain laughed, 'or you will not get your present.' And with that he folded his arms and tried to turn away from her.

Eilish put her hand under her husband's clean-shaven chin and turned his face back to her. 'Would you keep some pretty charm from me, would you, Donal O'Regan? And I suppose you will save it for that dark eastern beauty you have been dreaming about?'

At that Donal opened the leather pouch he always carried tied to his belt. He reached in, withdrew his clenched fist a moment later and held it out to his wife.

'What do you think it is?' he teased her.

'I can tell you what it isn't,' she answered. 'It isn't a pile of golden marks.'

'But every stack of riches starts with a penny,' Donal quipped and he opened his palm to reveal the two halves of the bronze coin which Balek had given him as a gift.

Eilish looked at the pieces for a moment before she caught her husband's eye. 'What sort of a gift is this?' she asked, perplexed.

'Two halves of a coin,' the chieftain explained.

'I can see that!' she wailed in mock pain. 'I mean to say, what use is a coin that is cut in two?'

'The two pieces fit perfectly together,' Donal told her. He moved them close to each other to show her what he meant. 'Balek says no matter where they are, or how long they are apart, each half will always belong with the other. And one day they will surely fit together again.'

Eilish put her arms around Donal's neck, holding him tightly so he would not see the tears beginning to well up in her eyes.

'If you always carry one half with you,' he went on, 'and I always carry one half with me, Balek reckons the two pieces will find their way by magic back to each other. And so we will be reunited, no matter what else befalls us.'

Donal handed her one piece of the coin. She held it in her hand without looking at it. 'I will keep this token with me every day you are away. Every night I will pray the other half returns to me within a year and you still carrying it.'

'I will return,' Donal promised. 'I will come home to you again even if Saladin himself should try to stop me. And whenever you doubt that, even in passing, you must take out the coin, hold it in your hand and ask it to bring the other half home.'

'I will, my love,' she whispered. 'I will.'

THE CASTLE OF FEAR

Chapter Ten

To Lord Robert's utter despair, six long months passed by before he had raised all the troops he needed. By then final negotiations for their passage to the Holy Land were under way with a ship owner from Normandy. But as the autumn rains were beginning to fall, letters began arriving from France reporting that the new king, Richard, was having trouble organising his crusade. Although King Richard was enthusiastic about war in general, he had been forced to deal with an uprising in York which had ended in the deaths of many Jews of that city.

The chaos in the north of England forced the recently crowned king to remain in Britain much longer than he would have wished. And terrible riots in York decimated his treasury for he relied solely on the Jews to lend him the necessary funds to raise an army for the Holy Land. Christians were expressly forbidden by Papal decree to perform the role of money-lender, so King Richard had had to look further afield to raise the gold he needed for his war.

Delicate negotiations took place between the English Crown and the Order of the Temple. Eventually the Temple was granted a Papal exemption to lend King Richard all the money he desired to conduct a long campaign in a far-off land.

The end result of all these setbacks was that the crusade

had had to be put off. Eventually, however, impatient to leave the troubles in England far behind him, King Richard sent dispatches to every part of the kingdom making it clear he would be setting out for Outremer within the next six months. The staging point for the crusade was to be at Vézelay in France. All those lords who wished to accompany their king were encouraged to assemble there as soon as possible.

Robert was ready to leave as soon as he heard the news just after midwinter. But there was a great concern among his soldiers that the seas might be too rough and unpredictable for the journey at that time of year. Lord Robert, however, was tired of waiting. He had spent his days in jousting, training for war, and prayer, but by now his men-at-arms were growing tired of fighting one another with wooden swords.

As another ship had to be engaged, their departure was delayed even further, but finally Robert tracked down a two-masted trading ship from France. The master of this vessel was returning to his home port and agreed to take Robert's company with him.

At last, on the day after the feast of Saint Brigid, with a thick icy blanket of snow upon the ground, Robert FitzWilliam's small force gathered at the castle of Bally Raine. Nine other knights, the sons of Norman lords from the nearby estates, joined Robert and his men. Each young knight brought with him a small group of men-at-arms, for none of the other families were as wealthy as the FitzWilliams. Suddenly there were more bright banners flying from the keep at Bally Raine than had been seen since Lord William first built the fortress.

In the brisk air of that morning Donal took Braonin aside to speak with him privately while Eilish waited in the courtyard of the castle. When the two cousins came back from their brief discussion, the chieftain held his wife in a tight embrace for a long while. Then the two of them walked together hand in hand down to the chapel.

Donal crossed himself as he passed under the lintel. It was not necessary for him to make this gesture because the church had not yet been consecrated. But this was the burial place of his father and as such worthy of respect.

Eilish followed his example and then made straight for Mathúin's tomb. Kneeling before the stone slab that marked his grave, she lit a candle for the old man's soul.

'The tilecutter has done a marvellous job so far,' Donal exclaimed, pointing out the details in the mosaic work.

'Is that all you have to say?' Eilish whispered. 'More bloody talk about the craftsman and his skills.'

Donal took his wife by the hand to show her the design laid around his father's grave. 'Do you see that?' he asked her.

Eilish nodded sullenly.

'That is the endless knot,' he explained. 'Balek told me it is a design he copied from the monks at Clonmacnoise. Our ancestors used it to signify that there is no beginning or end to anything in creation.'

'Balek sounds like a Culdee,' she snapped.

'Our ancestors were all Culdees,' Donal reminded her. 'Trace the pattern from here,' he instructed her, placing his wife's index finger on the design.

Eilish followed the pattern as he told her. Within a minute or so she had come back to the exact spot where her finger had started.

'That is what I will be doing,' Donal assured her. 'I might travel to the other side of the world but like the endless knot I will return one day. Do not forget it.'

'I will not forget,' she promised.

'And you still have the little half a coin?'

'I wear it in this pouch about my neck,' she informed him. 'I would never let it out of my sight for a minute.'

'Every day you must pray for my safe return,' Donal whispered as he held her hands together in his. 'And every day I will pray that the days shorten until I am with you again.'

Then Donal heard his name being called and he knew he had to go and perform his duties. 'I am being summoned to help bring the men to order,' he told his wife and she threw her arms tightly around him. It was a long time before Eilish reluctantly let her husband move.

When Donal finally broke away from her embrace he noticed Balek standing at the door to the chapel, his cap in his hand.

'I have come to say farewell, master,' the tilecutter said in his heavily accented Latin. 'Safe journey to you.'

Eilish bowed her head to Balek and the craftsman smiled broadly, deepening the laughter lines around his eyes.

'I will miss you, Balek,' Donal told him. 'Thank you for your gift and your well wishes. Perhaps we will meet again some day.'

'When you return,' the tilecutter replied as if, despite the hazards of the journey, there were no question of Donal coming home to Bally Raine.

The two men shook hands. Then Eilish and her husband made for the door.

'Do not lose that piece of a coin,' Balek said as Donal passed him. 'It will bring you good fortune.'

'I will keep it safe, close to my heart,' the chieftain answered.

'I was speaking to your wife,' the tilecutter laughed.

Eilish blushed as she realised this man was truly a kind and gentle soul. She felt guilty for having reprimanded Donal whenever he spent too much time in the craftsman's company. She gave Balek a warm smile, took Donal's hand and led him out toward the castle to do his lord's bidding.

At the keep nearly one hundred men were saying farewells to their families and friends. Countless tears were shed as soldiers gathered their armour, their weapons and all the gear they would need on campaign. As Donal waited for the warriors to finish their farewells, Eilish spent a while braiding his long dark hair with a leather strip to hold it in place.

Robert rode around through the ranks, impatient as ever to march out of Bally Raine bound for the coast and the waiting ship which would take them to France. He had not donned his war gear for this short march to the sea because of the steadily falling snow—the lord did not want to arrive in Normandy with rusted armour.

'May the sun shine on your face,' Braonin called out in parting to his cousin as the ranks of men formed to march. 'And the wind be ever at your back.'

'And may the wind of your backside not erupt so often from your face,' Donal jibed, turning the traditional blessing around.

'Nor may you grow so enamoured of yourself,' Braonin shot back, 'that you think the sun shines out of your own arse.'

With those words Donal O'Regan, chieftain of Cúil Ghréine, marched out of Bally Raine on his way to the Holy Crusade. The finest and strongest young men of the district went with him. And afterwards many who were left behind fell to weeping, certain that some, at least, would not return.

Braonin and Eilish watched from the castle green as the small force crossed the wooden drawbridge. They stayed to see the army trudge off down the road through the lightly falling snow. They leaned wearily on each other, watching as the column finally disappeared out of sight over the far hill. Then, full of sadness, the pair made their way to the chapel to say prayers for the safe journey and speedy return of all their kinsmen.

It was while she knelt at her prayers that Eilish noticed the building work had not advanced very much in the previous six months. Robert had insisted the stonemasons work exclusively on improving the castle fortifications as a precaution against any attack.

The lord felt, and many folk agreed with him, that with most of the able-bodied men gone from the estate, the castle was vulnerable. The lands of the FitzWilliams might prove too tempting a prize for a northern lord looking to expand his domain. By the time Robert left for France, however, he was confident his castle could withstand a siege of many months. All this work on the fortifications meant the chapel had lain open to the elements without a roof. Work could only start again now the improvements to the castle were complete.

With the roof unfinished it had been impossible for Balek to start laying the tiled floors or complete his wall mosaics. It would have been futile to set the tiles only to have them flooded in a sudden downpour or covered by a drift of snow.

After their prayers were said, Eilish went back to Cúil Ghréine with Braonin. Balek sat by the great fire in the lord's hall, waiting for the weather to change so the roof could be finished. Lonan the chamberlain went about his work in the castle, and Rufus sat in the room that had once been his father's. There the young FitzWilliam wished for the days to roll by to spring so he could begin to put his plans into effect.

The voyage to France was mercifully uneventful for Robert's entourage. The weather was not as bad as predicted and the ship's master was a skilled seaman. As soon as the vessel made landfall, the green banner of the FitzWilliams, to which Robert had added a small white cross, flew over Normandy for the first time in many years.

The lord put on his mail-coat before his company landed. Over the top of his armour he wore a deep green surcoat exactly the same as the one his father and grandfather had worn. On the breast Robert had attached a cross just like the one on his banner. His war helm was polished and the brass of his harness shone in the sunlight.

Donal thought his lord at least looked the part. 'But pretty clothes don't make a warrior,' the chieftain commented under his breath.

The small force did not stay on the coast for long. Donal convinced his lord they should try to reach the castle of Robert's cousin, Eustace, as soon as possible. The castle was a two-day march from the coast, but the weather held fair and the company arrived in good spirits.

Eustace, who held stewardship of the FitzWilliam lands in Normandy, was ten years older than Robert. But he immediately recognised the young knight of Bally Raine as his lord with an extravagant feast and two days of hunting. All Robert's distant relatives came to the castle to see him and this held the company up for a week.

Eventually Donal began to lose patience with all the niceties of court life and he pressed Robert to continue the journey without further delay. So, after only nine days at the FitzWilliam castle, they set out for Vézelay.

Eustace contributed a small company of crossbowmen to the expedition, some fifteen men. But Robert's cousin claimed it would be irresponsible of him to go off on a crusade and leave the Norman lands without a lord. Robert tried to convince him otherwise, but Eustace could not be persuaded to abandon the castle and Robert did not insist, as he could have done.

As the FitzWilliam force was marching south, King Richard arrived in France and met with the French king, Philip, to assemble their armies. The company from Bally Raine arrived in Vézelay the day after the two kings met. Robert sent a message to Richard to offer his services, but the next day fell ill with stomach cramps and was confined to his bed for a week. So he missed the pomp and ceremony with which the two monarchs announced their joint crusade. The day after that celebration heavy rain set in, confining everyone to their tents.

When the rain stopped four weeks later, Richard's army, including Robert's contingent, marched to the southern port of Marseilles. Robert and Donal then found themselves preparing to embark for Sicily. The rains were gone but the calm weather caused the fleet to be late for the embarkation. So King Richard left for Salerno with his best hand-picked troops, leaving the main army to wait for the ships.

Before landing in Outremer it was the King's intention to reclaim the Norman stronghold of Sicily from one of his illegitimate cousins. The main fleet caught up with him after his conquest of that island. Then the great host of warriors sailed on to Cyprus where Richard indulged himself in two weeks of warfare before securing that island as his own territory also.

King Richard promised the Templars a large slice of Cyprus as a reward for their help on his crusade. As a consequence it was the white-robed knights who did most of the fighting. Robert and his soldiers saw no action at all during the attack on the island and for that Donal thanked God earnestly.

With Cyprus secured, the English king sailed on to his next conquest. Two weeks before midsummer's day, the great fleet was anchored a short distance from the city of Acre on the west coast of Outremer. After offering only a token resistance, the Saracen commander of the city promptly surrendered the entire garrison to King Richard.

Robert was jubilant. He had set out from his home with the intention of helping to reconquer the Holy Land. Under the leadership of King Richard, who the common soldiers referred to as the Lion Hearted, that lofty goal was now within reach. And the Lord of Bally Raine had still not seen any fighting.

After the surrender of Acre, Saladin's forces retreated to a point just beyond bow-shot of the city walls. Richard and King Philip of France spent many days arguing over which of their underlings should rule the city, while the great army marched on south to Jaffa and then to Jerusalem.

And, true to the traditions of their two noble families, the monarchs could not reach any agreement at all. After a month of bitter argument King Philip became sick with a wasting disease. The sickness transformed him from a strong handsome warrior into a thin bald man whose fingernails dropped out. Philip took ship for France and abandoned the crusade altogether.

King Richard took the French monarch's disease as a sign from God. He triumphantly marched his army out of the gates of Acre and there he slaughtered all his Saracen prisoners in cold blood. Two thousand seven hundred men and a further three hundred women and children were put to the sword within sight of Saladin's helpless army just outside the city.

Robert FitzWilliam was shocked beyond words by this. He had never seen so many corpses. The young lord prayed day and night ever after for the soul of his king, believing that King Richard had been led on by the Devil to commit such a massacre.

This act of brutal injustice inspired the Moslem commanders to vow revenge. From that moment on the Saracens harried the Christian army day and night on their march. As a result the whole journey soon degenerated into nothing more than a series of rearguard actions.

Not even the highly disciplined Templars held much hope of dealing with an enemy who struck swiftly and then vanished out of sight. All along the route to Jaffa the Saracens mounted one attack after another, like waves washing against the shore. This constant fighting and the fact that the Christians could only move in the cool hours of the morning meant the army of King Richard covered no more than a few pitiful miles each day.

The country they travelled through was barren, dusty and red-brown. Small rocks littered the roadside and any horse that strayed from the path risked being lamed by the uneven surface. Dust blew up on every breeze, so that men and animals were always coughing up sand.

Donal had never in his life experienced such hardship, such heat, such barbarity, both on the part of the Saracens and the Christian knights. There was little enough water for every man, though the fleet had followed them down the coast and bore plentiful supplies of food. Nevertheless many exhausted men fell behind their comrades in the column. And Donal knew that those poor wretches would surely be killed by the ever-present enemy.

Like ghosts the dark-skinned Saracens would appear out of the desert to strike down their targets. Before any resistance could be organised, the terrifying enemy melted away again into the sands. Donal glimpsed their forms only a few times.

Once when the army was marching through a narrow pass the chieftain spotted an infidel standing alone and defiant high on a bare rocky outcrop. The man raised his arms to the sky and his long white flowing clothes were caught up in the wind. Donal realised then that the Templar dress owed as much to the Saracens as to the white Cistercian brothers.

Robert and a few of his men were permitted to ride in

the midst of the Templar contingent and the lord fought his first brief engagement among them. A dozen of the enemy charged out of the hills directly at the Templars, who cut the men down without mercy. Robert proudly showed Donal a tear in his surcoat where one of the Saracens had slashed at him with a great curved sword. The chieftain resolved to stay close to his master after that. He did not want to risk the loss of Robert's life.

Despite the unimaginable hardship, Lord Robert was obvously happier than he had ever been in his life. His dreams had been realised. Everything he had ever wished for was coming to pass. Many men in the Christian army shared Robert's feelings. And in the midst of this undeniable excitement the army of King Richard marched onward to Jaffa.

The King of England was a reckless fighter, often throwing himself into the thick of the fray with scant regard for his own safety. On the second day of the march Donal witnessed with his own eyes this fearless king leading a charge against a group of Saracen horsemen. Richard was quickly unhorsed and surrounded within a few short minutes. Had it not been for the arrival of twenty English knights, the whole crusade would have ended then and there.

Despite the thirst, the constant fighting, the flies and the forced march, Donal began to understand Robert's enthusiasm for this adventure. It seemed to the chieftain that he was trudging behind the standard of one of the most magnificent kings in history, truly a conqueror. Donal may have had misgivings about this expedition, but he was proud to be fighting for a high and holy purpose. He also understood why his father had never discussed the hardships of the campaign in much detail. When compared to the noble cause they were supporting, Donal reckoned such difficulties were of little consequence.

By dawn on the fifth day since leaving Acre, the chieftain

and his lord still had not seen a major engagement. But that was about to change.

While Donal and Robert were still waiting in the city of Acre for the kings of France and England to settle their differences, Braonin and Eilish were kept very busy. Final preparations for the first midsummer festival since the departure of the warriors were nearing completion.

In the interests of keeping festival expenses to a minimum, the two of them had decided only wild boar or deer would be provided for the spits at this year's feast. They also agreed there must be no more than eight barrels of ale. To compensate for the lack of festive drink, Eilish suggested the bonfire be larger than usual.

Braonin was concerned that most people would reckon eight barrels spread amongst so many tenants not enough. So he had the idea to allow two days instead of one for the traditional market. The merchants would surely sell more of their wares and the estate could reap much higher tithes as a result. This would cover the cost of a few more barrels of ale.

'We will have a riot on our hands,' he admitted, voicing Eilish's own concerns, 'if Rufus allows the soldiers to bully folk as they did last year. There is still a lot of resentment about the way the garrison managed to consume most of the brew unaided.'

'Then we will ask the soldiers to pay for their ale,' Eilish suggested. 'In fact, I cannot see any reason why all the tenants should not pay a few pennies toward the making and supplying of the food and refreshments.'

'By tradition the lord provides the feast as a gift to his

tenants and freeholders,' Braonin objected in an injured tone. 'Folk would not accept a charge against such a feast. It would be like raising the taxes.'

'You and I both know that if we cannot find some way to cut expenses on this estate, the taxes will surely rise,' she reminded him. 'Our sons and husbands are off to war and we must support them as much as possible. If we present this to the people as a way of ensuring the smooth running of the estate, I am sure they will be happy to help out in whatever way they can. Anyone who cannot contribute a coin to the feast may give in kind. Every family has a chicken, a duck, a pig or some grain laid aside.'

'I am not so sure,' Braonin sighed as he adjusted the leather tie on his long fair hair. 'It seems wrong to me to ask folk to pay for the lord's feast.'

'Then I'll leave it to you,' Eilish countered, 'to inform the people their taxes and rents are set to rise.'

She waited for him to react to this statement. When he frowned deeply she went on, 'Free feasting was all well and good when all our menfolk were here to bring in the harvest. But this year we will not have enough able bodies to do the work. We have a choice. Either we can hire folk from beyond the estates to bring in the oats and barley. Or we can buy additional grain from the neighbouring landlords to feed everyone.'

'In any case,' Braonin conceded, seeing her point, 'we will need a store of gold or cattle with which to pay for the shortfall in our work force. But with the warriors away there are not so many mouths to feed,' he argued.

'We must count on them returning before next year's harvest. If we do not have a store of food in waiting, we risk a famine on their return.'

'Have we enough cattle to make up the shortfall?' Braonin asked.

'Only if we eat our best milch-cows,' Eilish retorted. 'And

I know none of the tenants would agree to such a drastic measure.'

'And what if the soldiers don't return within a year?' Braonin inquired.

'Of course they will,' Eilish snapped. 'Donal promised me he would return within twelve months, no matter what befell him in the Holy Land.'

'Almost six months have passed,' Braonin reminded her, 'since we had any word from Robert and his expedition. The last letter to arrive at Bally Raine came from Normandy.'

'A letter,' Eilish pointed out, 'takes just as long as a man to travel from across the seas. It would be wrong to concern ourselves simply because no word has arrived from the expedition.'

'Eilish,' Braonin cut in, choosing his words carefully so he would not upset her further, 'it is conceivable Donal will be gone for much longer than he or anyone expected. We must accept that possibility.' He put a hand gently on her arm to soothe her. 'The tenants may endure one season paying for their ale and their feasting, but when the year passes to next spring and there has been no lord's feast, they will begin to grow impatient.'

'I told you Donal promised me he would return before the passing of a year,' Eilish insisted, 'and I will hold him to that.'

Braonin held up his hand to calm her, deciding this was not the time to speak further with her on this subject. He told himself it would be best to leave the matter until after the midsummer festival when they were both better rested.

'I will talk to Lonan and Rufus about making the tenants pay for their ale,' he told her. 'If they think your idea is worth trying, then we will certainly proceed.'

'I am sure Lonan will see the sense of it,' Eilish said

confidently. 'I have already asked the opinion of my father's family. They seem to think the reasoning is sound.'

'And how are you faring alone in Cúil Ghréine?' Braonin asked. 'Are you finding there is too much work for you to do?'

Eilish dropped her head. 'The clachan of Cúil Ghréine is far more than I can manage alone,' she admitted. 'Even with all the women pitching in to help, caring for the cows and the sheep is exhausting work. The O'Regan house went without new thatch this year. I don't know how we will fare when the harvest comes around. It was so much work to finish the planting, and the old folk were of little help. A few of the women from Gioll Martin on the Clonough will be coming to stay with us during the festival. If my father's family can spare one of them, I may have an extra pair of hands about the place for a while.'

'We should call an assembly during the festival to divide the labour evenly between every able-bodied adult on the estate,' Braonin suggested. 'For if Cúil Ghréine is finding it difficult, then so is Gioll Martin and the other smaller clachans. The only folk who will not suffer will be the brothers at the abbey at Shelton, for they did not send any of their men away to the war.'

'Then we shall ask the the monks to help us!' Eilish responded in a flash of inspiration. 'They can hardly refuse. It is their Christian duty to help avert a famine.'

'They never go beyond their monastery walls,' Braonin pointed out. 'They are bound by the rules of their order.'

Then I shall go there myself and speak with Lord William,' Eilish announced. 'He would never sit by and let his people starve.'

'You will not be allowed to see him. Women are not permitted within the walls of the monastery.'

Eilish sighed. 'You are right,' she conceded, recalling that the monks had taken up the practice of locking their gates against all outsiders. 'We will wait and see how things go. If we become desperate, I will go to see Lord William.'

On the morning of Lord Robert's departure from Bally Raine, Rufus FitzWilliam had made a vow to himself that he would one day be lord of the estate. With his brother out of the way, this goal was certainly within reach. Rufus was eager to take the reins of the estate but he was still uneasy about how he would retain authority if the tenants resisted him.

He had often observed the popularity of his elder brother with disdain. But in the weeks following Robert's departure Rufus had suddenly come to an understanding of how important it was for a ruler to be respected.

The younger FitzWilliam had realised he would never be lord if the tenants held him in contempt. Without the respect and support of the warriors who had remained behind on garrison duty, he would have no real lasting power and position.

'I must be patient,' he had told himself often. 'If I am going to take the lordship for myself, there must be no dissent among the common folk.'

And so Rufus had resolved to alter his ways, at least on the surface of things.

A month after his brother's departure he was no longer getting drunk on a regular basis. Then he took up the challenge of strengthening his body and improving his fighting skills. Slowly, without attracting too much attention, he had started to rid himself of Robert's loyal warriors who had been left behind to man the castle. In time he had replaced these men with mercenaries of his own choosing, warriors who would stand alongside him without question, experienced veterans he could rely on to handle themselves in a fight. Every day, right through the spring, the young FitzWilliam had spent the morning hours riding around the borders of the estate. His afternoons were taken up in practice with sword, mace and lance.

Then, after selling a horse or two and some of the family heirlooms to pay their wages, he had hired six of the best archers in the land. Every soldier in his employ spent each day, apart from the sabbath, honing their skills, preparing contingency plans against an attack on the castle, and standing sentry.

Lonan, the chamberlain, had expressed his reservations to Braonin about the hiring of these soldiers. But he could not criticise Rufus as long as it was his own gold or his family's that paid for the warriors' upkeep. Indeed, all the tenants were glad of these warriors. Their presence ensured there would be no raids from any of the renegade Norman warlords of the north. It was also comforting to everyone that Rufus seemed to have changed his ways.

The young FitzWilliam had cut his hair short and often wore a soldier's coif upon his head. Instead of bright clothes cut in the latest fashions, he had taken to wearing sturdy warrior's clothes made for comfort and wear. As midsummer approached the young FitzWilliam's transformation was complete, and everyone who saw him commented upon it.

When Braonin, in his role as chancellor, suggested that a small tax be levied against each person attending the festival, Rufus was very enthusiastic. He congratulated Braonin on this clever plan and promised he would do all he could to support it.

'And to put the tenants at ease,' Rufus promised, 'all the warriors on the estate will be placed on full guard duty for the entire festival. There will be no drinking or carousing on their part whatsoever. As long as the troops are fed well, I am sure they will be happy.'

Braonin could hardly believe his ears. When he told Lonan what Rufus had said, the old man lifted his eyebrows so high the wrinkles around his eyes disappeared.

'I will believe that when I see it,' the chamberlain laughed. 'A salmon may leap into the air every once in a while, but it cannot live out of the water it was born into.'

Nevertheless, as the first market day approached, it was clear Rufus meant what he had said. Folk arrived at the castle from all the country around for days beforehand. They were met at the gates by a small group of well-disciplined soldiers in polished armour who cheerfully directed people to the fields where they could erect tents and light cooking fires. Some days before the feast six soldiers were assigned to help with the setting up of stalls. Others supervised the orderly gathering of firewood and the safe storage of valuables in the keep.

Next morning Eilish was astonished to see twenty warriors in their full battle array lined up on the grass beside the moat. A sergeant-at-arms was issuing them orders for the day. She stood to watch for a short while, unaccustomed to seeing such discipline from the garrison.

'Rufus intends to put on a display of fighting skill at the feast,' Braonin informed her as he approached. 'I don't know whether I am more impressed or surprised with the change that has come over him in the last six months.'

'Well, a display of arms should keep the tenants amused for a while,' Eilish agreed. 'It would seem the man has had a turnabout in the last few months.'

Braonin took the bundle of timber she was carrying and slung it over his shoulder. 'A fox will always wear a fox skin,' he said seriously, quoting a variation on Lonan's jibe. 'I'll carry this up to the kitchens for you. I am after a bite to eat, so I might as well earn it.'

Eilish laughed, pushing him on. 'And a donkey may be recognised by the sound of his bleating,' she teased. 'You had better be careful I don't give you some more work to do, Braonin O'Regan.'

'A donkey has to earn his hay, I suppose,' the fair-haired man replied good-naturedly.

As they came to the kitchen door Braonin dumped the timber down on the stones outside. At that very moment the door opened unexpectedly. A young woman emerged with a great pan of steaming whey in her hands, left over from the cheese making. Strands of her hair had fallen over her eyes and she obviously did not expect Braonin to be standing there just then. In her rush she bumped straight into him, dropping the iron pan as she did so. The contents spilled all over the young man.

'You great stupid oaf!' the girl cried. 'Of all the places to be hanging about, why stand at the kitchen door?'

Braonin tried to mutter his apologies but was so surprised he could not make a sound. It was all he could do to stand opened-mouthed, staring at this beautiful black-haired creature he was sure he had never seen before.

'There is all this morning's whey gone to the pigs already,' she grumbled. 'What am I going to use to baste the meat now?'

Braonin still could not answer; partly because he did not know what to say, but mostly because he was captivated by the bright green eyes of this young woman.

Eilish saw the look that passed between the two of them and immediately stepped in to mop at Braonin's clothes a little. 'Wake up, lad!' she laughed. 'Have you never seen a pretty girl before?'

Braonin opened his mouth to protest and the girl suddenly realised he hadn't been struck dumb from having whey water spilled all over him.

'Braonin,' Eilish coughed, trying to get his attention, 'you remember my cousin Neesh, don't you?'

'This can't be Neesh!' Braonin gasped, brushing his golden hair out of his eyes. 'The last time I saw her she was a thin girl with spindly legs and a high-pitched voice.'

Neesh dropped the dish she was holding and it landed with a thud on Braonin's foot. He winced as it hit him, instantly understanding his mistake. 'I meant to say,' he stuttered hastily, 'it is astonishing what a beautiful woman she has become. When a fellow is in the presence of such loveliness he can forget himself.'

'No man ever died of wisdom,' Neesh remarked. Then she cast a mischievous glance at Eilish who was unable to restrain her laughter any longer.

Both women burst into fits of giggles, struggling in vain to regain their composure. 'Aye,' Eilish cackled, 'and young Braonin surely knows how to impress a woman with sweet words,' she cried. 'How could a girl forget a man who spills the curd leavings all over her and then tells her she's not as ugly as she used to be! No wonder the women are lined up at your door each night, Braonin O'Regan.'

Neesh smiled broadly, feeling better that Braonin had been rebuked for his comments and his clumsiness. She bent down to pick up the iron pan but as she did so the chancellor rushed to beat her to it. Their heads bumped into one another's as their hands touched the dish together. Once again Eilish began to laugh uproariously.

'Good God, man,' she gasped, tears streaming down her cheeks, 'get out of here before you cripple the girl.'

With a hand over his eye where his brow had been bumped, Braonin stepped back to shake his head. 'I'm terribly sorry. I'll be off then,' he muttered, obviously extremely embarrassed.

Braonin turned around to make his exit but only got as far as the roasting pits when he remembered he had come to the kitchen for a bite to eat. He wavered for a second, deciding whether he could ever face Neesh again. His stomach groaned and he made up his mind to go back. After all, he asked himself, what harm could come of it?

'She's only a woman,' he reprimanded himself aloud. 'She won't kill me.'

As he came close to the kitchen he heard Eilish laughing lowly, but thought nothing of it. Braonin turned the corner to approach the kitchen door.

Just as he caught sight of her, Neesh said loudly to her cousin, 'Do you think he would be that clumsy in bed?'

Braonin stopped stock still in his tracks and felt his face flush red. Both women looked up at him in surprise and the smiles instantly dropped from their faces. For a few uncomfortable seconds there was no sound or sign between the two women until Eilish could bear the silence no longer and began to giggle.

Neesh immediately broke down herself, and the pair of them were soon leaning against each other screaming with amusement. They were still bawling their eyes out with glee when they noticed Braonin had disappeared.

Chapter Eleven

When the great army of Richard the Lion Heart was only a short distance from the city of Jaffa, the renowned King Saladin launched his largest and most brutal attack. The highly disciplined Christian knights quickly took up defensive positions when scouts pointed to the enemy banners in the distance.

Robert's own banner, held proudly by his sergeant-at-arms, was raised among the formation of the Knights of the Temple. Twenty long lines of knights made up the Templar formation. Four hundred warriors and their attendant sergeants formed a square of solid iron.

The Hospitallers, dressed in their sombre black surcoats, took up positions to the right of the white-robed Templars. Every one of the horses of the Knights of the Hospital was black and also draped in fabric of that colour. To Donal these strange dour warriors looked like soldiers of the Devil, their helms covering their faces completely and their lances tipped with cheerless black pennants. All the horses in the press of black warriors must have sensed what was about to take place for every animal shook its head and many called out to others of their kind in terror.

As he waited to engage in his first pitched battle Donal felt his body begin to shiver uncontrollably, as if fear had jumped onto his back and was eating away at his courage. Donal forced his attention away from the disturbing Hospitallers to the men close by him in the Templar company.

The Knights of the Temple were perfectly calm, and it was as if they held some supernatural control over their animals. Among the white ranks, fear had been exorcised from the souls of man and beast. Their long beards and solemn prayers gave the knights an air of holiness which the chieftain had never expected to experience around such reputedly brutal warriors.

Unlike the Knights of Saint John, the Templars' conical helms covered only the top of their heads with a nosepiece shaped like a cross which jutted out in front of their face. This strange company of men seemed so confident that even the prospect of a bloody battle did not threaten their faith in this mission.

Donal was adjusting the padding on the inside of his helm when he heard screams. Out of the impenetrable dust cloud the first flight of arrows fell amongst the Hospitallers on his right. The enemy was still invisible in the rising wind that scattered a thick haze of earth and sand across the battlefield.

Despite the elements, the mounted Saracen archers had judged their targets well. There was immediate panic in the black ranks as the arrow shafts found their marks and many horses fell. Knights may don armour to protect themselves or raise a shield to deflect a blow, but there is nothing to stop an arrow striking down a horse in the press of the front line.

Before Donal knew what was happening, his horse began to froth and kick in great distress. Robert, on the other hand, was more fortunate. His mount was calm by nature and not given to fits of fear. The lord sat high and proud on his warhorse, dressed in his deep green surcoat. Like everyone else he was trying to peer through the dust storm to get a better look at the enemy ranks. Donal reined in his horse, patting its flank until it stood still again.

When the second wave of arrows hit the lines of the Hospital, several of the warriors in black lost control of their animals completely. Then a few knights darted off in a mad unsanctioned attack. And it was only moments before this hysteria spread along the line. Suddenly the situation erupted into a full-blown charge with all the Knights of the Hospital spurring their horses toward the enemy.

The Templar commander wisely held his troops back as long as he could, understanding the danger the black knights were galloping into. But many of the ordinary knights and men-at-arms were ready for a fight, and some ignored their commander, following recklessly in the wake of the black horses of the Hospital.

King Richard had been watching the steady disintegration of discipline from the moment the first flight of arrows landed among the mounted troops. By the time the Hospitallers broke into their gallop, he was riding with all speed down to the front line, surrounded by his ever-present bodyguard. When the soldiers and knights in the press of warriors saw the King's standard, they took it to mean King Richard had ordered the charge. After that there was no stopping the fateful advance of the Christian army.

The Templar commander raised the banner of the order and the white knights moved forward. The King now risked losing the best of his knights in a foolish headlong race into the waiting ranks of enemy spearmen.

So Richard did the only thing he could think of in such a situation. Instead of calling a general retreat which in itself could have cost many lives and been extremely difficult to orchestrate, he had his trumpeter sound a long blast.

The Lion Heart signalled the charge. And then he led it.

With great skill the King managed to manoeuvre his small entourage around until they were in front of the charging line. In moments there were seven hundred knights yelling at the top of their lungs and steering their mounts into the dust cloud.

Donal had no idea what was happening at all. Caught in the press of hundreds of warriors, choking in a pall of sandy dust, he never even glimpsed King Richard's banner. When the mounted troops suddenly broke into a charge in front of him, the chieftain's only thought was to keep close to Lord Robert. Unless Donal kept an eye on his master, he would be unable to come to his aid if the situation degenerated.

Robert FitzWilliam, on the other hand, had no consideration for any danger to his own person. Imbued with the wild excitement of battle, he dug his spurs into his horse until streams of blood ran along its flanks. The young knight waved his sword around his head, seeming to abandon all his senses in the frenetic upheaval of the sortie. Donal's only hope was to keep up with his lord and to remain as level-headed as possible throughout the fight.

As the horsemen galloped on, the dust suddenly cleared as if some magic spell had been lifted. When Donal saw the enemy ranks before them, he realised they were all in deadly danger. The Hospitallers who had started this foolish assault had almost reached the Saracen lines. But without a blow being struck, the infidel footmen began to fall back like a great wave retreating from the beach.

To either side of these fleeing Saracens, on the left and right flanks of Saladin's army, all the warriors stood firm and unflinching. The enemy commander was deliberately drawing the Christian knights into a deadly trap from which there would be no escape but through hand-to-hand combat.

Donal had used this tactic himself many times to trap wild boar, hemming them in from all sides, and he realised Saladin intended to do just that with the Christian knights.

As soon as the unwary army of King Richard had advanced behind the Saracen lines, the flanks would rush into the gap, effectively cutting off the escape of hundreds of warriors.

Donal recalled the story of the battle of Hattin which had led to the fall of Jerusalem. The King of the Saracens had used this strategy on that day also. Only a handful of the Christian army had survived. This tactic of a feigned withdrawal was one of Saladin's most famous and effective ploys. And now it seemed the Christians had walked straight into the trap once again. There was nothing to stop the knights being butchered by the infidel warriors.

Donal's heart beat in his mouth when it became clear there was nothing he could do about this predicament. He could not even rein in his own horse or turn to ride away from disaster. It was simply impossible for him to break away with so many knights packed tightly all around him.

Just then dust and sand blown up by the wind flew into the chieftain's face and he was completely blinded. Donal frantically put a gloved hand to his face but his skin was caked with sand. Moments later he was forced to keep both hands on the reins so as not to fall from his mount and be trampled. He shook his head violently, his eyes red and watering. With all his strength he clung to the saddle, praying that he would not fall, terrified because he could see nothing of what was transpiring around him.

After a long while he managed to clear his sight a little. When he could finally focus clearly, Lord Robert was nowhere to be seen among the hundreds of other mounted warriors all around him. There were white knights, others in black, grey or red liveries. But no sign of the dark green surcoat he was supposed to be watching out for. With a loud curse on his bad luck, Donal stood high in the stirrups to see as far ahead as possible.

A long way ahead he caught a brief glimpse of Robert in the crowd and he breathed a sigh of relief. At the front of the charge Donal saw the banner of King Richard for the first time. And he could not fathom why such a leader would order this mad assault.

Before the charging Christians stood thousands of armed Saracens. The points of their spears glinted in the sunlight like as many flashes of starlight. Donal heard a great rushing sound and thought the wind was picking up again. Abruptly men started screaming all around him.

The great noise like the wind was the sound of a fall of arrows. By some miracle the chieftain rode on unscathed while knights were struck to either side and in front. Almost immediately he saw the enemy ranks loose another volley of arrow shafts. Donal watched, powerless to flee or find shelter as the deadly cloud of missiles darkened the sky above him.

Instinctively the chieftain crouched forward on his warhorse and threw his oblong Norman shield across his back. He stayed like that, gripping the saddle between his knees until he felt first one thud, then another.

When he slipped out from under the shield there were three arrows stuck fast into the leather covering. The chieftain would have crossed himself if he had had the chance. He looked over at the enemy ranks again as the Saracen archers fell back behind their heavily armed footmen.

Donal noticed the King's banner then veering away from the front of the Saracen line. Richard wheeled the great company of knights around to the left so they would fall upon the archers on either flank of Saladin's army. If they continued on into the footmen, Donal realised, the Christian army would be annihilated by archers firing into their ranks from behind.

But King Saladin was an experienced military man. He saw through Richard's strategy. Unexpectedly a banner appeared in the midst of the Saracen ranks and a thousand enemy footmen gave a great shout. The ground shook with the fury of their cry. Then the centre of the entire enemy line lurched forward. In moments the soldiers at the front were running like crazed men toward the charging Christians. Countless faceless figures dressed in flowing robes of all colours, carrying round shields and long curved swords, hurled themselves into another dust storm.

Donal felt nothing but a paralysing fear at that moment. Fear of what would happen when this rushing mass of horses he was caught amongst was suddenly brought to a halt. Fear of what would become of his master in the resulting mayhem. He struggled as best he could to manoeuvre his mount closer to Robert but all his efforts were in vain. The lord's horse was a much stronger animal and there were too many warriors between them.

The enemy footmen were now only seconds away from clashing with the leading horses. Donal looked on their wild faces, eyes staring fiercely out of their brown faces, and could do nothing but pray and hang on for his life. At the very last moment he remembered to draw the sword Robert had gifted him with. The next thing he knew his warhorse came to an abrupt halt and was pushed hard up against the mounts in front.

There was havoc all around him, screams, bloodied faces, empty saddles and dust. Only three ranks of Christian knights separated him from a thousand Saracens sporting javelins, spears, swords, maces and axes. And all these weapons were raised in anger at King Richard's army.

All of a sudden the knights in front of the chieftain parted and the enemy were running toward him. Donal swung his blade wildly at a few of the footmen, striking one man to the ground where he was immediately trampled. A spear shaft brushed past the chieftain's shoulder; he dodged backward as the Saracen withdrew his weapon to lunge again.

All concern for his lord was banished from his mind as

Donal concentrated on his own survival in this hellish nightmare. His horse screamed and foamed at the mouth. The chieftain lifted his blade again and again. He cut at anything nearby that moved, screeching at the top of his lungs to drown out the chilling Saracen yells.

Despite the fury of the infidel attack, relatively few of the Christian knights fell. And many, many enemy footmen were trampled under their war mounts. Yet it seemed to Donal that for every Saracen he saw fall, another would appear to take his place.

Then suddenly, without any warning, the enemy ranks dispersed like the sand carried on the breeze. Donal found himself surrounded by friendly knights again. The immediate danger had passed. His arm heavy from wielding the blade, his shaking legs aching from squeezing his knees into the saddle, he looked about him and saw ahead a swarming mass of heathen, spear points raised to the sky, vying with one another to push forward. Donal reckoned the chances of a Christian victory very remote indeed.

Donal concentrated all his thoughts on getting himself through this engagement unscathed, but before the fighting resumed, a trumpet call resounded across the field. The chieftain again glimpsed the royal banner of the King of England moving back towards the rear. Richard the Lion Heart had decided to fall back. All the great press of his mounted warriors dutifully followed after their king.

In less time than it takes to draw a deep breath, Donal found himself amid the throng riding back towards the Christian lines. On every side trumpets blew, men were laughing and crying with the joy of battle. Some had grim bloodied faces. Others were so badly wounded or dazed they sat in their saddles like corpses strapped into place. The chieftain quickly counted a dozen abandoned warhorses among the mounts. He was amazed that so many warriors wore arrow shafts stuck into their bodies or leather armour.

Donal turned in his seat, searching the crowd in frantic haste to locate his master. But Robert FitzWilliam was nowhere to be seen. A hundred lengths of a warhorse the great company galloped on until the trumpet sounded again. Donal could not see anything through the dust the horses kicked up. So he could not tell if the infidels were following close behind.

Then the army reined their mounts and came to rest. Only Donal did not stop, pushing his way through the crowd in a desperate search for Robert. Among the wounded, the jubilant and the war weary, the chieftain called out the name of Robert FitzWilliam until his voice was hoarse from yelling. But try as he might, he could find no trace of his lord.

It appeared to Donal that only a few dozen knights in the army had lost either their lives or their horses. Mostly these unfortunate souls were from among the Hospitallers who had been goaded into the attack by the arrows of Saladin's mounted archers. About thirty others had fallen during the reckless ride, knocked to the ground in the crush before they reached the enemy. A handful of knights and sergeants had been injured or killed by the enemy footmen.

'What will become of our expedition,' Donal cried aloud, despairing for his lord, 'if Robert has been killed?'

The chieftain began to mumble another plea to God as the trumpets rang out once more. King Richard's banner was raised toward the enemy line for a second time. This, clearly, was the signal for another charge, and Donal felt the blood drain from his face in fear.

Rufus stirred from sleep not long after sunrise on the

morning of the midsummer festival. For the first time in months he did not care that his slumber was disturbed by the noise of servants making preparations for the coming feast.

The young FitzWilliam lay on his back in bed for a long while, recalling with great pleasure a dream he had been having just before he woke. In the wonderful vision his brother was missing, presumed dead, somewhere in the Holy Land. Acclaimed by all the tenants, Rufus had been elevated to the rank of Lord of Bally Raine and married to a beautiful woman with hair of pure gold. This goddesslike creature had gorgeous blue eyes like two sapphires and a voice as sweet as the pretty music of a harp.

For a few moments more Rufus savoured the illusion that this fancy of his imagination might be a prophecy of things to come. Then he growled with frustration, threw off the covers and climbed out of bed.

'It will not be so easy,' he reminded himself, 'to bring your plans to fruit.'

Rufus pulled a clean linen shirt over his head and went to stand by the small window which overlooked the courtyard. He scratched the back of his neck where the hair was cut close to the skin and looked out at the day.

It had been noise from the servants' quarters directly below that had disturbed his sleep so he leaned out of the window a little to locate the source of the disturbance. As Rufus stared out on the bleak cobblestone yard a sight caught his eye that almost stopped his heart. There below him, making her way into the hall, was the young girl he had accosted at the well many months previously.

The young FitzWilliam had not thought about her in a long while. But now a bitter memory of the insult she had inflicted on him stirred. Rufus was overwhelmed by a desire for revenge. He quickly dressed himself, eager to discover whether or not the girl would recognise him.

'I'll teach you a lesson, my pretty one,' he promised himself. 'Rufus FitzWilliam never forgets an insult to his honour.'

He went back to the window when he was dressed to see if the girl was anywhere about. He had been surprised at seeing the black-haired girl from the well but now he was stunned at the sight that met his eyes.

The door to the inner courtyard opened and out stepped the very woman he had seen in his dream. She had perfect locks of honey-gold flowing over her shoulders and down her back in a magnificent cascade. Her skin was as pale as milk and the cut of her tunic outlined an enticingly firm young body.

'Look up at me, my lovely,' Rufus begged under his breath, willing her to turn her face toward him so that he could get a better look at her.

'Just one glance up to the keep,' he begged, 'so that I can see your eyes.'

At that precise moment Eilish turned, as if she had heard his words. She looked up to the top of the keep and Rufus moved back into the shadows slightly so she would not glimpse him watching her from the window. A few seconds later she shrugged her shoulders and crossed the courtyard on her way back to the kitchen.

But those few seconds were all that Rufus needed. She was the woman of his dream. She would be his wife when the lordship came to him. Rufus knew her face well enough. He remembered clearly where he had seen her last.

'The wife of Donal O'Regan,' he recalled. 'Eilish was her name. How fitting that she and I should one day marry. She mourning the death of her husband in battle and I the loss of my dear departed brother.'

Rufus smiled, caressing the reddish stubble on his chin. Once again, he told himself, some guardian angel had gifted him with all that he desired on earth.

'She is chieftainess of the O'Regan clan in her husband's absence,' Rufus said, 'and as such has a great deal of influence over most of the estate. If I can win her over to me, the tenants will not dare stand against my ambitions, no matter what I do. Together she and I could make these lands the richest in Ireland.'

The young FitzWilliam strode across the room. He sat down on a rough wooden stool in front of the glowing embers of last evening's fire. With a hearth iron he turned over the ash until the turf started to burn bright orange again. His best ideas came to him when seated here.

'You must be very careful, my lad,' Rufus told himself. 'She will not rush to marry you. She is devoted to her Donal. And you, Rufus FitzWilliam, are nothing but a Norman fool to her. She would not even look at you unless . . .'

Then another voice spoke up from within Rufus's mind, scheming and full of cunning. 'Unless, of course, she were to be presented with undeniable proof of her husband's death.' He shook his head and put that thought to the back of his mind. For the time being there was the more pressing problem of the girl from the well.

The obvious answer crossed his mind, but he dismissed it quickly. He dared not risk a murder or disappearance, lest all his plans be shattered. There was already gossip in the castle over the disappearance of his father's messenger. Then Rufus suddenly wondered whether the girl had spoken to Eilish about the incident at the well.

'If she has said nothing, then I still have a chance of winning O'Regan's wife for myself,' he decided. 'Even if the girl has spoken of the incident, I may yet be able to salvage the situation.'

Rufus put the hearth iron down, stood up and went to the door of his chamber. He grabbed a cloak on the way out to drape around his shoulders. Downstairs in the hall he greeted the chamberlain. Lonan was seated by the great open fireplace enjoying some fresh steaming barley bread straight out of the oven.

'Good morning, chamberlain,' Rufus enthused.

The old man coughed, obviously taken aback by the warmth of the salutation. 'It would be a better morning if the drizzle would lift,' Lonan replied, rubbing his knee. 'This weather is too damp and cold for midsummer and my bones ache from it.'

'Are you busy just now?' Rufus inquired and then went on as if the reply was not all that important to him. 'I would like you to accompany me to the kitchens if you would. I am checking on the preparations for the tournament. I want to make sure that my men are properly fed.'

'Just coming, my lord,' the chamberlain sighed. 'I am sure there is plenty of food to go around. Eilish has been running the kitchen on feast days for years now.'

Donal rode with three more wild charges against the Saracens before the enemy broke ranks and scattered. After the last devastating assault Saladin's banner disappeared from the midst of his troops. Without effective leadership the armies of the infidel could not stand their ground.

The brilliant leadership of Richard Lion Heart inspired the Christian knights. They kept their discipline throughout the battle and did not fall into the trap of chasing after the retreating enemy again. The crusaders battered the weakest part of the enemy line, suffering very few casualties. Before the Christians knew what had happened the infidel army had fled the field in disarray.

As the day edged toward midafternoon another wind storm rose up. Despite this hazard most of the knights successfully regrouped. Then they moved off to prepare a campsite for the night. For the time being at least the march on to Jaffa would have to wait.

Donal resigned himself to searching the battlefield for his master's body. At sunset there was still no sign at all of Robert FitzWilliam. The chieftain had never in his life felt so cheerless, exhausted and utterly spent. But then he had never in all his days witnessed such a bloody and senseless struggle. All over a piece of ground upon which not even a blade of grass could have been enticed to grow.

Donal struggled against fatigue to stay in the saddle as he rode through the ranks of knights who had returned to the Christian lines. But it was not long before he was forced to give up his search for Robert. The chieftain's heart was clouded with sadness. He knew his lord's death was not his fault but he was already blaming himself for losing track of Robert in the midst of the fight.

'I have watched him carefully every day since we left home,' he rebuked himself, 'and at the first sign of a real fight I let him down.'

The chieftain reached inside his shirt to touch the little leather bag he wore around his neck. Inside was the half-penny the tilecutter had given him. Donal's thoughts strayed then to his home and his wife. He wondered if she was still wearing her half of the split coin close to her heart.

Donal reined in his horse near a group of soldiers who had built a small cooking fire. He swung his leg over the saddle and dismounted. When his feet touched the dusty earth the chieftain felt a great pain in his calves and thighs. He examined himself for visible wounds.

'That was your first battle!' an old veteran yelled out in glee. 'I can always tell a man who's come from his first fight.'

The other men at the fireside laughed and hooted at Donal.

'Next time don't grip the horse so tightly,' the old man advised. 'If you want to survive in war you have to learn to relax.'

Donal led his warhorse to a wagon and tied the reins. Then he came to sit at the fire beside the veteran. The old man had a jug of water which he handed to the chieftain.

'There's a first time for everything,' the veteran laughed. 'I felt the same way you do now the first time I lay with my wife. That's why I joined the crusade.'

Donal looked at the smiling old face, wondering what the veteran meant.

'War holds no terror for me,' the old man explained, 'compared to the scolding of a woman.'

All the other soldiers broke out in fits of laughter and Donal lay back smiling, despite his sorow. In a short while he had closed his eyes and was asleep.

The chieftain was jolted out of his short slumber by the sound of many horses plodding by the campfire. He opened his eyes to see hundreds of knights dressed in white passing along towards the rear of the lines.

The last soldiers to return from the field were, of course, the Templars. They had stayed to guard the bodies of the slain. Many of the immaculate white surcoats were stained with dust and blood. Every horse was frothing, sweating and champing at the bit. Donal saw the grim faces and dirty beards and smelled the familiar but peculiar stench that followed these unwashed men wherever they went.

All of them were perfectly quiet. Not one among their number spoke. They were ghostly, serene and godlike. Invincible and immortal, Donal thought, as he watched the knights riding by, like legends come to life.

What a contrast these men were, he realised, to the boastful brash knights of the Hospital. He recalled the Templars' restraint before the charge. Donal knew the victory had been snatched away from Saladin by King Richard's quick-witted valour. But the triumph really belonged to the Knights Templar who followed their commander's instructions without question, without a second thought.

'Donal!' a voice called out and the chieftain got up on his elbow and squinted through the dust.

'Donal O'Regan! Where have you been?'

'Lord Robert?' Donal cried, jumping to his feet. 'Is that you?' the chieftain yelled jubilantly.

In the next breath Donal noticed a knight riding towards him with a battered white oblong Templar shield held out in front of him. The helm this knight wore was of shining steel. It was not Robert's helm. Nor was the horse the same one his lord had brought with him from Bally Raine.

'Where did you disappear to?' Robert called out as he lifted the helm from his head. Donal was so relieved to see his master again that he was lost for words. As the horse came to a halt by his side, the chieftain reached up a hand to clasp that of his lord. The two men held each other like that for a long while as the whole company of Templars passed on by.

'I thought you had been killed,' Donal cried, his voice was still hoarse from calling out.

'I thought that myself a few times,' Robert laughed. 'I lost two horses from under me when we hit the Saracen lines. It's nothing short of a bloody miracle that I found another mount after each fall.'

'Thank God my prayers were answered,' Donal wheezed, his throat dry from the dust and all the yelling he had done.

'Have you ever seen such a thing in all your life, Donal O'Regan?' Robert shouted at the top of his voice. 'What a thrill it was to be at the forefront of the charge riding beside the King of England and the unconquerable knights of the Temple. Do you know what it felt like to be unstoppable? To be galloping amidst the fury of the soldiers of Christ?'

'I cannot say that I do, my lord,' the chieftain declared. 'I was too busy thinking of your safety for most of the time to realise what danger I had placed myself in. Or to understand that the Saracens did not care whether I was wearing white, black or imperial purple. If I had thought too much about the foolish charge, I probably would have galloped all the way back to Acre.'

'You can't be serious!' Robert exclaimed at the top of his voice. 'That was the most glorious action in the history of all the crusades. Men will talk about it in years to come and wish they had been here to see it. What a blessing it was to ride with the white knights to victory.'

'What happened to your shield?' Donal asked, changing the subject to calm his master down.

'When I fell from my second horse I grabbed at the first shield my hands touched. This took blow after blow from a wild Saracen with a huge war club. I thought it would surely shatter under his attack but the shield did not buckle or split. It saved my life. It is a sign, Donal, that I was destined to join the Temple and ride with the white knights.'

'You were very lucky, my lord,' the chieftain replied quickly, not at all happy with the direction in which this conversation was headed. 'It is time for us to return to the lines and seek out a place to rest for the night. Are you injured at all?'

'Just a scratch above my eye. My helm was knocked off and shattered by a Saracen with a great curved sword.'

Donal restrained himself from asking where Robert had got the helm he was wearing. He was not ready to hear another tale of luck, valour or destiny just at that moment. The memory of the bitter fight was still too real to him and he did not share Robert's enthusiasm for conquest. All Donal had seen was a bloody slaughter: men trampled, horses butchered, horror, death, fear and murder. The words valour, triumph and glory did not enter his head.

As Donal tried to put the images of battle out of his mind the tilecutter's words came back to him. Balek had once told him that Christian, Jew and Muslim all worshipped the same God under different names. All religions, the craftsman had insisted, hold the same ideals and virtues as holy.

'And yet they still fight among themselves,' the chieftain sighed, 'like children.' And Donal wondered if God had watched the battle or if He had turned away in disgust.

Chapter Twelve

Geoffrey d'Acre, dubbed Knight of the East, Guardian of the Secret and Brother of the Holy Order of the Temple, entered the chapel of the twin pillars. He was barefoot, blindfolded and dressed in sackcloth peasant clothes. In the months since his arrival at Mont Salvasch he had allowed his beard to grow in the manner of the Templars. But even after all this time it was little more than a thin scraggly growth on his chin.

Henry St Clair led his student by the hand, guiding the young, recently knighted petitioner into the great chamber. Geoffrey stumbled on the uneven stone steps of the dais where his promotion would be announced. He could sense the many men in the room, though there was no sound whatsoever to indicate their presence. A sharp wave of fear coursed through him and then passed away again before his heart had begun to race. There was no reason for him to be afraid, he told himself. The ceremony about to take place had been performed on many other knights. In any case, Geoffrey cared little for empty rituals, and if these strange ceremonies gave him clues to the mystery of his brother's last will, then any discomfort was worth enduring.

He had read Godfrey's testament over and over. He had studied his brother's final letter until he could recount the contents from memory. But to Geoffrey's disappointment there seemed to be no clues at all contained in those parchments. After all these months he still had no idea where the great treasure of the Temple might lie concealed.

'Geoffrey d'Acre,' St Clair's voice boomed, 'you are here to prove your worth to your brothers-in-arms.'

The young man jumped a little when his name was called out. He knew he should concentrate all his attention on this ceremony but his heart was not in it. He had only agreed to become a Knight of the Temple because he was certain this castle, hidden in the valleys of the east of Outremer, held the solution to the mystery.

He also suspected that if he rejected the Temple, he might end up a prisoner in this forgotten fortress. And he knew Guy d'Alville would not think twice about employing the instruments of torture if he thought Geoffrey was withholding information.

The castle of the Krak had fallen only the day before his arrival at Mont Salvasch. This incredible stroke of good fortune had diverted the attention of both Guy and Henry. And it had given Geoffrey time to think about what action he should take. He had come to the realisation very early on that escape was impossible. The only way he would ever make his way out of this fortification would be with the blessing and protection of the Master of the Castle. Geoffrey had also made a vow he would not leave without the treasure his brother had guarded and paid for with his life. And the vision of the Virgin Mary was still fresh in his mind. He knew it was his destiny to guard the holy treasure.

'If you are ready to see the path before you,' Henry intoned, 'your eyes will be opened to the mysteries of the Temple.'

'I am ready, brother,' Geoffrey answered, 'to look on that which has been concealed.'

'Then prepare yourself to leave the land of the dead and to walk among the living. You will take the path our master, Christ, prepared for us. Open your eyes and lie down within your grave.'

The blindfold was suddenly whipped away from Geoffrey's face. His eyes took a few seconds to adjust to the candlelight in the chamber. When he could focus he was shocked at what met his gaze.

Before him on the stone floor was a skull with two human thighbones crossed beneath it laid out on a black cloth. To his right he heard the sound of ropes being hauled through a block. He turned to see a great stone being raised up from the floor.

'Go to your grave and lie down to rest,' Henry commanded. 'If you are worthy, you will push the stone aside and rise again. And if you rise again you will be granted life eternal to walk among the chosen for all your days.'

This ceremony did not resemble any Christian ritual Geoffrey had ever witnessed. The dark sinister liturgy frightened him as nothing had ever done before. His heart began to pound in his ears. Did they really mean to bury him beneath that great stone?

He remembered the Gospel tale of Christ who rolled the stone away from his own tomb after the resurrection. He recalled the story of Lazarus, the man Jesus had called back from the dead after he had been entombed for three days. These thoughts made him even more nervous. What sort of a test was this? Was this elaborate ceremony merely a trick to subject him to some form of torture?

Henry took the young man by the hand, leading him to the edge of a pit which lay under the raised stone. Geoffrey could plainly see there was barely enough room for a man to stretch out in this depression. There would be very little room in the cavity once the stone was set back in place. And if it were lowered too far it would most certainly crush the life out of him.

Now Geoffrey felt certain this was the cruel torture he

had overheard Guy describing to Henry months earlier. To stave off panic, he tried to convince himself he was more valuable to Henry alive than dead. After all, he was likely to be the only one who could unravel the mystery of the missing treasure.

'Lie down then, brother,' St Clair whispered insistently. 'If your heart is pure and you seek only the Kingdom of Heaven, then you have nothing to fear, for you will be raised up.'

Geoffrey caught an odd quality in the old knight's voice and his throat went dry with apprehension. He hesitated for a few more moments. Then, realising he had no choice, Geoffrey did as he was told. His heart racing as his mind conjured images of the ordeal to come, Geoffrey placed his hands on the hanging stone, pushing it aside a little to make room for him to climb down into the hole.

Surprised the slab swung so easily on its ropes, he sat down at the edge of the pit and dangled his legs over the side. In moments he had jumped down and was lying face up in the grave. Two knights draped a black cloth over his face and body as soon as he was settled and once again his vision was restricted just as if he were blindfolded.

The next thing Geoffrey heard was the sound of ropes creaking under the weight of the stone slab. He realised it was being lowered down onto the grave. His first instinct was to pull the cloth away from his eyes, but he resisted the urge to do so, determined he would not show his fear.

'We commit, O Lord,' Henry prayed, 'the body and soul of our comrade brother, Geoffrey d'Acre, into your care. Bring him to your heart. Make him poor. Teach him the merit of meekness. For the Lord advised us we should give our trust to Him and pay attention to the Word. We should seek knowledge. We should respect the gift of life. If we do these things, then no-one will ever persecute us. If we follow this advice, no man will criticise us but ourselves.'

The assembled knights replied in one voice, 'Amen.'

And the ropes supporting the mighty stone creaked louder than they had before. The stone was lowered down the last few feet to cover the pit in which Geoffrey lay.

The young man stayed perfectly still for as long as he could. Then he convinced himself to lie motionless for just a little while longer. He did not want to capitulate. He did not want to give in to this intimidation. To scramble out of the pit like a coward would have been to admit defeat. He knew he had to trust in the Lord as the scriptures said.

Geoffrey shut his eyes tight, willing himself to have courage, but his resolve was faltering. Then a most unexpected thing happened. He heard a whisper. His eyes snapped open again and he turned his head sideways, unsure whether he had imagined the breathy voice.

The stone moved slowly into position. Geoffrey closed his eyes. And then he heard the whisper again.

'You will not die,' a woman's soothing tone came to him and he realised he was not hearing with his ears. The voice was somewhere inside him. Geoffrey thought of the vision he had experienced at the Krak and instantly felt the presence of the Virgin Mary.

'Do not fear,' the Holy Mother repeated. 'You will rise again.'

The face of a beautiful woman came into Geoffrey's mind and he felt a calmness take hold of him. The young postulant breathed deeply and felt his body relax.

Then he became aware of the stone locking into place above him with a grating slide. All the light that had filtered through the cloth covering his eyes was gone. He could hear the scraping of stone against stone to either side of him. Now he would face the real test.

Abruptly all noise ceased as the slab sat still in its slot. Geoffrey tried to calm himself. Long minutes passed. No voice. No sound. No movement.

The air inside the grave was quickly growing stale. Geoffrey could feel the temperature rising as he began to sweat profusely. He was certain he could sense the presence of the slab only a hand's length away from his nose. Carefully the young knight raised a hand to touch the surface of the stone above him.

Abruptly the ropes creaked as if the young knight's touch had loosened them. The slab moved a little. Then in a flash the great stone dropped until it rested on his ribcage.

Geoffrey turned his head to one side and opened his mouth wide in a frantic attempt to breathe. But the weight of the stone pressed down upon him so tightly he could only draw the shallowest of breaths. He thought of calling out but decided this would be a mistake; besides, he hardly had enough breath to make a sound. He summoned all his internal strength, determined not to give up or show his fear to these knights.

'You will not die.' There was the voice of the Virgin again. 'You will rise again if you have faith.'

Geoffrey struggled to regain his composure but by now he was covered in sweat. It was running down his face and into his thin beard. He tried to turn his head again but there was no room to move. The air was steadily becoming hotter. There was an earthy odour about it that Geoffrey would have considered sweet in any other circumstance. But in this moment the scent of freshly turned soil brought him to the brink of panic.

'You will not die,' the voice repeated, but by now Geoffrey was beyond reassurance. 'You will rise again.'

'God,' he whispered, trying to think of a prayer, but he was too panic-stricken to concentrate. Above him he heard muffled voices but he could not discern what was being said. An incredible sonorous boom shook the ground around him and Geoffrey thought his bowels were going to turn to water. He considered trying to push at the stone but he had merely touched it earlier and it had fallen enough to almost crush him.

'This is the end,' he said with what little breath he could spare. Guy d'Alville must have decided he was too much of a liability.

'They are going to kill me,' he wheezed, his head spinning. Geoffrey drew a desperate gasp to fill his lungs. He knew the air in this tiny grave was almost spent. His senses reeled. Unconsciousness finally began to descend upon him like the black shroud draped over his body.

Then all of a sudden there was another great booming thud that shook the earth. The ropes began to creak again. The stone lowered a tiny fraction, pinning Geoffrey's arms at his side. The weight on his chest was now too great for him to bear. His heart was bursting, his lungs screaming for air. Geoffrey tried to scream but the only sound he could make was a low broken hum.

The next thing he knew the stone was shifting again. But this time it was lifting up slightly. He felt the pressure on his chest diminish and then in a few short moments he could breathe again. He swallowed air the same way a man who has been lost in the desert gulps water.

Light began to seep back through the black cloth covering his eyes. Geoffrey felt the urge to sob for joy and laugh in relief both at the same time. Then a hand reached into the grave to haul him out. Another pulled the black shroud away. Geoffrey, drenched in sweat, was dragged to his feet, still gasping, to be confronted by Henry St Clair.

The old knight smiled broadly, embraced the younger man and then kissed him on the cheek. An attendant knight handed St Clair a sword sheathed in a scabbard of bright silver and set with a red jewel.

'Your brother's sword,' the old knight declared as he handed the weapon to its new master.

Geoffrey took the sword and held it tightly in both

quaking hands. His eyes filled with tears and his knees felt weak. He could not tell if he was expected to respond to St Clair but his throat was too dry to make a sound in any case.

'Upon receipt of this sword,' Henry intoned so all in the chamber could hear him, 'you must swear to keep secret the rituals of our order and the true nature of our treasures. You have come into the guardianship of the Tau. Do you swear?'

'I do,' Geoffrey answered immediately in a hoarse voice. He was ashamed it was so weak and breathy compared to that of St Clair.

'The hour of your resurrection is come and you are among the living. We are as many as the fish in the sea. Take the first steps of your new life, reborn to the service of the Temple. Kneel before the Master and hear his words.'

Bertrand Guesclin was seated in his customary place upon the throne between the two pillars. Geoffrey shuffled toward the old man, still trembling. As the young knight came to within ten paces of the throne the master motioned for him to kneel. Geoffrey laid the sword down at his side, at the same time bowing his head before the leader of the Temple in the lands of Outremer.

'The sign of the triple Tau,' Bertrand declared, 'is the secret symbol by which you will recognise all your brother knights. For though we wear the cross upon our breasts, it is the ancient sign of Tau which we truly venerate. The triple support of the block and tackle which lowered down the stone and lifted it again to free you is a manifestation of the Tau. It represents the way of Christ. Like the heavy stone that seals our tomb, the teachings of the Son of the Father lift all our sins from us.'

'In the time of Jesus the Teacher,' Henry took up the tale, 'the Tau was his signature and by this sign the Nasreans recognised him. We are but the guardians of the Nasrean ways. We are the fish and our God is the fisherman. In time we all swim into his net.'

St Clair placed himself in front of Geoffrey and traced a symbol on the stones at his feet. The sign was made up of three letters all exactly the same. Each was like the Latin cross with the topmost arm removed and they were joined by their longest arms in the centre.

The master smiled and spoke again. 'Arise, Sir Knight, accepted as a warrior of the true Church, a soldier of the Holy Cup and guardian of the sacred books.'

But Geoffrey did not hear all that was being said to him. While the master was explaining the significance of the Tau, the newly invested guardian's eye was distracted. Geoffrey's attention was drawn to the shadows just behind the throne on which Bertrand was seated. St Clair helped the young knight to his feet and as he stood up he got a clearer view.

In the half-light stood a rectangular granite tomb Geoffrey had never noticed before, though that was hardly surprising as this was the closest he had ever come to the throne. It was a very old grave for the knight sculpted in stone across the top was dressed in archaic armour.

But it was not the knight's clothing that struck Geoffrey as being odd. It was the pose the figure was carved in. One leg was crossed behind the other in what would have been an uncomfortable position in life. It immediately reminded Geoffrey of one of the cards he had seen among his brother's papers.

Then he recalled what Henry had said when he first saw that card. He had given it a name. The hanged man.

Suddenly, like a light illuminating the dark recesses of his mind, Geoffrey recalled the words his brother had written in his will. 'A sword length from the east, another from the west, hold the pommel a measured distance from the floor, lift the hanged guardian high upon the Three, look to the throne wherein lies the secret realm.'

Geoffrey brushed his jet-black hair away from his eyes. His heart was pounding again but it was not from fear. Now all he felt was an intense excitement. He had not worked out exactly where this piece fitted into the puzzle, but he was sure this was the clue he had been searching for. This was the beginning of the answer to his brother's riddle.

It was possible, Geoffrey told himself, he would find the entrance to an underground vault beneath the carved tombstone between the pillars. If he was right, this was where the treasures had been stored for safekeeping. Godfrey, his brother, had done his best to disguise the answer in his words. And it was pure chance that Geoffrey had discovered this vital clue. But it struck the young knight as very strange that Henry, Guy and Bertrand had not come to the same conclusion as him.

They would have surely known much more about the traditions of the order. Henry himself was master of the castle, so he must have an intimate knowledge of all the chambers within the fortress. Why had he not caught the hidden meaning in the will?

There was obviously much, much more to this mystery than Geoffrey had at first imagined. The answers probably lay carefully concealed in a maze of intricate puzzles, and all the riddles would need to be solved before he found the path to the truth.

Rufus and Lonan made their way across the courtyard to the kitchen door. On the way they stopped off to inspect the soldiers who were lined up inside the fortification waiting to begin the mock battle. The younger FitzWilliam intended this entertainment as more than a diversion for the tenants. It was meant to show them in no uncertain terms just how efficient these warriors were.

While Lonan waited nearby, Rufus spoke to each of his men under his breath. He wanted to make sure they all had their instructions clear and there would be no mistakes made during the tournament. These Normans were the best warriors money could buy, but even the best men make mistakes.

Rufus had a surprise in store for the inhabitants of the estate, a little drama that would be long remembered in Bally Raine. Only his soldiers had any inkling as to what he had planned. He had been very careful to keep his intentions secret.

If the truth be known, few folk other than the Normans were excited about the mock fighting. The older people had seen enough real warfare in their lifetimes and were not impressed by a group of large men throwing spears or wielding swords. And the young folk were more interested in dancing. Most of the tenants did not speak the Norman tongue, so very few had spoken with any of the soldiers.

When Rufus had finished with his soldiers, he congratulated them and wished them well, more than satisfied they would provide a good performance. With a smile on his face he strode off with Lonan following close behind.

'I wonder if you could do me a great favour,' Rufus asked the chamberlain in his most friendly tone.

'If I can assist you, Master Rufus, in any way . . .' Lonan began.

'I have decided to hold the joust within the courtyard of the castle.'

'There is not enough room for so many men to manoeuvre in the courtyard, Master Rufus,' the chamberlain stated in surprise. 'You must remember how crowded it was when Lord Robert was assembling his expedition. If the yard were full of spectators, folk might be injured. Surely you must consider the safety of the tenants who will be watching the fight.'

'You are right,' Rufus conceded, rubbing a hand across the close-cropped hair at the back of his neck. 'I would not like anyone to be hurt. These men are expert swordsmen but even so they should have plenty of room to swing their blades.'

The young FitzWilliam sighed loudly as they walked a few more steps and then he snapped his fingers. 'I have it!' he exclaimed. 'I'll have the drawbridge raised. We can seat the people on the grass at the edge of the moat where my father would have extended the keep. The fight can take place under the very walls of the castle on the green.'

'As you wish, Master Rufus,' Lonan answered dutifully, 'but I do not understand why you could not hold the joust out in the fields where the bonfire will be lit.'

'I have a little treat in store for everyone,' Rufus smiled. 'Do not worry,' the young FitzWilliam soothed, noticing the dismay that darkened the chamberlain's face. 'It will be a harmless display of skill. I promise no-one will be hurt intentionally.'

Lonan was going to ask what Rufus meant but they reached the kitchen door before he had a chance to speak. A few paces away Neesh sat on a three-legged stool, plucking a chicken.

The girl was so engrossed in her task she only noticed Rufus at the last minute. By the time he was at the kitchen door it was too late for her to make an escape. She felt her heart beat faster and prayed to herself that he would not recognise her. She dared not look up from her work but instead pretended she had not seen the two men.

To her surprise and dismay Rufus walked straight over to her and opened his mouth to speak. Before so much as a syllable had passed his lips, Neesh rose startled from her seat, dropping the chicken as she did so. Rufus grabbed her arm as she tried to pass him. She flicked his hand away from her wrist and glared at him full of hatred, but she was quivering with fright.

'You are the girl called Neesh,' the young FitzWilliam began, 'from the Gioll Martin at the clachan of Clonough?' He bent down to pick up the carcass she had been stripping.

Lonan noticed the girl was shaking and he raised an eyebrow with interest.

'I am,' she replied curtly, snatching the chicken away from him, 'as well you know.' Neesh may have been frightened for her life but she would not be intimidated by this ruffian.

'I have an admission to make in front of my brother's chamberlain,' Rufus declared, 'a humble confession for the wrong I did to you. And an apology.'

'Please, sir,' Neesh replied, surprised at his tone of voice, 'I do not bear you any grudge. I have long since put the incident out of my mind and I beg that you do the same.' His contrition caught her off guard but she smelled some trickery.

'What are you talking about, Master Rufus?' Lonan asked sternly. 'What wrong did you do to this girl?'

Neesh bowed and would have returned to the kitchen but the chamberlain stopped her.

'Wait a while, Neesh,' Lonan snapped. 'I wish to know what you are both talking about.'

Rufus turned to face the chamberlain. He rolled his grey-green eyes toward the sky, a shameful expression on his face. 'It was over a year ago at the well at Gioll Martin,' he confessed, sighing. 'I came upon this girl going about her chores.'

He paused, sensing Lonan was losing patience with him and playing on that as best he could.

'What happened?' the chamberlain hissed through clenched teeth.

'I don't know what came over me,' Rufus mumbled. Neesh looked toward the ground, avoiding the chamberlain's eyes.

'In a moment of carnal weakness,' the young FitzWilliam went on, 'I forced myself upon this girl.'

Neesh shot an icy glance at Rufus. She had no desire to speak about this incident—in the end she had not even told Eilish about it. She had decided it was best to forget the whole thing. If gossip spread around the estate that she had been set upon by this Norman, she feared no man would ever take her for a wife. She did not want the taint of having been touched by Rufus FitzWilliam, even if her honour had remained intact.

'You did what?' the chamberlain barked, appalled such a thing could have happened on the estates and perpetrated by no less a man than Lord William's son. 'Better men than you have been hung from the grey oak for that kind of crime,' Lonan informed him.

'Thank all the saints I did not succeed,' Rufus cut in. 'I was prevented from having my way with her by the hand of God himself. I learned a great lesson from this girl. From that night on I knew I had to change my ways.'

Lonan looked at the young FitzWilliam with a frown. A cloud passed over the old man's face and his wrinkles visibly deepened in shock. The chamberlain turned up his lip, clearly doubting every word he heard. 'Is this story true?' he barked at Neesh.

'It is true, Master Chamberlain,' the girl replied, still shocked at the Norman's admission. 'I pushed him into the well and afterwards I hid up at the old chapel for the night. It was the same evening Mathúin passed away. I remember because Master Rufus came to fetch Eilish from Gioll Martin later that night.'

'Did he do you any harm?' Lonan asked.

'I was frightened out of my wits,' Neesh admitted and regretted her words immediately. She had not wanted to give Rufus the satisfaction of knowing that.

'I carried some bruises for a while,' she added, 'and a cut under my chin, but these quickly healed.'

'Rufus FitzWilliam,' Lonan spat, 'I never thought very highly of you. I have occasionally considered it nothing better than a waste of good food and ale to keep you. But now I find myself wishing I had taught you a few sterner lessons when you were a lad. What kind of man would do such a thing? How in heaven's name did you expect to get away with this crime?'

'I admit my foolishness, Lonan,' Rufus mumbled in what appeared to be genuine contrition. 'I did not think of the consequences of my actions.'

'Did not think?' Lonan repeated, 'Did you imagine you would simply walk away from such a crime without retribution falling on you? Would she not have told her father and brothers of the attack?'

The young FitzWilliam sighed loudly. 'It was my plan to murder the girl so she would not have the chance to speak to anyone of what I had done.'

Lonan was suddenly overcome with an anger such as he had not felt in many years. He growled under his breath, raising a hand contorted with rage. Rufus saw the old man's eyes burning and read the violent intent in them, but before the young FitzWilliam could move out of Lonan's reach, the chamberlain grabbed his jaw. He tightened his grip as he glared into Rufus's pale green eyes. The two men faced each other down, all rights of birth or conquest, position or power dissolved for the time being.

After a long pause, Lonan hissed and relaxed his grip, but his eyes were still full of contempt. Rufus opened his mouth to speak, but before he knew what had hit him, the young

FitzWilliam's head was turned by a hard slap from the chamberlain's bony hand.

Rufus wavered in that moment. He had not expected this from Lonan and his pride did not allow for this sort of behaviour from an underling. But the Norman restrained himself from retaliating. He told himself he must not strike back. Not yet. Rufus bit his tongue, buried his fury and turned to look the chamberlain in the eye.

Lonan saw there was no fight in the younger man and suddenly began to think perhaps Rufus really was sorry for what he had done.

Neesh did not look up from the ground, in part because her eyes were flooding with tears, but also because she could not understand why Rufus would have made such an admission in this way. She was devastated he had recognised her, gone to this length to approach her and then humiliated her in front of the chamberlain.

'What do you want?' Lonan spat at the Norman, suspecting there must be more to this revelation than met his eye. 'Why have you made this confession?'

'To cleanse my soul, Master Chamberlain,' Rufus lied, channelling his indignation into an emotional plea. 'I decided I could not live with the shame of my act for another day.'

'And do you really believe it is enough to merely confess this sin?' Lonan queried. 'Or do you think you should be subject to the full penalty of the law on this matter?'

'I would freely give myself to any judge to pronounce sentence upon me,' Rufus quickly replied. 'But only if young Neesh thinks it necessary to pursue the matter. However, before I ask her thoughts on that, I wish to humbly apologise to her.'

The young FitzWilliam turned to the girl, determined this performance would be thoroughly convincing. 'Neesh,' he began, summoning up all the sincerity he could muster, 'I am sorry for the wrong I have done to you. If there is anything I can do to make recompense to you for what I have done, please let me know now. I will do anything to wash the shame of this sin away.'

'You will go before a judge,' Lonan declared bitterly, 'and you will pay for what you have done. But you will not appear before any Norman court that would let you off easily with a reprimand and some holy penance. You will come before a Brehon judge. One of our own people will decide your fate.'

'Is that absolutely necessary?' Rufus cut in nervously. 'I wanted to keep this whole affair as quiet as possible so as not to bring such shame on my father and brother. I have shamed them enough already.' Rufus was certain he could call on Lonan's absolute loyalty to William. The old chamberlain would never risk humiliating his old lord and master.

'I asked you to accompany me, Lonan,' the young FitzWilliam explained, 'so that my father's good name would not be damaged. I trust your judgment in all things. But would you like to make my foolish behaviour public knowledge and so dishonour my father whom you so loyally served for so many years? Surely you understand the position I am in.'

The chamberlain ran a hand through his beard, seeing the young man's point but suspicious of his motives. This was a chance to vent his anger at Rufus for a hundred insults, indiscretions and petty injuries. But while Lord William still lived, the old chamberlain could not bring himself to cause public disgrace to the FitzWilliam household if it could be avoided.

'I will be your judge,' Lonan announced after he had considered the situation. 'I will set a fine for you as is the custom under our laws. We do not hang men for this sort of crime. We make them pay damages equal to the honour of the one they have offended.'

'I will gladly pay any amount in order to clear my name,' Rufus vowed.

'You will never clear your name,' the chamberlain observed wryly, 'but you may just preserve your father's reputation.' Then the chamberlain turned to Neesh. 'My child,' he asked her, 'would you be happy if I made a judgment on your behalf?'

'I have long since put the matter out of my mind, Master Lonan,' she replied, seeing her opportunity to resolve this once and for all, 'and I would prefer that it were finished with. If you think you could make a fair decision, then I will respect your judgment.'

'Very well,' the chamberlain sighed, relieved that Neesh seemed to hold no ill feeling towards the young FitzWilliam. 'Rufus,' he began, 'I can see you are full of remorse for what you have done. I know it takes maturity and courage to admit to a sin that otherwise might never have come to anyone's attention. Taking this into consideration, my judgment is that you will pay the fine of three good milking cows to Neesh. Also you will pay the rent and taxes for her father's family for this year out of your own pocket.'

Rufus closed his eyes, struggling to control his protest.

'When that payment is made,' the chamberlain concluded, 'you may consider your earthly penance settled in full. However, you should look to your heart, my lad, and ask yourself whether you deserve such a lenient sentence.'

'How do I give three cows to Neesh without her family asking questions?' Rufus snapped, unable to govern his tongue and regretting the words as soon as they were uttered.

'That is your problem,' Lonan declared. 'Perhaps you should have thought about the results of your actions a long time ago.'

'But my father's honour will be stained,' Rufus protested. 'I do not want the details of my crime to become public.'

'It seems strange to me, Master Rufus, that you should suddenly be so concerned about your father's honour,' the chamberlain observed, 'but I see your point. It would be best if you gave the cows to her father and family as a gift. The festival is a perfect excuse for such a gesture. The payment of the rents and taxes is not so simple to disguise, but we have plenty of time to find a solution to that problem.'

The old man turned once more to Neesh. 'Does all of this meet with your approval?'

'It does, Master Lonan,' she replied, 'I am very glad this matter is not being made public. And I am satisfied Master Rufus is genuinely sorry for what he did.'

'Then we are agreed,' Rufus piped up, 'this matter is not to be discussed with anyone else? It is to be kept between us three?'

'I believe,' Lonan sighed, 'for once, Master Rufus, you have managed to turn a thoroughly dishonourable situation into one that reflects well upon your character. I will say nothing more to anyone if the fine is paid today.'

'And I will speak of this to no-one,' Neesh confirmed. 'I will keep the whole matter as secret as I have all these months.'

Rufus heard her words and his heart leapt with joy. Three cows, he told himself, was a small price to pay to be sure Neesh had not spoken to anyone. He still had a chance of approaching Eilish and winning her for himself.

'I cannot thank you both enough,' Rufus chortled, suddenly merry. 'You will never know what a great weight you have lifted from my shoulders. I feel as if I can walk with my head held high again. And this is only the start of the great change you will see come over me, I promise. I am determined to make amends for all the trouble I have caused.'

'It is well, Master Rufus, that you speak so,' Lonan grunted, still suspicious, 'but what spiritual penance will you do?'

'I will go now to Father Conlan and ask his advice,' Rufus answered feebly. He had not expected this demand, but he realised that such an act would prove his contrition.

'If you will excuse me,' the young FitzWilliam mumbled as he turned smartly on his heel. A few moments later Rufus was striding off in the direction of the chapel, leaving the chamberlain and the girl behind.

As soon as he was out of earshot Neesh voiced what had been on her mind throughout the conversation. 'Why has he done this?'

'Do you mean why has he confessed to something he could so easily have kept hidden?' Lonan asked, and then went on without waiting for an answer. 'I cannot be sure,' he admitted, 'but either he is planning something or he is afflicted with the curse of the FitzWilliam family.'

'What is the curse of the FitzWilliams?' Neesh asked, horrified.

'They are all quite mad,' Lonan informed her, putting a finger to his forehead. 'Quite, quite mad.'

Braonin stood for a long time at the drawbridge. He pretended to be looking out over the moat but he turned his gaze back towards the kitchen every once in a while to satisfy his curiosity. He saw the chamberlain and Rufus approach Neesh. And he clearly saw she was very upset at whatever they had to say to her.

'I've never trusted that bastard,' Braonin swore in a whisper. 'If ever there was an evil creature on this earth, born of Satan's wickedness, it is Rufus FitzWilliam.'

When the young FitzWilliam parted company from the other two, Braonin decided to follow him in the hope he might discover what had caused young Neesh to shed so many tears. He watched Rufus go down towards the chapel and saw him kneel before Father Conlan on the steps of the building.

To Braonin's surprise the priest became very agitated. In the next moment Conlan dragged the young FitzWilliam by the sleeve within the walls of the little church.

Braonin made his way as quickly as he could down to the roofless structure, hoping to observe the two men. He soon found a spot beside one of the empty arches where he would not be seen. No sooner had he settled himself than he heard the priest's voice raised in anger.

'You are a wicked one, Master Rufus!' Conlan spat. 'I swear you are a shame to your good father.'

'But I am trying to make amends for my actions, father,' Rufus insisted. 'Why do you think I went to Neesh and apologised? Why do you think I asked Lonan to give a judgment on my actions? Why do you think I have come to you to ask a penance?'

'For such a sin as rape, my lad,' the priest sneered, 'there is no penance great enough.'

Braonin's eyes closed tightly in pain when he heard Conlan's words. 'For the love of God!' he hissed almost inaudibly, reluctant to believe what his ears told him. 'That bastard!'

'It never went that far!' Rufus interjected. 'She resisted me.'

'But you intended to force yourself upon her?' Conlan pressed. 'You would have had your will with her if she had not fought you off?'

The young FitzWilliam was silent for a few moments. 'She gave me every indication that she desired a roll in the grass as much as me.'

'Something must have made her change her mind then,' the priest said quietly.

'I swear,' Rufus protested, 'she was flirting with me.'

'I will have to take your word for that,' Conlan answered after a short pause.

Braonin sucked the breath in through his teeth in anger and told himself to calm down. But he found it almost impossible to restrain himself. In the end he gripped the hilt of his hunting knife at his belt and pressed his body up against the wall to listen again to the conversation.

'You will pay a penance of nine cows to the abbey at Shelton to start with,' Father Conlan declared. 'And you will say morning and evening mass with me at this altar every day for a year. On holy days you will sit midnight mass with me also.'

'Don't you think you are being a little harsh, Father?' Rufus demanded, making no attempt to disguise his indignation. To bow down to Lonan was one thing, but Rufus had no respect for this dottering old priest and despised having to take penance from him.

'I think I am letting you off lightly by promising to keep this matter between you and I. If the tenants got wind of this appalling crime, they would probably not let you live on these estates a day longer. If they let you live at all,' Conlan added.

'The Brehon laws do not allow the taking of a life as punishment,' Rufus countered.

'But the Brehon law is not the only law in this land. If it were proved under the King's law that you had committed this act, you could well be hanged.'

Braonin realised with disgust that Father Conlan had no

intention of letting this crime come to light. The priest put a hand on the Norman's shoulder as Braonin watched carefully at the window arch.

'You forget, my son,' Conlan went on, 'that some of these folk were alive when your father's generation first came to Ireland. They still remember the way most of your people treated their kinfolk. Though William was readily accepted and revered as lord, he was a rare bird. If the tenants had a good excuse to rid themselves of you and your brother, they would happily take the opportunity to be free of the taxes, tithes and rents you impose upon them.'

'Are you trying to tell me these people would dare rise up against us?' Rufus snapped.

'I am saying,' the priest soothed, 'that your position is not as secure as you might believe. There are many travelling folk about who have been evicted from their lands for stirring up rebellion. The tenants listen to their tales and take them very seriously.'

'I am well aware of the existence of these travellers,' Rufus stated. 'In fact I have been told of one outlaw who has been living on these estates for over a year. He has the respect of many of the tenants. But that man will find himself in irons before the sun goes down today.'

'Cinneach is a misguided soul,' Father Conlan protested, 'a heretic, and I suspect he holds some pagan beliefs, but he is popular with the common folk. It would not be wise to attempt to arrest him, my son.'

'And what if the abbot discovered you knew of the existence of this man,' Rufus slyly asked, 'and were protecting him? How would he react?'

'I have not harboured Cinneach. The abbot would not believe you if you told him that. And you would lose my support if you complained about me.'

'Yet you have spent many hours with Cinneach before the fire in the great hall of my father's castle, have you not?'

Rufus countered. 'Would you be declared a heretic for keeping a Culdee safe?'

Father Conlan squinted, understanding that he was in a very difficult position. 'I have done nothing wrong,' he protested.

'I wonder if the abbot would say that,' the young FitzWilliam sneered.

'All it would take,' Conlan countered, 'would be one word from me and you would be expelled from these estates forever.'

'I believe you are right,' Rufus agreed. 'I stand to lose my rank and position should you decide to disclose my crime.' The Norman smiled and his eyes flashed with glee. 'But you will not,' he laughed. 'For two reasons. First, a priest is forbidden to discuss the details of any confession brought to him in the spirit of contrition and for which penance has been assigned.'

Conlan sighed, knowing this to be true.

'And second,' Rufus went on, 'I might be banished for what I have done but heretics and those who protect them are burned at the stake. Brehon law passes such evil wrongdoers to the Church for punishment. Norman law has no jurisdiction to intervene. If it could be proved that you supped with Cinneach knowing all the while of his activities against Norman rule and the Church, you would be hard pressed to escape with your life.'

Conlan's face drained of colour and he put both hands to his face in fear. Rufus put a hand on the priest's shoulder to comfort him.

'But there is no need for me to mention your indiscretion,' the young FitzWilliam assured Conlan, 'as long as I have your support.'

'Support?' the priest muttered. 'What do you mean?'

'I have an ambition to one day rule this estate,' Rufus explained as Conlan's jaw dropped open in shock, 'should my brother not return from the Holy War,' the Norman added quickly.

'How can I help you?'

'We can help each other,' Rufus stated. 'When I am Lord of Bally Raine I will remember and reward my supporters. Imagine what we could do together.' He put both hands on the priest's shoulders and turned him around. 'Try to picture this chapel as just a small corner of some great cathedral. We could build it, you and I. The largest church in all Ireland. Folk would come from far and near to worship at the high altar. There could even be a bishopric in it for you if we approach the matter with careful consideration.'

Conlan blushed as he considered this proposal. Rufus had successfully appealed to the priest's one weakness, his vanity.

'Bishoprics are granted on merit alone,' Conlan resisted.

'Is there no merit in building a great cathedral?' Rufus asked. 'A man who could govern such a project would certainly be worthy of high office.'

Father Conlan closed his eyes. In his imagination he could clearly see the high altar of a huge and beautiful cathedral. His mind echoed with the sound of the offices being chanted. He smelled the holy incense. Then the priest realised what it would mean to him, to God, if this church were built. He would be venerated as a great leader of the faith, perhaps even as a saint. But if he let this chance go by, he would never be anything more than a parish clergyman ministering to poor farmers.

'Do you guarantee you will commit yourself fully to this undertaking?' Conlan asked finally.

'As dutifully as I will govern these estates,' Rufus answered sincerely. 'But the first step for both of us is to rid Bally Raine of this heretic forever.'

Braonin lay back against the wall, appalled that Conlan was so easily bought.

'I will help you if I can,' the priest agreed. 'Only because I believe you will make a good lord of these estates one day. What is your plan?'

'I want you to publicly denounce Cinneach to the tenants,' the young FitzWilliam answered straightaway, 'before I arrest him. Then it will look as if I am merely doing the bidding of the Church.'

'What have you got against this man? He has done you no harm.'

'I want the people to see what my soldiers are capable of,' Rufus replied. 'I want them to know wrongdoers will be dealt with swiftly on this estate.'

'And if I refuse to denounce him?' the priest inquired, trying his hand one last time.

'Then I will have a letter in the abbot's hand by sunset,' Rufus sneered with obvious satisfaction, 'and you will be lodged in the strongroom of the castle before midnight.'

'Do you really believe this arrest will serve both of us?' Father Conlan sighed.

'That, father, depends on you,' Rufus remarked, 'and how willing you are to help me to reach my goals.'

'I cannot see how I would be of any help to you.'

'In time, father, you will see,' Rufus whispered and then he slapped the priest on the shoulder and turned to depart. 'I will meet you on the green before the mock battle,' he added. 'That is when I plan to trap the heretic.'

'Make sure you are free this evening,' the priest snapped back, 'to begin your penance.'

Rufus laughed loudly as he left the chapel. 'I will be here,' he promised. 'I would not miss it for anything.'

Braonin was about to slip away from the chapel when he thought of confronting the priest with all he had heard and convincing the old man not to go along with the young

FitzWilliam's plot. He waited until Rufus was well out of sight and then made his way through the main door to the chapel.

Father Conlan was kneeling at the altar. When he heard the footsteps behind him he turned around. 'What is it now . . .' he began, but as soon as he saw Braonin he coughed.

'Who were you expecting, father?' Braonin asked. 'Obviously not me.'

'No-one, my son,' Father Conlan lied.

'I heard every word, father.'

'What are you talking about?' the priest stuttered nervously.

'I heard the confession,' Braonin stated coldly. 'I heard what Rufus plans to do. I heard Rufus threaten you with the fury of your own abbot.'

'You dare to interfere with the holy rite of confession?' Father Conlan roared, but sweat was starting to appear on his forehead.

'Bugger the holy rite, father. Are you going to let him get away with arresting Cinneach?'

'I do not have any choice, Braonin. One word to the abbot and I could be in grave danger myself.'

'You cannot let him do this,' Braonin pleaded. 'He is using Cinneach to show how powerful his soldiers are. This is his first step towards taking over lordship of the estate.'

'Nonsense, my son,' the priest soothed, trying to calm the young man down. 'He has no such intention. He is trying to make amends for his past indiscretions.'

'Lord Robert appointed me as chancellor to prevent Rufus making a bid for control of the estates,' Braonin argued. 'You are in a position to ensure Robert's fears for the future of this landholding do not become a reality. Are you going to sit on your hands and do nothing? Are you going to allow Rufus to have his way?'

'I told you,' the priest bellowed, 'I have no choice. I must think of my own position. If I am sent away, then Rufus may get a priest who will support him in his plans.'

'Is that not what you are doing now?' Braonin snorted, then he shook his head with disgust. 'You are betraying your own people. Rufus will never build the cathedral he spoke of.'

'He will,' Conlan protested. 'I will make sure he keeps his promise. I am stronger than you think. If anyone can stand up to Rufus, it is me.'

'He will twist you around his finger like a loose thread on his tunic.'

'Cinneach is a heretic. He is a danger to all of us,' Conlan argued, trying to get the younger man to see reason. 'I must honour my vows to the Church.'

Braonin looked into Father Conlan's eyes and saw the fear reflected in them. 'If you won't do anything, then I will,' he spat. With a hiss of contempt he stormed out of the chapel, making straight for the castle to warn Cinneach.

Father Conlan knelt soberly before the altar to consider the options placed before him. After a long while he finally rose, crossed himself and went out to find Rufus to tell him of Braonin's intentions.

Chapter Thirteen

Donal eventually found resting places for himself and his lord among the many wagons and sleeping camels in the great Christian camp. At Robert's insistence they lay down their packs amid the countless Templar fires. The lord wished to observe the warrior knights more closely and perhaps speak with some of them before he slept.

At midnight Robert was still sitting up listening to Templar prayers sung in French, not Latin as was usual for a holy Christian order. His sergeant-at-arms drifted off into sleep, too saddle-weary to stay awake.

In the middle of the night Donal stirred, rolled over and noticed his master was sitting up. The chieftain lay watching Robert for a while before he spoke up.

'Do you have a man's blood on your hands, my lord?' he inquired.

Robert was startled by the question and turned to face his sergeant-at-arms. 'I barely had the chance to swing my sword, Donal,' he laughed. 'I did more damage to the desert shrubs than I did to the enemy.'

'Then what is troubling you?'

Robert coughed to clear the dust from his throat, unwilling at first to speak his mind. Then he sought out his water bottle and took a long draught. When he had a mouthful he passed the vessel to Donal who also swallowed a small measure.

'I have been thinking,' Robert began. 'It is past the time I joined the Temple as a knight. It is an urgent need in me to find a use for my life.'

Donal sat up immediately. 'Is that wise? Have you thought about this decision?'

'I have thought of nothing else since we landed at Acre with King Richard's army,' the lord admitted. 'I would have sworn to the order as soon as my father came back from the crusades if he would have allowed me. I can think of no other purpose that would make my life worthy unto God.'

'And what about the people on the estates?' Donal cut in. 'Do you not have a duty to them also? Is the protection of your people not a worthy way to spend your life?'

'What do you mean?'

Donal took a deep breath before he spoke, realising he would have to word his objections carefully. 'Please try to view this from your tenants' point of view,' the chieftain began. 'If you were not our lord, then who would be? Rufus?' Donal spat into the sand. 'I pray to God you are not considering that foolish lad as your successor.'

'Of course not,' Robert declared. 'He would not be capable of living up to his responsibilities. He is too selfish and reckless. Besides which, my father has lawfully excluded him from lordship.'

'Then who would be our lord? Some warrior from the north? Or some relative of yours such as Eustace, who might well hold ambitions for his own kingdom?'

'I have not thought about it,' Robert admitted, 'but the rule of the Templars states I must relinquish all my lands to the order.'

'Your father did not do so,' Donal pointed out.

'He was merely a postulant when he passed the lands to me,' the lord explained. 'He had not taken his final vows as a brother.'

'So the tenants will have a holy order for their landlord?'

'I suppose that is what will happen in the end. Yes.'

Donal spat again and then thought for a while. 'Could you give the tenants freehold of the land they occupy before you join the order?'

'I could,' Robert said cautiously, 'but what would that achieve?'

'It would give them some degree of control over how the land was to be used in future,' Donal explained, 'without devaluing the mills and forest at all. The order could hold these assets for their own.'

'Under this scheme the peasants could work the land as they liked. But they would still have to pay tithes to the mill if they wished to grind their grain?'

'Yes,' Donal enthused. 'It would remove the greatest fear we have had since your father retired to the monastery. All your tenants have been frightened some new lord would take William's place and prove to be a much harder master.'

'The Temple is notoriously generous with its tenants,' Robert soothed. 'Your people would not have to worry about the rents and taxes rising too sharply.'

'And what if the Templar order ceased to exist?' Donal suggested. 'What if they are one day subsumed into another order? What if at some distant time in the future the Temple decides to sell the land or raise the taxes?'

'It will not happen,' Robert insisted. 'The Order of the Temple is as strong as the Church itself. Such things are inconceivable. The Temple is above all things temporal.'

At that moment there was a sound nearby of a man yawning loudly.

'Do you fellows never sleep?' a voice asked in the darkness. 'Have you not had enough excitement for one day?'

'I am sorry,' Robert offered sincerely. 'We did not mean to wake you.'

'I was awake anyway,' the man sighed. 'I have worries of

my own and they are not unlike yours.' He paused for a second, 'I hope you don't mind, I was listening to your conversation.'

'Not at all,' Robert stated. 'Would you like to join us at our fire?'

'I will indeed,' the other man said, 'for there is no sleep in me tonight.'

With that the other knight rose and wrapped a blanket around himself. Donal could plainly see that beneath this cover the man was fully dressed in the white surcoat of the Temple. Under the surcoat he wore his coat of mail. The chieftain wondered whether the Templars ever removed their armour at all.

The other knight sat himself down and Donal observed him with growing interest. The stranger's voice had sounded like that of an old man, yet this fellow seated at the fire could have been no older than Lord Robert, perhaps only twenty-five years of age. But his youthful face was tinged with a sadness, betrayed in his deep-set eyes and revealing the truth of his hard life as a knight of the order. His beard was full, entirely covering his throat.

'How long have you been a Templar?' Robert asked as he passed the water bottle to the knight.

'Eight long years,' the man sighed. 'I saw the terrible slaughter of our knights at the battle of Hattin when I was sixteen years old. That day thousands of Christians were driven mad with thirst. They rushed toward the Saracen lines where the only water lay, only to be massacred. I thought we had another Hattin on our hands today.'

'You mentioned earlier your worries were similar to our own,' Donal cut in. 'Are you the lord of a great estate?'

'I was a lord for a brief period of my life,' the knight confirmed. 'Until I joined the order my family owned a large estate in the kingdom of Scotland. But I gave that willingly to the Temple when I took my vows. They have managed it fairly ever since.'

'Then how has this arrangement caused you worry?' Robert inquired.

'The Grand Master has ordered me to return to my ancestral home and take up my duties as lord once again,' the man laughed, but there was bitterness in the gesture, 'to leave Outremer forever, to marry and to father an heir.'

'What is so terrible about that?' Donal quizzed.

'I have grown used to the routine of a warrior's existence. I am a monk under a vow of celibacy. And I have come to appreciate the dry heat of this country. I love the sunshine on my face and the authority I wield as a leading knight of the Temple.'

Robert cast a glance at the knight's fair hair and his tanned skin. He could not understand why he would agree to such an arrangement if he really did not want to return to Scotland.

'I have no choice,' the knight sighed, answering Robert's unspoken question. 'I must follow the rules of the order and the first rule is obedience. There have been many commands I have followed that were distasteful to me, yet I always carried out the wishes of my superiors to the letter.'

'What is there in this land that could be so appealing it would make you want to stay here forever and never return to your home?' Donal asked.

The man smiled. 'I am a prefector of the order,' he explained. 'Though I know I look young for such a rank, it is nevertheless true. And I have responsibility for a castle in the south of Outremer which has not yet fallen into the hands of the enemy. Indeed I am told the Saracens do not even know it exists.'

'You are indeed very young to hold such high rank,' Robert confirmed, obviously impressed, 'and to have a castle and its garrison under your command.'

'I have not been back to my garrison for more than two years,' the man admitted. 'I have been a prisoner of Saladin for a long while. I was released after King Richard took Acre under the terms of the surrender of that city.'

'A prisoner!' Robert exclaimed. 'But you look so healthy and well fed! Were not the conditions in the Saracen dungeons appalling?'

'Dungeons?' the man repeated, incredulously. 'There are no dungeons in the Saracen cities. And I was fed better in the care of the great Saladin than I have been in many years.'

'We have been told the Saracens murder all their Templar prisoners,' Robert protested.

'Not Saladin,' the man explained. 'He is quite different. He is an honourable man and as great a king as Richard.'

Then the stranger turned his eyes back to the fire for a while. 'After we have taken Jaffa I am travelling to France. I may not have the opportunity ever again to visit the castle I once commanded.' He paused again before he went on. 'You were saying you had the ambition of taking the vows of a knight of the Temple,' he said to Robert.

'That is true,' the lord agreed, 'but my sergeant informs me that my tenants would be uneasy about the lands being given into the control of the order.'

'They have nothing to fear,' the knight said, 'the Temple is the most generous landlord they will ever know. If you are thinking seriously about your vows, then go to my castle in the south and witness the rules of the Temple first-hand. I need to send important letters there. So you would be doing me a great service.'

'Is it far away?' Donal asked.

'Six days' ride, maybe a little more,' the knight answered. 'But it would give you a glimpse of how the tenants are treated on lands controlled by the Temple. There is a sugar mill in the castle and the local farmers mostly grow cane for its sweet juice.'

'Thank you for your offer,' Robert replied courteously, 'I would gladly carry your letters for you. I am sure it would do me good to look upon an estate in Templar hands. It would put my mind at rest about my decision.' Then the lord realised he had not been introduced to this prefector.

'Forgive me,' Robert begged, 'but I have been so involved in my own thoughts and worries, I did not even ask you your name.'

'I am Henry St Clair,' the knight answered, 'descendant of Catherine of that noble name and of Hugues de Payen, the founder of our order.'

Just after midday one barrel of ale was opened and Braonin ordered it be set up on the green just outside the castle walls. This patch of grass lay between the defences of the castle and the moat. William had left it bare in case some future Lord of Bally Raine decided to extend on his fortifications. There was enough room to add new stables and a barracks for soldiers.

For the time being this open space was used for the seasonal celebrations, as a place where folk could gather close to the castle. As soon as the barrel was set up there all the tenants gathered to share a cupful of ale and some gossip while the soldiers climbed down the stairs from the castle keep to form ranks by the walls.

'Clear a space!' the garrison sergeant-at-arms bellowed in his best military voice. The people fell back to create a rough oval within which the warriors could display their skills.

Ten soldiers marched smartly into the centre of the cleared space, followed by Rufus FitzWilliam dressed in his polished mail-coat and helm. On his back he had slung an oblong Norman shield almost as big as his body. At his side was a sheathed sword sporting a gleaming brass pommel and hilt. With a flourish the young knight removed his helm as the sergeant-at-arms placed a wooden box upon the grass.

Rufus stood upon the box to address the crowd just as his brother had done at the previous midsummer feast. 'Friends and tenants,' he began, 'welcome to the festival. I wish you all well during this great celebration of midsummer.' He smiled benignly at the assembly and then went on, 'These past months I have been training a small group of soldiers in the skills needed to protect our little community from attack. You may recall that the warriors who were left behind by my brother tended toward drunkenness, brawling and bullying.'

More than one person in the crowd considered those warriors had been heavily influenced by Rufus himself, but no-one dared say so.

'As such they could not have been depended upon in an emergency. The most important aspect of dealing with a military threat is to recognise it before it becomes unmanageable. These soldiers you see before you have been trained to weed out threats to the community, to deal with them swiftly and efficiently with a minimum of disruption to the lives of the people they are paid to protect.'

Rufus cast his eyes over the crowd until he caught Braonin's eye. The young FitzWilliam smiled again and his eyes seemed full of joy as if he were savouring some private joke.

Then the young FitzWilliam caught the eye of Eilish who dropped her gaze immediately to avoid his attention. Rufus did not care, he was grinning broadly now and had placed his hands on his hips as he noticed Father Conlan pushing past Eilish toward him.

Most of the tenants began looking from one to another to see if anyone really understood what the young Fitz-William was talking about. But before anyone could ask him to explain, Rufus had stepped down from the box to allow Father Conlan to take his place.

As the priest passed by the knight he whispered something to Rufus which made the younger man laugh loudly. Then Rufus nodded his head and urged the churchman up onto the speaking box. While Father Conlan was taking his place Rufus went to the sergeant-at-arms. He issued orders to the man in a low voice no-one else could hear.

'I have been asked to speak to you today,' Father Conlan began and then cleared his throat nervously before continuing. 'I have been asked to inform you all . . .' He stopped again, clearly anxious to word his statement carefully.

'There is no greater crime in the eyes of the mother Church,' he started again, 'than the hideous sin of heresy. It corrupts the hearts and souls of all those who have contact with it. Like a disease of the flesh it rots the mind. In the end the spirit of the afflicted one is sent to hell for the rest of eternity where the torments are many and there is no rest from punishment.'

The tenants all looked to one another, trying to fathom why the priest was preaching this sermon to them.

'And a heretic is usually so shameless a man he will live among us, eat with us and share our trust, though we may never know his secret. A heretic must keep his misdeeds to himself for the risk of discovery by honest Christians is too great. And so the criminal, at first a rebel against God, falls into other crimes and ends his life a rebel both against his lord and his Maker.'

Of all those present it seemed only Braonin O'Regan understood this speech. Braonin's face turned red with anger as he stepped toward the priest. When he was only a few paces away from Conlan, the chancellor turned to face the tenants.

'Rather a heretic than a traitor to one's own friends,' Braonin yelled, searching the crowd for Cinneach's face.

'The chancellor will hold his tongue,' Rufus demanded, 'until the good father has finished speaking.'

'The weed that grows out of a dunghill lifts its head the highest,' Braonin shouted back at Rufus. A murmur passed around the tenants as they asked each other what was going on.

'Silence, chancellor,' Rufus replied, 'and perhaps I will give you a chance to speak later.'

Eilish suddenly felt sick in her stomach with a premonition of disaster. She realised Rufus was up to something but she, like everyone else, had no idea what it could be.

Father Conlan coughed once more to clear his throat before he went on. 'There is one among us,' the priest stated in a stern voice.

Ten more soldiers made their way down the stairs from the keep. Everyone turned and stared at them, including Father Conlan who stopped speaking again. The men took up positions between the crowd and the moat and the priest went back to his speech.

'There is one among us,' Conlan repeated, 'who has abused the trust of his neighbours. He has come to us from the west where his kinfolk are fighting an unjust war against their landlord. He has been sent to us to stir up rebellion. He is a Culdee and therefore a heretic. Those who harbour heretics are stained with their sin also. Those who shelter rebels have rebellion on their minds.'

With that the priest stepped down from the wooden box and Rufus took his place again.

'The man Father Conlan refers to was sentenced to hang by royal decree!' Rufus exclaimed. 'He is a rebel who attempted to murder his rightful lord. Those of you who know him might not think him such a terrible man. But if he was capable of preying upon his victim while the noble knight was asleep, then he is capable of anything.'

Rufus fell silent as he surveyed the crowd. Most of them knew by now exactly who he was talking about. Finally his gaze rested on Cinneach, who was, as Rufus had predicted, present among the tenants.

'The rebel I seek to arrest has been carefully followed these last two weeks,' Rufus declared. 'My soldiers have kept a close watch on his activities and gathered much evidence against him. The man I accuse of heresy and rebellion is ...' Rufus paused to keep the tenants in suspense, '... Cinneach O'Hare, Culdee, seanachie and rebel.'

Braonin hadn't been able to find Cinneach anywhere. And now it was too late to warn him. As he heard his name, the Culdee turned and made a dash for the moat. He knew if he was able to jump in he could easily swim to safety. But within seconds a soldier had grabbed him by the sleeve and the other warriors were already rushing to help their comrade restrain the man.

Cinneach and the soldier quickly fell to struggling desperately with one another and for a second it looked as if the warrior was about to throw his captive to the ground. But before the soldier had the opportunity, Braonin came to the rescue, grabbing the soldier from behind around the chin and pulling the warrior's head back until the man could not even cry out. In his agony the soldier had no choice but to let Cinneach go. In an instant the Culdee had leapt into the moat and was swimming for his life. By the time another warrior had cracked Braonin on the back of the head with a club to subdue him, Cinneach was clambering up the opposite bank.

The warriors stood at the edge of the moat, watching their quarry escape, powerless to follow after him. Their heavy mail-coats would have dragged them to the bottom if any of them had tried to brave the waters.

'Let down the drawbridge!' the sergeant-at-arms bellowed between curses. A short while later the great wooden bridge began to descend. Ten of the soldiers climbed back up the stairs to the castle to rush across the bridge, but by the time they reached the other bank Cinneach the Culdee was long gone.

Eilish rushed to Braonin's side to make sure the blow had not been fatal. The crowd gathered around and someone brought a cup of ale for the wounded chancellor. Eilish put the cup to her cousin's lips and in a few moments he had regained consciousness. As he opened his eyes Braonin saw the young FitzWilliam standing over him.

'Braonin O'Regan,' Rufus stormed, and everyone turned to face the man dressed in armour, 'I arrest you for heresy and high treason against your lord and the King. You have knowingly consorted with a heretic and a rebel. You have assisted in the escape of a criminal condemned by the King to death. I strip you of your rank as chancellor and confine you to the strongroom of the keep until a court can be convened to try your case.' He turned casually to the sergeant-at-arms, lowering his voice. 'Take him away.'

The assembled tenants stood back, too stunned to protest as the soldiers lifted Braonin onto his feet and carried him up the stairs to the castle.

'Chamberlain!' Rufus called out, summoning the old man. 'I will speak with you in my room immediately.' Then Rufus bowed slightly to Eilish and followed the soldiers back into the castle.

Some time later, in the chamber his father had once occupied, Rufus sat waiting for Lonan to attend him. The young FitzWilliam stirred up the fire again and sat before it, dreaming of his conquest of the estate. And his victory seemed much closer than ever before.

With Braonin out of the way and the potentially embarrassing matter of the girl, Neesh, settled favourably, Rufus was feeling very confident. He still marvelled at how everything he wanted seemed to be falling into his lap.

'It is my destiny to rule this land just as my father held it before me,' Rufus told himself, smiling as he spoke. 'And it is my duty to do what I can to subdue the populace should they rebel against my rule.'

A sharp knock at the door brought the young FitzWilliam back to his senses. He jumped, startled like a boy who has been caught stealing butter from the family larder.

'Come in, chamberlain,' he said and his voice cracked a little. 'I am ready to speak with you.'

'Master Rufus,' Lonan began before he had finished bowing, 'I have the Lady Eilish O'Regan with me. She wishes to plead with you for the life of her husband's cousin Braonin. Her kinswoman, Neesh, is with her.' The chamberlain shot a glance at Rufus, warning him to be careful how he dealt with this matter.

Rufus had half expected Eilish would come to him. He was overjoyed he had enticed her to his room so easily and so quickly. He was unsure at first whether he should allow young Neesh to accompany her, but he was feeling very confident and certain it would profit him to seem magnanimous.

'You may tell them to enter,' the young FitzWilliam commanded eventually. 'I will speak with them.'

'Master Rufus,' Eilish pleaded as soon as the door opened, 'Braonin is a good man with a clear record of service to your family. It is ludicrous to suspect him of being a heretic or of inspiring folk to rebellion. He is no traitor. He is the chancellor appointed by your brother to control the accounts in his absence.'

'I am aware of that, Lady Eilish,' Rufus answered with sympathy in his voice, 'and it pains me more than you know that I have been forced to arrest him. But you saw for yourself how Braonin struggled with one of my soldiers to set the heretic Cinneach free.'

'He was doing what he thought was right under the circumstances.'

'Come now, my dear lady,' Rufus soothed, 'Cinneach is a Culdee. That is undeniable. And Braonin was aware of the man's crimes when he helped him to escape.'

'Yes,' Eilish conceded, 'it is true Cinneach is one of the Culdees who have been declared anathema. But Braonin is not one of those men. The very idea of treason is abhorrent to him. He is one of your brother's most faithful supporters.'

'I would like to believe you, Eilish,' Rufus sighed sincerely, 'I really would. But the mass of evidence before me does not point to Braonin's innocence.'

'He is the chancellor of the estate,' Eilish cut in, the desperation showing in her voice. 'If you imprison him, you are going against the wishes of your lord and brother. The tenants are already expressing fear that you might be about to seize the estate for yourself.'

Rufus dropped his jaw in surprise. Then he looked directly into her eyes. 'I am deeply hurt by that suggestion,' he declared as he held up his hand in protest. 'I am merely doing my duty as a knight of the realm, nothing more. Cinneach is a traitor already condemned by a royal court to hang. Braonin assisted in the escape of an outlaw. As a true knight I am bound to follow the letter of the law.'

'Master Rufus,' Lonan interjected, 'the only evidence you have of misconduct on Braonin's part is his willingness to stand up for Cinneach against one of your soldiers. Surely you must realise we were all taken in by this seanachie? Would you arrest me also if it could be proved I spent my evenings in his company?'

Eilish looked at the chamberlain, surprised that he had

turned against Cinneach. Then she realised he felt no need to defend the Culdee, who was free and would most likely leave the estates quickly now he was a hunted man. It was better to argue Cinneach was the guilty one and the many people he had befriended were innocent of wrongdoing.

Rufus looked the chamberlain sternly in the eye. 'I would not hesitate to arrest any man I thought a traitor,' the young FitzWilliam stated.

'Braonin was no less shocked than anyone else,' Lonan went on, 'when Father Conlan denounced Cinneach. It was the last thing we all expected. I am sure that now Braonin has had time to think about the situation, he would agree his actions were foolish.'

'I believe you are right,' Rufus relented. 'For if even you were taken in by the Culdee, it only proves how skilful a liar Cinneach is.'

'Then you will consider letting my husband's cousin go free,' Eilish pressed, 'and give him another chance to prove his worth to the estate?'

'Considering Lonan's arguments,' Rufus said slowly as if he were considering the proposition carefully, 'I will let him free. But you must understand I would have to review his position as chancellor. I am sure my brother would agree with me on this. I must act prudently so Robert still has an estate to return to when he comes home from the crusade.'

'Lord Robert appointed Braonin as chancellor,' Lonan reminded Rufus, 'after long discussions with the tenants. Braonin was considered to be a choice acceptable to all parties. If you replace him, it would only be fair to find another person trusted by both sides to perform the duties of chancellor.'

'That will be difficult . . .' Rufus began and he squinted his eyes as if he were in pain.

'I could do the job,' Eilish cut in. 'Robert would have

appointed me were I not a woman and as such inferior in the eyes of the King.'

'Yet I do not consider you inferior,' the young FitzWilliam eagerly replied, allowing his expression to relax again. 'Indeed, I would be happy to have you perform the duties of chancellor. But I would be hesitant to agree to such an arrangement if my brother has already vetoed the idea.'

'Master Rufus,' the chamberlain sighed, clearly frustrated there seemed to be no easy answer to this problem, 'earlier today you asked my judgment on a certain matter.'

Rufus glared at the old man, silently warning him not to mention the matter in front of Eilish. Neesh blushed in horror that Lonan had brought up the incident in her cousin's presence. Lonan sighed loudly, showing his displeasure at being placed in such a difficult situation.

'Please hear my judgment regarding this problem,' the chamberlain went on tersely. 'Eilish would be a far better chancellor than Braonin, that is certain. But more than this, to imprison Braonin would only cause the tenants to distrust you. In time they may be inspired to defy you or a chancellor of your own choosing. Let Braonin go free. By all means strip him of his office for his foolish behaviour. He should have acted with more discretion.'

Lonan stepped closer to the young FitzWilliam and softened his tone. 'But let him go free. Such an act will reassure the tenants you are not intending to take the lordship by force. And it will show you are willing to forgive minor misdemeanours. I beg you to remember the discussion we had this morning. Forgiveness can wash away the stain of guilt. And then one's life may begin anew.'

Rufus smiled, nodding his head in total agreement, inwardly overjoyed that events had taken such a favourable turn. The young FitzWilliam noticed his fingers tingling with excitement. He suddenly realised he was being offered a perfect opportunity to work alongside Eilish and insinuate himself into her life. If she were the chancellor of the estate, the tenants would accept her rulings without question. And in time, Rufus told himself, he would be able to bend her to his will in all matters.

'You are right, of course,' the young FitzWilliam stated. 'And I really have no stomach for keeping men in gaol simply because they made one mistake. We have all made errors of judgment in our time. And forgiveness is the salve that cures the festering sores of guilt.'

Then Rufus stepped closer to Eilish to look her in the eyes. 'I am sure you would make an excellent chancellor,' he told her. 'Perhaps when Braonin has once again proved his loyalty, he may seek reinstatement. If Robert ever raises any objection to my decision, I will take full responsibility. After all, he could not have foreseen this situation. And you are right, it would not be fitting for me to take over Braonin's duties. That might be seen as an attempt on my part to gain control of the treasury and the estates.'

'So you will release Braonin?' Eilish beamed, wondering briefly whether she had misjudged this man.

'It will be done immediately,' Rufus agreed. 'And all the charges will be set aside. I will speak with Father Conlan about it now.'

'Bless you, Master Rufus,' Lonan said gravely, imagining he saw a real change coming over the young FitzWilliam. 'Your father would be proud of you for this act of charity and forgiveness.'

Rufus nodded, slightly disgusted by that thought but careful not to let his true feelings show. 'I suppose he would be proud, wouldn't he?' he laughed.

The army of King Richard the Lion Heart marched on to Jaffa the next day. But before they reached the city word arrived from the garrison. The infidel commander was ready to talk terms with the King of England. The Christian knights and soldiers were jubilant at this victory. But Richard understood Saladin's plan.

Even if the Christians secured the city immediately, it would be another two weeks before they were ready to march on Jerusalem. In that time Saladin could marshal his forces without the need to defend Jaffa. The King of England was an experienced enough soldier to realise that his lightning invasion was grinding to a halt. Saladin would soon have the upper hand in this war.

Robert decided to leave his small force under the command of the Templars. That released him, Donal and two other knights to ride to the castle in the south with Henry St Clair's dispatches. They set off two days after the battle of Arsuf.

The road was difficult, the land inhospitable. The horses tired easily on the badly maintained roads. The small party often had to dismount and lead their war-horses, so the going was painfully slow. Besides which, they could only travel in the late evening and early morning. The terrible heat of the day was unbearable for both man and beast.

Saracen patrols were few, but countless bandits travelled the land in search of plunder. Robert's party encountered several small bands of these wild desert men, though none of them would have dared approach three armoured knights and a sergeant-at-arms. Donal, however, did not know the awe in which western knights were held by the local tribespeople and so he never felt safe. He was always on his guard, day and night.

A wild wind storm blew up on the third day of their journey, forcing them to seek shelter in a rock crevice at the foot of a mountain pass. That evening the gale died down and they travelled on through the night.

As Donal rode he thought constantly of his home in Cúil Ghréine. He pictured the green hills, wooded valleys, the gentle River Clonough flowing sweet and pure to the sea, and the snowfall that had sent them on their journey. This land could not have been more different.

'It is as though God has visited some curse on this country,' the chieftain said to Robert as they climbed a steep rocky path. 'Everything is dry, parched and brown. Some of these hills are as red as if they were on fire.'

'I heard a tale,' the lord answered, 'from a seanachie called Cinneach. He told me of the Grail Cup which was guarded by the Fisher-King. But the king was wounded in the thigh and so his kingdom began to wither until it turned into a wasteland.'

'I know Cinneach well,' Donal replied, frowning, 'but I have not heard this tale.'

'We are in the midst of that wasteland, Donal,' Robert went on. 'This is the country of the Fisher-King who guards the Grail.'

'What is the Grail?' Donal asked, self-consciously attempting to pronounce the strange word.

'Some say it is the cup from which Christ administered the wine of the last supper. Others claim it is the chalice in which drops of the Saviour's blood were gathered. In any case it is surely a magical vessel which can cure any illness. It offers eternal life to those who are deemed worthy to guard it.'

The chieftain saw Robert's eyes glaze over as he spoke of this wonder and he suddenly realised that the Grail was the real reason his lord had come to Outremer.

'I am yearning for my home,' Donal murmured, diverting the conversation. 'This land is the Devil's own country. We have not seen a flowing stream, a bush that was truly green or grass on any hill since we left Arsuf. The goats are thin, the people haggard, the earth cries out for nourishment. God must have cursed these folk.'

'Perhaps we are coming close to the castle of the Fisher-King,' Robert mused. Donal fell silent, understanding his master cared nothing for the hardship they were suffering. All that was important to Robert was his holy quest for the Grail.

On the evening of the sixth day Lord Robert consulted the detailed map he had been given and tried to reckon their position from the landmarks. He had been warned of the difficulty he might experience in locating this valley, but Robert had never really believed finding a great castle in the middle of the desert would prove difficult.

On the morning of their seventh day the party took shelter in a cave. It was just big enough for the horses and for the four men to find a cool place to sleep in the midday heat. Robert could not rest, however. He was excited about arriving at the community of the Order of the Temple and eager to experience their way of life first-hand.

A few hours before noon he slipped away and climbed to the top of a rock near the cave. There he spent the morning mapping out the area in an attempt to find the concealed entrance to the valley. In the late afternoon he returned to his comrades with his news.

'It is very well hidden,' the lord announced triumphantly, 'but I managed to get quite close to the gate without being observed. There are soldiers everywhere. At first I thought they were Saracens. They are clothed in long flowing infidel robes. But do not fear, underneath these garments they wear the surcoat of the Temple. At the change of watch the sentries passed their outer robes over to the next watchmen.'

'Let us go then,' Donal sighed. 'Perhaps tonight we will rest in a room with clean blankets for our covers and straw in our mattresses. We might even get ourselves a decent meal. I am tired of eating dry bread and smoked meat.'

'The Knights of the Temple do not indulge themselves in wasteful luxury,' Robert explained. 'You will be lucky to find anything but wooden beds for your comfort, though the food will certainly be of a high standard, I am sure.'

As soon as they had saddled their horses they set out for the gates to the fortification. A narrow path led down to the valley floor through a dry riverbed of hot sand over which the horses had to be led. Just beyond the lifeless stream the track widened and there Robert raised his hand to halt the small company.

'The entrance to the castle is just ahead,' he declared, but before he had finished speaking, a dozen crossbowmen appeared on the road in front of them. They were followed moments later by a dismounted knight dressed in a white surcoat. The warrior had drawn his sword and was barking orders to his archers.

The crossbowmen formed two ranks, the soldiers at the front kneeling and the remainder standing behind. The knight stepped forward to challenge the intruders.

'You are trespassing on the lands of the Temple,' the man bellowed. 'Turn back and I will spare your lives.'

'I carry letters to the commander of the garrison and to a monk known as Geoffrey d'Acre,' Robert explained. 'We have travelled many miles to come here. We have news of King Richard's victories in the west of Outremer.'

'Do you carry the seal of the Temple?' the knight asked. 'For you are not dressed as one of our brethren.'

'I have come here on the recommendation of a high-born knight of the order,' the lord went on. 'He suggested I visit this castle to decide whether I would take my vows as a Knight of the Temple.'

The knight in charge of the watch turned to one of the crossbowmen. 'Sergeant, keep them here while I check with Lord St Clair.'

'Aye, master,' came the reply. The sergeant of the bowmen stepped forward to lower his crossbow at Lord Robert as his commander disappeared into a rocky crevice.

Donal rode forward to stand his horse beside his master's mount.

'Did you hear that?' the chieftain whispered under his breath. 'The knight told his sergeant he would go and check with St Clair. Does it not seem strange that the commander of the castle has the same name as the warrior who sent us with these letters?'

'Perhaps the commander is Henry's brother,' Robert offered, shrugging his shoulders, 'for Henry could not possibly have reached this place before us. I know he was intending to sail to France in a few days' time. Unless he has changed his mind.'

'I have a bad feeling about this,' Donal replied, glancing left and right to see if there was anywhere they might shelter if the crossbowmen loosed their arrows. 'Something is not quite right here.' With that he spurred his horse on a little to speak with the sergeant.

'What's the name of your commander?' the chieftain asked.

'Stand your ground!' the warrior yelled, raising the bow to his shoulder. 'Come no further or I will let fly an arrow at you,' the sergeant barked. The other crossbowmen raised their weapons to the ready at the same time.

'Calm yourself, brother, I was merely asking a question,' Donal protested, noticing the warrior's black sleeves beneath his surcoat. 'What is your master's name?'

'Henry St Clair,' the man answered. 'I thought you had letters for him. You should know his name.'

'I was just making sure we had reached the castle we were instructed to find,' Donal explained. 'Your master has not been seen for a long while,' he added slyly, hoping to glean as much information as possible.

'The lord has been here for over six months. No man bar a messenger or two and the knight Guy d'Alville have left the fortification in all that time.'

'And is there any news of Henry's brother?' the chieftain added.

'His brother died at the battle of Jerusalem years ago,' the sergeant answered, dropping his heavy bow to his hip again. 'That's common knowledge.'

'I had not heard,' Donal smiled and then turned his mount around and let it saunter back towards Robert.

'Did you hear that?' the chieftain whispered to his lord. 'Something is very wrong here. This man who calls himself Henry St Clair must be an impostor.'

'I have a feeling you may be right,' Robert agreed. 'Many men among the Templars in King Richard's army knew our Henry by name or had been captive with him in Acre before the King's victory.'

'And that sergeant is wearing black sleeves under his tunic,' Donal pointed out. 'Templar sergeants wear brown surcoats. And common soldiers of the Temple are forbidden to wear either white or black. We must be very careful. It would not be wise to hand the letters over to this man. If he is an impostor he will recognise the real St Clair's signature. We cannot risk letting him know we have met Henry St Clair. If he believes we know his secret, our lives could be in great danger.'

'You are right as usual, Donal,' Robert admitted. 'There is something strange afoot here and, until we know what is going on, it is better to feign ignorance.'

'What are you two muttering about?' the sergeant yelled. 'If you have something to say, speak it loud enough for me to hear or shut it.'

'How dare you speak to my lord in that fashion?' Donal replied, turning his horse around to face the bowman. 'Just who the bloody hell do you think you are?'

The sergeant raised his crossbow to his chest and pulled back hard upon the trigger. In a flash an iron-tipped bolt sped toward Donal, embedding itself deep in the shoulder of the chieftain's horse. The animal cried out in pain and fell forward, throwing Donal off balance so that he tumbled into the dust.

When the chieftain came to rest he was winded. His horse was lying motionless. Donal raised himself painfully on one elbow and looked up in fury at the bowman.

The sergeant laughed as he introduced himself. 'I am Giles of Turneux, sergeant-at-arms and captain of the guard, that's who I think I am.'

The other bowmen laughed along with their comrade but the merriment dropped from their faces as Donal rose to see to his horse. The animal was dead, mercifully slain straightaway with a very accurate bow shot.

Donal knelt beside the animal that had served him so well. When he had caught his breath he stood up, grabbing a handful of dust as he rose.

'You bastard!' the chieftain screamed, casting the dirt at the sergeant. Then in a flash he was running for the man with such force that the other bowmen scrambled to get out of the way. In seconds Donal had the sergeant by the collar, pushing him to the ground with such violence that the man bellowed in pain as he hit the dirt.

'You will bloody well pay for that horse, you senseless little bully!' Donal demanded. 'It cost my kinfolk dearly and I've no mind for them to suffer at the hand of a stinking wretch like you.'

Donal sank his boot into the man's stomach and grabbed his collar once more. But before the chieftain could drag the sergeant to his feet, a voice rang out from the rocks.

'Stand away from that man,' someone commanded, 'or I will order the archers to slay you immediately!'

The chieftain snarled, pushing the man into the ground

once more. Then he turned around slowly, realising the danger he was in.

'That's right,' the voice soothed. 'Now move away from the bowman, back towards your lord.'

As soon as Donal was close to Lord Robert's horse the voice from the rocks spoke again but in a softer tone. 'I have been told you have letters for Henry St Clair. Is this true?'

Robert was about to speak but thought better of what he was going to say. After a short pause he answered carefully, 'No. I carry letters for a knight called Geoffrey d'Acre, whom I have been told is garrisoned here. I was advised to come here to see for myself how the Temple Knights live. I am thinking of taking my vows.'

'I overheard your man's conversation with the sergeant of bows,' the stranger declared. 'Where did you hear the name Henry St Clair?'

'I heard his name in Acre a week ago,' Robert replied. 'I was told he was the commander of this garrison. I was given to understand he had been a captive of the Saracens for many months.'

'Have you ever met with him before?' the voice queried and Donal looked to Robert. This question confirmed their fears.

'I know him by his reputation only,' the lord said finally.

At that a middle-aged man with grey hair and a long beard stepped out from the rocks. 'You will hand me the letters,' he insisted.

'I regret that I may hand them to none but Geoffrey,' the lord replied. 'I have sworn it as my duty and I must respect the wishes of the knight who sent me here.'

'What manner of man writes to Geoffrey d'Acre?'

'I was charged by the chamberlain of the King of England to deliver the parchment,' Robert lied. 'I have no idea who wrote upon it.'

'If you enter this castle, you may not be allowed to leave for many months,' the grey-haired man explained. 'We cannot risk the Saracens discovering this sanctuary.'

'I am on the business of the King of England,' Robert repeated, 'surely you would not hold me against my will? Perhaps it would be better if I rode back to Richard's court and told him I was refused admittance? He has likely subdued all the Saracens in the Outremer by now and would not think twice about bringing a force of his Templars here to question your hospitality and perhaps regarrison the castle.'

'There will be no need for that,' the other man replied hastily. 'You are welcome to stay here until we can be sure it is safe for you to leave. I am merely warning you that it might take some time before I can be sure you will not be attacked. I cannot risk revealing the whereabouts of the entrance to my stronghold.'

'Will you allow me to deliver my letters personally to this Geoffrey d'Acre?' the lord inquired.

'Naturally,' the grey-haired man replied with a slight bow of his head.

'And what about my sergeant's horse?' Robert added. 'I trust it will be replaced.'

The man smiled again and there was a hint of something in the expression that chilled Donal to the bone. 'I give you my word,' the man promised, 'as surely as my name is Henry St Clair.'

Chapter Fourteen

Lord Robert released the two other knights who had travelled with them as escort from any further duty to him. The commander of the garrison, who called himself Henry St Clair, invited the pair to stay on with Donal and Robert. But the Lord of Bally Raine insisted these two warriors were needed in the Christian army. In the end the grey-haired knight relented and allowed Robert's escort to return to Acre.

'If your master has gone to France when you arrive,' the lord instructed them quietly in parting, 'make your report to the King.'

The two men turned their horses around at the gates to the fortress and headed directly back toward the coast. Robert had had no chance to speak to them of his fears or to give them any message to pass on. But he knew these men well. They had been with him since the beginning of the crusade and would surely sense that all was not what it seemed at Mont Salvasch. Robert was counting on them to make enquiries with the leadership of the Temple.

The lord still had no idea why two very different men shared the name Henry St Clair. Was it coincidence or did one of them have something to hide? As his escort disappeared out of view Robert had a sudden fear that he had made a terrible mistake. He glanced at his sergeant-at-arms for reassurance but Donal was scowling.

The chieftain climbed on Robert's horse to sit behind his lord as the grey-haired knight rode ahead of them. Within fifty paces they were on the paved road which led directly to the inner sanctum of the castle.

'Why did you agree to enter the castle?' Donal whispered when he was sure no-one could overhear their conversation.

'There is something amiss here,' Robert answered. 'This man knows we will be missed if we are gone too long. He will not dare keep us.'

'We will only be missed,' the chieftain pointed out, 'if our escort returns safely to Acre.'

'What do you mean?'

'If this man is an impostor,' Donal explained, 'he will very likely have our two friends murdered on the road before they can bring word to King Richard.'

Robert blushed. He had not for a moment considered that possibility. Then he realised how foolish he had been to trust this strange knight.

'We are among Templars,' the lord stated, trying to sound relaxed. 'What could possibly be of a threat to us? Perhaps we are worrying too much. The answer to this riddle may very well prove innocent. We will laugh about it later.'

'Promise me you will be careful what you say,' Donal said sternly.

Robert did not have a chance to reply. At that moment twenty footmen appeared out of nowhere at the side of the path. The soldiers waited until the horses passed by, then disappeared again across the opposite embankment.

Within minutes the party passed through the intricate concealed defences which were constructed to resemble the natural walls of a mountainside. The lord dared not speak any more to Donal for there were sentries everywhere and he did not want to risk being overheard.

The deeper they travelled into the maze of embankments, the more Robert marvelled at the workmanship of this fortress. He wondered, awestruck, how such ramparts could have been carved out of the solid stone of the hills.

When they came to a great chasm, the knight who called himself Henry St Clair halted his warhorse and dismounted. Then he led the animal to the very brink of the wide gorge. Robert and Donal shrugged shoulders at each other and dismounted; the next thing they knew they were gazing into a seemingly bottomless abyss.

'Welcome to the Castle Mont Salvasch,' Henry said formally.

But Robert and Donal could not see any castle and both men looked at the knight in confusion. Henry laughed at them.

'It is well hidden, is it not?' the old knight smiled broadly.

Donal could see nothing but solid stone on the other side of the chasm where the mountain rose almost straight up to the sky. But then he noticed a warrior with a spear in his hand looking down from the top of the rocks opposite.

On the other side of the gorge the flat wall of stone moved slowly and a large rectangular section seemed to fall away from the mountainside. Robert's horse panicked, rearing up in dismay. Donal held the bridle to stop the animal bolting away in fear.

'Stand aside,' Henry advised them, 'or the drawbridge will crush you under its weight.'

It was then Donal realised what the great rectangle of stone must be. The drawbridge of the castle was perfectly concealed to look as if it were a part of the mountainside.

'I am sure you understand why we do not encourage visitors to this place,' Henry explained. 'The fewer men who know the secrets of this place, the easier it is to defend.'

'This castle is a miraculous structure,' Robert gasped.

'You have only seen the outside,' Henry commented. 'Wait until I introduce you to the inner workings of my fortress.'

When the drawbridge had come to rest, they crossed it, leading their horses on. After fifty paces the three men had passed under the great arch which supported the workings of the bridge. There were soldiers everywhere inside the battlements and Robert guessed there to be twenty or thirty on the battlements alone.

They did not walk far before Henry handed his reins to a groom. The servant took hold of Robert's reins also but the lord resisted at first.

'You need not fear,' Henry assured him, 'my servants will take good care of your animal.'

Robert relented and the groom led the two horses away. Then the lord turned to see a great keep with a dozen stone steps leading to its front door.

'Forgive me,' Henry apologised, 'I fear I must leave you here. I am expecting a visit from a high official of the order and must attend to his needs. My servants will see to your accommodation and your every need. I trust you will join me at dinner this evening and at prayers afterwards.'

'And where may I find Geoffrey d'Acre?' Robert asked politely. 'To hand him the letter that I carry.'

'I will be speaking with him shortly,' Henry replied. 'Are you sure you would not trust me to give it to him?'

'I vowed no man would touch them but Geoffrey himself,' Robert explained again, then realised his tone was very harsh. He did not want to arouse suspicion. 'I hope you understand,' he added politely.

'Of course,' Henry agreed. 'I will send young Geoffrey to your chamber. Your squire may lodge with the stable-hands.'

'He is my sergeant-at-arms and my chancellor,' Robert cut in. 'I would prefer he stay close by me. Unless you have any objections, he can share my chamber rather than lodge with the servants.'

'Very well,' the old knight agreed, bowing his head

slightly, 'I will arrange for you to have adjoining rooms. But once you have taken your oath to the Temple, you will have to observe all the rules of our order. The Grand Master frowns on any fraternisation between the servants and the knightly class.'

'I am a chieftain in my own country,' Donal declared. 'I am equal to any knight in rank and respect among my people.'

'Then perhaps you should consider taking the vows also,' Henry smiled, looking at Donal in amusement. 'Once you have established your credentials, of course.'

Then the knight took off his riding gloves and shook Robert by the hand, squeezing the lord's fingers tightly. 'I wish you a comfortable stay in my residence. If there is anything you need, please let my servants know and it shall be yours. As a Templar I am forbidden to wash my body, but should you wish to do so the servants will show you to the well where they conduct their ablutions. Good day.'

Henry turned smartly on his heel and hurried up the steps of the keep. When the great door closed behind him both his guests breathed deeply in relief. As they waited for St Clair's servants to show them to their rooms, neither man spoke to the other but both were wondering whether it had been an entirely wise decision to enter this fortress.

By nightfall Robert had washed and dressed in his fine green surcoat. He had polished his mail to remove the dust and mud of the journey and brushed his hair and beard. Donal spent the early evening writing a letter to Eilish by candlelight. He hoped Henry would consent to send it off with his next messenger to Acre.

'I promised my wife I would return within a year,' Donal confessed to his lord as he finished writing, 'even if that meant deserting you on the field of battle.'

'You must miss her very much,' the lord answered as he adjusted his armour, 'and I would not blame you if you did desert me. My desire to become a Templar has led you into this castle. I am certain there is something very sinister indeed about our host and his lodgings. I hope I have not led us unnecessarily into danger.'

'The stables are huge and full of horses,' Donal stated, staring out the window of Robert's apartments, 'but I have not glimpsed one single knight in the castle grounds, apart from the sentries on the walls. They are all common foot-soldiers. Certainly there are many knights lodged here. Where can they be?'

Robert moved to the window. He looked out on the courtyard where they had parted with St Clair. 'I am glad we did not give him the letters,' he said.

'I am sure he is not who he claims to be,' the chieftain agreed.

'There is a horseman riding up across the bridge,' Robert observed. 'Take a look at him.'

Donal stood up from his chair and moved around the desk to stand beside his lord.

'He's no Templar, that one,' the chieftain observed, 'not unless the dispatch riders of the order have taken to wearing black.'

'That man is a Knight of the Hospital of Saint John,' Robert declared.

As he spoke they both saw Henry St Clair rush out of the keep, straight up to the rider. The commander of the castle was obviously upset with this man about something for he was shouting at him from the stairs to get inside.

Robert and Donal did not see any more for in that instant there was a knock at the door to their chamber. The chieftain went to find out who it could be. As he swung the door open he saw a thin man sporting a sparse black beard and close-cropped hair. He wore a white Templar surcoat and a silver-sheathed sword which dragged on the floor behind him.

'I am Geoffrey d'Acre,' the young man said, introducing himself. 'I believe you have letters for me.'

Donal let the young man in and shut the door after him. 'Forgive me, Master Geoffrey, but would you be able to prove your identity?'

Geoffrey looked at the chieftain, raising his eyebrows.

'I am sorry to have to insist,' Robert added, 'but I am to hand the letter to none but Geoffrey d'Acre.'

The young man smiled. 'I don't believe I know your names.'

'I am Donal O'Regan, chieftain of Cúil Ghréine,' the sergeant-at-arms informed him, 'and this is my lord, Robert FitzWilliam.'

Geoffrey bowed low. 'I am honoured to meet you both. You are the first visitors I have had in many months, apart from that sly old fox, Guy d'Alville.'

'Can you prove to us you are Geoffrey d'Acre?' Robert insisted.

'I have my brother's sword about my waist and his ring upon my finger, but apart from these things I have nothing which proves my identity.' Then he suddenly remembered Godfrey's letter which he always carried. For a moment he faltered, questioning whether he should reveal his well-guarded secret to these strangers. Geoffrey half closed his eyes as he considered the possible consequences of letting this parchment fall into the wrong hands. But when he looked up again and saw Robert frowning in concern, Geoffrey decided to take a risk. These men, he reasoned, were not like Henry or Guy.

'I have this,' Geoffrey admitted. 'It is my brother's last letter to me.' He removed the letter from inside his surcoat and held it out for Robert to take.

The young lord unfolded the parchment, scanned it for a name and, satisfied, handed it back to Geoffrey, who sighed in relief. Robert obviously had no idea of the significance of the letter.

'How is it a Knight of the Order of the Temple is receiving dispatches from a rider dressed in the colours of the Hospital?' Donal asked.

'I am not sure,' Geoffrey answered cautiously. 'I have seen three riders dressed in this fashion in the last three months. Has there been another?'

Robert nodded. 'Just now in the courtyard, Henry St Clair received him.'

'I am not convinced,' Geoffrey stated, deciding to take a risk and trust these men, 'that Henry is all he claims to be.'

Donal looked to Robert and they both bit their tongues, realising that to speak of their suspicions to a stranger was extremely dangerous.

'What brought you to this place?' Geoffrey asked, sensing their anxiety.

'We were given letters for the commander of the garrison and for Geoffrey d'Acre from . . .' Robert paused, '. . . a knight who spent many years in Acre and claimed to know your brother well. He had heard a rumour you were staying here and asked that I seek you out.'

The lord went to his saddlebag to retrieve the letter. 'I have the ambition of one day becoming a Knight of the Temple myself,' he went on.

'Then do not choose to take the vows in this place,' Geoffrey warned, 'for no man leaves this castle unless Henry permits him to do so. The Master of the Order lives here, but he is a foolish old man with no will of his own. He is dominated by Guy d'Alville. That man is the real master of the order in Outremer.'

'And what brought you here?' Donal inquired, changing the subject.

'My brother, Godfrey d'Acre, was a guardian of the treasure of the Temple,' Geoffrey explained. 'He lost his life in Acre performing his duties.'

'Godfrey d'Acre!' Robert exclaimed. 'That was the knight

my father spoke of.' Donal nodded to show he remembered the tale William had told of his fight in the marketplace of Acre.

'You know something of my brother's death?' Geoffrey exclaimed.

'William FitzWilliam,' Donal explained, 'is Lord Robert's father. He was involved in a fight to defend a mysterious box that was being transported to the docks at Acre. The assassins murdered everyone but Godfrey d'Acre who was mortally wounded and later died in Lord William's arms.'

'Afterwards my father was charged with escorting the cargo to France,' Robert added.

'I can hardly believe my ears,' Geoffrey whispered excitedly, moving across the room to sit down at the desk. 'Forgive me but this news is rather a shock to me. So my brother was within the city walls of Acre when he died?'

'That is how I understood my father,' Robert confirmed, 'when he told the tale.'

'So Godfrey did not die during the siege of Acre at all,' Geoffrey deduced.

'I would not think so,' Donal cut in. 'Lord William was long gone from Outremer when the siege began in earnest.'

'Henry St Clair lied to me!' the young man spat and he thumped the table with his fist. 'I had a feeling all along that his version of events was untrue.'

'What was in the box?' Robert stammered, excitedly. 'I have been yearning to know that part of the story since my father told it to me.'

Geoffrey looked at both men in turn. 'The box contained a part of the Templar treasure,' he explained. 'Thanks be to God it was rescued from the hands of the enemy. Did your father not know what was inside the crate?'

'He did not look upon the contents,' Robert sighed. 'But I had an insight at prayer one evening in my private chapel,' the lord admitted shyly. This comment caught Geoffrey's attention and he sat back in his chair to listen.

'I dreamed the box contained the Holy Cup of the Grail,' the lord mumbled, expecting this knight to laugh at him.

But Geoffrey did not laugh. He leaned forward to share the secret of his own vision. 'The Virgin Mary herself told me,' he whispered, 'that the box contained the Ark of the Covenant.'

The two men stared at one another, each deadly earnest and both convinced of the truth of their experiences. Then they reached out, clasped hands and smiled as if they had known one other all their lives.

'Read your letter,' Donal cut in, handing the sealed document to Geoffrey, somewhat impatient with all this talk of visions. 'It may contain important news.'

The young knight hummed agreement, took the parchment from the chieftain and quickly broke the seals.

'Would you share it with us?' Robert asked. 'For it may answer some questions we have about this place.'

'I will,' Geoffrey nodded, and he commenced to read the letter word for word, quite convinced now that he could trust these men.

' "Dear Geoffrey," ' he began, ' "I was a great friend of your brother and have only just learned the sad manner of his death. The truth of it was kept from me during my long imprisonment. I will have departed the city of Acre by the time this reaches you. Should you come to Acre, inquire for the Most Excellent Scottish Knight of Perfection. He will know where I may be found. If you have not arrived before I return to Outremer, I will come to find you. Be extremely careful. Trust no-one but the knight who bears this letter. He fought alongside me at the battle of Arsuf and is an honest man." '

Geoffrey turned the document over in his hands examining the back. 'It is not signed,' he finished.

'Do you know the man who wrote this?' Robert asked.

'I have no idea,' Geoffrey muttered, confused. 'Don't you know his name?'

Donal cut in before the lord could answer, 'I believe we should open the other letter we carry.'

'That is dangerous,' Robert opined. 'If we are wrong in our assumptions, we could find ourselves charged with treason. For the time being it is better we keep the letter safe. I will decide later whether or not to read the contents.'

'Who was the knight who gave you these letters?' Geoffrey repeated.

'He told us,' Donal breathed, 'his name was Henry St Clair.'

Geoffrey's mouth dropped open and he put his head in his hands.

'I knew it,' he mumbled, 'I knew that there was something terribly wrong here.'

'We may be in great danger,' Donal observed, placing a hand on Geoffrey's shoulder to comfort him. 'We must leave this fortress before the commander of the garrison realises we have discovered his secret.'

'We will go to King Richard and tell him what we know,' Robert suggested. 'It is obvious the Saracens have infiltrated the Order of the Temple.'

'They are not Saracens!' Geoffrey laughed, but there was no mirth in his voice. 'The men we face are a force more dangerous than any King Saladin could send against us.'

'What do you mean?' the lord cut in.

'They are Hospitallers,' Geoffrey asserted. 'Knights of the Hospital of Saint John. Black knights.'

'The messengers,' Donal nodded, 'dressed all in black like the knights who started the charge at the Battle of Arsuf. They must have taken over this whole garrison. But why go to the trouble of posing as Templars? What do they hope to achieve?'

'They are seeking the treasure of the Temple,' Geoffrey explained, 'which my brother and Henry St Clair secreted somewhere in this fortification. They have taken the white surcoats of the Temple so as not to arouse too much suspicion. And they are likely trying to avoid open warfare with the Temple.'

'They must realise,' Robert scoffed, 'they will be discovered eventually.'

'We have discovered them,' Geoffrey pointed out, 'but this castle will prevent us from sharing the secret with anyone. They have gone to much trouble to convince me to help them find the treasure.'

'You?' Donal exclaimed. 'Do you know where the Temple treasure is hidden?'

'Not yet,' the young knight admitted, 'but I have some clues.'

'And what of the Saracens who murdered your brother?' Robert asked. 'Are the infidels helping the Hospital?'

'Godfrey was not killed by any Saracen,' Geoffrey declared. 'I am almost certain the men who tried to steal the cargo he was guarding were also Hospitallers, dressed as Saracen soldiers.'

'All the more reason for us to leave this place immediately,' Donal maintained. 'It is obvious these men will not want the truth of their deeds to go beyond Castle Mont Salvasch.'

'Are you hard of hearing?' Geoffrey sighed. 'There is no way for us to get out of this stronghold without the master of the castle knowing. I have been here for months. I have searched every room and corridor. This place was designed to confuse anyone who does not know their way around. There are blank corridors and concealed doors at every turn. Some passages are lined with mirrors that confound the eye. Only one who has been that way before can find the path through the maze.'

'All the more reason for us to act quickly,' Donal insisted. 'The longer we wait the greater the danger.'

Geoffrey put his head in his hands again. 'We cannot leave here without the treasure,' he said slowly. 'I cannot allow it to fall into the hands of the Hospitallers. I must continue the work of my brother.'

'Where is the treasure hidden?' Robert asked, and Geoffrey lifted his eyes to the lord.

'I do not know exactly,' the young man said, 'though I have a rough idea. I need to spend some time examining the chapel within the keep. I believe there is a passage concealed in the stonework which will lead me to a hidden vault. That is where I am sure the treasure has been buried. I have a letter from my brother and his last will in which he has written some clues. But I have not made much progress in deciphering his meaning.'

Geoffrey laid the will and the letter on the desk in front of him where Donal had been writing to Eilish. The chieftain and the lord leaned over to view the documents and Donal moved the candle so they could all see what was written on the parchments.

When both men had read the will and laid it aside, Robert and Donal took the other page to examine it for clues to the mystery. But neither man could recognise anything significant anywhere in the letter.

'I have been poring over this will for months,' Geoffrey admitted, 'and I have only discovered one thing of interest. There is a tomb behind the master's chair in the chapel which may have something to do with the verse about the hanged man. The knight on the tomb is depicted in a similar pose to that of this card.' He pulled out the smaller parchments with the pictures drawn on them.

Robert looked carefully at the cards but ended up shaking his head in utter confusion. 'Perhaps there is something contained in the letter from Henry St Clair,' the lord suggested.

'We should perhaps discuss this later,' Donal reminded them. 'We are expected for dinner with the commander of the garrison. It would be best not to arouse his suspicions by being too late.'

'And we should speak no more of this to one another indoors,' Geoffrey advised. 'It is safer if we discuss these matters in the courtyard where we cannot be overheard. Bertrand Guesclin will be present tonight, Robert. He is the Templar Master of Outremer.'

'Guesclin is not the Master of the Temple,' Donal interrupted. 'We have met the master. His name is de Braque.'

'Are you certain?' Geoffrey gasped.

Robert nodded solemnly. 'Absolutely certain.'

'Who is Guesclin then?'

'Another Hospitaller, I would guess,' Donal replied. 'After dinner we should go for a short walk in the courtyard to discuss what we are going to do.'

'It is obvious,' Robert stated, 'we should make some attempt to rescue the treasure of the Temple. But even if we discover this secret vault of which you speak, how are we going to get the treasure safely out of the castle? It is nine days' ride to Acre at least, longer if we have fully laden horses. That is assuming we can find a way out of this place without being discovered. There is nothing more we can do now but to gather as much information as we can. We will make our move when the time is right.'

'You will help me then?' Geoffrey exclaimed.

'Of course we will,' Robert assured him. 'I came to Outremer to join the Temple order because of a dream. It was a dream in which the Virgin spoke to me of the Holy Cup. Until this day I did not understand the true meaning of that vision. But now I think she was sending me to aid you in your task. We will help you, Geoffrey d'Acre.'

'And in any case,' Donal added more pragmatically, 'it would seem we are as much prisoners here as you are. We might as well work together to plan our escape.'

'Do you have parchment and ink?' Geoffrey asked.

'There before you on the table,' Donal pointed. 'What are you going to write?'

'Henry will want to see the letter I received,' the young knight explained. 'I cannot risk him reading the parchment you brought. So I will compose one of my own and leave it in my cell where he can view it at his leisure.'

Geoffrey took up the glass-tipped pen, dipped it in the inkwell and scratched the first lines, speaking them aloud as he did so, ' "To my dear Geoffrey," ' he began, ' "from your friend and confessor Father Anthony. It is almost a year since we last met . . ." '

Eilish awoke in the middle of the night long after her hearth fire had died down to a soft glow. She opened her eyes in alarm at the sound of someone walking in the snow outside the house. Everyone in the clachan should have been asleep at this hour. The healer sat up in her bed in the loft and looked down on the interior of the O'Regan house. A horse neighed in the darkness. A child began to cry. All else was silent. So after a few minutes Eilish allowed her weary body to drift quickly back into sleep.

The next thing she knew the whole room was filled with a bright orange glow and a thick grey mist. The healing woman struggled against her exhaustion to open her heavy eyelids. It was a battle to throw off this annoying dream. And her body was so exhausted she could hardly fight off sleep.

'I have been working too hard,' she mumbled aloud. 'I always have nightmares when I overwork and do not eat.'

In the next instant Eilish took a deep breath of smoke. Her eyes immediately widened in horror. If this was a dream, she told herself, it was altogether too real and frightening.

In seconds the chieftain's wife threw off the covers to sit groggy and confused on the edge of the loft. The whole ceiling of the house above her was a smouldering mass of thatch. In places it shone with the bright reds and yellows of the fireplace. Like a slap in the face the scene that faced Eilish shocked into her consciousness.

Her house was on fire.

'Fire!' she screamed at the top of her lungs. Then she became aware of other voices calling out in the night. The house was full of dense impenetrable smoke. Flames had caught the thatch and were licking the roof beams. Glowing embers dropped like a shower of falling stars onto the beaten earth floor below her.

Eilish watched still slightly dazed as the sheepskin cover on her bed smouldered then burst into flames. The searing stench of burning hair caught at her nostrils. The healer covered her face with her hands to protect herself from the sickly smell.

Eilish grabbed her cloak and threw it about her hair so her golden locks would not catch fire for the air was full of burning sparks. Clothing hung upon the walls ignited as if touched by some magical fire spell. One of Donal's old tunics literally burst into flames.

Eilish slid down the ladder from the loft in a matter of seconds. She hurt her ankle as she fell but ignored the pain. Disbelief locked her into inaction. All the healer could do was watch, stunned, as the thick roof timbers began to smoke. Then, one by one, they were taken over by the flames.

'My house,' Eilish sobbed, shoulders drooping in defeat. 'My life. Everything I have is here.' Then she remembered her husband. 'Donal!' she screamed. 'Where are you?'

There was no answer at all, though she could hear other voices nearby calling out, cursing and crying.

'Donal!' she shrieked as the sweat poured from her face. Then she heard her name called back in answer.

'Eilish! Where are you?'

'I'm here,' she replied, coughing. 'Over here by the ladder.'

Amid the grey smoke and chaotic rain of sparks she glimpsed the figure of a man with his head wrapped in a blanket. He had his hands over his face to filter the air so he could breathe. As he made his way towards her the healer waved her arms at him.

'Eilish! Is that you? Where are you?' he called desperately.

'I'm here!' she cried, still frozen to the spot in shock. The man finally grasped her arm and her heart sank. It was not Donal who had come to rescue her. Eilish took the man's collar and shook at him until he put his hands up to stop her.

'Where is Donal?' she yelled over the dreadful noise of the fire.

'He is gone,' the man bellowed back at her.

'Gone?' she screamed in terror, misunderstanding his meaning. She could not believe her husband was dead. This must be a terrible dream, she told herself.

'Gone to the crusade with Lord Robert,' the man replied, shaking her back. 'Eleven months now it's been.'

Eilish suddenly felt a pain as if she had been kicked hard in the stomach. She trembled, resisting the urge to double up in agony as she began to retch. Then, as her mind struggled out of the haziness of sleep, she recalled Donal was indeed far away on the other side of the world. He was fighting against the infidels in the army of the King. The healer looked into the face of the man who had come to rescue her.

'Braonin,' she cried, 'what is happening?'

'Cúil Ghréine has been attacked,' he shouted as he tried to drag her toward the door. 'The bastards have set fire to every roof in the clachan. We must get out of here before the roof gives way, or we'll be trapped by the flames.'

Eilish instinctively reached for the little leather pouch that hung about her neck. But she could not locate it and with mounting horror she realised the half-penny her husband had left her was gone.

Panic gripped Eilish like a fever. She could face losing anything, any petty possession, but not the one thing that linked her to Donal. With a flick of her arm she broke away from Braonin and before he could stop her, she had half climbed the ladder to the loft.

The bedcovers were already burning fiercely. The ladder was smouldering. Her bare hands began to burn on the timber but she did not give up. High up near the roof the smoke was so thick the healer could not breathe. But she was certain that the little pouch must have slipped off her neck in her sleep.

'Are you mad?' Braonin screamed, fear transforming his reddened face. 'We have to get out of here.'

'I must find the penny,' she called back to him, spluttering from the choking smoke. Her voice was swallowed in the deafening noise of creaking roof timbers. Eilish said a few more words but her voice was drowned out as a large section of the ceiling buckled slowly and began to collapse.

The healer's footing slipped on the ladder and Braonin only just managed to catch hold of her. She fought him as if her life depended on it.

'Let go!' Eilish screamed.

Convinced she must be dazed by the shock of the fire, Braonin grasped her ankle firmly. When he was sure he had a good grip, he dragged her off the ladder kicking and screaming.

'We must go now!' he insisted in desperation. 'There is no time for saving anything more than your life!'

'The penny,' Eilish sobbed, reaching her hands toward the loft. The roof groaned again and began to sag in the centre. Braonin realised they had but seconds to escape this burning building alive. The disintegrating roof would certainly trap them in the inferno.

'We are leaving!' he stated again and put his arms around her waist. 'Now!' he shrieked at the top of his voice.

'I must find my penny,' she repeated, 'so that Donal can find me again.'

'Our lives are in danger!' Braonin bellowed, dragging her to the door. 'If we do not leave this instant, the only thing Donal will find when he returns is your well-tended grave.'

Those words seemed to jolt Eilish. Instantly she came to her senses. She leaned on Braonin and shivered. 'All right,' she said in a subdued tone.

He put his arm around her to shelter her from the falling ash and embers. Then he threw his cloak around them both as they searched for a way out in the clouds of dense smoke.

When they found the door it was jammed shut and would not open. Braonin let go of his cousin's wife for a second to give the timbers a great kick. The door buckled slightly but it took two more blows before it collapsed and fell outwards.

When the way was clear, Braonin grabbed Eilish and bundled her out of the cottage. Moments later he leapt out after her to land heavily in the snow. As he rolled over to look for the healer, the roof of the O'Regan house gave way with a mighty deafening crash that shook the ground.

The next thing Eilish knew she was lying on the cold snow-covered ground some thirty paces away from the burning building. Braonin had picked her up and carried her to safety. As soon as she was out of harm's way, he ran off to help the other tenants who were trying to put the fires out.

Eilish stared back at her house, a sickening nausea overwhelming her. Her stomach still felt bruised, as if she had been kicked by a horse. Then she was coughing and retching violently, spewing out wads of soot-black mucus that had settled on her lungs.

When the retching eventually subsided, Eilish lay on her back to steady her breathing, at the same time trying desperately to divert her attention away from the terrible disaster.

Finally, after what must have been a long while, Eilish felt as if she could breathe easily again. The pressure on her chest subsided a little, so she sat up. Her breath billowed out of her in a cloud of steam into the night air. It was as if the smoke she had swallowed was issuing out from her mouth.

The healer looked up toward her home and gasped in shock. Every building in Cúil Ghréine was on fire. Some of the houses, like her own, were already little more than smouldering shells. Other thatched roofs had only just caught fire as sparks from the burning buildings travelled on the breeze.

Then Eilish felt her stomach sink again as she remembered Neesh. In a flash the healer was struggling to get back on her feet. Her young cousin had been sleeping in the house with her. Eilish feared she must have been overlooked when Braonin came to search the building. She got to her knees and struggled to rise, but she barely had the energy to cry out the girl's name.

'Neesh!' she wheezed through a dry throat raw from the smoke.

A gentle arm wrapped around the healer's shoulders and hugged her close. 'Calm yourself,' the young woman's voice soothed, 'I am here. There is nothing to worry about. No-one has been injured. Everyone managed to escape their houses before the fires got out of control.'

'What happened?' Eilish sobbed. 'How did this calamity come upon our homes?'

'The fires were deliberately lit,' Neesh informed her. 'Drink this,' she ordered, putting a wooden cup full of icy cold water to the healer's lips.

Eilish looked into the girl's eyes, overwhelmed with relief that her cousin was safe. She sipped some water. Then the healer woman lay shivering in Neesh's arms for a long while. She was too distraught to think of anyone else. Too broken-hearted to tend to other folk.

When the shock began to subside, Eilish wept for the loss of her house. Then she wept for her neighbours' loss. And finally the healer woman wept for the loss of her one remaining connection to her husband. The little trinket he had given her before they parted.

The tilecutter's penny.

Next morning smoke from the burning houses of Cúil Ghréine could be seen as far away as Shelton, even though the clouds were low and there was a heavy snowfall after dawn.

Rufus and ten of his soldiers galloped toward the clachan an hour after sunrise. They set out from Bally Raine as soon as the watchmen at the castle reported the red glow of fires in the distance. By the time they arrived, the flames were all doused so Rufus ordered his warriors to help where they could with the cleaning up.

Snow was still drifting down when the young FitzWilliam

reined in his horse at the bottom of the cow path which led to the clachan. By that time Braonin had gathered most of the cows and sheep at the end of the muddy track, ready to be driven on to Clonough.

'How did this happen?' Rufus demanded as he struggled to retain control of his mount. All the warhorses were on edge in the drifting pall of smoke.

'A group of strangers came upon the settlement in the night,' Braonin replied, exhaustion clearly visible on his face. 'They threw burning rags up onto the roof thatch. I cannot think why anyone would do such a thing.' His voice cracked as he spoke, betraying hopelessness and confusion.

'Were they armed men?' Rufus pressed. 'Or peasants?'

'Peasants, I would reckon,' Braonin answered. 'I caught sight of a couple of them. Their dress was poor and they had no armour of any kind. And when I challenged them the bastards ran into the woods, too cowardly to confront me.'

'Bandits,' Rufus hissed, 'rebels.'

'What are you saying?' Braonin snapped.

'This is the work of Cinneach the Culdee, my friend,' Rufus spat. 'The man you helped escape from my soldiers. Yours is not the first settlement he has put to the torch in his ill-conceived campaign against Norman rule.'

Rufus paused for a second to look around him at the damage. 'Was anyone hurt at all?' he asked.

'No-one was injured seriously,' Braonin stated. 'Just a few slight burns and a great deal of grief.'

'I will arrange for food to be sent down from the kitchens at the castle,' the young FitzWilliam decided without a hint of emotion.

This unexpected gesture surprised Braonin but he viewed the offer with immediate suspicion.

'Where is Eilish?' the Norman inquired, sensing Braonin's hostility. 'Is she safe?'

'She is as well as can be expected, Master Rufus,' Braonin

answered tersely. 'The last I saw she was rummaging through the remains of her house searching for anything that might be salvaged.'

'Take some rest, my friend,' Rufus advised.

'I will rest when the animals are seen to and safe from the weather,' Braonin replied, unhappy at being addressed as friend.

'If you bring your people to the castle this evening, I will arrange a meal and temporary accommodation for anyone who needs it.'

'Thank you, Master Rufus,' the hunter answered. 'Most of us will lodge with our kinfolk at Clonough.'

'But you and Eilish must stay in the castle,' the Norman insisted. 'It is the duty of a lord to see to the wellbeing of his people.'

With that Rufus dismounted, leading his horse up the bohreen to find Eilish. Braonin was left to stand among the cows, wondering whether the young FitzWilliam now considered himself to be the Lord of Bally Raine. At the same time he realised that all the folk of Cúil Ghréine would now have to rely on the man's generosity.

When the Norman came to the house Eilish had shared with her husband, he tied the reins of his horse to a post. Then he removed his war helm and carefully stepped in among the smouldering cinders. Two women knelt among the ruins a few paces away. They did not look up so he made his way straight toward them.

'Eilish,' Rufus called, 'is that you?'

The healing woman turned to see who had called her name, 'I am here,' she replied. 'Who needs me?' Then she recognised the young FitzWilliam. 'Good day to you, Master Rufus.' Neesh stood up, putting an arm around her cousin's waist to support her.

'I am sorry you have lost your home and all your possessions,' Rufus began. 'It is a terrible thing.'

'It was only a house,' the healer answered bravely. 'It can be rebuilt. But who would have done such a thing?'

'I fear it was Cinneach and his band of rebels,' Rufus declared, 'seeking revenge upon the estate for my attempt to arrest him. I am just going now to see if I can track them down and bring them in to be tried for this crime.'

'Cinneach?' Eilish stammered, finding the suggestion hard to believe. 'He surely would not do such a thing. He is a priest of the Culdee faith. They are forbidden to wage war or to harm innocent people.'

'It seems that prohibition has little meaning for this man,' the young FitzWilliam stated. 'He has been involved in wars and insurrections against the rule of law for five years or more. In Bally Cahone he set a church afire. Everyone within perished. They were burned alive.'

Neesh winced at the thought of such a thing, finding it difficult to imagine that the man she had met at the chapel all those months ago could have been responsible for such a wicked deed. The girl grabbed tightly at Eilish's arm as much for her own sake now as that of the healing woman.

'Do not fear,' Rufus soothed. 'It is unlikely he will return here again. I will post a guard on the houses to ensure those savages do not return to loot the ruins. When we catch him he will be very sorry for his actions.'

'There is no need for a guard,' Eilish interrupted. 'There are plenty of folk nearby who can keep watch through the night. Not that we have anything left worth plundering.'

'But surely you are not thinking of staying here tonight?' Rufus remarked. 'There will be more snow today and the weather is not likely to improve for some weeks. I would like you to come to the castle for a few days, at least until the shock of this disaster has abated.'

'That will not be necessary,' Eilish replied proudly, brushing the golden strands of hair from her eyes. 'I have my family here and I would rather stay with them.'

'You have nowhere to shelter,' Rufus reasoned, 'no food and very few clothes. You risk freezing to death in the open. I insist you come to the castle before sunset. I will send a cart over to fetch you and any of your kinfolk who need somewhere to sleep. You, Eilish, will have my brother's chamber until other arrangements can be made.'

'You need not concern yourself,' the healer declared.

'It is my duty to see the tenants are protected,' Rufus reminded her. 'I have failed in my duty this night because I became complacent. A good lord would have kept a watch through the night. I have neglected the maintenance of the signal beacons. Cinneach took advantage of my incompetence. I am responsible for your plight. If you were to die of the cold, it would be one more black mark against me as provisional Lord of Bally Raine. How would I face my brother on his return?'

Eilish was about to protest again but in that instant her eye caught the glint of a small metal object in the ashes. She bent down quickly to sift through the soot for it. Her hand found the object and she brushed it with her shawl to clean the blackened surface. Then she grasped the trinket tightly in her hand.

'I found it,' Eilish sighed with relief, tears welling up in her eyes. Then she realised Rufus was still waiting for her reply. 'I will come to the castle,' she relented, 'and I thank you for the generous offer of your hospitality.'

A smile stretched across the face of the young FitzWilliam and his eyes sparkled as he turned to leave. 'I am glad you have decided to lodge with me for a while,' he told her enthusiastically, 'I am looking forward to your company. Now I must go. If I am to find the men who committed this crime, I had best start before the snow covers their tracks. If you will excuse me,' he bowed.

In a few moments Rufus was trudging across the blackened ground toward his horse, his dark blue cloak flapping in the breeze. The Norman did not mount immediately. As he untied the reins he summoned his sergeant to his side to discover the latest news. The familiar form scurried through the snow to stand at attention before his master.

'Were any of the men injured, Quicktoe?' Rufus whispered.

'No, my lord,' the large warrior answered with a grin, eyes staring to the front and chin up.

'Where are they now?'

'The other party should be well on their way back to the castle,' Quicktoe reported lowly. 'They were going to dump their clothes in the river before changing back into their armour and livery.'

'Very good,' Rufus hummed. 'Once again you have proved yourself, Quicktoe. My brother was a fool to treat you as he did. I knew I would not regret repatriating you into my service.'

'Thank you, my lord,' the warrior beamed.

'Let the soldiers know I am pleased with their work,' Rufus added, slapping his gloves playfully on the warrior's chest. 'There will be a little gift for each man with supper tonight.'

'You are most generous, my lord,' Quicktoe replied.

'Now,' the young FitzWilliam whispered hoarsely, taking the warrior by the sleeve, 'I want your party to make a great show of trying to find the insurgents. Search every building on the estate. Act as though everyone is under suspicion. But do not cause any harm. It is vital no-one suspects my soldiers of this attack. There are to be no arrests. Do you understand? For now it suits me to have a renegade band of rebels on the loose. Every little disaster will be blamed on them. And the myth will unite the tenants behind me.'

'Yes, my lord,' Quicktoe smiled, cheeks glowing in the cold.

'I want these simple folk to believe,' Rufus went on, 'I

am doing everything in my power to catch the men who did this.' Then he added as an afterthought, 'If you manage to find Cinneach or some of his followers, let them be but inform me immediately. I want to wait a while before we arrest him.'

'I believe I know where the Culdee may be found,' Jon Quicktoe assured his master.

'Then get to it. Do not waste another breath,' the young FitzWilliam commanded. 'Enlist the tenants to aid you if you wish. That will help cement the impression that we are all facing a common enemy.'

'As you command, my lord.' The warrior brought a hand across the sheathed hilt of his sword in a snapped salute. Then Quicktoe ran through the settlement, calling the soldiers of his party to assemble.

Rufus swung himself up into the saddle with confidence. High on the back of his warhorse he took one last look at the gathering of buildings that had once been known as Cúil Ghréine.

Then, satisfied everything had gone exactly to plan, the young FitzWilliam rode off home towards the castle of Bally Raine. But he had to struggle with himself all the while not to let the pleasure show on his face.

'Soon,' Rufus whispered to himself, 'soon I will be Lord of Bally Raine in more than name alone.'

Chapter Fifteen

When Eilish, Braonin and Neesh finished collecting what few of their possessions remained, they climbed onto the cart Rufus had provided for them. Then, amid another snowstorm, they set off for Bally Raine.

'Did you find the penny, Eilish?' Braonin asked as they travelled the rough road leading away from their smouldering homes.

'I did,' the healer replied cheerfully. Then Eilish blushed when she thought of how she had endangered them both in her frantic search for it. 'I am sorry, Braonin,' the healer mumbled, 'I do not know what I was thinking of. It was stupid to be looking for a small piece of brass when the house was burning down around us.'

'I understand,' Braonin soothed. 'It was a special sign between you and Donal.'

'You speak as if he were dead,' Eilish blurted, surprised to hear Braonin refer to her husband in the past tense.

'I did not mean to,' the hunter retorted, 'but it is nearly a year since he left on Lord Robert's adventure and we have not had any word at all from the Holy Land.'

'A year,' Eilish repeated, under her breath. 'The time has gone so quickly. Donal promised he would be home within a year if the chapel was finished.'

'The chapel will be complete within a few short weeks,'

Braonin informed her. 'Father Conlan is preparing the building for its final consecration.'

'Then I will write to Donal,' Eilish asserted, 'and tell him the news. It is time he was back here in his homeland. We will need him to help rebuild Cúil Ghréine. His duty is with us now.'

'I pray no harm has come to him,' Braonin added, 'and that he is still alive and well.'

'Of course he is still alive,' Eilish spat. Neesh put an arm around the woman and held her close to comfort her. Braonin turned away. He felt the tears gathering in his eyes but he knew he had to say what was on his mind.

'Eilish,' he began, 'it is nearly a year and we have had no word. No letter. Nothing.'

'They are fighting a war in a far-off land,' she shot back sharply. 'I am not surprised he has not had time to write.'

'Eilish,' Braonin tried again, knowing there was no way to say what was on his mind without causing her pain, 'before he left, Donal asked me to pass a message to you.' He paused, feeling awkward and trying to gauge whether she was listening. 'Donal told me if anything happened to him he would send you a sign.'

'What are you talking about?' Eilish demanded, pushing Neesh away.

'Your husband told me if he was killed in battle, the half a penny would be sent back to you with a letter describing the manner and place of his passing.'

Eilish swallowed hard, trying to control her tongue. She knew Braonin meant well in telling her this, but after everything else that had happened, this new piece of information was too much to think about.

'There has been no sign,' Eilish replied, gritting her teeth. 'There has been no letter. Donal is alive! He will return to me. Now, I will hear no more of this foolish talk. I am the chieftainess of Cúil Ghréine and the chancellor of Bally

Raine. I cannot allow my kinfolk and the tenants to see me upset. I must set an example to them. Tonight I will write a letter to my husband. I know he will be back among his people as soon as he can find a ship to carry him.'

With that she leaned back against Neesh who held her close again and stroked her hair. Then exhaustion took hold of the healer and she shut her eyes, drifting into a fitful sleep.

Robert and Donal had spent four months as the guests of Henry St Clair at castle Mont Salvasch. Each day Lord Robert requested leave to return to King Richard's army. And every day the commander of the garrison politely but firmly refused.

The two men were not official members of the garrison so they were not required to walk guard duty or to perform any other military tasks. Their days would have been idle had it not been for Geoffrey's quest to discover the whereabouts of the Templar treasure. The three men explored as much of the castle as possible. Robert also spent many hours in the master's library studying the old texts while Geoffrey trained with sword and axe. But Donal could not find any activity that would ease his troubled mind.

Then one morning the master of the castle summoned Robert and his sergeant-at-arms to his chamber. Robert, clothed in the white of a postulant, led the way into the room. Donal, dressed in the brown tunic of a Templar sergeant, followed after his lord.

Henry St Clair lifted his head from the papers he was reading as they closed the door behind them. 'Good morning, gentlemen!' he declared cheerfully. 'I am glad to see you both looking so well.'

'Good morning, St Clair,' Robert answered tersely. 'I hope you have called us in to tell us the road is open again and that we may leave.'

'How long has it been?' Henry smiled, trying to make light of the situation.

'Far too long,' Donal replied, echoing the feelings of his lord.

'We were expected in Acre three months ago,' Robert lied. 'I am certain there will be many people of that city concerned for our safety.'

'Yes, I am sure,' Henry replied and his smile lost its sincerity. 'I took the liberty of writing to the chief Templar of Acre,' he told them, 'to inform him you had been delayed indefinitely. I doubt anyone will be too worried as long as you are in my company.'

'I must ask you to allow us to leave this fortress,' Robert insisted, frowning. 'I came to this land in the hope of fighting the Saracens. I do not think Saladin's army is very likely to appear outside these walls. So I would like to be freed to go where the fighting is taking place.'

'What fighting?' Henry replied. 'King Richard of England has just concluded a truce with Saladin. The war for Outremer is over. The Saracens still hold Jerusalem but they are allowing Christian pilgrims to visit the holy places. King Richard is in Acre preparing to return home. The war is over.'

'Then we must return to Acre also,' Donal snapped. 'I have a wife at home and my kinfolk need me on the estate.'

'I have no wife and family,' Henry said, holding up both his hands to calm the chieftain, 'but I do understand how you feel. I am afraid your departure will have to wait for a few more days at least until my scouts have confirmed the roads are safe for journeying.'

'A few days,' Robert repeated, clearly disappointed. 'You have said that before.'

'This time I mean it,' St Clair answered sternly.

'And then we will be able to leave?' Donal cut in.

'I promise,' Henry asserted. 'Unless Lord Robert has decided to take the vows of a Knight of the Temple.'

'I will wait until I have returned to Acre and concluded my business in that city,' Robert stated. 'For now I wear the robes of a postulant and that is enough. It is better I return to the headquarters of the Temple. Since I have been held in this fortress against my will, I prefer not to make any decision here.'

'I beg you, my lord,' St Clair said softly, 'do not think it was my intention to keep you here as prisoners. You have been well fed and clothed and all your needs have been met. If the military situation had allowed, I would have escorted you to Acre myself. Unfortunately this fortress is in a unique position. It is still a well-kept secret.'

'Is it so secret that even the Hospitallers do not know of its existence?' Donal asked provocatively.

Henry laughed loudly. 'The Knights of the Hospital may know about this castle but they would never be able to use it to their advantage. Many aspects of this fortress are closely guarded Templar mysteries. This castle is a legendary fortress but, at the same time, a puzzle which cannot be solved by ordinary means.'

'Following the directions of our informant,' Donal went on, 'we did not have any trouble discovering the front gate. Why would anyone else?'

'You merely stumbled on the forward defences,' Henry smiled. 'The fortress is a long way from those walls, as you may remember. But you have reminded me of an unanswered question which I wish to put to you again. Who was your informant?'

'I have given my word never to divulge his identity,'

Robert replied carefully. 'I am sorry, but my honour will not allow me to give you that information.'

'If you look at it from my point of view,' Henry retorted, as if he had expected that particular reply, 'it is very suspicious that you are so unwilling to reveal the source of your information. I am, after all, a high-ranking officer in the Order of the Temple. Anyone who would have given you such directions would be known to me. You would not be risking any lives by telling me what you know.'

'I hope you will understand that I cannot,' Robert replied.

'You have spent quite a lot of time in the company of Geoffrey d'Acre,' St Clair went on, smiling wryly now as he changed the subject. 'I would like to know your impressions of him.'

'He is a sober young man,' Robert answered, surprised at the question, 'who is trustworthy and loyal.'

'But loyal to whom?' Henry asked. 'Is he as faithful to the Temple as he claims to be? Or does he have misgivings about his calling? Could he have been recruited to the Hospital before he came to be under my care?'

'He is devoted to the memory of his brother and to the white surcoat which he is honoured to wear. I have nothing but admiration for him,' the lord concluded.

'Has he spoken to you of the Templar treasury?'

'No,' Robert lied, 'he has not.'

'I know that he has,' St Clair said, turning away from the lord to look out the window of his chamber. 'I would like you to do me a favour,' he went on without giving Robert a chance to protest. 'I would appreciate it if you would let me know any information Geoffrey might volunteer regarding the treasure of the Templar order. You see,' the old knight explained, 'I have reason to believe his brother may have been involved in a plan to strip the order of its riches. There is some evidence that Godfrey d'Acre was transporting the plundered Temple gold back to France when he was killed by a group of assassins. It has even been suggested that he was in fact a traitor who had sworn allegiance to Hospitallers.'

'I would be very surprised,' Robert stated bluntly, 'if this young man were involved in such a conspiracy. I think you have misjudged him terribly.'

'In that case there can be no harm in pressing him for information to put my mind at rest,' Henry shot back, turning on his heel to face Robert and Donal once more. 'It would not be proper,' St Clair stated, 'for me to make such enquiries. Naturally Geoffrey would suspect my motives. But you and he have become close friends. It would not be out of place for a comrade to broach the subject.'

Robert breathed in loudly through his teeth, realising he had little choice but to agree to this request. He did not want to fall under any suspicion himself. 'I will speak with him,' the lord promised. 'And if I glean any information I feel would be of help to you, I will let you know immediately.'

'Make no mistake, brother,' Henry added with a hard edge to his voice, 'any information you may be able to supply would be of great value to me. I must settle this matter within the next three days or, I am afraid, more stringent measures will have to be taken with your friend. I have never been in favour of torture myself. It is a barbaric way to conduct business. But the Master of the Order has decided we have wasted enough time with young Geoffrey. We are beginning to think he is more deeply involved in his brother's treachery than we had originally thought.'

'He is a Knight of the Temple,' Robert gasped, shocked that Geoffrey might be subjected to the rack or the branding iron. 'Surely you would not resort to such a severe recourse.'

'I must use every means at my disposal,' Henry explained, 'if I am to retrieve the treasure of the Temple.'

The old knight paused for a moment to indicate to Robert

that his mind was made up. Then he sat down at his desk and went on. 'Geoffrey has been concealing letters from me that may contain information crucial to the discovery of the treasure. Convince him to share the contents with me. Assure him no harm will come to him if he is open and honest about all he knows.'

'And if I cannot convince him?' the lord inquired.

'I will have no choice but to bring in the brand and the rack,' Henry replied with shallow sadness in his voice. 'So young to have his bones broken on the stretching table. But some men are born stubborn. And of course I would have to request your attendance at the subsequent Temple court which would try the young man. You would be required to give evidence as to his character.'

'And this trial could take many months,' Robert smiled grimly, catching the threat in Henry's words.

'It would take time to assemble the necessary knights to form a tribunal,' St Clair explained. 'I would imagine we could start proceedings after the observances for Christmas are finished. Such a trial would probably take six months to complete, but I would not be able to guarantee you could leave here until the court handed down its findings. I suppose that would force you to postpone your journey to Acre indefinitely.'

'It would,' Robert agreed, frowning and clearly angered at this blatant manipulation.

'Then you will do your best,' Henry sighed as he returned his attention to the papers before him.

'I will,' the lord answered, resigned, hoping Henry would not suspect otherwise.

'I knew I could rely on your wisdom and steady judgment,' St Clair added. 'Let me know the moment there is anything to report. And, by the way, if you serve me well in this, I will personally recommend you to the Grand Master of all the Temple.'

Henry stood, indicating the audience was ended.

'There is one last thing,' Donal interjected. 'Some months ago I sent letters to my home through your messengers. I was wondering if any word had come for me from my wife?'

'No,' Henry stated flatly. 'But that is not surprising. Often a message from France can take up to a year to reach the hand of the one for whom it was written. You come from a land at the end of the earth, so I would expect a much longer delay. I must say good day to you now,' he ended, ushering them to the door, 'I have an audience with Master Guesclin which must be concluded before lunch.'

Robert bowed. He and Donal left the room, but as soon as the door shut behind them they stood silently looking at one another. After a long while the pair nodded to each other without needing to say a word. Then Robert and his sergeant went off to search urgently for Geoffrey d'Acre.

Chapter Sixteen

A week after Saint Brigid's Day a messenger galloped wildly along the road to Bally Raine. The rider had already gone to Cúil Ghréine in search of Eilish O'Regan but had only found a small collection of deserted burned-out buildings. So he decided to ride on to Bally Raine. There he would be able to pass the letters into the safekeeping of the lord of the castle until Eilish could be found.

As chance ordained, Rufus was out riding with five of his soldiers when the messenger approached them on the road. The young FitzWilliam stopped the stranger and asked him what his business might be on the estate. The reply brought an instant grin to the face of Rufus FitzWilliam. Once again, he told himself, good fortune had shone down upon him.

'I will take the letters to Eilish O'Regan,' Rufus offered. 'She is staying at the castle of Bally Raine with me at present.' Then it came to him that this man might prove useful. 'You will accompany me to my fortress,' he ordered the messenger. 'I wish to reward you for carrying these letters.'

'Yes, my lord,' the man replied, bowing his head.

Rufus ordered his men to complete their rounds of the estate without him and to make a full report upon their return. He parted company with his soldiers to ride with all speed back to the castle, eager to read what Donal had written of his travels in Outremer.

The young FitzWilliam commanded the messenger to wait in the great hall while he retired to read the letters. As soon as Rufus was inside his chambers he bolted the door. Then he sat down in front of the fire which had been stacked with wood to warm the room quickly. He tore open the seals, holding the first folded parchment closed. Then, relishing the exercise, he inspected the first document carefully.

'"My dearest Eilish,"' he read aloud, '"Lord Robert and I have been witness to a great battle at the town of Arsuf in which King Richard led the charge to victory. I have never seen such death and destruction in all my life. I am still quite sickened by it.'"

Rufus smiled broadly then continued reading. '"We have seen the Temple Knights in action. There is nothing so fine as their valour and calmness in the heat of battle. Lord Robert has decided to take his vows as a knight. This will mean the estates will be handed over to the Temple. Robert agrees this would be better than allowing Rufus to take the lordship.'"

The young FitzWilliam growled under his breath, more determined than ever that Robert would not pass the estates on to anyone but him. Rufus found a cup by his chair and filled it with warm red wine from a jug set by the fire.

'"This campaign has been bitter and bloody but it soon will be over,"' he read on. '"King Richard's army is sweeping over the land like a sandstorm and the Saracens cannot withstand the onslaught. For now, you will be happy to know, Robert and I are out of the thick of the fighting. We are at present lodged in a castle in the south-east of the Kingdom of Outremer, awaiting the pleasure of the commander of the garrison. We have been told it is far too dangerous for us to travel at present. We may be here for up to three months. Do not be alarmed if I do not return to you by Saint Brigid's Day as I promised. I will come home as soon as we can leave this fortress and a ship becomes available to take me back to France.'"

Rufus sipped his wine, his mind already working on the problem of Donal's and Robert's possible return.

'"How is work on the chapel going?"' the young FitzWilliam read on. '"Say a prayer for Mathúin the next time you are at Bally Raine. And give my greetings to Balek the tilecutter. I still look each day at my half of the penny he cut for us. I hope you still look on your half in the same way. I asked Braonin to let you know I would arrange for my half of the coin to be returned to you should anything happen to me. I hope he has explained what this means. I will return to you soon, as long as there are no more battles to be fought. Your loving husband, Donal."'

Rufus tore the seals and bindings off the letter and set them aside. In seconds the parchment was engulfed in the intense orange flames of the fire. In less time than it took to read them, Donal's words were consumed completely. Rufus turned his attention to the second letter once again, ripping the seals open in his haste to read the contents. This letter was much shorter than the first.

'"My dear Eilish, this letter must needs be short. The situation has not improved. We may have to remain in this castle for some time longer. Do not worry. All will be well. I shall return to you. Your husband Donal."'

Rufus salvaged the seals then threw this letter into the flames. He watched it disappear as the fire destroyed it.

'I must act quickly,' Rufus decided. 'I must secure this estate in my name as soon as possible.' The young Fitz-William stood up and went to a chest in the corner of the room.

After rummaging through the contents, he pulled out a rolled sheet of parchment and opened it carefully. It was the letter his father had intended to send to King Henry. The letter which effectively disinherited Rufus and all his descendants. The young FitzWilliam read the decree once more before striding back to the fire. With a last look at the parchment, he tossed it into the flames to share the fate of the other letters.

Now he had committed himself to this desperate plan, there would be no turning back. He had destroyed all evidence of any wrongdoing on his part. He told himself he had set things in motion and now the future would only be what he made it.

It was time to purge himself of all those who might oppose him. There was only one weakness in his strategy. He recognised it needed to be dealt with before he could move on to take the estates for himself.

Rufus sat down at his desk, took up pen and parchment and wrote a letter in his finest hand addressed to Eilish. In the short note he explained Robert and Donal had been killed at the battle of Arsuf. He then went on to state that Donal's penny had been entrusted into the hands of the messenger who carried this note. Then Rufus carefully folded the parchment and sealed it with the wax from the first letter.

When he was satisfied with his handiwork, he went to the water barrel that stood in the corner of the room. There Rufus immersed the letter for a few seconds. Certain the parchment had been wet through, he laid it down before the fire to let it dry a little.

Then he set to work on another letter addressed to himself giving the same account of things. This letter he also immersed in water. Then he sat it alongside the first forgery to dry.

A long while later Rufus broke the seals on the second letter, drained his cup of wine and went to the door to summon the messenger and Lonan the chamberlain.

The messenger was knocking at the chamber door a short while later and Rufus ushered him in to stand by the fire.

'I have a task for you,' the young FitzWilliam declared as he tossed a small but heavy leather pouch at the man. Rufus raised his eyebrows, encouraging the messenger to take a look. The man untied the leather cord around the top of the bag, his eyes bulging out of their sockets as he looked inside.

'There is more gold where that came from,' Rufus informed him, 'if you are willing to work for me.'

'I am your servant,' the messenger replied without hesitation.

When Lonan arrived shortly after, Rufus was still speaking with the messenger. So the old chamberlain waited patiently outside the chamber until the door swung open.

'Good day to you, chamberlain,' Rufus greeted the old servant. 'Please come in and take a seat by the fire. I have something very important to discuss with you.'

Lonan crossed the room, nodding to the messenger who was standing by the window. The chamberlain sat in the seat Rufus usually occupied and started to warm his hands before the fire. The young FitzWilliam leaned up against the wall near the fireplace and faced his guest.

'Would you like a cup of wine?' Rufus offered, lifting the jug to show there was plenty.

But Lonan shook his head. 'I try to refrain from any drink other than ale before sunset, Master Rufus,' he explained. 'I have found it is the only way to keep my wits about me.'

'Very wise,' the young FitzWilliam nodded with a glint in his eye, but he did not hesitate to pour himself a cup of the warm red liquid.

'Why have you summoned me, master?' Lonan said, slightly uncomfortable at the silence.

Rufus sipped his drink and then frowned. 'I have had some very bad news,' he explained, trying to sound as upset as possible. 'Some very disturbing and sad news. I don't quite know how to tell you.'

'It is Lord Robert,' Lonan sighed, 'is it not?'

'Yes,' Rufus went on. 'I have had a letter.'

'May I read it?' the chamberlain inquired.

'I will tell you what it says,' the young FitzWilliam cut in.

'There is no need,' Lonan declared in a defeated voice, 'I think I know what the news is.'

'Oh yes?' Rufus prompted, more than a little relieved the chamberlain did not want to inspect the parchment.

'Lord Robert has been killed,' the chamberlain stated with certainty and resignation.

'And Donal also, I am afraid,' Rufus added. 'In a great battle at the town of Arsuf.'

Lonan crossed himself, put his head in his hands and quietly contemplated the memory of the two men. This reaction took Rufus by surprise. He had not realised there would be such grief at Robert's death, and he suddenly understood that he would have to be seen to mourn also if his story were to be believed.

'Forgive me, master,' the chamberlain begged, wiping his eyes, 'I have known your brother since he was a boy. And as for Donal, it is terribly sad his wife will never see him again.'

'I have not told Eilish yet,' Rufus said gravely. 'I do not know how to break it to her.'

'She is a brave woman,' Lonan assured him, 'and I believe she half expected this would happen. And it is past Saint Brigid's Day. Donal had promised to return to her by then.'

'I believe there was a token Donal sent to her,' Rufus stated. 'Unfortunately it would seem this trinket was lost at sea in a storm.'

'That news will grieve her as much as anything,' Lonan replied, 'for the possession of the token would have proved to her without doubt that her Donal was dead. How did you learn of the token's loss?'

Rufus snapped his fingers and the messenger stepped forward. 'I was one of two messengers sent to this land from Normandy,' the man said. 'My companion carried the token in a pocket about his waist. I carried the letters. He was washed overboard in a storm a week ago. The token, a half-coin I believe it was, went to the bottom with his body.'

Rufus nodded and the messenger stepped back. 'We must think of Eilish first,' Rufus suggested. 'She may be a brave woman and strong but she is only human. This will likely hit her hard. I need your help in breaking it to her.'

'It is a shame,' the chamberlain sighed with conviction, 'that your father precluded you from the lordship. For though I agreed with his judgment at the time, I have since come to see you would have made a good lord of these estates.'

'There is a new king now,' Rufus reminded Lonan, 'a younger son who was treated in the same way by his father as I was by mine. I do not think it will prove difficult to convince King Richard that I am the only candidate for the lordship of Bally Raine.'

'Lord William would never allow it, Master Rufus,' Lonan stated, shaking his head. 'He would rather see the estates broken up between the northern lords.'

'Father need never know,' Rufus replied, clipping his words so there was just a hint of displeasure in his voice. As the young FitzWilliam spoke, Lonan felt a cold chill of suspicion ripple down the back of his neck.

'May I see the letter you received?' the chamberlain asked.

'It is here,' Rufus replied, picking the parchment up from his desk. Lonan took it but noticed the hand that passed the letter to him was trembling slightly.

'You should step closer to the fire,' the chamberlain advised warily, 'the cold has brought a tremor on you.'

Then Lonan unfolded the parchment and read its contents, raising an eyebrow as he came to the last few lines.

'The letter is unsigned,' Lonan noted. 'Is this not unusual?'

'I have been told it is common practice,' Rufus lied carefully, 'in case the documents should fall into enemy hands.'

'I cannot see what failing to sign such a letter would achieve,' the chamberlain opined. 'If this parchment had come into enemy hands, it would hardly matter to the Saracens who had written it.'

Lonan turned in his seat to face the messenger. 'Who gave you this parchment?'

'Lord Eustace FitzWilliam,' the man replied. 'The letters arrived in Normandy from Outremer a month ago.'

'I am sorry,' the young FitzWilliam went on, 'that I do not know who wrote this.'

'Then we must send to the Holy Land for confirmation,' Lonan concluded. 'Until we are assured this is not some forgery it would be inappropriate for us to tell Eilish anything.'

'There was a letter for her also,' Rufus interjected. 'I have not given it to her yet because I wanted to speak with you first.'

'I will pass it on to her,' Lonan asserted. 'You may give the letter to me.'

'I would rather take care of this myself,' Rufus declared. 'As lord of the castle it is my duty.'

'You are not Lord of Bally Raine yet, Master Rufus,' Lonan snapped.

Rufus sighed heavily, sure the old chamberlain was deliberately trying to block him. 'I will be lord of this estate,' Rufus grunted, losing his patience. 'Robert is dead and Donal is also gone. Bally Raine needs a lord and Eilish needs a husband.'

'So that is what you intend, is it?' Lonan chortled. 'You

thought you could fool me with a forged letter and a wild story of Donal's token being lost at sea. Well, you might have been able to trick someone like Eilish, who has little experience of the world beyond this estate, but I have served Lord William for twenty years both here and in Normandy. I know that a letter without a signature and in a poor hand is very likely a forgery. I also know some men will do or say anything in order to gain that which their heart desires most.'

Rufus snapped his fingers at the messenger. 'You may go now,' he said as calmly as possible. 'I wish you a safe journey home.' The man bowed, thanked the young FitzWilliam and then scurried off as quickly as he could.

'You have misjudged me,' Rufus hissed as soon as the messenger was gone.

'I have judged you too well!' the chamberlain spat. 'You have done some terrible things in your life all to satisfy your lust for wealth, power and . . .' the chamberlain paused, remembering what had befallen Neesh, 'for women. But this is far worse than I thought you capable of.'

'You are wrong!' Rufus insisted, trying desperately to conceal his rage. 'I have not forged this parchment. It was handed to me along with the letter for Eilish on the road earlier today. You have spoken with the man who carried it. Half-a-dozen of my soldiers were with me when I met him.'

'A dispatch rider does not earn very much,' the chamberlain pointed out, 'so it would not take much to bribe him. And those finely dressed thugs of yours would say anything to protect you. They may be well behaved right now, but I'll warrant they can't wait to get on with the sort of work their kind enjoy most. Rape, plunder and arson.'

Rufus sucked the air sharply in through his teeth at this last comment. Lonan started at the sound and then suddenly made a connection between the fire at Cúil

Ghréine and what Rufus had said about Eilish needing a husband.

'Your soldiers set fire to the O'Regan houses,' the chamberlain said slowly as the awful realisation hit him. 'You manipulated the entire situation so you would have Eilish all to yourself in this castle. No wonder you agreed to her taking over as chancellor from Braonin.'

Lonan noticed Rufus was avoiding his eyes. 'My God!' he exclaimed. 'You had Braonin arrested to remove him from the office of chancellor. It was always your intention to replace him with Eilish.'

'You are wrong, Lonan,' Rufus declared, his voice breaking, his rage on the verge of exploding. 'This estate needs a lord until we can be sure Robert is dead.'

'Eilish is the chancellor,' Lonan pointed out. 'You are not fit to be lord of a dunghill.'

Rufus looked down as the old man spoke, hearing an echo of his father in the words. Then he felt the cold hands of anger grapple with his senses, choking the reason out of him. The young FitzWilliam struggled to contain himself, to control the temper rising in him. But he had withheld his rage for too long. He had spent too many months hiding his true motives from everyone. He was sick of pretending to have high ideals, tired of putting up a false front of decency and compassion.

'You have hated me since I was a child,' Rufus whispered. His eyes flashed with hatred and Lonan sat back in his chair in terror. 'You poisoned my father's thoughts against me. You made me look like a spoiled, evil-minded child while my brother was always cast as the rightful heir and the pure heart.'

The young FitzWilliam strode forcefully across the room to where the chamberlain was seated, trembling by the fire. 'Whenever I had any dreams or ambitions, you stood in my way,' he shouted, venting his rage. 'Well, you will not stand in my way ever again,' he vowed, screaming now. 'Never again!'

In the next second Rufus had his hands about the old chamberlain's throat. Before he understood what he was doing, the young man found himself slowly squeezing the life out of Lonan.

He almost reneged. He almost let go of the old man when he thought of what it meant to kill the chamberlain of the castle. But Lonan had angered him beyond reason. Here was the one flaw in his plan. This man had to be destroyed.

The chamberlain was too shocked to do anything but grasp the wrists of his attacker. He struggled in vain to draw air into his lungs. Rufus watched the old man's eyes roll back into his head as the life seeped away and Lonan slipped into unconsciousness.

Only then did Rufus realise he had gone too far. If he killed the old man outright by strangling him, there would be obvious marks upon the murdered man's throat. So he made sure Lonan was not quite dead.

When he was sure the chamberlain was still breathing a little, Rufus went to the door and bellowed out for the servants at the top of his lungs. The old cook was first to answer the summons. She came rushing in to see Lonan slouched in the chair, unconscious but still alive.

'What happened?' she screamed in horror.

'We have had very bad news,' Rufus explained, 'from the Holy Land.'

The cook crossed herself. 'Just like it was with Mathúin,' she cried.

'He was struggling for air and grasping at his throat to breathe,' Rufus went on. 'I do not know what to do.'

'I'll rush out to find Eilish,' the old woman said, 'she's a midwife and she is a healer.'

'I will watch over the old man until you return,' Rufus confirmed. 'Make haste,' he called.

As soon as the cook left the chamber Rufus went to his bed and carefully chose a large pillow. As he returned to the fireside he dusted it out to make it a little softer. Then he pressed it hard over Lonan's face until he was certain the old man had stopped breathing altogether. When Lonan was obviously dead, Rufus calmly lifted the lifeless corpse forward and placed the pillow behind the old grey lolling head.

Satisfied with the arrangement of the body, Rufus stood looking at the chamberlain for a short while before he picked up his cup and wine jug. The young FitzWilliam poured himself a good draught of the red liquor, then raised it to Lonan.

'The Lord of Bally Raine is dead,' Rufus announced, 'long live the Lord of Bally Raine.'

He drained the cup in one gulp down and placed it on the edge of the windowsill where his father and mother had loved to sit. A few moments later Braonin and Eilish appeared at the door to the chamber. Eilish did not have to come far into the room before her instincts and experience told her the old chamberlain was dead.

Braonin approached the old man, placing his hand in front of Lonan's nose and mouth. There was no breath at all, nor any sign of hope, so he closed the staring lifeless eyes. It was then he noticed Lonan's throat had been badly bruised and he immediately suspected that the chamberlain might have been strangled.

'There are marks on Lonan's neck,' Braonin observed, his voice full of suspicion.

'The shock of the bad news was too much for him,' Rufus muttered almost inaudibly. 'His breath became short and he clawed at his own neck to breathe. There was nothing I could do.'

Eilish touched the slumped corpse and said a little prayer for her friend's soul before turning to Rufus who stood gazing silently out the window. When she approached the young FitzWilliam he avoided her gaze.

Eilish placed a hand on his shoulder to comfort him. It was then she noticed there were tears gathering in the young man's eyes as he stared out on the fields beyond Bally Raine. Eilish left her hand on his shoulder in comfort.

Then she realised what the terrible news from the Holy Land must have been, and suddenly she could not see anything but her own tears.

As soon as Donal entered Geoffrey's candlelit chamber Robert told their young friend what they had learned from Henry.

'It is not safe for you to remain here,' the lord explained. 'It is Henry's intention to have you tortured. Unless you tell him all you know about the Templar treasure.'

'Where will I run to?' Geoffrey laughed. 'I am trapped here and Henry St Clair, or whatever his name might be, is my gaoler.'

'There must be a solution to this problem,' Donal reasoned, 'there surely must be another way out of this place.'

'The answer lies under that tomb in the chapel,' Geoffrey declared. 'I am willing to wager that when we find the treasure we will discover a hidden exit from this castle.'

'It stands to reason!' Robert exclaimed. 'Your brother must have ensured the treasure could be retrieved even if the castle fell to the enemy.'

'It *has* fallen to the enemy,' Donal reminded his lord.

'If only I could examine that tomb,' Geoffrey sighed. 'But I have not been able to get close to it. The doors to the chapel are locked each evening as soon as the knights finish their devotions. The chamber is not unlocked again until morning.'

'We might slip in unnoticed,' Robert suggested, 'if we covered our faces well enough.'

'In the whole time I have been here,' Geoffrey replied, 'I have never met any of the dubbed knights outside that chapel. The men-at-arms walk all sentry duty in the fortress. If the chapel knights truly are Hospitallers as we suspect, they would recognise us as strangers immediately.' He put a hand to his brow and rubbed his forehead. 'Your suggestion is a good one but far too risky, I fear.'

'Then we have no choice but to solve the puzzle your brother left for us,' the lord replied.

'Was there anything else your brother left to you that might contain some clues? There must be another way into the chapel other than the locked door,' Donal reasoned.

'I am sure there must be at least one more entrance,' Geoffrey agreed. 'This whole castle is riddled with secret doors and hidden passages. But the only things my brother left me were those bottles of ink, a roll of parchment and some writing tools. There are ten quills, a penknife for trimming them and some blotting sand.'

'You did not show us the parchment and ink,' Donal remarked.

'I will find them for you,' Geoffrey answered, 'but there are no answers to be found there. I have carefully examined everything Godfrey left me. I even thought my brother might have rolled a message up and stuffed it inside one of the quills.'

Robert shook his head in frustration. 'It might serve us well if we made a list of all the clues we have accumulated. It is possible we have missed something obvious yet of vital importance.'

Geoffrey led Donal to his desk, placing two candles on the table near the inkwells and quills. Then he laid a fresh sheet of parchment out before the chieftain so he could copy down everything that was said.

'Show me the letters again,' Robert asked. 'I would like to examine them once more.'

Geoffrey removed the sheets of folded parchment from inside his surcoat where they had been tucked under his belt. Then Robert looked carefully at the seals on each letter. He smiled broadly to show he had discovered something.

'Here is a fine start,' he began. 'The seal on this letter, the last one you received from your brother, is the seal of the Knights Templar.' Robert passed the letter to Geoffrey and the young man examined it.

'It shows two knights sharing a horse,' Geoffrey observed.

'That is right,' the lord answered. 'One version of the tale explains this symbol as representing the Templar vow of poverty. But my father told me it is a sign illustrating the two levels of initiate within the order. Some knights are given the reins while others must be content to go wherever the horse would take them.'

'But that is exactly what I would have expected,' Geoffrey sighed. 'There is no clue here.'

'Not on this parchment,' Robert agreed, 'but on the will your brother had drawn up for you there is another seal with a design I have never seen before.'

He handed the will to Geoffrey. 'Two pillars,' Geoffrey exclaimed. 'Just like the two pillars in the chapel. And there is a design between the pillars which I cannot quite make out. It seems to be an eye within a triangular device.'

'The all-seeing eye of Almighty God,' Robert explained. 'the symbol of the holy sanctuary within the great Temple of Solomon. According to legend, beneath the spot marked by this sign, the Ark of the Covenant was buried in a secret vault.' Robert paused. 'I have been reading the manuscripts in Henry's library,' he explained.

Geoffrey hummed with excitement. 'Then this piece of parchment may tell us how to reach the hidden vault.'

At the desk Donal had managed to open one of the inkwells but was looking at the contents dubiously. 'This is not ink,' he announced. 'It is a strange grey coloured fluid.'

'I do not know what this is,' Geoffrey explained. 'It is certainly not ink. When I tried to write with it there was not enough colour in the fluid for the letters to show.'

The chieftain put the tip of his little finger into the liquid and then sniffed at it. After a moment he tentatively tasted the watery fluid. 'This is not ink at all. It tastes like lemon juice,' he remarked, somewhat surprised to find it in an ink bottle. 'Why would someone put the juice of a lemon in an inkwell?'

'To write with, of course!' Robert exclaimed, nearly knocking over the bottle in his excitement. He picked up a blank piece of parchment and examined both sides to make sure there was no mark on it. Then he took a pen and dipped the nib into the juice.

'My father showed me this trick,' the lord stated. 'He learned it from some Templar friend of his. Of course lemons do not grow in Ireland but old William had a few bottles put aside.'

The lord scratched his name across the page and then blew on the liquid until it dried. When he was satisfied with his handiwork, he offered the parchment to Geoffrey.

'What good is that?' Geoffrey asked. 'The writing has disappeared completely.'

'Sometimes it is necessary to conceal information within the body of a letter,' Robert explained, 'but the words I have written are only invisible until I am ready to restore them.'

Then he held the parchment over a candle flame for a few seconds. Instantly Robert's name appeared on the page as if it had been written in a dark brown ink.

Donal's eyes lit up with excitement. 'That's the answer,' he stuttered. Carefully he held Godfrey d'Acre's will over the flame.

In a few seconds the outline of a map appeared. All three men opened their eyes wide, awestruck at the discovery. When the flame had warmed every corner of the page, Geoffrey snatched it away from Donal.

'This is a map of the castle,' he confirmed, 'showing a part of the stable with a doorway marked in the side of the cliff face. I passed through that door by chance on my first morning here. We are going to have to find the entrance somehow.'

He studied the way in which the will had been written in relation to this map. Then he realised the little poem that had been so puzzling at first fitted in the space beside the secret door to the stables.

'"Here begins the tale of your descent,"' Geoffrey read from the will. '"Here begins the story of the Holy Grail. Here begin the terrors. Here begin the marvels. A sword length from the east, another from the west. Hold the pommel a measured distance from the floor. Lift the hanged guardian high upon the Three. Look to the throne, wherein lies the secret realm, the lance that wounds. The dish that feeds the multitude, the cup that heals the maimed king. And above all others the scroll on which is writ the book of ages."'

He paused for a few moments and then concluded, 'With this map we will find a way into the chapel after the main door is locked. But how will we find the treasure once we have lifted the tombstone?'

Donal handed Geoffrey the letter the young Henry St Clair had given to them to deliver. 'I would wager the answer to that question lies hidden on this parchment,' he said.

Geoffrey held the letter over the flame. Sure enough,

another drawing appeared. This sketch was much more detailed and there were words written in a neat but almost indecipherable script around the edge.

'I cannot quite make out what is written here,' Geoffrey confessed. 'This is an obscure Germanic style of handwriting which I have not seen before.'

Forcing his eyes into a squint, the young knight read each character one by one until he thought he had a sentence. '*Clavis ad Thesaurum*, I think,' he said slowly.

'The key to the treasure,' Robert translated.

'And here,' Geoffrey pointed out, 'there is a drawing of a strange box with the words, *Res ipsa pretiosa*.'

'The precious article rests here,' the lord declared. 'We have found the treasure!'

'Not yet,' Geoffrey pointed out. 'We still have to make our way into the chapel, if Henry St Clair is to be believed, and we do not have much time.'

'And we must avoid discovery,' Donal added. 'I do not trust St Clair.'

Donal had barely finished speaking when they heard the sound of many horses riding up over the drawbridge into the main part of the citadel. Geoffrey went to the window and as soon as he looked out on the courtyard he called to his companions.

'There are thirty black Hospitallers in the yard below us!' he gasped. 'We may have already left it too late to act.'

Robert rushed to the window and looked down at the soldiers as Geoffrey recognised one of the knights.

'That is Guy d'Alville!' he exclaimed, pointing at a black knight who seemed to be in charge of the warriors. 'He was posing as a Templar when I last saw him. That confirms our worst fears. There must be trouble brewing if Guy does not feel the need to disguise his true allegiances any longer.'

At that moment there was a loud knock at the door. The three men looked at each other with apprehension. Without a word Donal took up a position behind the door. Robert stood in the middle of the room in full view as Geoffrey went to answer the summons.

A knight dressed in the black livery of the Hospital pushed his way into the room as soon as the door was unlatched. He was closely followed by two men-at-arms.

'Geoffrey d'Acre, you will come with us immediately,' the knight demanded.

'There must be some mistake,' Geoffrey protested. 'A Templar such as myself does not take orders from one such as you. You are merely a Knight of the Hospital.'

'The Hospital of Saint John now commands this castle,' the knight sniggered. 'You would be well advised to do as you are told or you will suffer the consequences of your disobedience.'

'And what of the master of this place, Henry St Clair?' Robert asked. 'He is a Templar. Is it not strange that a Templar should order a Hospitaller to come and fetch us?'

'Henry St Clair is no longer master of this castle,' the Hospitaller stated with obvious pleasure. 'The commander of this castle is Guy d'Alville, Prior-General of the Hospital.'

'I will be along presently,' Geoffrey said, indicating with a wave of his hand that the knight was free to leave.

'You will come now!' the knight insisted. 'And I will escort you.'

'Very well,' Geoffrey agreed, seeing he had no choice, and he reached for his brother's sword.

'You will not be needing your steel,' the knight added, 'not where you are going.'

Geoffrey looked at the Hospitaller and understood he had little hope of escape without endangering the lives of his two friends. 'I take your meaning,' he said, holding up the palms of his hands to show he would offer no resistance.

'You are very wise,' the knight replied. 'In your wisdom

please tell your companion behind the door that he would be advised not to attempt to free you.'

'He will not move until I am well clear of this chamber,' Geoffrey replied, raising his eyebrows in surprise. 'I commend you for your astute mind.'

'Enough of the idle compliments, if you don't mind. Let us go.'

Geoffrey handed his sword solemnly to Robert. 'This was my brother's blade. Take care of it for me. One day I may need it again.'

'You won't have any use for it where you are going,' the Hospitaller laughed. 'Now come along or I will have to set my men onto you.'

Geoffrey bowed to his captor and walked out of the chamber with his head held high.

As soon as Geoffrey and his guards were out of the door and headed down the corridor, Donal gathered up all the papers and stuffed them into the leather pouch that hung at his side.

'What do we do now?' he asked his lord.

'Follow them,' Robert replied, heading out the door.

The Hospitaller was waiting in the passage, leaning against the wall with a smirk on his face. 'You will return to your own chamber now,' the black knight commanded, 'and remain there until you are summoned.'

Robert nodded politely and turned down the corridor in the opposite direction, followed closely by Donal.

In a few moments the Hospitaller and his prisoner had gone down the stairs leading to the courtyard. Robert stopped to watch them from a window. As they crossed the cobbled yard soldiers dressed in the black livery of the Hospital began to assemble.

'What now?' Donal repeated, grabbing at Robert's sleeve to get his attention.

'We have to find a way to help free Geoffrey,' came the

reply. 'But we must also try to find the treasure before Guy d'Alville lays his hands on it.'

'We cannot act without Geoffrey,' Donal pointed out. 'He knows this fortress better than I know Cúil Ghréine.'

'Then we must find Geoffrey before we do anything else,' Robert decided. 'And we must avoid being captured ourselves. But I am afraid we have to cross that crowded courtyard somehow without being detected.'

The lord strode off towards the stairs at the other end of the corridor to stare over the balcony. Suddenly his eyes lit up. 'I believe I may have an answer,' he smiled, pointing down.

Donal leaned over the balcony and saw two guards dressed in the Hospitaller colours standing at a door at the foot of the stairs. He looked back to Robert and nodded.

'We must hurry,' Donal whispered, 'if we are to have any hope of reaching the chapel before Guy and his men.'

Chapter Seventeen

Braonin left the castle before sunset on the evening of Lonan's death. He told Eilish he was going out to Cúil Ghréine to stay among the ruined buildings for the night. He assured her all he wanted to do was collect some spear points from the wreckage and to cut new shafts for them the next morning.

But Braonin did not ride all the way to Cúil Ghréine. Not far from where the settlement had once stood, he left the road and spurred his horse into the forest. For a long time he rode among the trees, letting his horse go at her own pace. Nervous, he constantly checked to make sure he was not being followed.

While there was still a little dusk light left the hunter continued on at this relaxed speed until, just on dark, he found a small natural clearing in the midst of the trees. He judged there was little chance of sparks igniting the branches of the surrounding vegetation, so he dug himself a small pit. Then he gathered some bracken and firewood.

Satisfied the fire pit would contain his little blaze, Braonin took out his flint and steel. When the tinder was ready he struck a spark into the dry bracken. Suddenly there was smoke around the kindling and then the first flames burst into life. Once Braonin had built the blaze up, he lay back with his hands behind his head to look at the stars and wait.

It must have been around midnight when he finally heard

a sound in the forest nearby. But he did not get up or stir at all. A short while later he was sure he could discern the sound of voices somewhere close by. Men were whispering but they must have thought he was asleep for they were not being too careful.

Braonin lay perfectly still, hoping he had not committed an act of outright foolishness in coming to this place at this time. Not too far away he heard the cry of a wild boar and his thoughts strayed to the last boar hunt he had taken part in. Since the day of Mathúin's death when he had almost touched the spirit of his prey, he had never again lifted a spear to any animal of the forest. This refusal to hunt had earned him a large share of good-humoured criticism from his kinfolk. And the occasional dark suspicion whispered behind a hand so that he would not hear.

The hunter began to wonder, as he had when the boar had stared him down, whether there were faerie beings about in these wild woods. His heart beat a little faster. What if he had attracted a band of faeries from their homes? What if they were angry at him for invading their territory?

The hunter knew full well the faerie folk were a wondrous race who often granted many favours to humankind. But he was also aware their wrath was unmatched. Especially if they perceived a threat to their homes or the forests they considered their domain.

'You are surrounded,' a voice boomed in the darkness and Braonin nearly jumped out of his skin with fright. 'Do not move or you will be struck down dead before you can draw a blade.'

The hunter sat up slowly, raising his hands high in the air so whoever was watching him in the dark forest could see that he offered no resistance.

'I wish you no harm,' Braonin asserted.

'Braonin?' came the voice. 'Is that you?'

'Yes,' the hunter answered, 'it is me.'

'Put down your bows,' the voice commanded. 'This is the man who saved my life. This is Braonin O'Regan.'

'Is that you, Cinneach?' Braonin asked.

At that very moment the Culdee stepped into the light of the fire. He smiled broadly. 'They have not captured me yet,' Cinneach declared.

'Nor will they either,' another voice from the forest added.

The Culdee reached out a hand to his friend, helping him to his feet. Braonin noticed the other man had grown pale since his time in the forest. If Cinneach had looked unkempt when the hunter had last seen him the Culdee was now truly filthy. Covered in caked mud that clung to his hair and clothes, he could have passed for one of the faerie folk.

'I did not get a chance to thank you for coming to my rescue,' Cinneach said apologetically.

'You had other things on your mind at the time,' Braonin laughed.

'What are you doing here in the woods?' the Culdee queried. 'Are there Normans nearby?'

'None that I know of,' Braonin replied. 'I came to tell you the news.'

'What has happened?'

'A letter came from the Holy Land to say Lord Robert and Donal were killed some time ago in the fighting against the infidel.'

'That is very sad for all of us,' Cinneach sighed. 'Robert was a good man. How is Eilish taking the news?'

'She seems to be coping remarkably well,' Braonin answered. 'I believe she half expected Donal would never return. But, in any case, she has had to set her personal grief aside for the time being.'

'Why is that?'

'Rufus received the letter from Outremer,' Braonin explained, taking his friend by the arm to whisper in his ear. 'The first person to read it after Rufus was Lonan, William's old chamberlain. Lonan apparently took the news quite badly. On hearing the tidings it appears he suffered a terrible seizure. Within minutes he was dead. Eilish believes Lonan died from shock in much the same way as Donal's father, Mathúin.'

'But you do not believe that is what happened,' Cinneach observed from the tone of his friend's voice.

'I do not,' Braonin asserted. 'When I saw the chamberlain's body, the reddened marks of a man's hands could clearly be discerned on his throat. Rufus and he were alone when Lonan had his seizure.'

'Would Rufus dare to murder the chamberlain of Bally Raine?' the Culdee gasped.

'I believe he might,' Braonin suggested, 'if the succession to the lordship were unresolved or if . . .' he paused here, choosing his words carefully, '. . . if Lonan guessed the letter from the Holy Land was not authentic.'

'It is well known that Lord William did not favour his younger son,' Cinneach stated, 'but if Robert were not actually dead, Rufus would gain very little from such a ruse. He might rule for a short while as lord but one day Robert would surely return and punish him. Not even Rufus is so foolish as to act that rashly.'

'Perhaps he plans to murder his brother . . . I do not know, but one thing I am sure of is that Rufus planned your arrest as part of a scheme to have me replaced as chancellor,' Braonin went on. 'Now Eilish fulfils those duties.'

'I cannot see what his reasoning might be in having you replaced,' Cinneach murmured, considering the problem carefully. 'Unless he wants to reinforce his claim on the lordship by being seen to work closely and effectively with Eilish. She is, after all, the chieftainess of these lands in her husband's absence. All the tenants respect her.'

'That is quite possible,' Braonin agreed, 'but I am sorely

worried for this estate and for all the tenants if Rufus should come to be Lord of Bally Raine.'

'He will cut this forest down, that is certain,' Cinneach said sadly. 'One of my men has heard that the land has been surveyed so it may be cleared for farms. And Rufus wrote to a shipbuilder in the north offering the timber at a good price.'

'This is the only remaining source of firewood and building timber on the estate,' Braonin recoiled in dismay. 'If the tenants lose this woodland, they will not be able to cook their meals.'

'They will not have much to eat anyway,' the Culdee spat. 'Most of the game in this forest would likely perish in the clearance. But the folk of Bally Raine will also lose their fishing rights in the river nearby as new tenants move in.'

'What would Donal do in a situation like this?' Braonin asked himself aloud. 'What would Lord Robert do if confronted by his brother's plan?'

'Are you certain Lonan was murdered?' the Culdee pressed. 'And it was Rufus who did the deed?'

'I am not certain,' the hunter admitted, 'but I have a strong feeling that the chamberlain did not die of natural causes. Rufus was not himself when Eilish and I came into the room. But it would be very difficult for me to prove Lonan was strangled.'

'Did you ask Eilish what she thought of Lonan's death?' Cinneach inquired.

'She told me I was imagining things. And that I still held a grudge against Rufus for arresting me,' Braonin sulked.

'She did not want to give credence to your accusation?'

'She was distracted by the news of Donal's death,' Braonin asserted. 'She is not thinking clearly.'

'Mere words may not be enough to win her over,' the Culdee declared. 'We may have to leave it to Rufus's actions to convince her. If it is true that freckled boy was involved in Lonan's death, then his motives are certainly impure. He has been very clever but he will make a mistake sooner or later. And when he does, we will be waiting to swoop on him like a raven diving on its prey in the long grass.'

'A rising?' Braonin gasped.

'I have a good number of men and women with me here in the forest,' Cinneach informed his friend. 'We could storm the castle if we had enough weapons and a way of ensuring the drawbridge was open and waiting for us.'

'I cannot help you with weapons,' Braonin admitted, 'but the drawbridge is another matter.'

'For the time being let us wait and see what happens,' the Culdee decided. 'It is best we bide our time until the warmer weather before we make a strike. It will give us time to plan carefully and to watch Rufus.'

'I will be your eyes in the castle of Bally Raine,' Braonin declared. 'And when the time comes we will strike down the enemy together.'

The two men clasped hands and smiled at each other, sealing their pact and their future.

Eilish assumed Braonin's sudden departure for Cúil Ghréine early that evening had more to do with the news of Donal's death than his desire to sift for spear points in the ashes. The awful news from the Holy land, she reasoned, must have affected him more deeply than he wished to show.

As for herself, Eilish was too busy arranging the laying out of Lonan's body and notifying all his kinfolk to take time to think about her own grief. It was late in the night before she finally made it back to Robert's chamber, which she had occupied for some weeks since the fire at Cúil Ghréine, and was able to sit by herself in silence.

'Whatever possessed Donal to leave?' Eilish asked herself as she knelt down before Robert's statue of the Virgin Mary. She had sat in this spot every night since the fire had destroyed her house. Each evening before sleep she prayed for her husband's safe return.

Now Eilish found she had no words left to say. The healer was amazed at herself. She had believed completely that the Holy Virgin Mother of Christ was listening to her prayers with compassion. Now Eilish felt betrayed, angry and foolish.

'You have taken my husband away from me,' the healer whispered as she looked the lifeless statue square in the eye. 'I thought you would protect him and you did not.'

There was no reply. Eilish felt her heart breaking. 'Lord Robert and Donal were fighting for your Son when they were killed,' she cried. 'They may have earned their place in heaven but I will never see the man I love again. I have paid a higher price than they for their devotion to the Cross.'

No sound, no acknowledgement from the wooden statue. The healer felt her head pounding in pain. 'I have been left a widow,' she screamed. 'Tell me, Holy Mother, how do you reward the widows of the fallen? With a lifetime of loneliness?'

The statue of the Virgin smiled down silently and serenely as always. With tears sreaming down her cheeks, Eilish got up off her knees. She deliberately neglected to make the customary sign of the cross as she did so. Then she went to find a length of coarse woven cloth she had salvaged from the fire. When she had found the cloth she stood in front of the statue again.

'Since you have turned your gaze from me and mine,' she told the Holy Virgin in a hoarse voice, 'I will take my gaze away from you. I will not bow down to any sacred relic ever again. I will offer my prayers to no-one.'

With that Eilish draped the cloth over the statue and covered it completely. Then she found a leather strap to bind around the cloth and wrapped the Virgin tightly.

'Now you will know what it is to be separated from those who care about you,' she snapped.

Eilish put her hands over her eyes and lay down on her bed. Before she knew what had come over her she was kicking, screeching and rolling around as her emotions exploded. In her anguish she threw a candlestick at the wall and it clattered loudly to the floor. She asked herself a hundred times why she had not prevented Donal from leaving. Then she began crying all over again.

Some time later, when she had sobbed herself into exhaustion, she lay on her back with her hands over her eyes. She was just nodding off to sleep when she heard a knock at her door.

Eilish arose, adjusting her tunic and brushing her hair back as the serving woman entered the room. 'Are you all right, mistress?' the servant inquired gently.

'I am,' Eilish replied with a cough.

'Shall I bring a light?'

'No,' the healer replied. 'But thank you.'

'Master Rufus would like to say his goodnight,' the woman explained. 'Shall I tell him you are already asleep?'

'Yes,' Eilish answered without hesitation, but then she suddenly changed her mind. 'No. Tell him I will speak with him. He was going to show me the letter he received from Outremer. He did not get a chance earlier in the day. Will you go and find Neesh? I have not seen her since we finished washing Lonan.'

'I will find her for you,' the servant murmured reassuringly as Rufus pushed past the woman into the room.

'You had better find a candle after all,' Eilish advised the woman.

'I trust I am not disturbing you,' the young FitzWilliam said softly as the servant left the chamber. He raised his eyebrows when he noticed a cloth covering the Virgin Mary. 'I know this must be a difficult time for you,' the Norman continued in a subdued tone.

'You are not disturbing me,' Eilish assured him, but the sharpness of her voice clearly indicated she would rather be left alone.

'I will get to the point,' Rufus stated. 'In the shock of Lonan's untimely passing, other matters slipped my mind. I have not spoken to you personally regarding the news we received from Outremer. I hope you will forgive me.'

'Of course, Rufus,' the healer replied. 'Your loss has been as great as mine. Your only brother is gone.'

'My brother and I were not very close,' the young FitzWilliam interjected. 'We never saw eye to eye on anything. But I suppose he was my flesh and blood. I have no-one else now he is gone, except for my father who is, as you know, living in the monastery at Shelton.'

'William will doubtless take the news very hard,' Eilish surmised.

'He has asked not to be told any tidings of the outside world,' Rufus explained. 'He shut himself in the abbey because he wanted to retreat entirely from the struggles and triumphs of life. He has had his fair share of both, so I imagine he only wishes to rest in his grey years. Naturally I will inform the Abbot of Shelton of Robert's passing but I will leave it up to him to pass the news on to my father.'

'You have been very generous and understanding, Rufus,' Eilish muttered.

'There is one last thing I should tell you,' Rufus went on, 'and I pray you will not be too angry with me for what I have done.'

'What is that?' Eilish frowned.

'When I met the messenger on the road this afternoon . . .' the Norman paused to make sure she was paying attention to him, for her eyes had drifted to the floor, 'he handed me two letters.' Rufus pulled a sealed parchment from his tunic.

'In my confusion and grief I neglected to pass this one on. It is addressed to you.'

Rufus held the letter out. Eilish stared at the parchment until the silence became uncomfortable. Then she reached out a trembling hand and took it from him.

Once she held the parchment in her hands she could not summon the will to break the seals. Eilish knew in her heart what words the letter must contain. She dreaded reading it.

'I will look at it later,' the healer told Rufus.

'Are you sure?'

'I am not ready,' Eilish muttered, casting her eyes to the floor again. 'I do not wish to have my husband's death confirmed in writing just yet.' Then a thought struck her. 'Was there a token with this letter?' she asked.

'There was,' Rufus lied. 'I believe there were two messengers sent here with these parchments. The man carrying the token was washed overboard during a violent storm at sea. His body was not recovered.'

'Then the half-penny has gone to the floor of the ocean,' Eilish concluded, struggling not to sob as she spoke. She stood up and went to the window so Rufus would not see her reddened eyes. 'So the token never came home,' she said. 'Perhaps it was only meant to return to me with Donal. I must speak with the tilecutter about it.'

Rufus crossed the room and put his arms around the healer's shoulders. Eilish did not resist and after a moment she turned to face him, resting her head on his breast as she cried.

'I do understand,' the Norman soothed. 'You must

remember that if there is anything you need from me, all you have to do is ask.'

Eilish clung to Rufus tightly and sobbed like she had never sobbed in all her life. It was a long while before the spasm of despair passed. When she finally quietened, Rufus sat her down on the bed and knelt before her.

'I would like you to keep my brother's room for a while longer,' he whispered. 'This chamber has brightened up immensely since you came to live in it. The castle would be so empty without you.'

Eilish blushed, deeply embarrassed that she had ever thought ill of this man who was proving to be so supportive in her time of need. 'I could not possibly impose myself on you any more,' the healer protested, drying her eyes with the hem of her dress.

'It would not be an imposition,' Rufus cut in before she had a chance to say anything more. 'With Lonan gone and Robert also, I need someone to run the household as well as the estates. You have already proved your value to me and to the tenants. You are well respected.'

'What are you saying?' Eilish asked, choking back her emotions.

Rufus was about to answer when Neesh opened the door. The girl held her candle high, took one look at Rufus on his knees before the healer and coughed in surprise. The young FitzWilliam stood up, flustered.

'We will talk about this later,' Rufus mumbled, 'when you have rested and had time to think over all that has happened.' He put his hand on the top of Eilish's head as a parting gesture of sympathy and then turned to leave the room.

Neesh eyed the Norman with suspicion as he brushed past her. As soon as the door was shut she rushed to the healer's side and threw her arms around her cousin.

'What was that all about?' Neesh demanded to know.

'Rufus came to give me this,' Eilish answered, holding up the letter. Then she wiped her nose with her handkerchief as Neesh examined the parchment.

'You have not opened it,' the girl observed.

'Later.'

'What was Rufus doing on his knees before you?' Neesh asked.

'He was offering his friendship and support,' Eilish replied curtly. 'He said I could stay in Robert's chamber for a while longer if I so wished.'

'Don't you want to return to Cúil Ghréine?'

'There is nothing for me there any more,' Eilish sighed. 'Nothing but memories and sadness. I think it would do me good to stay at Bally Raine for a while until I am feeling better. And besides, Rufus needs help in running the place now Lonan is gone.'

Neesh felt a prickling at the back of her neck. 'If I were you,' Neesh said slowly, 'I would be very careful of Master Rufus.'

'How can you say that,' Eilish exclaimed, hurt her judgment was being questioned, 'after all he has done for us? If it had not been for Rufus, we would have had to sleep in the snow after we lost our home. And that with the snow falling heavier than ever this year. He has fed us and clothed us. He has put his own grief aside to give me solace. Be careful what you say.'

'I have never trusted him,' Neesh declared. 'There is something about him that is sinister and conniving. Rufus has not changed all that much since Lord Robert left, no matter what he says and does to convince us otherwise.'

'Neesh!' Eilish snapped. 'I will not hear you speak ill of Rufus. He has his faults, as we all do, but deep inside he is a caring man. In the past he did many foolish things but I believe he is a changed soul. I don't doubt that the added responsibility of the lordship will mature him even further.'

'He will be Lord of Bally Raine?' Neesh stammered, surprised at this piece of information.

'Of course he will. His brother is gone. His father is in the monastery. Rufus is the only one of his family who can take the reins.'

'I never thought I would see the day,' Neesh admitted, shaking her head.

'And neither did I,' Eilish agreed. 'But it is always what we least expect in life that teaches us the most about ourselves.'

Neesh nodded and held her cousin close again. 'I suppose he will be looking to marrying,' the girl said almost to herself, 'and having a son who will be heir to the estates one day.'

'I suppose he will,' Eilish agreed. A new flood of tears began as her thoughts went to Donal once more.

Outside on the stairs Rufus stood with his ear pressed against the door until he heard Eilish begin to cry. Satisfied, he climbed the stairs to his chamber. Once inside he closed the door softly and went to the fire.

'I will have to watch young Neesh,' Rufus told himself. 'She understands me too well and is far too suspicious of my motives. I do not want anyone interfering with my designs.'

The Norman poured a cup of wine and sat down before the fire.

'Lonan was so easy to snuff out,' Rufus said, holding his hands up to his face to stare at them. 'Like a candle flame pinched between my fingers,' he muttered under his breath. 'I never thought it would be such a simple matter to remove such an obstacle.

'Neesh will not present any problem,' Rufus decided, 'if ever I need to dispose of her, she will be as easy. For the time being I will watch her carefully. The very moment she steps out of line I will deal with her.'

Then Rufus FitzWilliam drained his cup and leaned back in his chair to watch the fire and dream of his glorious future.

Donal walked straight up to one of the sentries at the bottom of the stairs, knocking the man to the ground with his fist before the black knight had a chance to react. Robert levelled Geoffrey's sword at the other warrior and seconds later the two guards were disarmed.

'Take off your tunics,' Donal ordered and the sentries did as he told them. While Robert watched the prisoners, Donal dressed himself in the black of the Hospital. Then the chieftain held a sword as Robert changed into a black surcoat.

'We will have to hide these two fellows,' Robert realised, 'or else we will be discovered.'

Donal pointed to the room the two men had been guarding. 'In there?' he asked.

The lord nodded and tried the door, but it would not open. Donal began to search the soldiers while Robert kept a watch for danger. Finally the chieftain found a bunch of keys at the belt of the senior guard. He fumbled with the lock until he came across the right key and the door swung open. Robert motioned for the guards to go inside but stopped when he saw the expression on Donal's face.

Inside the chamber was a sight that utterly surprised both men. Almost forty soldiers were crowded into this small room. Some were lying on the floor, some kneeling in prayer, others seated with their knees drawn up to their chests in quiet contemplation. But every man was dressed in the white robes of the Temple.

'Who are you?' one of the knights demanded defiantly. 'Is it time to take us to the gallows?'

'The gallows?' Robert repeated, not comprehending. Then the lord realised he was wearing a black surcoat, not a Templar tunic. 'We are Templars also,' he assured them. 'We took these clothes from your guards. Are you prisoners?'

'We have been here under lock and key for months,' the Templar knight replied. 'We were told we would be executed this evening.'

'Executed?' Robert murmured. 'Something is definitely amiss here. We will have to ask St Clair a few questions.'

'He was taken also,' the knight said, then added, 'by black Hospitallers.'

'Well, you are free now,' Robert declared. 'This castle is thick with the Knights of Saint John. We are going to attempt to recapture the fortifications for the Temple. But first we must locate our comrade who was taken away earlier. Will you help us?'

Every man in the little chamber got to his feet to reply with a solemn, 'Aye!'

'Though you have no weapons,' the lord advised, 'it would aid us greatly if you could create a diversion by distracting the guard of Hospitallers who have assembled in the courtyard. My sergeant and I will try to cross the yard without being detected.'

'If you make it across the courtyard,' one of the Templars informed him, 'follow the largest alley which runs behind the keep. It will take you to the cells in which prisoners are usually held. There were too many of us for the Hospitallers to keep all their captives there. I am sure that is where they have taken your comrade.'

'Thank you,' Robert replied sincerely. 'As soon as you are ready we will make our move. Remember, we are relying on you all to confuse the enemy as much as possible so we can get away,' he added gravely.

'This is madness,' Donal murmured under his breath. 'We will all be killed.'

'We will all be killed anyway,' one of the Templars retorted. 'Do you think the Order of Saint John would allow us to live after the way they took this castle? If word got to the Pope of their unprovoked attack, of their infiltration of this garrison, the Hospital would be abolished in disgrace.'

'We are already dead,' another knight chimed in. 'Guy d'Alville brought every Hospitaller in the Outremer with him. There must be three hundred enemy soldiers within the fortifications. At least this way we will go to our graves fighting for the honour of the Temple.'

'These men are unarmed!' Donal protested to Robert. 'They will be slaughtered.'

'But we have one weapon which could win the day for us,' Robert assured him, 'and that is surprise. The last thing the Hospitallers expect is that their forty Templar prisoners will suddenly rush around the castle spreading mayhem.'

'What about the armoury?' Donal pleaded. 'Surely that is where all these men's weapons are being held. Would it not be better to try to capture it first? Then at least these knights would have arms to fight with.'

Robert looked at his sergeant as the other knights hummed in agreement.

'You are right, Donal,' the lord conceded. 'That may be all the diversion we need to cover our escape.'

Donal adjusted his belt around the black surcoat, then took a helm from one of the guards. Robert waited at the door while two of the Templars made sure the guards were well bound and gagged.

A few minutes later Donal and his lord headed out into the courtyard, their faces covered by the nose guards of their helms. They were no more than thirty steps into the yard when a Knight of the Hospital ran towards them wide-eyed.

The warrior seemed to be headed directly at them. Certain they had been discoverd, Robert was sure his heart would stop beating as the soldier grew closer and closer. But as the knight came within a few paces, Robert realised why the Hospitaller was so distraught. From out of the building where the Templars had been held prisoner came thick billowing clouds of smoke. The castle was on fire.

'Wonderful!' Robert exclaimed, then he leaned in close to whisper to Donal: 'That will keep Guy's men busy. Now we must move quickly!'

He had hardly finished speaking when he noticed the Templars were streaming out of the building in all directions. Only about ten of the white knights seemed to be making any sort of stand. The rest were headed for the castle armoury.

Chapter Eighteen

Geoffrey's guard negotiated the alleyways behind the keep until they came to a heavy iron door in a dimly lit passage. A gaoler challenged the party before the door swung noisily open on its rusty hinges.

The Hospitaller knight who had arrested Geoffrey motioned for his prisoner to enter the room. As soon as he was inside, the door slammed shut behind him. Geoffrey listened to the sound of the key turning in the lock again and then leaned against the cold stone wall in frustration.

'How will I get out of this one?' the young Templar asked himself.

'I am afraid there is no easy way out of this prison,' a familiar voice replied.

Geoffrey looked around the large cell. It was empty except for a figure seated in a far corner. The man rose and moved slowly into the light.

'Henry St Clair!' Geoffrey exclaimed. 'What are you doing here?'

'I, like yourself, find that I am a prisoner of the Hospitallers,' the old knight answered. 'And I should tell you my real name is not St Clair. I am Arnauld Lusignon.' He bowed. 'I am a Prefector of the Order of the Temple.'

'Why were you using the name Henry St Clair?' Geoffrey inquired suspiciously.

'Sit down,' the old knight smiled. 'It is a long tale.'

Geoffrey did as he was told, sinking down to the floor and leaning against the wall. Lusignon sat propped against the door.

'The upper echelons of the Temple,' the old knight stated, 'have known for a long time how the black knights had tracked our treasure to this fortress. The Hospitallers infiltrated our organisation over many years, some rising to prominence. Henry St Clair was elected to head a small group of the inner circle to cleanse the Temple of these intruders.'

'And Guy d'Alville is one of those Hospitallers?' Geoffrey asked.

'Guy is a latecomer,' Arnauld laughed, 'a man more motivated by greed than honour or duty to the Hospital. D'Alville is not trusted by his own people.'

'So it was no accident when St Clair was captured by Saladin,' Geoffrey concluded.

'Indeed not,' the old knight sighed. 'The Saracens rarely keep Templar prisoners because they know the Temple does not pay ransoms. The Hospital paid Saladin handsomely to see no harm came to St Clair.'

'Why?' Geoffrey asked, confused.

'Because Henry knew the whereabouts of the treasure,' Arnauld explained. 'They were not about to murder one of the only two men who could lead them to the treasury of the Temple.'

'They killed my brother!'

'That was an accident,' the old knight explained. 'It had never been their intention to murder Godfrey. They merely wanted to get their hands on the items he was guarding. Guy d'Alville is an impatient man. And he is searching for a particular item rumoured to be a part of the treasure.'

'The Ark?' Geoffrey asked.

'Some say the Ark of the Covenant is among the Templar treasure,' Arnauld replied. 'Others, Guy d'Alville among them, believe the Holy Grail is the centrepiece of Templar wealth.'

'The Grail?'

'Guy,' Arnauld sneered, indicating he had little respect for the man, 'has heard a tale which attributes great power to the Cup of the Last Supper. He believes that if he drinks from the Cup, he will attain eternal life.'

'And what do you believe?' Geoffrey pressed.

'Let me only say,' the old knight stated, 'I have never beheld the Grail Cup. So I cannot comment on its existence or its alleged powers.'

Lusignon coughed to clear his throat and then he continued his tale. 'As soon as Henry St Clair heard of your brother's death, he went to Saladin to beg to be released. The Vizier is an honourable man and he was naturally outraged that agents of the Hospital had disguised themselves as Saracens. But he did not release Henry.'

'Why not?'

'Saladin believed St Clair would be in great danger,' Arnauld replied. 'The Vizier did not want to be responsible for Henry's death. So St Clair was given the freedom of the Saracen court but not allowed to leave. In the meantime, Saladin spread the rumour that Henry St Clair had escaped.'

'That is where you enter the tale,' Geoffrey guessed.

'I was chosen to stand in for St Clair because I served him for many years and know his ways,' Arnauld nodded. 'In the guise of Henry and with the sanction of the Temple I allowed myself to fall into d'Alville's hands. He was, of course, delighted to play host to such a distinguished prisoner. His suspicions were never aroused. He had not met St Clair, so it was a relatively easy matter to convince Guy of my identity and influence. Then I set about putting as many obstacles in Guy's path as I could arrange. I allowed the Hospitallers to have access to this castle but not to its secret places. Within a short time, however, Guy's troops arrived to replace the Temple Knights who garrisoned the fortifications. I had not counted on that.'

'But why was it necessary to play traitor?' Geoffrey inquired.

'I was never a traitor to the Order of the Temple. I was working to stall Guy's treasure hunt,' Arnauld explained. 'I have three other reasons to feign the role of d'Alville's ally. First, the central enclave of the Templar order saw the opportunity to trap the Hospitallers in the act of plundering the treasury of the Temple. We knew the Pope would not act to stop their thieving ways unless the Hospital was completely compromised. The Pope is the only person who can intervene to curtail the activities of the Knights of Saint John. They are becoming too powerful, too greedy.'

The old knight glanced at Geoffrey, noticing his listener sat wide-eyed. 'Second,' he went on, 'we wanted to dispel all the fantastic rumours of the Templar treasure. The real treasure of the Temple is more holy than any cup or gilded box. And it must be preserved at all costs. It is a dangerous hoard. If the Pope knew what it contained he would have it destroyed. If anyone outside the Temple were to discover its true nature, the result would be disastrous. We knew Guy had tracked the treasure here to this castle. That is why I was appointed to delay him and to protect the secret.'

He paused again as Geoffrey looked directly at him. 'And how do I fit in to this plan?'

'You,' Arnauld smiled, 'are the third reason for our ploy. You were born with the blood of a guardian in your veins. Since your brother's death you stand in line to inherit the highest office of the Temple. Our knights were spread too thinly across the Outremer when Saladin attacked. It would have been impractical to spend warriors on your protection. Keeping you first with the Hospitallers at Krak and then here under my protection was seen as the best way of ensuring your survival.'

'Why have you been imprisoned then?' Geoffrey asked. 'Were you discovered?'

'No,' the knight laughed. 'Guy still has no idea I was reporting his every move to my superiors in Acre. D'Alville truly believed I had turned against the Temple to betray the treasure. I was imprisoned because I did not locate the treasure quickly enough. I also failed to persuade you to part with whatever information you may have had. But most importantly I was gaoled because Guy's time has almost run out.'

'What do you mean?'

'The valiant knight and Prefector of the Order, Henry St Clair, has assembled a great army. At this very moment he and his men are marching toward the walls of this castle. Henry helped build this fortress. He will not have to carry out a siege to make his way within the walls. He knows of the secret pathways to this place. Guy must realise St Clair will soon be here. And there is nothing he can do about it.'

'So we will be free soon,' Geoffrey surmised.

'I am afraid not,' Arnauld sighed. 'We will likely be dead long before St Clair arrives. Guy will not risk us bearing evidence against him. He only has a few hours to find what he has been seeking for many years. D'Alville knows I have no information about the treasure that is of any value. But you, you do hold some clues. I expect Guy is preparing to torture you to gain the knowledge he needs.'

Geoffrey felt the blood drain from his face.

'You don't have any information that could help him, do you?' Arnauld stammered nervously. 'I mean to say, you do not know where the treasure of the Temple has been concealed? Do you?'

'I believe I have discovered where it may be hidden,' Geoffrey answered.

'Oh dear,' the other knight sighed. 'Then we really should not be sitting here waiting for Guy and his men to arrive. His torturers have quite a reputation. Folk say Guy could persuade the Devil to sing the Te Deum.'

'What are we going to do?'

'There is no question,' Arnauld replied. 'We must escape from this cell and locate the treasure before Guy gets his hands on it.'

The old knight stood up and walked to the door of the cell. He placed his mouth close to the tiny opening through which the guards kept an eye on their prisoners. Then he yelled at the top of his voice, 'Help! Guard! There is a man dying here.'

'What are you doing?' Geoffrey whispered.

'Be quiet. Hold onto your wrist tightly. And get over in the corner out of my way.'

'What's the noise about?' a deep voice demanded from outside.

'My cell mate has cut his wrist open,' Arnauld replied. 'He is bleeding to death.'

'Let him,' the guard answered. 'It will save the hangman some work.'

'You are right,' the knight answered, 'Guy d'Alville probably won't mind that this fellow dies. It will save him the effort of extracting secrets from the poor lad.'

There was silence for a few moments as the guard contemplated Arnauld's words. Then Geoffrey heard the key turning in the door. As the sentry entered the cell Arnauld pointed to where Geoffrey was sitting on the floor in the far corner.

The soldier strained his eyes in the dark. While he was distracted Arnauld struck him a blow across the back of the head with his elbow. The guard fell face first onto the floor in front of Geoffrey.

Arnauld unsheathed the man's sword and leaned out into the corridor. 'Hello,' he called. 'Anyone there?'

The answer came a few seconds later. 'What do you want?'

'Help me with this prisoner,' Arnauld demanded.

The other guard arrived a few seconds later to be held at sword point by the old knight. 'Do not make a move or you will not live to see your unlucky friend awaken,' he warned the second guard.

In a flash Arnauld had disarmed the second sentry and taken his surcoat from him. Within minutes, dressed as a Hospitaller, Geoffrey stepped out into the corridor as Arnauld adjusted his own black surcoat. Then the man who had posed as Henry St Clair locked the door to the cell behind them.

'Which way?' Geoffrey asked.

'I know how to get out of here,' the old knight reassured him. 'We must make our way down this passage,' he added, heading off through the corridor towards some stone steps.

The stairs led down one level to another corridor which they followed until they came to a large heavy oak door. Arnauld swung it open but what he saw on the other side made the old knight swear under his breath. An iron grate had been secured over the exit to stop anyone entering the building.

'They must be expecting Henry's attack,' he reasoned. 'All the doors to this wing will be closed in the same way. We may not be able to get out.'

'We must try!' Geoffrey insisted.

Arnauld frowned but there was no time to discuss the matter any further. Without another word he was off down the corridor again, muttering to himself. After a few minutes the old knight had located the passage he was looking for. It was a narrow alleyway that led off from the main corridor.

'Here it is!' he proclaimed with relief, but as he turned the corner he saw two knights dressed in black standing beside a shrine to the Virgin Mary. The pair of Hospitallers saw Geoffrey and Arnauld immediately and drew their blades without hesitation.

Arnauld lifted the sword he held and in a flash he charged at the black warriors hoping at least to intimidate them, if not drive them off. But to his surprise the two men stood their ground as if they had nowhere to retreat. Then one of the Hospitallers spoke.

'You take the little one, Donal,' the warrior commanded, as he ran forward, 'I'll look after the old one.'

Geoffrey heard the voice and yelled at the top of his lungs, 'Donal O'Regan!'

The two enemy soldiers stopped in their tracks as Arnauld dropped the point of his blade to the ground.

'Geoffrey?' Donal ventured. 'Is that you?'

The young knight lifted his helm to reveal his face and in seconds the three men were slapping each other's shoulders in congratulations and relief.

'Who is that?' Robert asked, indicating the old knight.

'Gentlemen,' Geoffrey began, 'may I introduce Arnauld Lusignon, Protector of the Order of the Temple.'

Arnauld removed his helm and both Robert and Donal let the surprise show clearly on their faces.

'Holy Mother of God!' Donal exclaimed. 'Which side are you on?'

'The winning side usually,' Arnauld replied with a smile. 'Though I am having a rather difficult time deciding which is which today. I see we are all coming up with similar strategies,' he quipped, tugging at Donal's sleeve. 'I can understand why you do not usually wear black. Brown is much more your colour.'

'How do we get out of here?' Robert cut in. 'All the doors are barred.'

'There is no other way I know of, I'm afraid,' Arnauld admitted.

As he finished speaking Donal heard a noise in the main corridor behind them. 'Soldiers!' he warned.

'Get down on your knees and pray!' Arnauld ordered as each of them slipped their helms back onto their heads. No sooner were they in position in front of the Virgin's shrine than a large group of warriors marched down the corridor adjoining the narrow passage.

'You men there!' a knight called out. 'What are you doing?'

'We are at prayer, brother,' Arnauld replied, disguising his voice.

'Get up, you lazy bastards!' the knight screamed. 'There are Templars at the gates and two score prisoners have been set loose within the stronghold. I need every man ready at his post.'

'Yes, my lord. We are on our way,' Arnauld answered in his most rustic accent.

The knight passed on with the rest of his warriors. Arnauld breathed a heavy sigh of relief when he was sure the man was gone.

'What's the matter?' Robert asked, seeing the shocked expression on Arnauld's face.

'That was Guy d'Alville,' the old knight said. 'Someone must be watching over us.' With that he crossed himself, kissed the tips of his fingers and touched them gently to the Virgin's feet.

To his utter surprise the foot of the statue gave way under the pressure of his touch and the Virgin moved back slightly. There was a low sound of stone grating against stone. The four men all looked at each other in wonderment as a section of the wall behind them slid open to reveal a hidden passage.

'Shall we try down there?' Arnauld asked, but Geoffrey,

Donal and Robert were already peering into the darkness.

'I can see a torch hanging from the wall further down,' Donal pointed out. 'I will go and get it.'

He disappeared into the passage and returned a few moments later holding the rush light.

'No-one has been down there for a very long time,' he announced as he took flint and iron from his pouch to set fire to the torch. As soon as it was lit they ventured down the passage, pushing the stone panel shut behind them as they went.

'Donal is right,' Robert noted, 'but perhaps this passage leads out of the castle.'

'Be quiet!' Arnauld hissed. 'We do not know how thin these walls are. We must not risk being discovered.'

They went on silently after that, pushing the cobwebs aside with open palms until they had walked about a hundred paces. Then they came to a fork in the path. One passage led off to the left and one to the right. Donal turned around suddenly and resin spilled from the top of the rush light, setting a cobweb on fire.

'Be careful with that thing!' Robert cried. 'You could hurt someone.'

Geoffrey lifted his helm to examine the walls of the passage. In a moment he was brushing the dirt away from an inscription on the left wall.

'Look here!' he said. 'This is the symbol of the two pillars.'

'That signifies the chapel,' Arnauld stated.

Geoffrey went to the opposite wall and rubbed away the dust and cobwebs. 'And this sign is two knights mounted on a single horse.'

Arnauld stepped up beside him and wiped away some more dust. 'They are enclosed within a horseshoe,' the old knight observed. 'This is the passage to the stables. And this,' he went on, indicating the passage forking to the left, 'is the way to the chapel. We may have saved ourselves a great deal of time.'

'I would like to be sure,' Donal interrupted. 'I am not certain I trust you, Arnauld Lusignon. If that is your real name. What if your interpretation of the signs is incorrect?'

'There is only one way to find out,' Arnauld smiled. 'We must select one passage and follow it. But make your decision quickly and choose well. In secret passages, as in life, you never know what is waiting around the corner.'

'Then let us go down the corridor that most likely leads to the chapel,' Robert suggested. 'What good would it be to go back toward the stables?'

There was silence for a few breaths as each man contemplated the possibilities. Finally, without another word spoken, they agreed to do as Robert suggested. Once more the four men set off with Donal leading the way, a torch in one hand and drawn sword in the other, the other three spread out behind, a few paces apart.

Before long the passage became very damp and the air was full of mould that caught at the back of their throats. The sound of flowing water could be heard in the distance and they noticed the corridor was descending at a slight angle.

After a hundred more paces they were up to their ankles in water. The floor was soft and soggy like a quagmire. Within ten minutes the stagnant stinking flood was up around Donal's waist.

'At least no-one will suspect us of having broken our vows as Templars,' Arnauld whispered down the line. 'We will come out of this bath smelling far worse than when we went in.'

'I am not so worried about being accused of illicit cleanliness,' Donal replied tersely. 'I am more concerned about where this passage will lead us.'

No sooner had he spoken than he noticed a block of stone

which sealed the corridor a short distance ahead. Within twenty paces he was leaning up against the smooth surface, cursing under his breath. Geoffrey came up beside him and ran his hand over the polished surface of the stone.

'It is beautiful,' he observed. 'I have never seen stone worked so smoothly, so perfectly.'

'It is a dead end!' Donal exclaimed in frustration. 'We might as well go back to the fork and try again.'

'Wait a minute,' Robert cut in. 'What did the parchment say about the hidden door?'

Donal handed his leather pouch to Geoffrey who removed the soaking pieces of parchment. Then Geoffrey carefully unfolded his brother's will and read the relevant part of the little poem that fitted in with the detailed map.

'"A sword length from the east, another from the west. Hold the pommel a measured distance from the floor." A sword length from where?' Geoffrey muttered to himself. 'There is no sign on this wall to indicate whether there might be a door concealed here.'

'What is this?' Donal asked, exploring under the water with his feet. 'I can feel a deep channel in the floor.'

Robert, realising he still had Geoffrey's sword, quickly passed the weapon to the young knight and Donal helped position the tip of the blade so it stood in the channel.

'The width of the door is almost exactly two sword lengths,' he declared triumphantly. 'So if I stand the sword in this channel, it should point to a lever of some kind near the pommel.'

'That's where you will find a catch or lock to open the door from this side,' Robert agreed.

Geoffrey fumbled around under the water for a few minutes but could not discover any obvious levers. He was about to give up when a section of the stone behind his sword moved slightly, sliding under his hand. Geoffrey leaned against the rock and a narrow stone block shifted.

There was a grinding screech as the door began to move up towards the ceiling. Donal looked at Geoffrey, realising with horror that they had made a terrible mistake. The water in the chamber suddenly started to drain out in a great fury.

'Hold on!' the chieftain screamed as he clutched at Geoffrey and Robert.

But the rushing torrent sucked Donal downward. In seconds he had lost his footing and slipped under the water. As he went down he dropped the precious rush light which hissed loudly as the flames sputtered out in the water. The passage was plunged into total darkness. The chieftain managed to claw at Geoffrey's legs and the young knight grabbed Donal's arms.

Suddenly there was a great splash as the chieftain surfaced again. 'Help!' he gasped, gulping in a deep breath. But before anyone could get a better hold on him he slipped away again, thrashing wildly.

Geoffrey cried in anguish as he lost Donal in the murky blackness. But he was soon too worried about his own safety to be able to search for him. Another stone slid into place above them and the young Templar was almost dragged under himself.

Then the whole right-hand wall moved. Suddenly the entire room filled with a torrent crashing down from above as other hidden passages released their stagnant store of water. In the darkness each man fought as best he could to stay alive, chilled by the screams of his comrades.

Before he knew what was happening Donal was kicking about under the surface of the stinking water. His leg snagged on rope near the door. The water draining from the chamber all around him sucked him down into another corridor but his leg was stuck. He could not strain his neck above the torrent to breathe.

Donal felt the wall near his leg begin to subside and for a moment he thought he would be released by the movement. But he was still stuck fast. His heart beat hard with terror as he realised he would not be able to hold the air in his lungs for much longer. He could see nothing and the only sound that met his ears was the bubbling of the water around him.

The chieftain knew he could only struggle for a few minutes longer at the most. In the thick putrid water there was no light at all. He fumbled around until he found the rope wrapped around his lower leg, but he had no hope of seeing his way clear to release it. As he began to suffer shock Donal felt his body spasm. His arms thrashed wildly in a vain effort to attract the attention of his comrades.

In pain and panic Donal made a last great effort to reach the surface to breathe. At that very instant two things happened. First the walls to either side of the corridor rose upwards slightly. Then abruptly the water level in the chamber dropped low enough so that Donal's mouth was just above the stagnant mire. He spat out sour brine then sucked the air into his lungs in urgent gulps.

No sooner had he done that than the wall near his leg moved again and he was suddenly whipped under the water by the force of it draining out of the corridor. In a matter of seconds he was rolling around, buffeted hard against the walls of a smooth stone passage.

Arnauld sensed that Donal was gone and understood immediately the danger they were all in. His hand brushed by a rope and he grasped it tightly, wrapping the line around his wrist so he could hold onto it securely. He did not have time to check whether the other end was secured to anything, but he prayed with all his heart that it was.

In the next second there was a great gurgling screech as the water rushed down the opening through which Donal had been sucked. Arnauld felt his feet whipped out from under him and, as he fell, his free hand found the arm of one of his comrades.

As the two men slipped into the drainage corridor Arnauld was struck on the head by another falling body. In the next instant there was a third man grasping the rope with all his might.

Only a matter of seconds later the water was gone, thundering off into the distance. The three men were left dangling in the entrance to the corridor, coughing and spluttering. As quickly as possible they wordlessly hauled themselves up the rope and out of the narrow stone shaft, fearful of another fall of water from somewhere above them. When they were all safe again, each man lay on his back breathing hard and nursing bruises.

'Where's Donal?' Robert gasped finally.

'Gone,' Arnauld replied. 'God knows where.'

'We can't just sit here,' the lord spat. 'We must go after him.'

'We have no choice,' Arnauld informed him. 'The corridor is sealed behind us.'

Geoffrey crawled back to where the old knight was leaning against a smooth stone block. 'He's right,' he confirmed. 'The way is blocked.'

'There is only one way out,' Arnauld laughed incongruously. 'Down.'

'We must hurry,' Robert coughed. 'He may be injured.'

'Relax,' Arnauld ordered. 'We have no way of knowing how far this shaft runs. I am not so worried about following after Donal as I am about how suddenly we may come to a stop.'

'We can't abandon him!' Robert protested.

'I applaud the sentiment,' Arnauld noted, 'but I am not

so sure I relish the task.' The other two men heard the old knight sigh deeply. 'I suppose there's no sense in staying here to enjoy the air,' he added and brushed past Geoffrey, making for the shaft. 'I'll go first, shall I?' he sang cheerfully.

Robert heard him slip away down the shaft as Geoffrey crawled to the edge.

'I wish there was enough light to see by at least,' the young Templar complained and then he too slid down the shaft. The lord was suddenly alone.

'Wait for me!' he cried and as he let go his hold he heard Geoffrey screaming in the distance. The terror in his companion's voice was too much for him. He fought to stop his descent but it was too late.

The next thing the lord knew his body was sliding down a steady but gentle incline. But before he could do anything to slow his fall, the angle of the passage increased sharply and he found himself being battered to the left and right. The wild ride was all the more frightening in the pitch darkness.

Robert's hands were bruised, his knees scraped and cut by the fall. Then, as suddenly as the sharp descent had begun, the lord landed on a solid surface. The wind was knocked out of him as he came to rest with his knees up around his chest. But he was still conscious.

There was water cascading all around him in what appeared to be another chamber and he slid along a smooth floor, pushed along by the force of it. Then Robert felt his legs dangle over the edge of a precipice but he had no way of knowing how deep it was because he still could not see a thing. The lord breathed easy, though, glad to be alive. But he should have guessed it would not be so easy to escape this trap.

'Robert!' Arnauld cried. 'Where are you?'

'I'm here by the edge,' the lord replied.

'Get over to the wall! There's another fall of water coming.'

Before he could make a move a fresh gush of water suddenly hit Robert from behind. He shrieked in terror as he lost his grip on the smooth surface of the floor. He clung with all his might to the edge of the precipice as more and more water cascaded down upon him.

Just as his fingers were slipping away and he knew he could hold on no longer, Robert felt a hand grasp his wrist.

'Hang on!' Donal cried. Then another hand reached out to him and another. In seconds he was dragged up onto the smooth stone surface again. And there he lay, trying to catch his breath and clear his stinging eyes. The lord coughed and spat the foul-tasting water out of his system and in between thanked his companions for their quick thinking.

'Donal,' he spluttered, 'thank God you are safe.'

'That depends,' Arnauld quipped, 'on what you mean by safe. We are all safer than we were in Guy d'Alville's custody, that is true.'

It was only when Robert could open his eyes properly he noticed he was lying on his back in a small chamber. There was a faint light filtering in from far above and this illuminated the only features of the room. The floor was of polished marble set in squares of alternating black and white. It ended in the sharp edge where Robert had been clinging and over which so much water had drained away.

The lord crawled the short distance to the edge and looked over. The hole below him seemed bottomless in this light and Robert began to tremble as he realised just how lucky he had been.

'Saint Brigid,' the lord prayed quietly, 'lead us safely to the chapel.'

'This is not the chamber we are looking for,' he heard Geoffrey say behind him, 'but it is probably an anteroom.

Are you all right, Lord Robert?' the young man asked, panting heavily.

'I will live,' Robert replied as if he wasn't really sure whether he would. 'No bones broken. But I fear what that foul water will do to my stomach.'

'The passage must have been closed for many years,' Arnauld coughed. 'The water probably built up over time with nowhere to drain to.'

'The stench is disgusting,' Robert commented as Arnauld got to his knees and stood up rather stiffly.

'That passage is probably linked to the latrines,' the old knight added. 'I expect we will have to have a wash sooner or later.'

'You sound disappointed at the prospect,' Donal noted wryly.

'It has been some years since I took my vows, young man,' the old knight replied. 'Considering a Templar is never permitted to remove his underclothing, young Geoffrey and myself will probably be suffering from this ordeal for much longer than you. I personally would much prefer a quick knock on the head to a week wearing damp undergarments.'

'This passage leads nowhere,' Donal told them, changing the subject. 'There does not seem to be anything down there,' he pointed into the pit, 'but more blackness.'

'Perhaps there is a ledge on the other side of the abyss,' Arnauld suggested as he took a ring off his finger and tossed it into the dark. The gold ring tinkled on the other side to confirm his theory. Then he took a dagger he had lifted from the gaoler and let it fall into the pit.

The four men waited a long while before they heard a far-off clatter as the weapon hit bottom.

'It looks to me like there is only one way forward,' Arnauld decided, 'and that is to jump this gap in the floor.'

'We can't see the other side!' Robert protested. 'We

cannot just leap off into the void without knowing what is on the other side.'

'It is a trick of the light filtering from above,' Arnauld explained. 'In any case, I have heard it argued that most things in life boil down to a leap into the void.'

'You really can't be serious,' Robert gasped.

'If we had a light to see by,' Arnauld agreed, 'it would be easier. We are going to have to trust in God to see us through this particular passage.'

'The stones on the floor are set exactly the same as in the chapel,' Geoffrey observed. 'We must be close to our objective.'

'It cannot be far,' Arnauld agreed, then he rubbed his hands together. 'So, who is going to go first?'

'I will,' Geoffrey volunteered. He unstrapped his belt and unsheathed his sword. In a few moments he had tossed the blade and belt across to the other side. Everyone could hear the clatter as they landed. The others then unstrapped their weapons and tossed them over.

Geoffrey did not seem at all frightened by the prospect of this great leap. But Robert could feel his own stomach churning with nerves. After his lucky escape he was not keen to tempt fate again. The lord stared into the darkness and decided he could not possibly jump this gap. It was too wide, too frightening.

'Call out when you make it across,' Donal told Geoffrey and the young Templar nodded confidently. Then Geoffrey stood with his back against the wall, preparing himself for the leap. After a few deep breaths he started his short run towards the edge.

Robert watched his friend until the moment before Geoffrey jumped. At that instant the lord closed his eyes tightly and listened. He could not bear to watch. His heart was beating in his throat for the young man. A split second later there was a crash and he heard Geoffrey call out.

'Are you hurt?' Robert shrieked. 'Geoffrey, are you hurt?'
There was no answer.
'Geoffrey!' Arnauld called. 'Can you hear me?'
Then they heard a muffled reply. 'I am winded,' Geoffrey cried out feebly. 'I will be fine in a few moments.'
Arnauld let a broad smile play upon his lips. 'I'll go next,' he announced. Before Robert had recovered from the terror of Geoffrey's leap, the old knight was running to the edge of the stone. Arnauld jumped as far as he could into the blackness, his legs and arms flaying wildly about him. Robert was still unable to watch.
There was a loud thud followed by a grunt as Arnauld landed on the other side. Robert could feel his palms sweating and his legs shaking. Then he felt Donal's eyes upon him.
'Are you all right?' the sergeant asked. 'You have gone pale.'
'There is nothing wrong with me,' Robert lied. 'You go next.'
Donal nodded and then made ready for his run-up. In a few moments he had launched himself off into the dark, leaving Robert behind. The lord watched his sergeant soar off into the unknown and suddenly disappear into the darkness.
'Robert!' Geoffrey yelled. 'Are you coming?'
'I need a few moments,' the lord called back as he tried desperately to steady his nerves.
'We don't have much time, man,' Arnauld retorted. 'Come along!'
Robert stood on the edge of the abyss, struggling for a glimpse of the other side. There was only blackness.
'I can't!' the lord cried, his voice cracking. 'I cannot jump.'
There was no reply from his three companions.
'Did you hear me?' Robert bellowed. 'You will have to

go on without me. I haven't the stomach for it.'

The chamber was perfectly silent. No word, no sound crossed the divide. Robert began to become concerned that something had happened to his comrades.

'Can you hear me?' the lord screamed.

There was a loud shuffling sound on the other side of the abyss. Then Robert heard Arnauld's voice cry out in terror.

'Help!' the old knight shrieked. 'Help us!'

Robert realised his friends must have been ambushed. In that instant the lord forgot his own fear. His companions were clearly in danger. He could not sit on the ledge to let them be captured or murdered. So, with shaking knees, he made his way back to the wall to start his run to the edge of the abyss. Robert's whole body was trembling but now it was out of fear for the safety of his friends.

The lord closed his eyes tightly and when he opened them again he made his move. With all his force he ran toward the edge, one foot before the other until, just before the stone dropped away into a bottomless pit, he leapt out. He did not intend to make a sound but he screamed his lungs out as he jumped.

For what seemed an impossibly long time Robert sailed through the air, howling as he flew. Abruptly his legs buckled painfully under him. A crushing pain in his chest put an end to his yell as he rolled across the marble floor. The lord ended up on his back, relieved he had landed on the other side.

'Oh Christ!' he bellowed in shock and anguish. He bumped his head on the floor as he tumbled over to lie face down, arms and legs spread wide. His whole body ached and he could hardly breathe from the heavy landing. Then he remembered his friends. As quickly as he could he rolled over again onto his back in an attempt to get on his feet.

But as he did so he felt a large hand press down on his chest.

'Stay right where you are,' a voice commanded and then a rush light appeared. Robert was blinded at first by the flaming torch after so long in the half-light. It was a few seconds before he could focus on the face of the man before him.

It was Arnauld.

'I am sorry for doing that to you,' the old knight apologised, 'but it really was not a long jump at all and we will be needing you. I could not leave you behind.'

Donal was holding a new rush light. 'Are you injured?' he asked, concerned.

'Only in my pride,' Robert struggled to answer. Then he turned to Arnauld again. 'I will never trust you again as long as I live.'

'With that policy you should live long,' the old knight laughed.

'There is another channel in the floor over here,' Geoffrey observed as he fitted the point of his brother's sword into it. 'It is exactly the same as the one we found earlier.'

This did not reassure any of the others at all.

'Can you move?' Donal asked his lord.

Robert nodded and got to his feet with his sergeant's help. It was a few minutes before he could walk unaided. Geoffrey waited until the lord had recovered, then he indicated it was time to move on.

'Stay quiet,' Geoffrey urged his companions as he made ready to press the release on the concealed entrance. 'We have made enough noise. And draw your blades. We have no way of knowing what is on the other side of this door.'

Where the top of the pommel lay against the wall he pressed his hand onto the stone. A rectangle was outlined in the blank marble where before there had been no sign of a door. The entrance slid open quietly and smoothly. When the stone had slipped away there was nothing but a wooden panel on the other side.

Geoffrey shoved on the wood and it disintegrated, splintering into a thousand pieces under his hand. This was the last thing he had expected. The young Templar had put too much weight into his push. As the timber collapsed he fell forward onto the ground with a mighty crash.

Arnauld and Robert jumped over the top of him into the next chamber, their blades at the ready. This room was about twice the size of Geoffrey's cell. It was empty and, as with the previous chamber, lit by a single torch. Donal followed after them, bearing the other torch.

'What was that you said about staying quiet?' Donal jibed as he helped his friend to his feet. 'Where are we?'

Geoffrey looked about him, immediately noticing a long wide length of cloth hanging from one wall of the room. 'This is the master's dressing room,' the young man explained, 'where he prepares himself before entering the chapel.'

Robert lifted the wall hanging with the point of his sword and peered out into the huge room beyond.

'There are candles everywhere,' he reported, 'and the beautiful black and white marble floor seems to go on forever. Is this the chapel?'

When Geoffrey looked into the chamber beyond he nodded. 'This is the place,' he confirmed excitedly. 'This is the chapel.'

'Where is the tomb between the two pillars?' Donal asked.

'I will show you,' Geoffrey stated as he pulled back the cloth and stepped into the chapel. The sound of his leather-soled shoes on the polished surface of the floor rang out.

Eagerly he rushed to the tomb and knelt down beside it, attempting to lift the heavy stone lid. But he could not budge it.

Robert and Donal arrived seconds later. Robert knelt down beside his companion to help him but Donal stood back a little. The chieftain was captivated by the strange expression on the face of the knight on the lid of the sarcophagus. It sent a chill through his body.

Arnauld knelt down beside the other two to lend a hand, though he did not try very hard to shift the stone.

'This is hopeless,' the old knight declared in a defeated tone. 'If there were twenty of us we might stand a chance of lifting this gravestone. But why move it in the first place?'

'Beneath this stone,' Geoffrey explained, 'is the entrance to the underground vault where we will find the treasure.'

'Rubbish!' Arnauld exclaimed. 'This is the tomb of my cousin Cesare Lusignon. I watched them lay him here a few days after work on this chamber was completed.'

Donal noticed, too, that the legs of the figure on the tombstone were crossed in a most unusual manner. He recalled one of the cards Geoffrey had been left by his brother. It had depicted a man hanged upside down by one foot from a cross. It was almost as if this tombstone had been modelled on that card.

'That is a man's tomb,' Donal spoke up, suddenly feeling the cold in this chamber. 'We must not desecrate a man's last resting place.'

'This is not a tomb,' Geoffrey argued. 'If I am right, this is the doorway to the vaults under the chapel. Come and help us instead of standing there dumbfounded.'

Donal reluctantly knelt down to lend a hand, but even with his aid the stone would still not move an inch. It was far too heavy. Geoffrey sat back defeated and panting from exertion. He pulled out his brother's will again and scanned it quickly in the hope of finding an answer.

'"Lift the hanged guardian high upon the Three",' he read aloud, '"look to the throne, wherein lies the secret realm, the lance that wounds. The dish that feeds the multitude, the cup that heals the maimed king. And above all others the scroll on which is writ the book of ages."'

'I do not understand,' Robert admitted, confused. 'What is the Three?'

'Who is there?' a man's voice suddenly echoed out across the chapel as the main door swung open.

'Guards!' Arnauld declared. 'We have been discovered.'

The four men barely had time to draw their weapons when five black-clad knights burst into the chapel and ran towards them.

'Throw down your swords!' one of the Hospital knights demanded, 'or I will introduce you to the point of mine.'

Arnauld held up his left hand. 'He is right, brothers,' the old knight stated. 'We do not stand a chance against so many brave warriors of the Hospital.'

'What are you talking about?' Geoffrey cried. 'There are only five of them.'

Arnauld looked around him as if he were shocked. 'Well, in that case,' he went on, 'I'll take these two and you boys will have to make do with one each.'

That was enough to catch the Hospitallers off guard. In seconds one of Arnauld's opponents lay bleeding on the floor and the old knight was pushing another knight into a corner.

Robert chose the largest of the enemy to tackle and was soon struggling for his life with a worthy opponent.

Donal fought like a gentleman at first, parrying the blows of his enemy and deftly dodging the man's sweeping blade. But he soon lost patience with the fight and punched the Hospitaller in the jaw with his left fist. The warrior fell sprawling to the floor. His helm flew off and he knocked his head hard on the marble. When Donal was sure the knight was unconscious, he took the belt from about the man's waist, then bound the Hospitaller's hands tightly behind his back.

Geoffrey fared better than his comrades. His opponent

must have been a recently inducted recruit for he fell down on his knees in front of the young Templar after only a minimal resistance. Geoffrey took his sword and tied his hands behind his back.

In the meantime Robert was in trouble. His opponent was strong enough that each blow he landed knocked the lord back a step or two. Robert was tiring. His body still ached from the fall down the shaft and the jump across the abyss, and he found his reactions were slowing as he approached exhaustion.

Donal finished binding his prisoner just as Robert missed a parry. The Hospitaller's sword glanced off Robert's blade and the point struck the lord just below the right eye. Robert fell back against the three-legged machine that had been used to raise the stone in Geoffrey's initiation.

In a flash Donal had leapt to his lord's defence, sprinting towards the enemy warrior with a wild cry. The Hospitaller glanced round then and, seeing his defeated comrades on the floor, realised he could not possibly win this fight.

The man sheathed his sword before Donal had a chance to challenge him. Then he turned and ran to the main chapel door. The chieftain did not follow after him. Instead he went to see to Robert.

'Are you hurt?' he cried as he knelt down beside the block and tackle.

'Catch that man!' the lord replied, stemming the flow of blood from his face. 'If he gets away, he'll warn d'Alville.'

But it was already too late. The Hospitaller had shut the great door behind him and disappeared. Moments later they both heard a loud groan and turned in time to see Arnauld withdrawing his blade from the body of a falling black knight.

'I have always preferred a stabbing sword to a cutting edge,' the old knight commented calmly.

'We must hurry,' Donal told them. 'One of the Hospitallers escaped. He will surely raise the alarm.'

Geoffrey came to kneel beside Robert. 'Where do you suggest we hurry to?' he asked as he tore a piece of his tunic to press against the lord's wound.

As the young Templar got up he steadied himself against the timber support of the lifting machine. And an answer struck him. He recalled his investiture into the order. A great slab of stone had been lifted out of the floor to create a space for his symbolic grave.

'Here is the solution,' he whispered almost to himself. 'The device with three arms and a rope and pulley. This can surely lift the stone.'

'Of course,' Arnauld agreed. 'That is the only way we will lift this grave slab. But I tell you there is nothing to be found in that tomb but a mouldering body.'

The device rolled easily across the floor on wheels attached to each of the supporting arms. With a little manoeuvring the four men managed to place the machine directly above the stone sarcophagus.

It was then Donal noticed a ring of iron in the centre of the stone. He slipped a hook through the ring as Geoffrey and Robert began to haul on the rope. But even with the help of this machine the two men could not raise the slab.

Soon all four were hauling slowly and steadily on the ropes. With great effort they raised the stone a few inches from its resting place. Then they wheeled the device aside a little to peer into the grave.

What they saw deeply disappointed all of them save for Arnauld. As the slab slid off the sarcophagus all that was revealed were the dry bones and rusted armour of a former Knight of the Temple.

'I told you this was Cesare's tomb,' Arnauld commented smugly. 'This is not the door to the vault.'

Undeterred, Geoffrey insisted they finish uncovering the grave. When the slab had rolled away completely, he leaned against the side of the tomb, sweating and panting, searching desperately for some answer to this frustrating problem.

'I don't understand!' he exclaimed. 'It should have been here. It should be beneath the sign of the hanged man.'

It was Donal who noticed the great square-ended key which the dead knight clutched in his sword hand instead of a blade. 'There it is!' he pointed triumphantly. '*Clavis ad Thesaurum*. The key to the treasure.'

Geoffrey's eyes lit up. 'Of course,' he replied excitedly as he reached into the tomb to pick up the huge key. A few of the knight's finger bones clung to the key but Geoffrey unceremoniously prised them off. Donal rolled his eyes at this mark of disrespect.

'It would be too obvious,' Geoffrey declared, 'to have the very entrance to the vault within this tomb. There must be a lock or device here that fits this key and opens the doorway to the vault.'

Geoffrey looked at the two maps which had been drawn with special ink and concealed within other documents. Once again he searched frantically for an answer. But there did not seem to be an obvious solution to the problem anywhere on the soaked and crumpled pages.

'I have come this far only to be stumped by a tiny obstacle like this,' Geoffrey grunted as he pored over the letters again.

'Where there is a key,' Donal piped up, 'there is a lock it was made for. We should be searching for the lock in this chamber.'

'*Look to the throne*,' Robert said, remembering the verse from the parchment, '*wherein lies the secret realm*.'

'Of course,' Geoffrey exclaimed. 'This strange-shaped box drawn on the map. It must be the master's chair.' He ran around to the front of the chair and tore off the covers of gilt cloth.

'Steady on!' Arnauld cried out. 'That chair cost a fortune. It belongs to the Temple.'

'If I am right, the Temple treasure is laid under this chair,' Geoffrey retorted. 'If we can get it out of this castle before Guy discovers it, I will buy you a new chair.'

Underneath the expensive golden cloth a rectangular stone was concealed with a strangely worked iron slot in the front of it just large enough to fit the key. Robert and Donal pushed the wooden throne backwards so that it toppled against the tomb. But their action cleared the stone underneath so Geoffrey would have plenty of room.

With great care and trepidation Geoffrey slipped the key into the slot and turned it. He waited, expecting to see a door swing open or a section of the floor miraculously slide away to reveal a cavern beneath them. But nothing happened. The men stared at each other, dumbfounded.

'Let us try to move the stone,' Robert suggested finally. 'It may have simply got stuck if it has been untouched for many years.'

The four men put their backs to the task and in a few moments the stone began to give way to them. It slid silently across the floor to reveal a steep staircase leading into the darkness below. Donal grabbed a candle and gave it to Geoffrey.

'After you,' he said politely. 'This is your treasure hunt.'

Robert took a candle for himself and gave another to both Donal and Arnauld. Then they followed Geoffrey down the impossibly new-looking steps into the chamber below. It was a long climb down and Geoffrey remembered the words his brother had written in his will.

'*Now begins the tale of your descent*,' he whispered to

himself, understanding finally that the phrase had nothing to do with ancestry as he had first thought. He counted thirty steps down, then three more before the floor levelled out. He lifted his torch and gasped.

Seconds later Geoffrey's three companions were standing beside him, their eyes wide open, mesmerised by what they saw.

THE CASTLE OF JOY

Chapter Nineteen

At the bottom of the secret stair Geoffrey stood astounded, gazing upon the largest single chamber he had ever seen in his life. The great vaulted cavern was carved out of solid rock to resemble the interior of a majestic cathedral.

Thin stone pillars reached up into the blackness above, spanning out at the top in elegant flowerlike shapes which touched the roof. The ceiling was impossibly high. The silence profoundly heavy. The air was stale but there was a slight breeze.

'The whole of Acre could fit in here,' Robert whispered and his breathy voice echoed long after he finished speaking.

'This chamber is far older than the castle above us,' Arnauld noted, keeping his voice low out of deep respect. 'I have never seen workmanship like it.'

'Who built this place?' Robert asked

'I have heard that the sect of the Nasreans concealed their holy books in a chamber similar to this. But that would have been in the time of the Romans,' Arnauld answered, 'during the lifetime of Christ.'

'Could this chamber be that ancient?' Geoffrey coughed in surprise.

'I believe it may well be that old,' Arnauld confirmed. 'There is a book in my library which describes the Nasrean chamber in detail. The manuscript claims this was the first chapel dedicated to the Holy Virgin.'

'Mary,' Robert whispered in awe. 'She set me on this quest.'

'My vision,' Geoffrey added. 'The Virgin was leading me to this place right from the beginning.'

'The chamber goes on forever,' Donal chimed in, his breath taken away by the sight. The chieftain held up his torch and caught a glimpse of polished metal thirty paces or so in front of them. 'What is that?' he asked as he stepped forward.

'We must be very careful,' Arnauld advised them. 'Do not stray away from each other. It would be too easy to get lost in here.'

Donal nodded but there was no holding him back. Robert and Geoffrey were still savouring this moment. For the lord this was a more mysterious experience than he had imagined possible. He was on the brink of viewing the sacred treasures of the Temple. Geoffrey was just as awestruck. He could sense a holy presence the like of which he had never come across before.

'Come along,' Donal insisted impatiently.

The chieftain had not walked ten paces when he realised what he was looking at. A massive bronze vessel stood on four great metal legs immediately in front of them. Robert guessed the giant basin would have taken up all the space in the courtyard of his own castle at Bally Raine.

Donal approached the cauldron and climbed up to dip his hand into the liquid which filled it to the brim. It was cool, clear and fresh. The chieftain put his fingers to his lips. It was water. Then Donal noticed a slow drip from the ceiling which fed this tiny lake. The water was always moving and so could not stagnate. The floor beneath the vessel was covered in the run-off liquid.

'This is the great Sea of Metal,' Arnauld informed them,

overawed. 'This once stood in the Temple of Solomon in the days before the Romans sacked Jerusalem. Christ would have looked on this basin. He would have dipped his hand into it just as you have done, Donal, to ritually wash himself before going to his prayers.'

'How do you know that?' the chieftain asked.

'I read it in one of my books,' Arnauld replied.

'The book you showed me when I arrived here,' Geoffrey cut in. 'The manuscript which describes the missing treasures of the Old Temple of Jerusalem.'

Arnauld nodded as Geoffrey passed by the great bronze dish, eager to discover the other wonders of this vault.

'Wash your hands,' Robert advised them. 'We should all wash our hands as the ancients did.'

Geoffrey nodded in agreement and one by one they touched the water and sprinkled it over their faces in silent reverence.

In the far distance Geoffrey could just make out the forms of two massive pillars exactly the same as the pair which adorned the chapel. These pillars, however, were almost twice the height and girth of the two in the chamber above. This vault was so huge they still did not reach the ceiling of this enormous cellar.

As Geoffrey moved closer he could see there was a square- shaped enclosure behind these pillars. It seemed to be constructed entirely from cloth stretched between posts set into the floor. Without waiting for the others Geoffrey moved closer to pass between the pillars. The young Templar made straight for this strange structure.

He was about to lay his hands on the cloth when he felt a hand on his shoulder and he jumped in shock.

'Stop!' Robert yelled, grabbing the young man by the arm to drag him away from the cloths. 'If these cloths conceal the Ark of the Covenant then it is very dangerous to get too close. I remember the stories from the Old Testament of those men who came too close to the sacred Ark and were burned to ashes in moments by the wrath of God.'

'This is not the Tabernacle of the Ark of the Covenant,' Arnauld stated confidently.

'He's right,' Geoffrey agreed. 'This flimsy barrier has been set here to frighten any man who has come this far but who does not know what is truly hidden behind the cloth.'

'How can you be so certain?' Robert asked with scepticism in his voice.

'Because he read it in my book,' Arnauld answered. 'The one in my library which describes this chamber.'

'The Ark of the Covenant,' Goeffrey went on, 'was taken to the land of Ethiopia in the time of the Queen of Sheba. It has rested there until this day, if the account in the old manuscript is to be believed.'

'I never cease to be amazed at your learning, young man,' Arnauld smiled. 'You will make an incomparable grand master one day.' He patted Geoffrey on the shoulder and then went on. 'Your brother and I knew a knight who had travelled with his companions to the city of Axum in search of the Ark. That was some ten years ago. He returned but his comrades remained behind. He told me they took oaths as Guardians of the Ark. Since then they have been forbidden to leave the city.'

'You see,' Geoffrey insisted, 'the Ark could not be here. This fine cloth holds no deadly secrets.'

'I hope you are right,' Arnauld conceded, standing back from the younger man. 'I personally would not put so much store in an old book and the tales of a wandering Templar.'

'There is nothing else in this entire chamber,' Geoffrey explained, 'but the great bronze dish, the two pillars and this cloth enclosure. What we seek must lie behind the cloth.'

'Unless there are further hidden chambers,' Robert piped up.

'No,' Geoffrey replied. 'This enclosure is laid in exactly the same position as the Holy of Holies in the Tabernacle of the original Temple in Jerusalem. This is where the remaining treasure is concealed.'

'The remaining treasure?' Donal said, raising an eyebrow. 'What do you mean?'

'Most of the hoard left Outremer long ago,' Geoffrey explained. 'My brother was killed transporting a portion which was given into his responsibility.'

'Which has since been secreted in several different vaults in England and France,' Arnauld added. 'This is the last shipment.'

'And,' Geoffrey continued, 'if I am right, this is the most important portion of all.'

The young Templar quoted from his brother's will.

' "Wherein lies the secret realm, the lance that wounds. The dish that feeds the multitude. The cup that heals the maimed king. And above all others the scroll on which is writ the book of ages." ' He put the papers down and repeated the last line. ' "And above all others the scroll on which is writ the book of ages." '

'What does it mean?' Robert muttered.

'The most precious treasure of all was left for last,' Geoffrey repeated. 'The book of ages is more esteemed than all the other items, at least to the Order of the Temple. Whatever it may be,' he told his comrades, 'its existence has been the reason the Order of the Hospital has rallied to hunt the treasure down.'

With that the young knight slowly approached the enclosure once more. When he stood in front of the cloths he waited a moment to relish the experience of having solved the mysteries of the vault. Then, with a great burst of elation, Geoffrey grabbed the cloth and tore it away from the posts to which it had been attached.

There before him lay a large box, bigger than a wagon.

Two long wooden shafts protruded from each end of it so it could be carried. But Geoffrey could not imagine who would have been able to lift it.

'It is shaped exactly like the Ark of the Covenant,' Geoffrey noted, 'except that it is far too large to be the Ark.'

Donal and Robert approached cautiously, their curiosity getting the better of them. Both men were suddenly aware there was a strange presence in this chamber that engendered an unexplained fear in their hearts.

'Is this the treasure?' Donal asked urgently.

'It is,' Geoffrey replied, 'all that remains of the treasure. Now we must find a way to get it away from Castle Mont Salvasch.'

Donal shook his head. 'We will never move it,' he scoffed. 'It would take a hundred men to shift that box.'

Geoffrey was about to suggest they split the treasure up into smaller lots when the eerie silence of the great cavern was shattered by the noise of many voices.

Donal looked to Robert and Geoffrey in dismay but it was Arnauld who spoke what was on all their minds. 'We have been discovered,' he sighed. 'Now we are in for a fight.'

As Donal and his companions entered the treasure chamber, far away in Bally Raine Eilish sat on her windowsill looking out over the moat and the rolling hills. In the distance she could just make out the line of the silvery serpentine River Clonough. Illuminated by the full moon the stream passed through the countryside toward the hamlet of Shelton.

There, a generation earlier, monks of the Cistercian order

had built a monastic settlement. And here old Lord William had retired to a life of secluded contemplation.

The ginger cat, Angus, who had once belonged to William, sprang up to sit on the healer's lap. Straightaway he began kneading his paws in her skirt, purring loudly and pushing the side of his face against her arm. Eilish put a hand gently on his back and the cat rubbed against it with all his force as he mewed his contentment.

'I miss him,' she whispered to the appreciative cat. 'I miss his bright eyes and his laugh. I will never see him again,' she sighed, filled with a terrible sorrow.

Angus lifted his head to look deep and directly into her eyes and their gazes locked. Eilish would not have been surprised in that instant if the cat had spoken up to soothe her with some feline tale of two lovers separated, only temporarily, by death.

'The mind of God may be glimpsed,' Eilish said aloud as she recalled an old verse, 'in the eye of a cat.' Angus purred on, heedless of her wisdom, staring at her as only cats can. Eilish ran her hand down his back again and this was enough to distract him.

All of a sudden the cat's mood changed sharply. He dug his claws into her leg and sat up, ears erect and twitching. His purring ceased as soon as he sensed someone outside the chamber. Sure enough Eilish took only three breaths before there was a knock at the door. Angus stood up on the healer's lap and hissed threateningly.

'That's enough!' Eilish squealed as she unpicked each of the claws from her dress and lifted the ginger cat up to release him. 'It is only someone come to visit me.'

Eilish went to open the door, but as she laid her hand on the catch Angus screamed in an almost human voice. As it opened a little he rushed out of the chamber and onto the stairs. The healer was looking down at him, frowning, when she caught sight of a pair of black riding boots before her.

She raised her eyes to see Rufus leaning against the doorpost.

'Good evening, my lady,' the young FitzWilliam hummed.

'Good evening, Master Rufus,' Eilish replied immediately. 'You are awake late.'

'I could not sleep,' Rufus admitted as he attempted to catch the woman's eye. 'My mind is weighing heavy on my brother's death.'

'I have been thinking about Donal also.'

'May I sit with you?' Rufus ventured.

Eilish thought about her answer for a second. She had been quite content to sit alone in her room and probably would have drifted off to sleep sooner or later. But Rufus had been very understanding and generous toward her since the news of her husband's death. The healer decided it would do no harm to offer some words of comfort to him.

'This has been a very difficult time for you,' Eilish offered as she opened the door a little wider to let the young FitzWilliam in.

'It is not that long ago I lost my father,' Rufus said quietly. 'To have lost a brother so soon after was a double blow.'

'But William lives in the Abbey at Shelton, does he not?'

'He may as well be dead,' the Norman sighed, crossing the room. 'He receives no visitors nor word from beyond the walls of his sanctuary.'

'Have you told him of Robert's death?' Eilish inquired, leaving the door ajar as she went to the window to resume her seat.

'The abbot was given a letter explaining the situation, but I have no idea whether my father received the news,' the young FitzWilliam sighed.

'I will go and speak with the old man,' Eilish offered. 'He was a great friend of my father-in-law.'

'No!' Rufus blurted, holding up his hand. 'That will not

be necessary. He would not speak with you anyway. Father believes all things feminine were created by the Devil as parodies of God's handiwork. They say there is not a female creature in the entire abbey. The sour old abbot cannot bear the company of womenfolk. You would not be allowed inside.'

'What a stupid and bitter old man the abbot must be,' Eilish stated, surprised at such a pointless act of denial. 'Where do the brothers get their milk from,' she asked, 'if there are no cows?'

'The tenants who live nearby sell it to the abbey,' Rufus explained. 'They also sell them eggs.'

'What of the abbey rats, I wonder?' Eilish jibed. 'Do you think they keep the abbot's injunction and refuse to mingle with females?'

'In the time of the previous abbot the monks did not follow the Rule of Saint Benedict so closely as they do now.' Rufus laughed nervously as he observed the woman's face for any reaction. 'I have heard,' he went on, sensing that she would not be too shocked by what he was about to say, 'that every brothel from here to Wexford had black-robed visitors from the Abbey of Shelton.'

'That was before the white Cistercians came to Ireland,' Eilish noted with a laugh. 'Theirs is an order doomed to die out.'

'How is that?' Rufus asked as he walked across the room to stand closer to the fire.

'They have no females among them,' she explained. 'They cannot propagate. Within a generation there will be none of them left.'

'They receive new postulants every day,' Rufus told her. 'Lord William of Bally Raine among them. I was foolish to have detested my father's rule so vehemently. Now I would give anything for him to renounce his vows and come back to the castle to serve as lord again. If he had not been drawn into the web of the Templars, he would not have chosen the life of a Cistercian.'

'You will have to do the best you can,' Eilish reminded him. 'I am sure you are up to the task.'

'Thank you for having faith in me,' the young FitzWilliam said as sincerely as he could, though in truth he blessed the day his old father had left for Shelton. 'But I fear without old William's wisdom and Robert's gentle guiding hand I cannot hope to run these estates. If it had not been for you . . .' He paused, looking Eilish directly in the eye. '. . . I would have given up months ago.'

Now it was Eilish's turn to blush. 'Thank you, Rufus,' she stammered, slightly embarrassed. 'I am very glad to be able to repay some of your kindness.'

The healer was suddenly very uncomfortable alone in this room with this man. Only a year or two ago she would not have given him the courtesy of a greeting. She still had little time for the Normans and their ways, but living in the castle had brought her to some understanding of them.

'It is strange to think,' the young FitzWilliam commented as he moved to stand by the window close to Eilish, 'that if you had been born a Norman or I had been born a Gael, we might have thought better of each other from the start.'

'I have never thought ill of you, Rufus,' Eilish lied, fearing he had read her thoughts in the expression on her face. 'You have been the very pillar that has held up the roof of this castle. You are tired and drained because there has been one disaster after another since the men went away. It has all begun to catch up with you.'

'You are right,' Rufus sighed, 'I am just tired.' He leaned against the stonework framing the window and looked directly at Eilish.

'If you are going to run these estates as lord,' she suggested, moving away from him slightly, 'you should be looking to find yourself a wife who can take over the duties I have been performing in this castle.'

'I would not be able to go on without you, Eilish,' Rufus declared quickly. 'You have been a better wife to me than any woman could have been. You have been a partner to me,' he went on, 'in all but name.'

Eilish drew a deep breath then looked at Rufus with a questioning glare, trying to discern whether there was any hidden inference in the Norman's words. 'What exactly do you mean?' she stuttered.

Rufus reached over to take her hand. 'I am asking whether you would consider becoming my wife,' he stated.

Eilish's jaw slackened in disbelief, then the healing woman snatched her hand away from his, swung her feet down onto the floor and walked briskly to the door. As she opened it wide she turned to Rufus, considering her words carefully.

'I am flattered by your offer,' she began, trying to sound grateful even though her stomach was turning as it had on the night her house had burned down, 'but I cannot accept the proposal. I have not yet grown used to the absence of my husband,' she explained. 'I am sure you understand that Donal stills lives in my heart.'

Eilish felt her heart racing. She did not want to talk any more. She felt Rufus had betrayed her, using her grief to his own advantage, assuming she had been weakened by all that had happened to her.

'As does Robert in mine,' Rufus replied soothingly. 'But they are gone. And no matter how much we may miss them, we are the ones who have been left behind to carry on. How long would you wait before considering my proposal?'

'I cannot be sure,' Eilish mumbled, avoiding the issue. 'Donal will never leave my thoughts entirely.' She could feel an anger building inside and she did not want to let Rufus see it. The healer kept telling herself how kind the young FitzWilliam had been to her.

'Neither of us is young any more,' Rufus argued gently. 'I would like to have a son before I die.'

'I too would like to have children,' Eilish agreed, sure this conversation had gone far enough. Her throat was swelling with emotion and she did not know how long she could control herself.

'Then wed me,' the Norman insisted. 'I will be a good husband to you. Together we will rule the entire estate as we have been doing so well these last few months.'

'I am not ready to speak of such things,' Eilish said, flustered. 'The time is not right. Now, if you will excuse me . . .'

'I understand,' Rufus replied in a comforting tone. 'I can see you need to think carefully about the offer. I did not mean to ask you so soon but the conversation just happened to come around to it.'

'You have been thinking about this for some time?' Eilish stuttered.

'A few days,' the Norman lied, then he realised he should leave. Best not to pressure her too much, he told himself. He decided to let her think on what he had said.

'Goodnight, Eilish,' Rufus wished her as he passed by her onto the stairs.

'Goodnight, Master Rufus,' she answered. Her tone was polite but her voice trembled. As she closed the door her eyes filled with tears and she hissed as she let her breath escape.

'How dare he?' she whispered. 'Bloody Normans! All they can think about is their precious bloodlines. Empty-hearted, self-centred, calculating bastards.' The rage got the better of her at last and she rolled her hands into fists to punch the door.

'Never!' Eilish vowed. 'Not as long as I have my wits and two strong arms.'

The healer was still standing there with clenched fists when she heard a familiar mewing and scratching outside her room. She pulled the latch on the door, opened it and scooped Angus up in her arms. The cat took up a position with his chin on her shoulder as she went back to the window to sit.

On her way Eilish blew out all the candles and the room was bathed in the radiance of the slow-burning turf fire. Angus quickly settled down to sleep on the healer's lap again, but Eilish stared out into the night sky.

'What am I going to do?' she asked the sleeping feline. Now that her rage had been spent, she began to think more clearly. 'Must I marry Rufus and forsake the memory of Donal forever? All for the wellbeing of my people? That bumbling idiot would never be a good lord without a guiding hand. At best he would bring ruin to the estates. At worst . . .' She paused. 'Who can tell?'

Angus ignored the healer as best he could. He rolled around until his ears were covered and he could not hear her speaking.

'I am afraid I must do whatever is best for my people,' she decided. 'He will pursue me whatever I do. The child in him is just beneath the surface. If I refuse him, that petulant child could destroy me and my clanspeople by seeking revenge.'

Eilish watched the moon rise into the night sky.

'I need some advice,' she decided. 'I cannot come to any conclusion on this alone. But who would be able to advise me?' she mused. 'Lonan is gone. Lord William is gone. Mathúin is gone.'

Then Eilish remembered the tilecutter. Donal had often spoken of Balek's wisdom.

'I will ask the tilecutter,' she concluded at last, 'and I will do whatever he advises me.'

Braonin had been sitting with Neesh in the great hall of the castle when he heard the door to Eilish's chamber open. Together they had listened carefully to hear what Rufus could be saying, but all they had been able to understand were the final parting goodnights.

As soon as the door had shut Rufus had marched down the stairs. The Norman had crossed the hall without acknowledging either of them and then disappeared out into the night air.

'There is evil in that man,' Braonin hissed now.

'He has two sides to him, that is for certain,' Neesh agreed.

'What do you mean?' the hunter asked.

Neesh considered telling Braonin of her first meeting with Rufus FitzWilliam. But she remembered her promise not to speak of it as long as Rufus paid his penance.

'The day he arrested you, for example,' the girl said, steering the conversation away from treacherous waters. 'He was very different then. But at other times he seems so caring. Especially when dealing with Eilish.'

'I have noticed that,' Braonin nodded. 'You don't think he has his eye on her, do you?'

'It is possible,' Neesh laughed. The thought had never crossed her mind. 'A marriage to Eilish,' she said, thinking aloud, 'would unite the FitzWilliam with the O'Regan family in a bond of blood. That would settle the question of the lordship of the estate.'

'I don't understand,' Braonin replied blankly.

'No-one would be able to challenge Rufus in his claim,' Neesh elaborated. 'For he would not only be the obvious candidate for the lordship under Norman law, he would also be married to the chieftainess of the estates. That would make him acceptable under Gaelic law also.'

'You don't think that is what he has in mind, do you?'

'He would be a fool if he had not thought about it,' Neesh replied. 'And Rufus is no fool.'

'There is a great difference,' Braonin cut in, 'between a wise man who may act stupidly once in a while and a fool who is stupid all of the time. Rufus is not a wise man.'

'He has shown he has compassion for our suffering,' Neesh objected. 'And if it had not been for his generosity, you would still be in prison.'

'It was Rufus who placed me in the cells in the first place,' Braonin countered. 'Do you think Eilish would ever consent to such a marriage?'

Neesh laughed. 'I don't think she would do any more than giggle at the suggestion.'

'I hope you are right,' Braonin replied under his breath. Then he leaned over to kiss Neesh on the cheek and she blushed at this familiar gesture. 'I am going out for a walk,' the hunter told her. 'You keep yourself warm.'

'I am off to bed now,' the girl told him. 'It is you who should be keeping warm on a night like this.'

'I have a warmth in me,' Braonin declared, 'that will preserve me on the harshest night.' Then he crossed the room and opened the heavy oak door. His eyes met with hers and for a few moments Neesh and Braonin looked at each other intently. After a while the girl opened her mouth to speak but before she had uttered a sound, Braonin pulled his cloak over his shoulders, smiled once more and turned to leave.

As the door slammed shut again Neesh closed her eyes and wished Braonin safe passage, knowing he was likely thinking of visiting the Culdee again.

Out in the courtyard the hunter recalled the conversation he had had with Cinneach only a few weeks earlier. Now he was determined to discover what Rufus had in mind for the future. If the Norman planned to marry Eilish, Braonin promised himself, then action would have to be taken to prevent such a disaster.

Chapter Twenty

Geoffrey had not expected so many torches, so much shouting and the deafening din of weaponry rattling. Before he or his companions had a chance to make any bid for freedom, twenty soldiers dressed in the livery of the Hospital were charging across the underground chamber to surround them, weapons drawn and pointing threateningly at them.

Then the sound of one man's laughter filled the great vault.

'Thank you, Geoffrey,' the voice sniped. 'I held high hopes for your intelligence. And, true to your potential, you did not let me down.'

The young Templar knew the voice immediately. But it was not until the knight was close enough for his face to be illuminated by torches that Geoffrey spoke his name.

'Guy d'Alville,' he spat. 'This was a trap!'

'Let us say I spurred you into action,' Guy laughed. 'I knew the entrance to the vault must be below the chapel somewhere, but I had no idea where to look.'

The black knight approached Arnauld and put an arm around his shoulder. 'And you, old man. you were brilliant. Faithful to your vows to the very last.'

Arnauld recoiled from Guy in disgust.

'I did not count on you rescuing this worn-out warhorse,' d'Alville told Geoffrey. 'I must compliment you, Arnauld

Lusignon. You fooled me for a while. I was shocked, I will admit, when I learned you were an impostor. But I must say I am impressed. Not many men can lie to me without arousing my suspicion. You should have been a Hospitaller.'

'How did you find out?' Arnauld inquired.

'One of your brother Templars let it slip in conversation.'

'On the rack,' Arnauld hissed.

'He is a changed man now,' Guy smiled, enjoying his own humour. 'Much taller than his mother remembers him.'

'What are you going to do with me?' the old knight asked solemnly.

'You will be put to death as a traitor,' Guy replied bluntly, 'and as soon as possible. If my fellow Knights of the Hospital discovered how you had duped me so completely, I might find it rather embarrassing. Sadly no-one will ever know of your clever ruse.'

'I will tell them,' Geoffrey declared.

'I have heard the Grand Master of the Temple is a necromancer who talks to the spirits of the dead,' Guy laughed. 'He will have to be very adept at the black arts to hear what you have to say from beyond the grave.'

'You have what you were searching for,' Robert cut in nervously. 'There is no reason to murder us in cold blood.'

'I don't intend to murder you in cold blood,' Guy gasped in mock offence. 'I am a man of honour. I intend to murder you in a fair fight.'

Then the Hospitaller looked at his gathered men, raised his hand and all his soldiers readied their blades.

'Actually,' Guy quipped, 'it will not be an entirely fair fight.'

'I wish I had never found the Templar treasure,' Geoffrey spat. 'I would rather have died in your prison than led you to this place.'

'Do not berate yourself too much, young fellow,' Guy

said in a serious tone. 'You solved a puzzle that has confounded the wisest men in the Order of the Hospital. Who knows, but under different circumstances you may have one day become the Grand Master of the Knights of Saint John. I would have been proud to serve with you. But now prepare to meet with your dead brother.'

'I have one thing I would ask,' Geoffrey added quickly, 'since I managed, with the help of my friends here, to locate the treasure. May we look before our deaths on the wondrous items stored here by our Templar brothers?'

Guy did not move a muscle as he carefully considered the proposal. Then he unexpectedly smiled and slowly nodded his head. 'I can think of no reason why not,' he said confidently. 'You have earned it and I don't think you will have the opportunity to steal it away from under my nose.'

The Hospitaller walked up to Geoffrey and put a hand on his shoulder. 'And I think one such as you will probably appreciate the experience. You see, I have been searching for the Grail Cup for many years. I am not so foolish as to believe it is literally a cup,' he added, 'but I am certain it contains the secret to eternal life without pain.'

'You have misunderstood the legends,' Arnauld sighed, 'like so many before you.'

'The game is ended, old man,' Guy spat. 'You do not need to lie any longer.'

D'Alville turned to one of his soldiers. 'Break open the box,' he barked.

The warrior stepped forward and lifted a war axe over his head to strike at the chest. The weapon came down heavily, shattering the timbers into splinters and smashing the side of the container. Then the warrior pulled at the broken boards to make a larger hole in the crate.

Guy stepped forward to examine the contents but he could not see inside.

'May I,' Geoffrey asked, handing his torch to the Hospitaller, 'be the first to retrieve something from the treasure?'

'Of course,' Guy replied, amused. Then he took the light from the young Templar and held it high.

Geoffrey reached a hand into the box. In seconds he had grabbed hold of a ceramic jar no longer than his arm and as wide as his thigh. He pulled the jar through the gaping hole in the chest but it caught against the jagged timber. The young Templar freed the jar but its wooden lid rolled onto the floor.

Geoffrey placed the jar on the floor and put his hand inside. When he withdrew it again he was holding a cylindrical article wrapped in decaying cloth. The young Templar unbound the cloth, becoming more and more excited.

His fingers trembled as he finally tore the covering away to reveal a long container made of dark wood. Inside this shell there was a copper roll with letters inscribed along the side in what Geoffrey assumed to be Greek. He tried to read the script but could make no sense of it.

'Do you know what this says?' he asked Guy as he passed the scroll to him.

The Hospitaller took the object and examined it under the light of one of his torches. 'I believe these are Greek letters,' he announced. 'This is a title. It says this is the Gospel of Saint Thomas.'

'The Gospel of Saint Thomas?' Donal repeated, only half believing what he heard. 'I know of that.'

'How could you know of such a thing?' Guy scoffed.

'I know a man who can quote from that book,' Donal replied icily. 'He told me it was one of the original eight Gospels of Christ.'

'Books,' Guy mumbled, disappointed at what he saw before him. 'The treasure of the Temple has been reduced to a pile of ancient books?'

'These books are the most dangerous written works on earth,' Arnauld cut in. 'They describe Our Saviour as a human rather than a divine being. They ascribe the status of wife and disciple to Mary Magdalene. One of these Gospels even claims Christ gave the entire ministry of the Church into Mary's keeping. Another teaches that the soul leaves the body at death and is born into a new form. These books espouse other doctrines also. One states there is no hell other than that which we create in our daily lives. And no heaven other than that which we earn each day and thoroughly believe in.'

'You knew all that was left of the treasure was a pile of heretical writings,' Guy snarled, 'and yet you let me believe there was more to it? You knew I was searching for the Grail and you let me waste my time here?'

'How do you know you have not found the Grail?' Arnauld smiled.

'These are books!' Guy shouted, throwing the scroll as far as he could. The precious article landed on the floor in the distance as his voice echoed through the vault.

'You were searching for everlasting life,' the old knight said quietly when the reverberations had ceased. 'And you have found it.'

Guy's frown deepened. 'Do not mock me, old man. Or I will crush you.'

'I am not afraid of death,' Arnauld replied, 'for I believe what these Gospels preach. There is no death. We pass from one body to another but our souls live forever. It was the early Church fathers who steered the faith away from this doctrine.'

'Why would they do that?' Robert interrupted, refusing to believe this tale.

'Because they modelled the Church on the Roman state,' Arnauld replied. 'Fear was their greatest weapon and the best way to control their followers. Fear of what happens after death. Fear of punishment for sins. Fear of damnation. Fear of God. In these books Christ never speaks of God as an avenging wrathful deity.'

'I have heard rumours of these books,' Guy laughed, 'but I never expected the Temple would be stupid enough to allow them to fall into the wrong hands. I thought the scrolls would have been among the first items to be spirited away to Europe. These books will do more damage to the Temple than you can imagine.'

Guy touched his lips with the tip of his tongue in a gesture of contempt. 'The Grail may have eluded me for the present,' the black knight snarled, 'but I will gain immeasurable satisfaction in bringing the true nature of the Order of the Temple to light.'

Guy turned to Geoffrey. 'Did you know,' he smiled, 'the inner circle of the Temple teaches that Christ was merely a military leader who had a falling out with his spiritual master and so was sacrificed in the name of the sect to which he belonged?'

'I have never heard of these strange ideas,' Geoffrey replied with venom, 'and yet I believe Arnauld if he says they are important to the teachings of the Temple.'

'I am sure you are also unaware,' Guy went on, 'that it is James, the brother of Christ, whom the Templars venerate as the founder of the Nasrean sect. Not Saint Peter the Rock. Did you know the Templars have revived many of the false ceremonies and rituals of that early time after Christ's death? The Temple denies the Resurrection of Our Lord. The Temple claims Christ had a son by the whore, Mary Magdalene. The Temple is biding its time, building its wealth and gathering its forces to challenge the Church of Rome for supremacy. The Pope may be their first target.'

'Some of these things of which you speak,' Arnauld admitted gravely, 'are true. I have known of the authentic teachings ever since I entered the College of the Living, the central enclave of learning in the Temple.'

'That is the name you give to your higher initiates,' Guy remarked. 'The Living. You are all heretics and when this evil is exposed, your comrades will burn for their crimes.'

'Now I believe I understand you,' Geoffrey stated. 'Your plan is to present these books as evidence to the Pope who will, of course, be outraged. He will naturally be persuaded to disband the Temple. I expect the Hospital will be granted all the Temple incomes and properties as a result. In one swift stroke you will destroy the greatest rival the Hospital has ever known. At the same time you will have redistributed the wealth of the heretics to your own people.'

'These books will help me present a strong case to His Holiness for the disbanding of the Order of the Temple,' Guy confirmed, realising Geoffrey was right and he might be able to salvage something from this situation, 'but I also expected to find the Cup of the Last Supper and the rest of the Templar treasure.'

'Long gone, I am afraid,' Arnauld cut in, shrugging his shoulders.

'I will satisfy myself with these books for the moment then,' d'Alville spat back at the old knight. 'They are proof of the Templar perversions. The Pope will surely be very grateful to me for exposing the evil heresies of the White Knights. I don't doubt that I will able to ask for any bishopric of the Christian world as my reward. The wealth and power which accompanies a bishop's mitre will allow me to continue my search for the treasures of the Temple. I will track them down. I promise you that.'

Guy turned to Geoffrey. 'You are a clever young man. It is a pity we ended up on opposite sides in this game. With your help I could have attained my goal much sooner.'

'You will not succeed,' Geoffrey laughed. 'You have overlooked one important detail.'

'What is that?' Guy inquired, frowning as his tongue touched his bottom lip.

'The Pope may not wish to risk such a violent end to the Temple,' Geoffrey explained. 'After all, there are thousands of knights who wear the white. The Holy Father may treat the discovery of these books as no more than a ploy on the part of the Knights of Saint John. He will be reluctant to move against a powerful military order with only your word against that of the Grand Master of the Temple. Possession of these scrolls does not prove anything. You could have bought them in the marketplace of Jerusalem. You will have to prove these doctrines are venerated by the Temple.'

'You may be right,' Guy smiled. 'Alas, but you will never know. You will not be leaving this chamber alive. This will be your tomb. You are very lucky. Not many men have the opportunity of inspecting their grave before they are sealed in it.'

The Hospitaller raised his hand and the assembled knights in black prepared as one to fight.

'It is time for you to face my soldiers,' Guy informed his captives. 'I think we will dispense with last words. I am told there is a Templar army at the gates and I would like to make good my escape before they find their way in here.'

A man coughed in the darkness. The sound echoed through the vault. Guy d'Alville froze, realising it had come from darkness beyond the light of his torches.

'I am glad to inform you that it is too late to flee this fight, Master Guy,' a voice boomed out across the chamber. Just beyond the cloth enclosure a figure dressed in white robes stepped into the edge of the torchlight. The strange knight held a long drawn sword in one hand and an oblong Norman shield in the other.

Geoffrey crossed himself, certain that here was the avenging angel of God's legions come to bring down heavenly justice upon Guy d'Alville and the Order of Saint John. The torchlight lit the warrior's face so that it seemed he was not of this world.

'St Clair?' Robert stammered in recognition. 'It is Henry St Clair, the knight Donal and I met after the battle of Arsuf.'

'I am glad to find you in good health,' Henry said pleasantly, as if there were no Hospitallers in sight. 'I must apologise for taking so long to come to your aid.'

Then the knight turned to the Hospitaller. 'Guy d'Alville,' St Clair stated, 'I arrest you for the crimes of murder, theft and the torture of your fellow Christian knights. You have violated the treaty of cooperation between our two orders. You will command your men to lay down their arms or to suffer the consequences.'

'Surely not,' Guy laughed, throwing his head back. 'It takes more than one insignificant knight to intimidate my soldiers.'

As d'Alville spoke dozens of lights sputtered into life behind St Clair as the Temple soldiers passed a taper through the ranks behind him.

'Would a hundred knights of the Temple persuade you?' Henry asked politely. 'A hundred against twenty is greater odds than I would willingly face.'

Guy smiled but it was an empty gesture. 'That might be just enough to make me reconsider your offer,' he replied through gritted teeth.

'Your castle has fallen, Guy. It is back in the hands of its rightful owners, the Order of the Temple. There are five hundred Templar troops in the citadel. You are vanquished.'

'You managed to negotiate the natural defences of this castle,' Guy congratulated him. 'That is remarkable.'

'I used the natural defences of this fortification,' Henry corrected him. 'There is an underground passage that leads directly through the mountains to chambers adjoining this vault. I should know about it. I helped construct it. Will you lay down your arms or must we fight this out?' Henry asked sternly.

The Templar commander paused for a moment to see if Guy would do as he was ordered. When the Hospitaller merely smiled, Henry bellowed at the top of his lungs, 'Lay down your arms!'

Most of the Hospitaller troops followed the order without even a moment of hesitation. The Templar leader turned to his men. 'Anyone who offers any resistance whatsoever is to be slain. Take them!'

The Templars rushed forward and for a brief moment it looked as if Guy might try to make a stand. But the odds were overwhelming. His sword was snatched from his hands before he had a chance to consider fighting his way out.

As the Templars rounded up their captives and led them out Henry approached Geoffrey, Robert and Donal. The three men were obviously confused and surprised at their sudden freedom. But Arnauld obviously expected no less. The old knight came forward to embrace St Clair and the two men held each other like old friends.

'You took your time,' Arnauld chided. 'A few minutes more and there would have been no-one to rescue at all.'

'I am sorry,' Henry apologised. 'I have been back to France since we last met. I only recently returned. When I realised there was no word from you I set out immediately. If I had known the situation was so desperate, I would have come much sooner.'

'You are Henry St Clair?' Geoffrey asked and the knight nodded his assent. 'Then you are the knight who wrote the letter to me, the one that gave us clues as to where to find the treasure?'

Once again Henry nodded.

'Then you knew the treasure was here?' Geoffrey added.

'Your brother and I placed it here ourselves,' St Clair explained.

'Is it true?' Geoffrey demanded.

'Is what true?'

'That the Templars are heretics,' Geoffrey cried. 'That they believe the terrible lies written down in these books?'

'You have not read these manuscripts,' Henry stated confidently, 'or you would not call them heretical. You have been listening to my good friend Guy d'Alville, a man responsible for the deaths of countless of our brethren in his misguided desire to destroy the Order of the Temple.'

'Is it true?' Geoffrey repeated more insistently.

'That you must decide for yourself,' St Clair informed him. 'These books and scrolls are coming home to the Kingdom of Scotland with me. I am their guardian now. If you wish to continue your Templar education, you are welcome to accompany me and to spend your days studying the stories laid out on their pages. In the end you will be able to answer the question of heresy for yourself better than I could ever hope to.'

'Perhaps you will also be required to make a great leap of faith,' Arnauld cut in, 'as Robert had to.'

'And what about us?' Donal interrupted. 'What will become of Robert and I?'

'We will go out to fight the Saracens again,' Robert informed his sergeant. 'I will join the Temple at last.'

'You may be accepted in the Temple,' Henry explained, 'but there is peace once more in the lands of Outremer. King Richard concluded a treaty with Saladin some months ago and has left these shores forever. The war is over.'

Robert did not speak. He did not move. It seemed to him his world had suddenly fallen apart. 'I have been wasting my time in this castle,' the lord whispered in shock, 'while the world passed me by. All I wanted to do was serve the Temple and fight for the restoration of a Christian kingdom. The Grail Cup I dreamed of is nothing more than a tale told to confuse the uninitiated.'

'You have done a greater service to the Temple than you will ever know,' St Clair assured him. 'Our real enemy has never been the Saracens. We have much to learn from the people of these lands. The true enemies of the Temple are those who would twist the teachings of Our Lord to their own ends. You should be grateful you only saw one great battle and will live to tell the story of it. Thousands were left on the field at Arsuf. None of them will ever see their homes again.'

Robert turned to look Donal in the eyes. 'Donal and I will go home,' the lord said at last, 'and I will pass the estates over to the Temple to administer.' With that he sheathed his sword and walked alone towards the stairs.

Donal watched his lord as he strode away. The chieftain could not help but feel sorry things had not turned out as Robert had wished. But Donal was not touched by any of the lord's sadness. He was overjoyed to be going home at last.

Chapter Twenty-One

Balek the tilecutter ran his fingers over the smooth surface of Mathúin O'Regan's tomb. His sensitive hands noticed a slightly uneven patch in the grout between the tiles and he found a chisel to remove it.

Satisfied with his work, he stood up off his knees and hummed approval of the craftsmanship. 'I am sure Donal will approve,' he congratulated himself.

'My husband is dead,' Eilish spoke up in her best Latin, startling the tilecutter so that he nearly fell over in his rush to turn around.

'Forgive me, lady,' Balek stuttered in his broken Gaelic, 'I had no idea you were standing there.'

'I have been watching you for some time,' she admitted. She still spoke the Roman tongue for she knew Balek did not have much Irish. 'You were so engrossed in your task, you did not even look up when the door to the chapel slammed shut behind me.'

'A piece of work is never finished,' the tilecutter explained, 'until I am completely satisfied with it.'

'Where do you think we should place Donal's tomb?' Eilish inquired.

'I do not understand you, lady,' he replied.

'I know we have no corpse to place in the grave,' the healer explained, 'but there should be a memorial to him at least.'

'Yes,' Balek agreed, frowning.

Eilish noticed the frown because it was uncharacteristic for the tilecutter not to smile. 'My husband thought very highly of you,' Eilish went on.

'He is a good man,' Balek interrupted.

The healer scratched her head wondering if he understood the situation. 'I have come to ask your advice,' she went on. 'Donal told me you were a very wise man.'

Balek laughed. 'Perhaps I am just a fool who knows when to be silent.'

'I have had a proposal of marriage,' Eilish continued, determined to get her question out, 'from Rufus FitzWilliam.'

'A Norman lord,' the tilecutter nodded. 'You must be very happy.'

'If I marry him,' the healer pressed on, 'I am certain I will be able to influence his decisions in future. The tenants of the estate will not need to fear that their rents and taxes will become too high. Rufus has many faults and I am wary of him, but I am certain I can outwit him. Perhaps I could change him into a good man.'

'All men are good,' Balek grinned, 'only the weak-willed are ever truly evil.'

'Yes,' Eilish agreed, 'I believe you are right.'

'It is easy to stray from the path of righteousness,' Balek confirmed. 'A man who strays is not a suitable choice for a husband. Men and women of character and good intention will stand by their morals even if the whole world condemns them.'

'I am not sure I understand what you mean,' the healing woman muttered. 'Should I marry him for the sake of my kinfolk's future? If I bore him a son, that child would one day be the Lord of Bally Raine. And he would have the bloodline of my father, the Gioll Martin.'

'A good argument,' the tilecutter observed, nodding his head again.

'But,' Eilish admitted, 'I am concerned about Braonin's dislike for Rufus. If they cannot work together there will be trouble.'

Balek continued to look at her but said nothing, so the healing woman decided to explain further. 'Braonin's judgment may be clouded by his conflict with Rufus. Donal's cousin is always finding fault with the man. He even accused Rufus of murdering Lonan, the old chamberlain.'

She covered her eyes with her hands and paused for a second. 'But Rufus has been very good to me and my kin,' Eilish stated. 'He gave us food and shelter when Cúil Ghréine was attacked and destroyed. He has acted honourably ever since the clonough burned to the ground.'

'Yet you doubt him,' Balek pointed out.

Eilish sighed, unwilling to admit that indeed she did have reservations about Rufus FitzWilliam and his offer of marriage. 'I dislike his manner,' she told Balek. 'He always acts as if he is superior to everyone, as if it is his God-given right to rule. He is arrogant and in many ways he has not matured at all. He was a drunkard once and I fear he could turn to the drink again. Normans have very little respect for their womenfolk. I do not want to end up as another possession on his long list of conquests. I cannot say for certain, but I feel he is not an honest man.'

'Then your decision is an easy one,' the tilecutter exclaimed, throwing his hands up to signify an end to the matter. Then he began to pack away his tools, ready to go for his midday meal.

'But if Rufus marries a Norman woman of his own class,' the healer reasoned, 'the livelihood of all the tenants may be at risk. How could we be sure she would be able to stand up to him? We would have no guarantee that such a woman would have any regard for our kinfolk at all.'

The tilecutter huffed in a noncommittal manner.

The healing woman's frustration was beginning to show

on her reddening face. 'I cannot find an answer!' she cried. 'I am just dancing round this problem in endless circles.'

Suddenly Eilish remembered she had come to the tilecutter for advice. So far he had not offered any. 'What do think I should do?' she asked him outright. 'Should I marry the Norman and try to keep a tight rein on him? Or should I spurn his proposal and take my chances with the woman he ends up wedding?'

Balek smiled awkwardly as he put his toolbag down again. 'How many tiles do you think it will take to cover the entrance portico?' he inquired.

Eilish stared in astonishment. Was it possible, she asked herself, that this man had not understood a word she had said.

'I have no idea,' the healer replied. 'I know nothing about tiles.'

'And for that reason alone,' the tilecutter informed her, 'I would not expect reliable advice from you on the matter. Tiles are my life,' he went on. 'I understand them very well. I can make them from the very dust of the earth.'

Eilish shook her head. 'What?' she mumbled, confused.

'You are a chieftainess,' Balek said, 'and the wife of a chieftain. You have known responsibility most of your life. You know better than I which is the right path for you to take. I have no experience of such things. My advice would be unreliable. I am a tilecutter. Ask me about tiles.'

'What would Donal say to me,' the healer sighed, 'if he were here?'

'If you are patient,' Balek shrugged, 'one day you will be able to ask him yourself.'

Eilish stared at the old craftsman in utter disbelief. Donal had thought this man wise, but at the present moment she could not comprehend why.

'I cannot wait,' the healer declared finally, 'until Judgment Day. I must decide soon.'

'I trust you will consider the problem carefully,' Balek said cheerfully. 'Now I must go to my meal. Good day, lady.'

'Good day, Balek,' Eilish sighed. 'Thank you.'

Donal lay back on the deck of the three-masted sailing ship, waiting for the wind to rise again. With his hands behind his head he half closed his eyes so he could watch the sunlight streaming down through the sail cloth. While the ship was becalmed there was little else to do, which frustrated him immensely. And the time passed very slowly.

To Donal's right, off the stern of the vessel, a flag hung limp from its rope. Donal pondered the meaning of the black naval ensign of the Templar order with its gruesome arms of a white human skull and cross thighbones. The air was so still the flag did not move at all.

At that moment he had the impulse to read his wife's letter again, though it was full of bad news. Donal fumbled around in the leather satchel attached to his belt until he found the battered parchment. Carefully he unfolded it. Then Donal lay back again, shielding his eyes from the sun with the precious letter.

He skimmed over the opening lines, going straight to the part where Eilish described the destruction of Cúil Ghréine. He read the passage several times. The broad pen strokes were not hers, he knew; they were obviously written by Lonan the chamberlain. But the words were unmistakably those of his wife.

The slightest breeze shook the paper, for a second distracting him. Donal looked up at the skull ensign but the wind had already dropped again. So he went back to his reading.

'"Rufus has been good to us,"' he read aloud. '"He has opened the castle to Braonin, Neesh and myself until our houses can be rebuilt. He says it was a company of brigands led by Culdee rebels who started the fire. We believe they may have been followers of Cinneach O'Hare."'

The rigging swayed gently in time with the softly rocking boat, creaking with the strain. But still there was no breeze.

'Cinneach might be a heretic,' Donal reasoned under his breath, 'but I cannot believe he would set fire to Cúil Ghréine in an act of rebellion.'

'Yet even your wife believes that is exactly what happened,' Robert cut in. The knight was sitting on the raised gunwale, holding onto a rope to steady himself. Donal got up off his back when he realised his lord was present.

'Stay where you are,' Robert insisted. 'Take what rest you can whilst you have the chance. You have been working like a mad dog ever since we left Acre.'

'I am anxious to get home,' Donal explained. 'If I lend my hand to the sailors the journey will be shortened.'

'Robert is right,' Geoffrey interjected as he walked up the deck toward them. 'You still have a hard road before you. You should rest.'

Donal stood up, folding the letter as he did so. He placed his wife's parchment back in his leather pouch and moved toward the gunwale.

'Once we land in Marseilles,' Geoffrey continued, 'we will be escorting Henry and his entourage to Normandy. From there we will take ship to Scotland. We have a good two months travelling ahead of us before you can even think of heading home.'

'Cúil Ghréine was burned to the ground,' the chieftain said, shaking his head, still not comprehending how such a thing could have happened. 'My kinfolk are without shelter.

It is my duty to travel directly home to my people after we land at Marseilles. I have no mind to be going off to Scotland.'

At that moment Arnauld appeared from below decks, his face almost as white as his Templar surcoat. He went straight over to a pile of ropes and sat down among them, leaning against the mast as he did so.

'I have no mind to go off to Scotland either,' Arnauld cut in, 'and no stomach for sea voyages of any kind. I would rather face a hundred Hospitallers single-handedly than a day at sea with a good headwind. Thank God the breeze has died down a little. I thought I would be retching for a week the way this little tub was rocking when we left Acre.'

'The sailors tell me that the seas here are mild compared to those between Calais and Scotland,' Geoffrey stated casually, a gleam in his eye.

'Mother of God!' Arnauld muttered, dropping his head into his hands. 'If it were not for Henry St Clair commanding me to go with him to his estates, I would still be seated in a tavern in Acre.'

'A week ago you referred to that city as a dry and dusty home of thieving heathens,' Robert smiled. 'You reckoned the ale to be rancid and the food so foul that even the rats shunned it. you were overjoyed to be returning to France.'

'My guts have a short memory,' Arnauld answered. 'Now that I am reacquainted with the rolling waves and the stench of the open sea, I regret my hasty assessment of the fair city of Acre. There may be many evils in that place but at least the ground doesn't shift beneath your feet when you walk.'

'Come with me to Ireland,' Donal asked, hoping he would be able to tempt the old knight into lending his sword arm.

Arnauld smiled. 'I am a Templar Knight. When I took my vows I promised to obey my superiors in the order. Henry St Clair is my superior. He has commanded Robert,

Geoffrey and myself to accompany him to his estates as his escort. We must do as he bids us. But you have taken no such vow.'

'You are still in my employ, Donal,' Robert interrupted. 'You are my sergeant-at-arms. But I will not force you to come with me on my errand when there is trouble brewing at home. I would prefer you to accompany us and lend your hand to the protection of the treasure, but in the end you must do as you see fit.'

'Your lord is a just man,' Arnauld said, 'but he is unaware of the difficulties you will face if you go on alone to Ireland.'

'What do you mean?' Donal asked with a frown.

'You will likely wait many months for a ship home from France or Normandy,' the old knight explained. 'There are few ships which regularly ply that route. On the other hand Henry has guaranteed safe passage to Ulster for both you and Robert as soon as the scrolls are safe in his stronghold. Even with the ride home from there, you will be home much faster than if you were to wait around in Normandy for a ship.'

'There is one other factor which you have not considered,' Robert added thoughtfully. 'If there really is a rebellion brewing on the estates of Bally Raine, you will ride into the thick of it. Alone you will have not achieved anything. You might even get yourself killed.'

'You left your company of soldiers back in Acre on garrison duty,' Donal reminded the lord. 'How will we quell a rebellion with warriors?'

'You know that most of the men were too weak to travel,' Robert replied. 'Sickness claimed more lives than the Saracens on this campaign. We lost forty men to the stomach cramp; the rest of them would have slowed us down too much. Apart from you, I have two well-seasoned soldiers to escort me. Four armed warriors just returned from the Holy

Land have a much better chance of restoring order than one solitary sergeant.'

Donal closed his eyes and nodded, seeing the sense in this argument. 'I will come to Scotland with you,' he said finally. 'But I would like to write to Eilish as soon as we land in France.'

'You will be home before the letter arrives,' Arnauld pointed out. 'Letters travel by the same route as any traveller.'

Donal turned to Robert. 'Then you must promise we will not stay a moment longer than necessary in Scotland.'

'I promise,' the lord vowed, 'that as long as my superiors do not give me orders to the contrary, we will return to Bally Raine as quickly as possible.' Then he turned to Arnauld and Geoffrey. 'Would you like to accompany us home? I am sure our cause would benefit from the strength of your sword arms.'

'I am to stay by Henry's side,' Geoffrey replied apologetically. 'He has specifically requested me to aid him in the guarding of the scrolls.'

'Once we arrive in Scotland I am free to travel where I will,' Arnauld answered, 'but I have my heart set on riding south to the Kingdom of England to stay a while at the Temple headquarters in London. Believe me, if there were no ocean voyage involved in journeying to Ireland, I would be with you.'

'I have heard that the food is terrible in England,' Robert teased gently to hide his disappointment.

'Then it will be much better than anything I had in Acre,' Arnauld quipped. 'Now I really have something to look forward to.' His face paled again and he got to his feet. 'So, if you will excuse me,' he added, 'I will go to the stern and look on the scenery.'

The old knight swallowed hard and his body shivered slightly. 'And I would appreciate it if we could turn the conversation away from culinary matters in future. At least until we are safely on dry land.' Then, with as much dignity as he could muster, Arnauld walked slowly and carefully toward the stern, keeping his eyes firmly fixed on the deck in front of him.

The other three men smiled at each other but did not comment. It was Robert who finally broke the silence. 'Cinneach told me a story once about the Holy Grail,' he said. 'If I had known then that he was a Culdee, I probably would have handed him over to the Abbot of Shelton as a heretic. It was Cinneach's story which convinced me that my destiny lay in Outremer.' The lord laughed a little at his own foolishness.

'I knew Cinneach also,' Donal admitted. 'He seemed to be an honest man, despite his reputation as a rebel. Just before we left he told me something of the Culdee creed. It seems to me now their ways are not so different from the beliefs which lie at the core of the Temple.'

Geoffrey raised an eyebrow but did not comment.

'I do not know enough about either subject to say,' Robert sighed. 'But if he and his kind are branded heretics by the Church and by the Templar order, I must do all in my power to bring him to justice. When we return I will set about capturing him.'

'I know nothing of the Culdees,' Geoffrey stated, 'but I understand that this man must believe wholeheartedly in the teachings of his sect. Otherwise he would not risk life and limb every day to keep their ways alive. In some ways these Culdees do not seem very different from ourselves. This Cinneach sounds as if he might be quite courageous.'

Robert opened his eyes wider as that thought struck home. 'Cinneach did not strike me as a fanatic,' he admitted. 'He was a very knowledgeable and respected storyteller, but he was not a man blinded by faith as so many are.' Robert paused for a few seconds. 'I thought I was being brave when I charged into battle at Arsuf with all the other knights, but that was not true bravery. It was easy to go along with all the others because I felt I was part of something bigger. Now I am beginning to understand that true courage runs deeper than that.'

'Every moment of that terrible ride toward the Saracen lines,' Donal admitted, 'I was frightened for my life. Every moment. I was so scared, I could not think clearly.'

'That is exactly how I felt at the edge of the abyss in the passageway beneath Mont Salvasch,' Robert agreed. 'The only thing that spurred me to jump was the thought of my friends in danger on the other side. I had to trust completely that I would land safely. It was a true leap of faith.'

'The tilecutter told me once,' said Donal, 'that each man has his own understanding of faith. We may argue about the details of our belief but if we are pure in our faith, God will judge as us equals. Faith is a very important force.'

Robert frowned deeply. 'Perhaps when we return I will have to consider Cinneach's position thoroughly. I am beginning to wonder whether he really is a heretic after all.'

Geoffrey smiled to himself. Truly, life was full of surprises.

Six weeks after Robert and Donal arrived in Marseilles, Rufus FitzWilliam was leaning back against the castle wall at Bally Raine, looking out over the moat. He had his sword drawn and was sullenly digging at the grass with the tip of it.

'So it will be at least a month before we have enough soldiers gathered?' the young FitzWilliam asked his sergeant-at-arms.

'Twelve more footmen and fifteen archers are coming, my lord,' Jon Quicktoe replied. There was a strange mirth in his deep guttural voice. 'There are no mounted men left in the whole kingdom. All gone off to the crusades,' he explained.

'Then you should begin training twenty of the footmen to ride well,' Rufus decided. 'I have only a dozen horsemen at my disposal at the moment. If we are going to subjugate the people of this estate, we will need a force of men who can move rapidly to any flashpoint. Choose your best men and work them hard. I give you three weeks.'

'Yes, my lord,' the sergeant answered, bowing his head.

'I do not want you to train them,' Rufus added. 'Leave that to men who are better suited to the saddle. You are going to be steward of this castle. I want to put you in charge of tax collection.'

'Thank you, my lord,' Quicktoe gushed. 'You will not regret this decision.'

'If you do not discharge your duties with enthusiasm and efficiency, you will deeply regret it, I assure you.'

Quicktoe held his gaze to the ground. This, he knew, was no idle threat. 'I share your distaste for these peasants, my lord,' he grunted. 'I will be ruthless in the pursuit of my duties.'

'Very well,' the young FitzWilliam smiled. 'And you will be responsible for ensuring the festivities are well planned and provisioned.'

'When is the happy day, my lord?' Quicktoe sniggered.

'The lady is still undecided,' Rufus replied. 'But I have always favoured the early spring for weddings. The flowering trees are fresh and the weather is mild, perfect for hunting. The honey is sweeter and the cows give their best milk at that time. For now let us assume the marriage celebration will take place around the first day of spring.'

'That gives me plenty of time to bring things to order, my lord,' the sergeant grinned.

'Three weeks,' Rufus warned. 'There will be many changes on this estate in the next moon. Bally Raine will enter into a new era of prosperity. If we are careful, this estate could easily begin to absorb the smaller holdings nearby. After that, who knows? The southern counties of Ireland would benefit from having a ruler who was strong and benevolent.'

'The people of the south would welcome a knight who could protect their lands from the marauding northern barons,' Quicktoe cut in. 'A man who could provide such a shield would be king.'

'King,' Rufus repeated under his breath, obviously relishing the sound of that title. 'Do you really believe the people of this land would accept a Norman king other than Richard?'

'If the Norman king had Norman soldiers to stand behind him,' the sergeant asserted, 'he would be king in all but name. Such a ruler, married to an Irish chieftainess, would have wide support. I am sure most folk would be happier to pay taxes to a man from their own country than to King Richard who squanders their hard-earned tithes on his wars.'

Rufus smiled as he paused for a moment to sheath his sword. 'Perhaps I have been too selfish,' he stated. Quicktoe frowned, trying to work out what Rufus meant.

The young FitzWilliam now realised he had been thinking on a pitifully small scale. 'I have concentrated too much on the good of this estate when truly I have a duty to the whole country.'

Quicktoe smiled. 'Ireland is in need of a strong hand,' he agreed, 'to free the people from the burden of Richard's costly war in the Holy Land.'

'Then I had best convince the Lady Eilish to wed me

soon,' Rufus decided. 'It is for the good of the whole country.'

Quicktoe grinned, eager for the adventure to begin. 'Are you sure your army will be fit to the task, my lord?'

'One step at a time, Jon Quicktoe,' Rufus hummed. 'First we must secure the estates, then we will begin work on the greater plan. Go to your post now and tomorrow you may set the footmen to training. They are already a tough bunch but I want them to drill until there is no peasant on this estate who would dare to stand against them. We must also prepare against any unforeseen attacks from the north. The soldiers must be able to hold their own against a larger force. You have a mere three weeks before we set this plan in motion.'

'By the time I am finished, you will have the beginnings of a great army at your command,' Quicktoe promised.

'Loyalty,' Rufus added. 'Every man must prove his loyalty to me. Including yourself, Jon Quicktoe.'

'I have a score to settle with your brother,' the sergeant admitted. 'He had me flogged and humiliated. My sword and armour were confiscated and I went hungry for a long time. You will have my loyalty,' he stated, 'as long as you treat me well.'

'Go to your watch, then,' Rufus ordered as he slapped the warrior on the shoulder, 'and goodnight to you.' Then the young FitzWilliam strode back towards the keep as his deputy returned to the guard post.

Braonin waited until he was sure both men were gone, then he emerged from the shadows and checked he had not been discovered.

'Eilish will be asleep now,' Braonin said to himself. 'I will talk to her in the morning. Tonight I will go and tell Cin-neach what I have heard.'

With that the hunter made his way to the stables, saddled his horse and led the mare quietly out into the night. As soon as he was a good distance from the castle he mounted his horse and rode off at a gallop in search of Cinneach the Culdee.

He must have been overconfident or perhaps distracted by what he had heard. For Braonin did not notice a rider following him at a discreet distance.

Early the next morning, shortly after sunrise, Eilish awoke and made her way down to the great hall of the keep to share some breakfast with the castle servants. Out in the kitchen the cook had prepared a great pot of boiled oats. When the healer came in she was handed a bowl of steaming porridge with a great dab of new butter on top.

Although it had become the custom of most folk since the coming of the Normans to drink a cup of ale with their first meal, Eilish preferred to go without it. She found ale certainly filled the stomach as it was meant to do, but it left her head fuzzy and she could never concentrate after consuming it.

Colm the game-keeper had already departed to walk his rounds of the estate by the time Eilish finished her meal. She was just rising when she heard a great commotion in the hall. The cook cast a worried glance at the healing woman and the two of them went to the door to see what trouble was brewing.

In the great hall Braonin was talking to Rufus in a barely contained whisper. 'I will not do as you say. You are planning to take these estates for yourself.'

Eilish stepped out of the kitchen then and slammed the door shut behind her. Both men turned around at the noise.

'Eilish!' Braonin exclaimed. 'Thank God I have found you.'

'Braonin, what is it?' she asked, worried that some catastrophe had occurred.

'I forbid you to marry Rufus FitzWilliam,' the hunter insisted vehemently. 'He is plotting to take the whole of Ireland for himself.'

'What are you talking about?' Eilish stuttered, hardly believing what she was hearing and looking to Rufus for some kind of explanation. The young FitzWilliam shrugged his shoulders and returned her gaze warmly.

'I overheard him talking with that monster Quicktoe last night,' Braonin went on. 'Rufus plans to marry you to get some credibility for his rule and then begin his domination of the entire country.'

The Norman laughed. 'This is ridiculous!' he exclaimed. 'Your cousin must have been listening at your door,' he ventured. 'He must have heard me make my offer to you, Eilish. But it was my understanding I do not have to ask any man's permission to marry a Gaelic woman.'

'That is true,' Eilish stated, glaring at the hunter. 'Only you Normans enforce the choice of a husband on a woman, even against her will.'

Then she turned to Braonin. 'You have no right to forbid me to marry whomsoever I please. I am a widow and I am a chieftainess. I will make my own decision when the time comes.'

'Donal was my blood cousin!' Braonin objected. 'He was my best friend. I am responsible for you. I won't see you wed a Norman.'

'No man is responsible for me!' Eilish snapped. 'And who would you have me wed? Or would you rather I spent the rest of my life a widow with no children and no home of my own, forever living off the generosity of my kinfolk?'

'You are an O'Regan now,' Braonin stated.

'Does that make me subject to your whims?'

'You must think of your clanspeople first before anything else,' he pleaded. 'To marry Rufus would be a terrible mistake. Such a match would surely end in disaster.'

'You seem to know a great deal about matters which do not concern you,' Eilish noted with venom. 'And what makes you think I am not a good enough judge of a man? Are you afraid I would make the mistake of marrying a man who might turn out to be a tyrant?'

Rufus shifted uncomfortably. For the first time in many months he felt as if all his plans might come to nothing. Perhaps, he thought, Eilish had seen through him from the very start. The young FitzWilliam swallowed hard and bit his tongue.

'Do you think I would even consider wedding Rufus if I had not examined every aspect of this situation in the greatest detail?' Eilish went on. 'I have put my own feelings aside in this matter,' she hissed and Rufus raised an eyebrow. 'I have thought only of my kinfolk. Their welfare has been the single most important thing on my mind all along!'

The young FitzWilliam breathed a little easier and inwardly smiled.

'No man will ever match my Donal,' the healer explained. 'But Donal is gone. He is dead and, short of a bloody miracle, he will not return to us.' She took a breath to cover her grief and to show her resolve.

'Rufus has been kind to us,' Eilish declared, softening her tone. 'He has given us a roof over our heads when we could have been forced to sleep in the snow. He has shown his intentions are honourable and he has shared our grief. If I choose to marry him, it will be because I am sure he will rule Bally Raine wisely. Such a marriage would also benefit my kinfolk, for my children would be the heirs to the lordship. The next Lord of Bally Raine would be half Irish.'

'He is plotting to use the tenants' loyalty to you,' Braonin protested, 'to raise the taxes and annex the surrounding estates. He plans to absorb them all into Bally Raine.'

'Rubbish!' Rufus exclaimed. 'I do not know who you have been speaking to but they have led you down the wrong road.'

'I heard you say these things to your sergeant last night!'

'You were not in the castle last night,' Rufus pointed out. 'I saw you ride in just after dawn. Tell me how you could have heard a conversation that supposedly took place here when you were in another part of the country.'

'I went out as soon as you and Quicktoe parted company,' Braonin countered. 'I waited until you had finished speaking.'

'This can be settled quite easily,' the young FitzWilliam declared calmly. 'I will send for Jon Quicktoe. We will ask him if he has any recollection of this conversation.'

Eilish went back to the kitchen door and called to the cook. 'Will you go and find Jon Quicktoe and send him to the hall? Master Rufus would like to speak with him.' The cook nodded and went out to the courtyard.

'Where were you last night, Braonin O'Regan?' Rufus inquired.

'I was out in the forest,' the hunter stammered nervously. 'I often go out at night when my mind is troubled and I cannot sleep.'

'You were alone?' Rufus pressed him. 'Entirely alone?'

'I was,' Braonin lied. 'I rode to Cúil Ghréine to walk among the ruins.'

As he was speaking the main door to the hall opened and Jon Quicktoe entered. The warrior immediately took his cap off as he wiped his feet at the threshold.

'You wished to see me, my lord?' the sergeant asked.

'He is not the Lord of Bally Raine,' Braonin interrupted. 'His brother is lord.'

'My brother is dead, Braonin,' Rufus hissed. 'When are you going to get used to that? My father is in a monastery. I am the only FitzWilliam left. I am your lord!'

'You will never be my lord,' Braonin retorted defiantly.

'Careful, my lad,' Rufus grunted. 'You are one short step away from treason.' Then the young FitzWilliam turned his attention to Quicktoe. 'Sergeant, were you on duty last night?'

'I was, my lord,' Quicktoe replied.

'And did I speak to you at any time during your watch, Quicktoe?'

Rufus looked into the sergeant's eyes, trying to convey the urgency of the situation, but there was no need. Quicktoe had perceived what was going on in the hall as soon as he had entered. The warrior was determined not to give away any secrets.

'You complimented me on my rehabilitation, my lord,' he answered. 'Six months of training with your soldiers, you said, had changed me from a common thug into a man worthy of carrying the FitzWilliam banner.'

'Did I mention any plans to marry the Lady Eilish?' Rufus asked.

The sergeant stared into his lord's face, searching for some sign as to how to answer this question. 'All you said was,' Quicktoe swallowed, 'that any wedding would have to be a splendid affair and it would need careful planning for many months. You asked me whether I would be able to oversee such an event. You did not mention the Lady Eilish.'

Eilish blushed and Rufus turned to her apologetically. 'I am sorry for not consulting you on this matter,' he stated. 'I wished this to be a surprise if you gave your consent to marry me.'

'I am not offended, Lord Rufus,' she said.

Hearing Eilish use his full title for the first time made

the young FitzWilliam swell with confidence. Now he knew she was taking him seriously and probably dismissing Braonin's story as a product of jealousy or over-protectiveness. To make sure the hunter's credibility was further called into doubt Rufus put another question to Quicktoe.

'When did your watch conclude, sergeant?'

'A short while ago, my lord,' came the answer.

'I saw a rider come in through the gates this morning after sunrise,' Rufus went on. 'Can you tell me anything about him?'

'Two riders came in this morning,' Quicktoe corrected. 'Braonin O'Regan was the first. He was followed by the warrior I sent to follow him through the night.'

'You sent a soldier to track Braonin without my permission?' the young FitzWilliam snarled as if enraged by this action.

'I did, my lord,' Quicktoe stuttered. 'I hope you will forgive my impudence. I had a feeling Braonin might find himself in trouble riding out alone at night. So I sent a man to make sure he would come to no harm.'

'Why did you not send the man to ride alongside of Braonin?' Eilish cut in, her suspicions aroused.

'Braonin is a proud man,' the sergeant replied without a thought. 'He would surely have rejected such an offer.'

'And where did he go?' Rufus inquired. 'Did your man follow him all night?'

'He did, my lord,' Quicktoe confirmed. 'And he spent the sleeping hours at the old settlement of Cúil Ghréine.'

'I am glad you were telling me the truth,' Rufus said to Braonin. 'I would have been most upset with you if I had found you were consorting with those rebels or that heretic Cinneach.'

'My lord,' Quicktoe interrupted, 'Braonin was not alone. The warrior reported that Braonin met with the Culdee called Cinneach. They sat up all night together planning the capture of Bally Raine.'

'Is this true?' Rufus bellowed. 'You were with the rebels?'

The new Lord of Bally Raine did not receive an answer. As soon as Braonin could see he had been caught, he knew he would not have a chance of presenting his side of the story. The hunter rushed toward Eilish and grabbed her by the shoulders. 'I was only thinking of you,' he declared. 'I was trying to save you from making a terrible mistake.'

Then, before either Rufus or Quicktoe had a chance to draw their blades, Braonin had flung open the kitchen door and was gone from view.

Rufus ran to Eilish and put his arms around her. 'Did he hurt you?'

'I am fine,' the healer replied, though she was confused at Braonin's behaviour. His rash departure confirmed that he had something to hide or had committed some deed he was ashamed of.

'Cinneach was talking about Braonin becoming the new Lord of Bally Raine,' Quicktoe finished. 'As the last male O'Regan he claimed to be entitled to that rank.'

'I am chieftain of the O'Regans!' Eilish declared, understanding now why Braonin might have a troubled conscience.

'What are you doing standing there?' Rufus shrieked at his sergeant. 'Call out the guard and arrest Braonin O'Regan on charges of treason, heresy and rebellion.'

Eilish shuddered at the foolishness of Braonin's actions. A charge of any one of those three crimes could attract the death penalty. But if all three were pursued and proved, Braonin would surely hang or burn.

That moment the healer heard the sound of a horse clattering over the cobblestones and knew Braonin had escaped the wrath of Rufus FitzWilliam for now. As it became clear to her he had acted treacherously, she resolved to ensure he would never have any influence on the estates again.

'I will be fine,' Eilish informed Rufus as she took his hands away from her waist. 'This has all been a great shock to me. I find I am in your debt again, Lord Rufus. If it had not been for your soldiers, I might have been deposed as chieftainess of the O'Regans. My husband and his father would have been ashamed for what Braonin has done.'

'It is not entirely his fault,' Rufus countered slyly. 'He has been led astray by that damned heretic, Cinneach. That Culdee has travelled the whole country around stirring up trouble where there never was any before. If Robert were here, he would not have stood for it. He would have wiped the heretics out as soon as he had become aware of them. But then Robert was always the more pious of the two of us.'

'It seems to me,' Eilish observed, 'that if you do not show you are a strong leader, you will find yourself in trouble in the future.'

'I have been reluctant to send my troops into the forest until they are properly trained,' Rufus explained. 'I do not want a massacre on my hands. The rebels must be brought in alive to face justice. I do not care whether the judgment is given under Norman or Irish law. All that matters is that my tenants feel secure their homes will not be burned down as was Cúil Ghréine.'

'You will make a fine lord,' Eilish said, 'if you keep that sense of fairness about you.'

'I have learned much from you, my lady, in the last few months,' Rufus sighed sweetly. 'I have appreciated your guidance on so many matters.'

'Thank you, my lord,' she replied. 'We do seem to understand each other.' The healer turned to go back into the kitchen but before she had reached the door she turned to say one more thing.

'If you are willing to wait a short while,' Eilish whispered, not daring to look Rufus in the eye, 'and if we can come to some arrangement suitable to both of us, then I will consider wedding you,' she said. 'But you must agree that I will be your equal in all things on the estate.'

'I would promise you anything,' Rufus declared, 'if it meant we would one day be husband and wife. I have always thought Beltinne was the best time of year for a wedding.'

Eilish nodded but allowed no expression to show on her face. She bowed her head and closed the kitchen door behind her, leaving Rufus alone in the hall once more.

Rufus was so overcome with excitement it was a few minutes before he woke out of his euphoric state. Then he remembered Braonin. He rushed off to the stables to saddle his horse and join in the hunt.

Chapter Twenty-Two

Evening shadows filled the hall by the time Rufus returned from the search for Braonin. The turf fire did not give off enough light for Neesh to work her supple fingers braiding the hair of her cousin Eilish, so Rufus had given the women three massive candles which stood as tall as a man, with wicks like miniature ropes. The light from them filled the chamber so Neesh could see her handiwork more clearly.

Outside in the crisp night air the wind rose a little, wailing around the parapets in a ghostly cry. Unexpectedly the shrieking gale dropped, and Neesh made the sign of the cross.

Eilish turned to the girl as she finished the little token of banishment. 'Why are you making the sign?'

'To put the spirits at rest,' Neesh replied flatly. 'To wish them peace in their time of sorrow.'

'What are you talking about?'

'It is barely half a year since your husband died!' Neesh exclaimed as she mercilessly pulled the older woman's braids tightly into place. 'His ghost is likely still afoot searching you out. And his cousin is hunted like an animal. How can you seriously consider another marriage so soon?'

'Donal was killed in a battle eight months ago,' Eilish corrected the girl. 'He will not be coming back! How long do you think I should mourn him? For the rest of my lonely life? Would Donal have wanted that? And Braonin will not be easily captured.'

'But what would your poor husband's ghost say to you if he knew you were wedding the young FitzWilliam?'

'If Donal were here in the spirit, he would understand my reasoning,' Eilish snapped. 'I have not felt his presence since I heard the news of his death. Not once. But I am sure Donal is looking down on me now. And he would give his blessing to this marriage, even if others would not.'

'Surely you cannot have any feelings for Rufus?' Neesh scoffed. 'He is a sour, mean-spirited, lazy drunkard. He is a bully and a braggart and the very opposite of your husband in every respect.'

'I am not marrying Rufus FitzWilliam for my sake,' Eilish said in a subdued tone. 'I am wedding him for the good of my kinfolk. With an O'Regan married to the lord of the estates, the tenants can be sure they will always be treated fairly.'

The healer turned in her seat to face the younger woman. 'How would you like it if Rufus went off and found himself a Norman wife? What do you think would happen to the estates then?'

Neesh avoided her cousin's eyes, preferring to concentrate on the task of braiding the golden locks of hair. 'Why would a Norman woman be any worse a wife than you?'

'Their womenfolk are not all as good-hearted as William's woman, Eleanor, was,' Eilish stated. 'If Rufus landed himself a vain, high-born lady who was fond of new clothes, fine embroideries and pretty trinkets, he would have to find enough gold to pay for her indulgences. The burden for those expenses would surely fall on the tenants of this estate.'

'But how can you even consider the prospect of sharing his bed?' Neesh hissed, making a ghastly face. 'How could you think of bearing him children? Surely you would not be happy as the Lady of Bally Raine?'

'I don't expect to be happy,' Eilish replied bitterly and for a moment Neesh thought the older woman would burst into tears. But Eilish regained her composure before she went on, 'How could I ever be truly happy again without my Donal?'

She did not wait for Neesh to answer that question. 'My feelings are of little consequence,' she stated coldly. 'Rufus is a weak man driven by his own desires. He has had a very privileged upbringing. He has never known hunger from the failing of the crops as we have. Everything he ever wanted was provided for him by his father. For that reason he never learned the value of a warm bed and a hearty meal. Or the worth of a hard day's labour. It is unfortunate, but old William had no skill in teaching such values to his children.' She paused again as Neesh tugged hard at her braids to tighten them.

'His brother Robert was no better. He squandered his fortune,' Eilish continued. 'He wasted his life and the lives of his soldiers on a stupid expensive expedition to the other side of the world. Rufus still has a chance to learn to distinguish between what is right and what is wrong. He needs to understand that his rights as lord must be balanced with his responsibilities. This is not an impossible goal for him to achieve. He has already changed a great deal since his brother departed for the Holy Land.'

'Ever since I first met him,' Neesh hissed, 'I knew he was an evil man who would come to no good.'

'I don't know about that,' Eilish replied, surprised that Neesh felt so strongly about the Norman. 'It will not be a difficult matter for me to bend him to my will,' the healer assured her cousin. 'His weakness will be my strength.'

'So you will sacrifice your happiness and independence to this man?' Neesh railed.

'If it means his children grow up speaking our language and respecting our ways,' Eilish explained, 'it will be worth it. The Normans leave the education of their young ones to the womenfolk. This woman,' she stated emphatically, touching a hand to her own breast, 'will instil in her children a love of the land in which they were born. This woman will bring her offspring up as Gaels. Within a generation or two the FitzWilliams will be just as Irish as you and I. They will speak our language, know our stories and think twice about paying tax to some far-off Norman monarch who never visits their shores.'

Neesh pulled at the golden locks again as she tied the tip of one braid with fine brown leather to keep it in place.

'I am not wedding Rufus because I have any love for him,' Eilish went on. 'May the saints preserve me! I am marrying the Norman so I can keep him under control. I will ensure the people of the estates are well fed and clothed. Their interests will come first in all things. And when my son ascends to the lordship, the tenants will have nothing to fear from any foreign tyrant. My offspring will live among the people so they understand the lives of their tenants. Donal would have seen the sense in that.'

'Rufus FitzWilliam is not worthy of you,' Neesh whispered under her breath.

'You must learn,' Eilish insisted, 'that we cannot always have the things we most desire in life. If I had my wish, there would be no Normans here and my husband would have had no reason to leave these shores.'

For a moment Neesh stopped her work, considering whether she should tell Eilish of her own encounter with Rufus FitzWilliam. Perhaps if Eilish knew he had tried to force himself upon her and had intended to murder her afterwards, she might reconsider her decision.

But the girl's conscience rebuked her. Rufus had begged in front of old Lonan for her forgiveness. The Norman had voluntarily undergone a regime of penance and abstinence in recompense for his sins. She had promised Rufus she would never speak of her ordeal. He had kept his obligation of atonement to her. The girl's strong sense of justice would not allow her to break her word and tell what she knew.

'There is more to Rufus FitzWilliam than meets the eye,' Neesh said eventually as a compromise. 'Watch after him carefully.'

Eilish laughed, brushing off the warning. 'I have been watching him carefully,' she declared. 'I do not want you turning the same way Braonin did. His action in supporting the heretics was unforgivable. All the evidence points to Cinneach and his men being responsible for the destruction of our houses!'

'They are fighting for our liberty from the Norman landlords,' Neesh corrected her. 'Braonin is a brave man, born of the same blood as his cousin Donal.'

'The best way to defeat the Normans is to overpower them in their own private chambers,' Eilish pointed out. Then she smiled and added teasingly, 'I noticed you have cast more than an admiring eye on our Braonin, have you not? You would not think of running off into the forest to join him, would you? Surely you would not leave me?'

'Perhaps Lord Rufus could find it in his heart to forgive the rebels,' Neesh suggested, hoping Eilish would take the hint and offer to present their case.

'You know as well as I do,' Eilish soothed, 'Cinneach and his men are rumoured to have been responsible for the deaths of at least four of the King's messengers. They have robbed merchants and poached the deer from the lord's woodland. Even if that is not true, the Culdee is a heretic. Cinneach has cast himself out from the Church by preaching false doctrines.'

'Our grandfather was a Culdee,' Neesh interrupted vehemently. 'There was a time when there were no other priests but the Culdees and their wives. I do not remember them as being any worse than that mumbling fool old Father Conlan. Or that loud-mouthed Lucius who was here before him. There were more churches when I was a small child and they were always full. The new chapel may be grand but the seats are always empty.'

'I don't know what to believe,' Eilish sighed. 'Some people say the Culdees are evil, others reckon they are the only true Christians on earth. But folk only cling to the old ways because they fear the new. I am not an expert on theology,' she went on, 'but I know the Culdees hold many different beliefs to the Church of Rome. Whether we like it or not, the Normans are our rulers now. They are orthodox Catholic Christians. They keep the feast days of the Roman Church, not the thinly disguised pagan festivals of our ancestors.'

'Our ancestors were content before the arrival of the Normans,' Neesh muttered, annoyed with her cousin's attitude.

'That is enough,' Eilish quietly reprimanded her. 'You are allowing your feelings for Braonin to cloud your judgment. We have to live with what circumstances come our way and that is that. I have made my decision. I would appreciate your support in this matter.'

'In three weeks you are going to wed a Norman lord in the very church your dead husband helped to build.' Neesh shook her head. 'I do not understand why you have chosen this path. I can only guess that the grief of your loss has affected your senses. But I will stand beside you whatever you do.'

'Thank you,' Eilish said sincerely as she reached behind her to take the other woman's hand.

'Will you ask Lord Rufus to grant Braonin a pardon?' Neesh pressed.

'I will,' Eilish conceded with a sigh. 'Perhaps he will do it as a gift to me on our wedding day.'

Neesh smiled and silently went on with her work of braiding. As she finished the task she thought about whether she should go out in search of Braonin. It was just possible, she reasoned, he had not heard of the wedding plans. Perhaps, she told herself, his presence would bring Eilish to her senses.

The weather was still cold. A harsh winter had stubbornly refused to let the world out of its icy white grip. The tenants of the FitzWilliam estates stayed close to their firesides even though the festival of the first day of spring, known as Beltinne, was only days away. Those who were not so fortunate to have hearth stones to sleep by huddled as best they could next to campfires deep in the woods.

Only desperately hungry hunters, fools and outlaws slept without walls about them at this time of year. There were few fools on the estates mad enough to brave the fury of winter. And thanks to the keen wits of Eilish, their chancellor, there were no families wanting for food. But there was a large number of outlaws sheltering from the wrath of Rufus FitzWilliam in the forests near the River Clonough.

From all over the south-east of the country, men and women who had been persecuted by the Normans gathered under the leadership of Cinneach the Culdee. The smoke from their fires could occasionally be seen from the battlements of Bally Raine. But no soldiers dared ride out in this harsh weather to challenge them, with the snow still falling heavily.

Rufus looked at the horizon with contempt, wishing the

black clouds would depart so he could challenge the rebels and drive them from his land. The weather did not lift. It showed no sign of doing so either for the time being. As long as it held, Cinneach and his people were safe.

They may have been safe but they were also close to starvation. With nearly one hundred and fifty folk harbouring in makeshift shelters, Cinneach was hard pressed to ensure no-one suffered from lack of food. Some of the tenants helped out where they could, providing portions of their precious winter stores of oats and barley. Nevertheless, the rebels relied mostly on their teams of hunters who went out every day in search of deer and other game. After several months of such hunting, the forest was depleted of its wildlife and the bands of hunters were forced to ride ever closer to the castle of Bally Raine to find food.

Finally, with supplies dwindling, Cinneach, a veteran of many campaigns against the Normans, began to despair. The Culdee knew he had to wait until the weather broke before his followers would be able to move on to better lands. To travel in the cold would be disastrous. None among his followers could have survived the ordeal. A march in this weather would be akin to suicide. So every evening the Cinneach earnestly prayed for bright sunshine to herald the dawn. Every morning, however, he was disappointed.

'We are no match for thirty trained warriors,' he told Braonin as they sat close to their campfire. 'The Normans have spent the entire winter indoors. They are well fed and rested. But most of all they are well armed. We have little more than farm tools to fight them with. If they come upon us unawares in the forest, we will be slaughtered.'

'Don't talk like that!' his wife rebuked him harshly. 'At least not where your people might overhear you. The spirits of these folk are close to breaking. If you really want a tragedy on your hands, then go on talking as if there is no hope.'

'Fidach,' Braonin soothed, 'there is no sense in harsh words between us.' The hunter was deeply disturbed at seeing Cinneach so despondent, but he knew that there was no use fighting among themselves.

'What would you suggest?' the Culdee sighed.

'Well, instead of just sitting here on our arses most of the time waiting for the hunters to return each day,' Fidach cut in, 'why not set our people to some useful tasks?'

'Stay calm, will you?' Braonin begged her. 'You will not achieve anything by leaping at each other's throats.'

'What would you have them do?' Cinneach retorted sarcastically. 'Weaving and spinning? At least we will not freeze to death if we have new cloaks.'

'You know what I mean,' his wife pressed.

'Fidach is right,' Braonin chimed in and Cinneach immediately scowled at him. 'Not far from here,' the hunter went on, 'is the main road leading to the north. We could set patrols out to watch for travellers. If any soldiers are spotted on the road, word can be sent back to us here. We should have lookouts posted all around the estate to report on the movements of FitzWilliam's men.'

'You are right,' Cinneach conceded through clenched teeth. 'I am not too proud to admit when I have made a mistake. But I have been so concerned with the survival of the people in my care, I forgot they need a strong purpose to their lives as much as they need food in their bellies.'

'We have all heard the tales the tenants have been fed,' Braonin continued. 'They say your people have been robbing merchants and waylaying messengers.' Braonin paused when Fidach laughed loudly. 'Most folk know the stories are not true. But the time has come, I think, to stop travellers and ask them for a contribution to the cause.'

'We are not brigands!' the Culdee exclaimed. 'I will not

stoop to the same thievery the Normans have forced on us. I will not allow my followers to take on the habits of the enemy.'

'The tenants have given us all they can,' Fidach reminded him. 'Their own stores are almost gone. This cold could go on for weeks more. What will happen when folk on the estates begin to starve? Do you think they will blame Rufus?'

Cinneach's wife paused to see whether her message was being heard. The Culdee turned his eyes downward, unwilling to admit he had already come to the same conclusion.

'They will blame every hardship on Cinneach the Culdee and his band of beggars,' Braonin went on, taking up the argument, 'because Rufus will give whatever food he can to the tenants. He will spread more lies about you. He will do what he can to make himself look like a benevolent saviour. It won't be long before the tenants turn against us. In a short while we won't be welcome on these estates. Our own people will become our enemies.'

'If only the weather would break!' Cinneach hissed under his breath.

'If the snows continue we will either starve,' his wife reasoned, 'be cornered here like wild boar, or we will be driven out. There is only one other alternative.'

Once again Fidach paused, rubbing her hands together to warm them and to make sure her husband was listening. 'The time has come to strike back.'

'We have no weapons,' Cinneach spat. 'What do you suggest we use to overthrow the FitzWilliam? Our bare hands? Or the bones of the carcasses we have eaten?'

'We must obtain weapons,' Braonin rejoined. 'There would have to be a score of hunting bows and spears hung high in the cottages of this estate. We should get our hands on them now while we still have the sympathy of most people. With spears and bows we have a chance of landing ourselves a few soldiers. Once we have captured Norman soldiers we will have armour and swords.'

Cinneach looked at the hunter and squinted. 'You are right,' he admitted reluctantly. 'We have to begin fighting back. What would all this suffering be worth if Rufus cornered us here in the forest? If the Normans fell on us now, we would not be able to resist the warriors. We would be slaughtered like chickens.'

'Rufus and his men may be well trained in warfare,' Braonin went on. 'Their arms may be new and plentiful. And they may have the discipline to hold the castle against us indefinitely. But we have an advantage. We are fighting for our lives. They are only fighting for their property.'

'How do you suggest we go about our campaign?'

'We must rely on our wits,' Braonin explained. 'If we are to win a fight against armoured soldiers, we have to plan well ahead so there is no risk of any of our folk being captured or hurt. Rufus would stand to gain a great deal from holding one of our people prisoner. He would display the poor wretch and no doubt extract a false confession from the captive. I suggest we lay a trap for one of the patrols that ride out to Shelton each day.'

'Six soldiers ride that road to the bridge and back to the castle,' Cinneach stated. 'Can an undisciplined mob of hungry peasants defeat six Norman men-at-arms?'

'If we plan carefully,' Braonin smiled, 'Rufus will find us at his gate before snow melt. And once he is trapped inside his fortification he will soon surrender to us. It will not take long for him to run out of food for it is the end of winter. He cannot have had a chance to restock his larders. If we move now, Rufus FitzWilliam will not be the Lord of Bally Raine for very much longer.'

Chapter Twenty-Three

Rufus paced impatiently along the uppermost parapet of the castle keep. The crisp snow crunched under his boots. Occasionally he stopped in his tracks to look out over the lands which would soon be his own.

'Once I am wedded to Eilish there will be no question of any former marriage arrangements,' the young FitzWilliam declared.

Father Conlan cast a glance over his shoulder at Jon Quicktoe. The huge warrior shrugged his shoulders in reply.

'But if Donal O'Regan is alive,' the priest tried to explain, 'the Church cannot recognise your vows to Eilish. Your marriage to her would have to be annulled.'

'If I wed Eilish I will be Lord of Bally Raine,' Rufus hissed. 'No man will dispute that. Eilish has been chieftain of the O'Regans since the death of her husband. She is respected by her people.'

'But clearly this letter from Scotland would seem to state,' Father Conlan said slowly as he held the parchment out before him, 'that neither Donal nor your brother Robert were in fact killed in the Holy Land. They are both alive and well.'

'How do I know I can trust your informant?' the young FitzWilliam spat.

'I have known Father Lucius since I was a lad,' the priest

replied. 'He served here as parish priest before my appointment. He knows you and your brother well. And he often spent time with Donal's father Mathúin. If Lucius says he has met with Lord Robert and Donal O'Regan and that they are heading home to Bally Raine, then I must believe him.'

'Damn!' Rufus grunted as he knocked the snow from the top of the parapet in frustration. 'Just when all my plans were about to bear fruit. Well, Robert and Donal are not going to spoil everything I have worked so hard for.'

'I do not understand why you are so upset,' Father Conlan stuttered as he nervously ran a hand through his long grey beard. 'Your brother is alive. Soon he will return to take up his lawful inheritance.'

'The situation has changed since Robert went off on his adventure,' Rufus snarled. 'I am Lord of Bally Raine now. And as soon as I am wedded to Eilish I intend to annex the estates north of the River Clonough.'

'She is already wed to Donal O'Regan,' Conlan asserted. 'If he is still alive . . .'

'I want you to annul Donal's marriage to Eilish,' the young FitzWilliam interrupted.

'I do not have the authority to do such a thing,' Conlan protested in horror. 'Even the Bishop of Ard Macha would have to consult with higher powers before taking such action.'

Rufus turned slowly to face the priest. Instinctively Conlan took a step back when he saw the rage in the young man's eyes. As the priest retreated he bumped into Quicktoe and the big soldier placed two broad heavy hands on Conlan's shoulders.

'You will do exactly as I say, father,' Rufus growled. 'You will marry me to Eilish in three days' time and you will bless our union. At the same ceremony you will proclaim me Lord of Bally Raine. If you fail to do as I command, you will find yourself in deep, deep trouble.' Quicktoe slowly squeezed his hands around Conlan's neck.

'Do I make myself clear?' the Norman added.

'What will happen when Donal and your brother return?' Conlan choked. 'Robert is the legal heir to these estates. You cannot deny that. And neither will any court in the land. The tenants will rise up to support him.'

'Robert and Donal will not be returning,' Rufus stated with a grin. As he spoke Jon Quicktoe let out a snigger of delight and released his hold on the priest. Conlan fell backwards into the snow.

'I am going to mount a guard on the north road,' Quicktoe cut in. 'If they come by that way, as they surely must, my soldiers will deal with them. They will get a decent burial and no-one need ever know they survived the rigours of the Holy Land.'

'What if they bring the whole company back with them?' Conlan pointed out. 'Remember they left here with over a hundred men.'

'But Lucius has stated in his letter to you they were travelling through the Kingdom of the Scots in the company of two other knights,' Rufus countered. 'The rest of Robert's men are coming home by a slower route through France and will undoubtedly stop in Normandy for some time before we see them. At most Robert will have one or two retainers in his company.'

'When Eilish discovers your plot,' Conlan frowned, 'she will renounce you and raise her kinfolk against this castle.'

Quicktoe picked the priest up by the shoulders. When he was standing Rufus grabbed Conlan by the front of his robe and pulled him close. Their noses were almost touching when Rufus spoke. 'But she will not find out. Will she?'

Once her hair was brushed Eilish dressed in the long white shift Rufus had given her. Neesh banked the turf in the fire ready for bed and went to her own sleeping place in the corner of the room. Eilish pulled back the covers on the large bed which had once belonged to Robert.

Angus, the castle cat, arrived almost as if he was drawn by the sound of Eilish yawning. In an attempted claim of ownership he began to press his paws into her pillow. Then Eilish snuffed the candles out before she crawled under the feather-down covers.

'Get down to the cat end of the bed, Angus,' she told her ginger friend. Angus looked at her as if he did not understand a word she was saying. But Eilish knew this creature better than that. She was not about to let him curl up too close to her face. The healer picked him up and his claws caught on the covers but eventually he relented and moved down to her feet.

When Eilish had first come to Bally Raine, this cat had followed her everywhere. He often woke her in the middle of the night with his stretching and his strange calls. Both she and Neesh had grown very fond of him for he seemed to be a human soul trapped in the ginger fur of a very intelligent feline. During this cold weather Angus was particularly fond of Eilish. But she found she had to firmly demand he sleep at her feet. Otherwise she would often wake to find the cat had managed to take the pillow all to himself.

With the cat purring indignantly at the other end of the great bed, Eilish was soon drifting off. The castle was silent but for the wind which still whistled outside the shutters. It had been a long day for the healer. She had helped the cook in the kitchens, preparing bread for the people of Clonough who had come to the end of their grain stores. Then she had spent many hours with some of the sick folk from the nearby houses. She had given out the last of her summer and autumn herbs. And then she helped one of the tenants with a cow with an infection in its leg.

Her feet ached, so it was soothing to have the warm body of the cat curled around her ankles. Eilish forced herself not to think about anything Neesh had said to her earlier. The decision to wed Rufus had been a painful one for her. But, she told herself, whatever happened from now on, she would have to live with the results as best she could.

She put a hand to her breast where a new leather pouch, containing her half-penny, was secured.

'Good night, Donal,' she whispered, half dreaming.

'Good night, Eilish,' she imagined the reply, though she had no doubt in her mind her husband was long gone from this world.

The healer awoke what seemed like a very short while later, to the sound of something popping in the fire. Drowsy and unable to ascertain what the noise had been, she closed her eyes again. Abruptly she felt her heart beat louder and stronger. In her groggy state she struggled to lift her eyelids again. But they would not budge. Suddenly she recalled the night of the fire at Cúil Ghréine and in less time than it takes to draw breath she was wide awake.

Everything was quiet and dark in the chamber. Eilish lifted herself up on her elbow and looked about. Nothing stirred. Neesh was breathing low and deep on the other side of the room. But Angus had disappeared. Gone off on some cat errand, she told herself. Relieved, she let her head fall onto the pillow again and she lapsed into an even deeper sleep.

Perhaps because her slumber had been disturbed Eilish slipped into a dream as vivid and real as her day-to-day life. However, there was no question in her mind from the start that it was a dream. Her rational self was observing events as they unfolded and she seemed at liberty to comment on the story as it progressed.

In her imagination Eilish was viewing a great plain from the top of a high hill. All around her there were strange soldiers dressed in unrecognisable attire. Down below she could see an army of knights whose pennants flew in the wind as they recklessly charged their enemies.

'That is the battle of Arsuf,' a voice whispered in her ear and she instantly recalled the name of the town where Donal had been killed.

'Where is my husband?' Eilish asked.

'Among the white knights,' came the answer. A peculiar growl followed the statement but Eilish was watching the battle too intently to take any notice.

Sure enough a great company of mounted knights rode out from the midst of the Christian army. They were led by a man dressed in a red and blue surcoat emblazoned with gold designs.

'That is King Richard,' the voice told her. 'They say he has the heart of a lion.' The strange voice broke into a derisive laugh but still she did not seek to discover the identity of her informant.

Eilish searched among the many warriors for the face of her Donal. But no matter how hard she strained, she could not find his position in the charging crowd. This is long past, she reminded herself. The healer knew she was looking on events of nearly a year ago.

'Where did my husband fall?' Eilish found herself asking.

'He did not fall,' the stranger laughed, 'neither here nor at any other place. Your husband Donal O'Regan is alive and so is his lord Robert FitzWilliam.'

Eilish felt her heart jump in her breast and she turned in her dream to see the face of the man who had been speaking to her. As she did so she felt a familiar tickling on her face and a wetness against her cheek.

Instantly her eyes were wide open and she was staring directly at Angus who sat on the pillow beside her, returning her gaze. For a brief moment she had the impression it might have been this ginger cat who had spoken to her in her dream. But then she shook her head to clear her thoughts and laughed under her breath at her own silliness.

The cat sat upright then as if he was somehow wounded by her lack of faith in him. The offence showed in his eyes and made her take a sharp breath.

'I am sorry for disturbing you, my friend,' she whispered, to soothe the cat, 'but my spirit was away on a night journey. I imagined I was looking down on the battlefield where Donal was killed.'

Without any provocation the cat leaned forward to gently nip his mistress on the nose. Then, while Eilish was still rubbing her face in shock, the creature jumped off the bed and ran out of the chamber. Eilish could see the door to her room was open but she could not think how that might have happened. She was sure she had shut it before she went to bed.

At first the healer thought she might still be dreaming. But the draught blowing up the stairs from the hall below was icy and real enough. So she dragged herself out of bed to close the door again. As she crossed the room Eilish heard the ginger cat on the stairs crying eerily like a human child.

'What is wrong with you?' she sighed in frustration, knowing she would not get any rest now until she had let him out into the courtyard.

With another huff of resignation Eilish fumbled about in the dark to find herself a small candle. Then she lit it from the turf on the fire and quietly crossed the chamber again to seek out the troublesome cat.

The stairs were silent and it seemed as though all the house was asleep. But now there was no sign of the cat. So Eilish began to walk down the stairs toward the hall. She had not gone five steps when she heard the creature cry again. This time she was certain he was behind her on the upper levels.

'Where are you,' she grumbled, 'you little mischief-maker?'

Angus answered her with a loud wail and Eilish turned around to climb the stairs towards the roof. She did not have to go quite that far, however. Outside the door to the chamber William had once occupied and which Rufus now called his own, Eilish saw the cat. In typical fashion he was calmly attending to his grooming and paying her no attention at all.

Eilish swore under her breath. 'They boil cats for dinner in the lands of the English, you know,' she warned him. 'You had better watch out or I will send you off over there to fend for yourself. King Richard eats three cats for breakfast. That is why they call him Lion Heart.'

Angus cried again as if he were mocking her. Eilish bent down to scoop the wayward creature up into her arms. As she did so the healer noticed a thin beam of light escaping from under the door to the chamber. In the next instant she heard Rufus mention her name and she froze where she stood.

'Who is he talking to?' she asked herself and the cat immediately cried in reply.

'Be quiet, little one,' she begged as he squirmed out of her arms and down the stairs again.

From within the chamber Eilish could hear loud laughter. She could not help but wonder who Rufus might be entertaining at this hour. But as she was standing there speculating, she heard the sound of heavy boots headed for the door. Without hesitation she turned around and fled down the stairs to her room, closing the door behind her as silently as possible. There she waited until she was sure she had not been discovered.

After a few minutes of hiding the healer could not control

her curiosity, so she pulled back on the door a little to see out into the corridor. Once again she could hear a voice and she was certain it was Rufus who was speaking.

'Remember,' the young FitzWilliam was saying, 'I want no trace left of either of them. None whatsoever. This is crucial to our plans.'

'Yes, my lord.'

'Then be on your way,' Rufus commanded. 'And do not forget to take the dogs with you. They need the exercise.' With that the man began to descend the stairs toward the hall. Eilish closed her door again and leaned heavily against it.

Eilish struggled to interpret the meaning of what she had just heard. The soldiers, she reasoned, must have tracked down Braonin and Cinneach. Rufus was issuing orders for their murder. She closed her eyes and offered up a prayer for her cousin and the Culdee, realising helplessly that there was little else she could do.

Outside his chamber Rufus stood watching Quicktoe until the loyal warrior disappeared around the bend in the stairs. He was about to return to his room when his eye caught a glimpse of something on the stones just outside his door. In the light spilling from his chamber he could not quite make out what it was, so he bent down to examine it more closely.

His fingers touched the white substance and it was still warm. Candle wax.

Had someone been listening at his door? he asked himself. Without waiting to speculate further he grabbed a candle and made his way down to the chamber where Eilish and Neesh slept.

When he came to the door he pressed his ear to it and gently turned the handle. The door swung open silently as Rufus peeked inside the chamber. Nothing stirred in the room and both women were fast asleep. With a shrug the young FitzWilliam quietly closed the door again and then held the candle high to check there was no-one else on the stair.

Satisfied, he turned to climb the steps again. But as he did so his foot caught on something and he heard a loud cry that chilled him to the bone. Heart pumping, he stepped back hard against the door as he stared down at his feet. There, hissing wildly and arching his back, was Angus, the castle cat.

An hour before noon the next day a heavy drift of snow blanketed the entire estate of Bally Raine. From the northern reaches past Shelton Abbey to the far south few folk ventured out in the hard weather. The Clonough shrank to a trickle as it iced over completely.

The only people abroad that morning were a desperate band of outlaws. At the place where the Shelton road skirted the woodlands a large group of Cinneach's men and women lay in wait in the freezing air. The Culdees dared not risk lighting a fire for warmth lest the smoke alert the Normans to their presence. But they were fairly certain they would not have to wait in the cold for too long.

Rufus usually sent his patrols off in time to arrive at the Abbey of Shelton around midday. After the soldiers had eaten and rested their horses, the patrol usually set a slower pace on their return ride to Bally Raine.

Cinneach hoped to catch them after their meal when they were likely to be tired and off guard. To be sure he would not miss them he decided to observe them riding to the abbey, that way he could discover exactly how many soldiers were in the patrol before launching any ambush.

A man dashed across the road from out of the sparse bushes on the other side as Cinneach looked up from his hiding place. A few moments later Braonin slid into the cover of the trees very close to where the Culdee was concealed among the pine needles.

'We are all done on the other side,' Braonin reported when he saw Cinneach smiling at him. 'We'll dance all over them.'

'I bloody well hope so,' the Culdee sighed. 'They will surely make a mess of us if we let them.'

'I have fifteen bowmen in the trees,' Braonin went on to explain. 'Seven on this side, eight on the other. Twelve men and women armed with boar spears are waiting just down the road. They are far enough along to allow for the horses to gallop on after the arrows hit their mark. One fir tree on either side is cut and ready to tumble and block the Normans' escape in either direction.'

Cinneach looked back toward Shelton and then on down the road. He screwed his eyes shut, shook his head and groaned under his breath. 'This is madness.'

'We will see what you say when we have mail-coats, helms and swords,' Braonin grinned. 'Then Rufus will have a fight on his hands.'

As he finished speaking Cinneach heard a low whistle from the lookout perched in the tree above.

'Twelve men,' the man in the branches reported, 'coming up from Bally Raine.'

'Twelve!' Cinneach repeated, anxious there were so many soldiers in the patrol.

The lookout nodded. The Culdee rolled over in the snow and grabbed Braonin by the front of his tunic. 'You said there would be six at the most,' he whispered hoarsely, but his subdued voice did not conceal his outrage. 'You bloody fool! There is no way thirty half-starved peasants can have a hope of beating twelve armoured men in a clean fight.'

'I never mentioned anything about fighting clean,' Braonin countered. 'And besides, we have the advantage of surprise.'

'That is interesting,' the Culdee retorted as he let go of his friend's clothes. 'It gratifies me greatly to know they will be shocked by our welcome. For a moment I had the impression I was the one who was astounded.'

There was another whistle. Cinneach looked up again for the latest word from his observer.

'The warriors have hunting dogs with them,' he reported.

'What else could possibly be waiting for us?' Cinneach sighed.

'And there are a further four armoured men travelling south from Shelton,' the lookout exclaimed, clearly distraught. 'They look as though they will meet with the patrol right in front of us on the road.'

'Holy Mother of God!' Cinneach blurted. 'Sixteen fully armed soldiers of the FitzWilliam estate, plus their dogs, bearing down on us from the north and the south. Truly, Braonin, they will be surprised by our ambush. And I will be surprised if any of us escape with our lives!'

'It does not look very good,' Braonin admitted.

'Not good!' Cinneach exclaimed. 'I think the expression one uses at a time like this is bloody disastrous.' The Culdee put his head in his hands and prayed silently for a few seconds.

'We are going to have to fight,' Braonin decided as he reached out to touch Cinneach's sleeve.

'Shut up,' the Culdee said quietly. 'Can't you see I am praying?'

'There is no time for that!' Braonin replied urgently.

'I am praying to God to give me the wisdom never to listen to you again as long as I live.' Cinneach got up on his elbows to rise but a thought came to him. 'Longer,' he added. 'I pray I never commit to one of your stupid strategies ever again, in this life or the next. If they halt in front of us, we will be discovered. We will have to spring the ambush now.'

'I will see to the felling of the trees,' Braonin declared indignantly. 'I have ropes around the upper branches ready to topple them.'

'Go to it,' the Culdee sighed. 'I will do what I can on the road. Our objective now is to save as many of our people from slaughter as possible. Do not stand against the enemy. We do not have a chance against them in a pitched battle.'

As he got up onto his knees the Culdee realised Braonin was already gone. 'Saint Brigid, in your mercy watch over us,' he prayed finally. Then Cinneach grabbed his own boar spear that lay in the snow nearby and rushed to his position by the roadside.

The group of twelve Norman horsemen riding up to Shelton slowed their pace somewhat when they spotted the four other warriors riding towards them on the road ahead. Braonin could see the leader of the larger group was moving his soldiers into a precise formation resembling a crescent moon with the horns pointed forward.

The other four travellers were also soldiers, if their helmets and the weaponry slung at their sides was anything to judge by. They gathered their pace to a faster gallop. All of a sudden Braonin got the distinct impression these two parties were not riding to a prearranged meeting. They were charging towards each other intending to come to blows.

Out in front of the patrol from Bally Raine on the left wing of the crescent rode a large man with fat hands. Even at this distance Braonin recognised him immediately as Jon Quicktoe. The smaller group all sported long beards. Three of them wore surcoats under their cloaks which were white. The fourth man was dressed in brown.

Whoever these strangers were, Braonin reasoned, it would be best to fell the tree on the road behind them as planned, to cut off their escape. Such action would at least ensure the warriors were disoriented for a short while. Perhaps the resulting confusion would allow Cinneach to successfully spring his trap.

What Braonin did not know was that most of the folk in the Culdee raiding party had been frightened by the appearance of a dozen soldiers on the road. Many of the rebels had withdrawn from their positions to flee. Only a handful of Cinneach's party remained waiting for the right moment to attack.

From among the group of four knights a standard flew up. A small pennant—top half white, lower half black—fluttered on the end of a lance. Braonin had only seen this design once before. Such a pennant had been among the war gear old Lord William had brought back with him from the Holy land. It was the battle standard of the Knights Templar.

'Templars?' Braonin whispered to himself with a frown. Then he noticed the larger group of warriors now displayed the green pennant of Bally Raine. As the hunter watched the two parties pick up speed on the slippery road, he realised he was about to witness a terrible clash of arms.

The ground thundered with the noise of warhorses at full charge. Braonin could only gasp at the foolishness of such a reckless ride on the slippery road. Three of the four Templars lowered lances at the tilt. The fourth, the warrior dressed in brown, drew a sword and let his mount fall back behind the others.

Quicktoe's men unsheathed their blades, brandishing

them above their heads. Then the Normans raised a blood-curdling cry. Braonin shivered in awe at the spectacle.

Seconds later the four Templar warriors bellowed their own threatening battle call. They passed the hunter in a blur of horseflesh and armour, bearing down relentlessly on their opponents.

Braonin ducked his head so he would not be seen. He felt the earth beneath him rumble with the passing of these warriors. Snow dislodged from the trees all around and fell to earth, covering the hunter. But he was so struck by the look of these knights he did not notice. As Braonin peered after them in wonder, he almost forgot to give the signal for the tree to come down.

'Let her go!' he yelled, regaining his composure. The hunter waved his arms about to let the man on the rope know it was time to pull the tree over.

But the tree did not fall. Within the space of four more breaths the two groups of warriors ran headlong into each other with a resounding crash. The cries of men and beasts filled the forest. The dreadful noise of steel striking steel rang out dull in the frosty air.

Of the larger group most of the soldiers continued riding on past their adversaries. Only the four or five horsemen packed into the middle of the crescent were stopped. For the most part they pulled their horses up before they collided with the four Templars. So all but one was thrown off his horse.

Braonin slid back under cover as Quicktoe drew level with him to turn his mount around on the road. Though he could not see the man, Braonin could hear the warrior barking out orders to his men.

'Form two tight lines!' Quicktoe bellowed. 'We're going to ride back at them slowly. A steady pace and you can dodge those lances. Any speed gives them the advantage.

Remember, we still outnumber them two to one. Take it easy. Don't let any of them slip away.'

It was only then that Braonin realised the tree still had not fallen as arranged. He ventured to lift his head above cover a little. When he was sure Quicktoe had moved down the road Braonin got up and sprinted over to where the rope was lying in the snow. There was no-one about. The lookout had abandoned his post. Braonin quickly grasped the rope and pulled as hard as he could on it. With a great creaking the old fir lurched toward him. Braonin barely had time to dive out of its way as it came crashing down to cut off the road to the north.

There was a boar spear lying in the snow nearby, no doubt abandoned by the lookout in his haste to depart the scene. Braonin picked the weapon up, weighed it briefly in his hands to find the point of balance, and then charged out onto the road.

'Bring down the other tree!' the hunter screamed at the top of his lungs as he ran forward clutching the spear. There was no sign of recognition from any of Cinneach's party.

'Bring down the other fir tree!' he bellowed again.

Everything on the road suddenly fell silent as both the Norman warriors and the Templars ceased their fighting to look at him. The Norman leader cursed loudly when he saw the fallen bough on the road behind him. But then his spirits lifted a little.

'Braonin O'Regan!' Quicktoe shrieked with delight. 'Two foxes struck with the same arrow!'

Braonin did not have the faintest idea what the soldier meant by this and he did not care to waste time working it out. There had been no reaction from the party of rebels waiting in ambush, so the hunter decided to charge straight for Quicktoe. He hoped this would inspire the others to action.

The Templar Knights took advantage of the confusion

and renewed their attack on the Normans. Their lances were useless in this close fight so they each drew other weapons. One man had a long sword with which he mercilessly battered two Normans off their horses. Another Templar spun around in the saddle to dispatch an assailant with a blow from a heavy club. The Norman fell backwards silently to lie on the road in a pool of his own blood.

By the time the hunter reached Quicktoe's horse he had given up hope of Cinneach's outlaws coming to his aid. Jon Quicktoe laughed heartily, dodging his mount around Braonin just out of reach of the boar spear.

'You will have to do better than that,' Quicktoe scoffed. 'Would you like to borrow a meat knife?' Then the great bulk of a man arrogantly slipped out of his saddle to stand beside his warhorse. Braonin had not noticed until now that the warrior seemed as strongly built as his mount. The hunter was beginning to regret his hasty charge.

'This will be very easy,' Quicktoe sniggered. 'You did not even bother to dress in your armour. You must have known you would have no chance against me.'

Lost for words, Braonin stepped back two paces as the other man drew his sword from a baldric at his side. But at that precise moment one of the Templars rode in to lash out at Quicktoe and the Norman was distracted.

Braonin turned to run just as he felt a horse blocking his way behind him. Instinctively he spun his spear around to challenge the rider, raising the weapon to the warrior's throat with a smooth sweep of the shaft.

The soldier before him was dressed in a grey cloak under which he wore a brown surcoat with a red cross stitched onto the left breast. The man's beard was dark, long and unkempt, and his skin was dirty, as if he had not washed in months. The reeking odour surrounding the Templar made Braonin gag. It reminded him of the sickly sweet smell of decaying flesh.

Braonin immediately thought of the old story of the woman whose three sons went off to the crusades. Each fell in battle against the infidel. When the three sons reached the gates of heaven they implored Saint Peter to allow them to return to earth for a time. They only wished to say their farewells to their mother. The saint agreed and the knights visited her briefly. They were said to have had the appearance of corpses dressed in fine clothes. And they reputedly stank of decay.

The nose guard of the stranger's helm covered the area from his eyes to his lips so Braonin could not see the warrior's face. Nevertheless he sensed this man meant him no harm. The hunter dropped the spear point to the ground to show he offered no threat. As he did so the warrior lifted his helm and Braonin felt the blood drain from his face in shock.

'Sweet Holy Mother of God!' he stammered in disbelief as he crossed himself. 'A lost spirit!'

The stranger's face was so like Donal, his cousin, it was uncanny. Yet the warrior's beard was impossibly long, matted and filthy. The Templar's skin was covered in a thick coating of dirt and dust. The eyes were weary beyond words. Everything about this man was familiar but at the same time terrifying.

'Braonin,' the apparition said in a voice that seemed remarkably alive, 'do you not recognise me?' But the hunter swallowed hard and could not find the words to reply.

Just then a great crash distracted them both as the second tree, further along the road, came tumbling down. Normans were scattering this way and that to avoid the falling fir. But a few seconds later the tree was the least of their problems.

With a mighty yell fifteen of Cinneach's men charged out of the cover of the woods. Valiantly they held Quicktoe and his men at bay with their spears. Braonin scanned the melee for the leader of the outlaws and when he spotted the Culdee he turned again to face the warrior on the horse.

'How do you know my name?' he demanded.

'I am Donal. Don't you know your own cousin?' the man replied in an incredibly fatigued voice.

Braonin's jaw dropped further. 'You are dead.'

'I have returned from the land of the dead,' the stranger answered with a laugh and his eyes lit up a little. 'I have come back as so few men do. And I brought good Lord Robert with me to look over his lands once again.'

An arrow flew past Braonin's shoulder and landed in the pine needles behind him, but he was so transfixed by the creature on the horse he hardly noticed. In the next instant another shaft struck a tree nearby and then three more fell on the road.

'I must see to my lord,' the ghostlike warrior declared, looking around him as he struggled to keep his mount steady. 'There seems to be a disagreement developing between Robert and these soldiers who are foolish enough to bear the FitzWilliam banner without his blessing. We really should make sure this matter is settled without too much bother before we move on.'

Braonin nodded dumbly. The spirits of Robert and Donal had obviously returned in this time of dire need to lend a hand to the fight. But, as in the story of the three sons, these ghosts could not stay for long. Braonin glanced over his shoulder before he swung around to rejoin the fight.

'For Lord Robert of Bally Raine!' he cried as he rushed forward. Only a few men heard his battle cry or made any sense of it. But Donal repeated the call.

By the time Braonin charged over to where Quicktoe was standing, the air was thick with arrows. Cinneach's archers were raining missiles down on every man who stood between the two fallen trees. But as most of them were untrained peasants, few of their shafts found a mark. The rare hits were due more to bad luck on the part of the victims than good shooting on the part of the bowmen. One or two of Cinneach's outlaw band were struck by their own people and injured badly.

Quicktoe still had a broad smile on his face as he stepped forward to strike at Braonin. 'I am not going to kill you, little man,' he informed his opponent as his blade cut through the air close to the hunter's face. 'I am going to take you back to Lord Rufus in chains and let him decide how to deal with you.'

The two men circled each other, reaching out to taunt with the tips of their weapons every now and then. But neither warrior dared commit himself to a blow that might leave his guard open.

'Lord Robert is back from the Holy Land,' Braonin gasped. 'Lay down your weapon and beg for his mercy.'

'What is Lord Robert to me?' Quicktoe spat. 'That bastard had me flogged. I have no love for him. Your lord is as good as dead. Dead men do not make good leaders. Tomorrow Lord Rufus will rule unopposed in Bally Raine.'

Braonin lunged forward viciously at the big soldier. But Quicktoe parried the spear out of the way easily with the broad blade of his sword.

'You will have to do better than that, little man,' the warrior sniggered. 'It takes more than a boy with a pig-sticker to defeat Jon Quicktoe.'

The huge warrior had barely finished speaking when an arrow struck him hard in the shoulder from behind. Braonin saw his chance and slashed the boar spear as close as he dared to the Norman. But the hunter missed, lost his balance and teetered forward as he slipped his footing on the thin ice.

As Braonin fell forward he felt a heavy blow strike him in the middle of the back. Quicktoe had managed to bring the flat of his sword down on the hunter as he fell.

The very moment that Braonin hit the ground he rolled over and held the shaft of his spear out in front of him. In the next breath he felt the blade of Quicktoe's sword strike at the shaft. If it had struck a split-second earlier the blade would have sliced the hunter's chest open.

'Well parried,' Quicktoe complimented, an arrow shaft still protruding from his shoulder. 'I thought you would be much easier to deal with.'

Braonin pushed the spear shaft up to force the sword away from him so he could stand. But Quicktoe brought his weapon around under the shaft and pressed the point of his blade into Braonin's stomach.

'This has been very entertaining,' Quicktoe added amiably, 'and you have been a fair opponent. But it is time we were on our way, don't you think? Drop your spear and stand up.'

Braonin hesitated, looking behind him to see if there was anyone nearby who might be able to help.

'I said get up!' Quicktoe bellowed and Braonin reluctantly did as he was told. He slowly moved to place the spear down on the ground beside him, then made as if to roll over and stand. He slowly moved onto his stomach, realising this was his last chance for freedom.

With his hands grasped firmly around the end of the spear shaft, Braonin swung the weapon around and thumped Quicktoe behind the knees. The ploy worked brilliantly. The big warrior's legs buckled from the blow.

In a flash Quicktoe was on the ground, wondering what had hit him, and Braonin was off, making for the shelter of the woods without even a glance behind him. As soon as he was in the forest, Braonin lay down in the snow by a tree, keeping his head low. He knew for certain he would not achieve anything by rushing back to the fight straightaway. He was winded and he had left his weapon behind on the road. He did not even have a knife about him. The hunter was defenceless.

Braonin resolved to wait until he had caught his breath before returning to Cinneach's aid. But that opportunity never came. Just as he thought he was ready to return to the fight, Braonin heard the unmistakable savage yelping of dogs.

Hunting dogs.

He stood up in the snow and saw, to his horror, Quicktoe setting the dogs loose to chase after him. Without another thought Braonin turned to the woods and ran as fast as his legs would carry him.

For a long while he ran heedlessly, jumping fallen logs and ducking beneath low branches. Twigs scratched his face and caught in his hair as he sprinted with all his might to outrun the hounds. He knew only too well that the Normans trained their dogs not just to hunt their quarry down, but to kill it. If these animals caught him, they would tear him to pieces.

But he was exhausted and he could not keep up the pace for long. He stopped to lean against the trunk of a tree, doubled up breathless. Braonin's ears pricked up but he could not hear anything above his own heavy gasping. It was a long while before he had calmed down enough to be able to stand up straight.

To his utter relief he could hear nothing. No dogs. No voices. Nothing. Now he was faced with a terrible decision. Should he make his way back to the campsite or return to the road to see what had happened.

Almost immediately he discounted the first option. If Cinneach and his outlaws had been defeated, then Quicktoe would surely be looking for the place where the rest of the

Culdees were camped. Braonin did not wish to lead the dogs directly to his comrades.

'If I take a long way around,' he said out loud, his breath pouring from his mouth like steam from a cauldron as he spoke, 'then I might get close enough to the road to see what happened.'

For a few more moments he waited to make sure he could not hear his pursuers behind him. Then he chose a route which would eventually bring him out of the forest just south of the road. From there he would easily be able to discern what had transpired.

All the way back Braonin berated himself for his cowardice in leaving the battle. But deep down he knew it would have been useless to stand against Quicktoe and his dogs. Even if he had been carrying a sword, the hounds would have quickly overpowered him. In the end the hunter told himself it was better to have lived through the fight.

Lost in a dispute with his own conscience, Braonin did not notice the barking until it was too late. When he did realise the dogs had picked up his scent he found he was too tired even to climb a tree. The combination of the fight, the flight and the bitter weather had sapped every ounce of energy from his body.

Braonin ran up to a tree trunk and threw his body down beside it. There would be no escape this time, he told himself. Now he was truly trapped. If the dogs did not kill him, Quicktoe would have him as a prisoner. The hunter leaned back, brushed his long fair hair out of his eyes, and felt the snow biting into his hands and feet.

His head began to spin but Braonin had no wish to be captured. With both hands he started to dig a hole in the snow in the hope of being able to bury himself.

What had happened to Donal? he wondered. Where was Robert? Did he dream they came to fight with them against Quicktoe and his men?

The dogs were getting closer. He could hear their heavy panting and excited whines as they sought out his scent. With one last great effort Braonin crawled into his hole in the snow. And then the dogs were upon him.

It was like drowning in a sea of wild hounds. The animals snapped at his feet and hands. One of the hounds ventured to nip him on the shoulder. They were drooling and crazed as if they had not tasted meat in weeks. Braonin fought them off as best he could, kicking and punching in every direction, but he was too exhausted to keep this up for long.

The effort of raising his arm to swipe at the hounds was so great, Braonin felt his strength drain away instantly. Finally, utterly spent, he lay back in his little hole and hissed at the animals. This seemed to keep them at bay at first. But the biggest hound came forward, showing its teeth and rolling its wild eyes at him.

The sight put the hunter in mind of the wild boar he had faced down on the day of Mathúin's death. These eyes were not wise as the boar's had been. These eyes were pure evil. Braonin thought that if the Devil existed he must have the face of a dog.

Suddenly there was an unexpected yelp from the rear of the pack and when the hunter heard it he realised he had been slipping into unconsciousness. Abruptly the hounds turned away from Braonin and began barking at something else, though the hunter could not see what it was that had disturbed them.

A moment later one of the dogs from the rear of the pack was flung into the air, landing close to Braonin. Once it hit the snow it did not move and the pack of hounds became frantic. But it was not the joy of the hunt spurring them on now. It was fear.

Braonin could plainly see that the dog's body had been ripped open by a very sharp instrument. The hunter's heart began to pump loudly in his ears and he summoned his last ounce of strength to raise himself on his elbow so he could see out over the edge of his hole in the snow.

There, surrounded by the pack of hounds, was a great boar almost exactly the same size, weight and colour as the one he had encountered that long while ago.

'The boar has returned to save me!' Braonin cried in delirious triumph.

As soon as he finished speaking, Braonin felt a hand on his brow. He turned to see who could have come to help him, half expecting to see the spirit of his dead cousin Donal.

'The boar will not save you, Master Braonin,' a voice said. 'Nothing will save you now.'

It was Quicktoe.

Chapter Twenty-Four

When the five surviving Normans returned to Bally Raine with their dogs, they had Braonin tied to the back of a horse. Rufus met his warriors at the drawbridge. Long before he drew level with his lord, Quicktoe could see the young FitzWilliam was enraged. So the sergeant decided it would be best for the moment not to mention the four knights who had challenged his patrol on the road.

'What happened?' Rufus demanded bluntly when the warriors reined in their mounts.

'We were ambushed,' Quicktoe answered with a shrug. 'There was nothing we could do. There must have been a hundred of the rebels. They cut down a dozen trees to block our path. We didn't stand a chance.'

'Did Cinneach escape?'

'I killed him myself,' Quicktoe smiled, lying easily. 'I cut off his head with my own sword.'

'There were thirty of us,' Braonin cut in, laughing. 'A few of our followers ran away when they saw your lot bearing down on them. The rest fled when the four knights appeared. And we cut down two trees, not twelve,' he added. 'One to the north and one to the south.'

'Who were these other four knights?' Rufus inquired, suddenly nervous.

Quicktoe looked down. 'I have no idea, my lord,' he lied again, wishing he had thought to gag Braonin.

'Lord Robert,' Braonin cried out, 'and Donal O'Regan. And there were two other knights with them. Robert and Donal are alive!'

Rufus said nothing but his steely glare betrayed his rage. The lord calmly removed his leather gloves, slowly easing his fingers out of their warm encasement as he walked toward Braonin. The hunter sat high in the saddle, proudly looking down on Rufus with contempt.

When the young FitzWilliam stood in front of his prisoner he pulled the hunter savagely to the ground. Braonin's hands were tied so he could not fight back but he began to swear loudly. Until Rufus stuffed his gloves into the hunter's mouth, making him gag.

'Take him to the cell,' Rufus ordered one of the soldiers, 'and see he remains quiet. No-one will be permitted to visit him. I do not want word of this getting out.'

The soldier dragged Braonin to his feet and as the prisoner stood up he spat the gloves out of his mouth.

'You are finished, Rufus FitzWilliam,' the hunter shouted. 'Lord Robert is back from the Holy Land! I'll see you hang.'

Braonin did not get the opportunity to say another word. Rufus gave vent to his anger and landed the hunter a kick in the stomach with his riding boots.

'You are the one who is going to hang,' the young FitzWilliam calmly informed his prisoner. Then the Norman turned to stride briskly back into his hall.

'You will present your report to me in my chamber,' Rufus barked but Jon Quicktoe stood still as if frozen to the spot.

'Move yourself, Quicktoe,' the Norman snarled. 'You may still have a chance to redeem yourself. But by Christ and all the angels you had better get your arse up those stairs or I will see it roasting over a slow spit before the day is out!'

Faced with this threat Quicktoe handed the reins of his warhorse to the nearest soldier, then followed reluctantly after his lord.

At the door to the hall Neesh met them. 'That was Braonin,' she stated, surprised and relieved. 'Where did your men find him?' she asked Rufus.

'He and Cinneach's bandits ambushed a patrol of my warriors,' the Norman explained, trying not to allow his frustration to show. 'My men were slaughtered mercilessly. The survivors managed to capture Braonin.'

'After a wild fight,' Quicktoe added, to which Rufus growled under his breath and rolled his eyes skyward.

'What will happen to him?' the girl inquired anxiously.

'There is no question of any further leniency with Braonin O'Regan,' Rufus said bluntly. 'He will hang.'

Neesh's eyes widened in shock as the Norman pushed past, followed closely by the huge bulk of Jon Quicktoe. As the door to the hall closed with a shudder, Neesh vowed she would do everything in her power to save Braonin's life. Even if her own life were to be endangered as a result.

Rufus would be unlikely to listen to Eilish now. Even if the healer were to plead on her knees for mercy on Braonin's behalf, the Norman would probably ignore her. But, Neesh decided, it was worth a try. Without waiting another moment she ran upstairs to her cousin's room to tell her this latest piece of news.

Within half an hour Eilish was climbing the stairs to Rufus's chamber. She could hear the Norman yelling unintelligible curses at his sergeant-at-arms. Then, as Eilish got closer, she picked up some of what he was saying. Her understanding of the Norman tongue was still limited but she recognised enough words to grasp what was being said.

'You will see that this castle is garrisoned throughout the

night,' the lord screeched, 'and that a watch is kept from all the towers. Before sunset you will ride out to Cúil Ghréine and round up the bloody lot of them. That is where they will most likely run to. When you find them, you are to kill them all. You will not spare one of the rebels, do you understand? Not a single man or woman is to be left alive at the end of this. Anyone who has spoken to them, aided them or so much as turned a blind eye to them is under a sentence of death.'

'Yes, my lord.'

'And if you fail me this time, Quicktoe, I will do more than have you flogged and run off the estate. You will hang alongside Braonin O'Regan.'

'I understand, my lord,' the sergeant spluttered.

At that moment the healer knocked at the door.

'Who is it?' Rufus shrieked.

'It is Eilish,' she replied quietly and in a flash the door swung open. Quicktoe bowed his head as he stood back to let her in. As soon as she was in the chamber the sergeant-at-arms made for the door.

'Stay, sergeant,' she ordered. 'I wish to speak with you also.'

Quicktoe looked to his lord and then to the floor, but he did not leave the room.

'What can I do for you, my dear?' the young FitzWilliam asked in as calm a tone as he could muster.

'What is happening?' Eilish asked. 'Is it true your men have captured Braonin?'

'That is correct,' Rufus admitted. 'He and his followers attempted to ambush my daily patrol to Shelton. Most of them were captured or fell to the sword, but one or two did get away.'

'What will happen to Braonin?'

'I must see justice is done,' Rufus began. 'He has broken the law. Along with Cinneach he has incited outlaws to rebellion. It is my duty to ensure others are dissuaded from taking similar action. Braonin will be hanged the day after tomorrow.'

'He is my cousin,' Eilish pointed out.

'Only by marriage,' the young FitzWilliam countered, 'not by blood. But if he were the cousin of King Richard himself, I would not be in a position to offer him any mercy. That is what you came to ask of me, wasn't it?'

Eilish nodded. 'Could you at least wait until your anger has subsided a little?'

'If I do not act swiftly, the tenants will think I am weak.'

'If you show forgiveness,' Eilish cut in, 'they will be grateful and they will know you are wise.'

'I do not expect you to understand,' Rufus admonished her. 'Women do not grasp the necessity of such actions in times of civil unrest. If we do not act now, the peasants will think they can slit our throats as we sleep. And, by God, they will try to do it.'

'The tenants would never try to cut my throat,' the healer smiled. 'I am one of them. I have saved many lives with my knowledge of herblore and healing. I am well respected.'

'But in a few days' time you will be a Norman,' Rufus reminded her. 'They will no longer consider you any different to me.'

'I would like to speak with Braonin.'

'You may not.'

'Why not?' Eilish demanded.

'Because,' Rufus sighed, becoming tired of all these questions, 'he is ranting and raving like a madman. The poor fool must have taken a knock to the head. At the moment he is dangerous. If he has calmed down by tomorrow, I will make sure you get to see him.'

'Thank you,' Eilish replied warily. 'I do understand your point of view,' she lied, hoping to placate the Norman.

Rufus smiled at her. And then walked to the door to open

it. 'You do not know how important your support is to me,' he said. 'Now, if you don't mind, I would like some time alone to work out how I am going to deal with this little problem. I do not want the Culdees to interfere with our wedding plans.'

'You will not send your men to Cúil Ghréine,' the healer said, 'will you?'

The young FitzWilliam's face turned red but his voice betrayed no sign of anger. 'What are you saying?'

'By all means,' she went on, 'arrest Cinneach if you must, and bring him to trial. But spare the common folk who followed him. Each one of them has a pair of hands which can be put to work at harvest time. Your brother took most of the able-bodied men with him on crusade. I can only assume they will never return. We need as many folk as we can muster sowing and reaping in the fields this year if we are to avoid a famine on the estates.'

'I will consider your request,' Rufus mumbled.

Eilish moved outside to stand in the corridor. Quicktoe brushed past her and rushed down the stairs.

'One of the servants told me,' the healer said to Rufus, 'that Braonin was calling out your brother's name when he was brought in.'

'He was calling down a curse on me,' the Norman lied, thinking quickly. 'He was invoking the dead spirits to come and destroy me.'

'I see,' Eilish nodded. Then she turned to walk down the stairs to her own chamber and Rufus shut the door behind her.

As soon as he was certain she had gone, the young FitzWilliam leaned on his own door and breathed out heavily. All his plans had been going so well up to this point. He could not imagine why the dream was suddenly turning sour. Right now Rufus was on the verge of giving up. He was ready to renounce his claim to the lordship and to the hand of Eilish O'Regan. If Robert really did return, he would never forgive his younger brother. He would see Rufus severely punished.

Rufus thought back over all that had happened in the last few months. The hard work of training his soldiers for war had come to nothing. His best troops, he rebuked himself, had been defeated by a group of peasants and four men-at-arms.

His eyes roamed around his chamber in despair, searching for an answer to this catastrophe. For a brief moment he thought he heard his father's voice berating him again, putting him in his place. That was all it took for Rufus to stand tall again.

With long strides the young FitzWilliam stormed across the room to the fireside. When he turned his back to the flames he thought he glimpsed the ghostly form of Lonan the chamberlain sitting in the same seat in which he had been strangled.

'It is too late to go back now, Rufus FitzWilliam,' the spirit seemed to be saying. 'You have sealed your fate and you will suffer for your crimes.'

The young FitzWilliam grabbed an iron poker from the fire and hurled it with all his strength at the empty chair. The seat fell backwards onto the floor with a thud, leaving Rufus sweating with fright.

In that instant the Norman realised there really was no turning back. He had worked hard to be proclaimed Lord of Bally Raine. And no-one was going to take that honour away from him.

Just on sunset, as ordered, Quicktoe rode out from the castle. The bad weather still showed no sign of abating, so all the soldiers were draped in heavy cloaks to keep out the cold.

Rufus watched from the window of his chamber as the line of torches disappeared into the night. Then he went back to his chair before the fire and drained his cup again. Before long he fell into a fitful sleep brought on by the wine and the worry of Robert's return.

Rufus seldom experienced dreams and rarely recalled the details if he did. This evening, however, he dreamed that his brother and Donal O'Regan rode right up to the drawbridge which fell open before them. The two warriors then charged into the keep and up the long stairs, cursing and swearing all the way that they would skin him alive. The next thing Rufus knew there was a pounding on his door and he woke with a start. He sat in his chair for a few seconds before he realised he must have drifted off.

He ignored the knocking. With his heart still beating loudly he closed his eyes again. But no sooner had he shut them than the pounding began again. Rufus unsheathed the long dagger he always carried at his waist and crossed the room warily.

'Who is it?' he asked. His voice sounded weak and frightened, even to his own ears. 'Who is there?' the Norman said again, trying to sound more threatening.

'Neesh,' came the answer.

As soon as he heard her name Rufus felt his body relax. The young FitzWilliam wiped the sweat from his brow and put his knife away quickly. Then he unlatched the door and opened it slowly, suspicious of who else might be with the girl.

'What do you want?' he demanded when he saw she was alone.

'I wish to speak with you,' Neesh said. 'I have a boon to ask of you. It is something very close to my heart.'

'If it is anything to do with that rebel Braonin,' Rufus snapped, 'then you are wasting your precious breath. I am no longer in a position to show him any mercy. He will hang the day after tomorrow and that is an end to it.'

'I think you have misunderstood me, my lord,' Neesh

replied, looking surprised at the young FitzWilliam's words. 'I have come to ask that you contribute to the alms-giving Eilish has planned for the day before the wedding.'

'Alms?' Rufus repeated. 'She did mention it some time ago. It must have slipped my mind. I have been very worried about these rebels.'

'Indeed,' Neesh agreed. 'If it had not been for their incessant raids, the tenants would not be in any need of help.'

'And if the weather had begun to improve,' he rejoined. Suddenly the Norman realised the girl was still standing on the cold stairs. 'Come in,' Rufus offered, 'and sit yourself by the fire.'

'Thank you, my lord.' Neesh crossed the chamber and stood close to the fireplace, soaking up the warmth of the glowing turf. But at every opportunity she glanced nervously over at the great desk which was strewn with papers.

'How much do you think we should give the tenants?' Rufus inquired.

'I think Eilish would prefer that we feed as many people as possible rather than hand them gold. They cannot eat the king's coin.'

'That is true enough,' Rufus agreed. 'She shall have her wish. Anything I can do to win the tenants over is well worth the expense.' As he was speaking he went over to his desk and sat down to write on a piece of parchment.

Neesh followed him and stood close to the side of the table where most of the papers lay. As he was writing she carefully slid her hand out to grasp one of the rolls of parchment, all the while watching the young FitzWilliam intently. He did not notice her move, but her heart beat so loudly in her breast she was sure he would hear it.

'A cow?' Rufus asked as he looked up and Neesh was certain he would notice her hand was around a scroll.

'I think that would be most generous,' she replied. Rufus

put his head down again and Neesh slipped the scroll under her cloak.

'Take this to the victualler,' the lord advised her as he sprinkled sand on the letter to soak up the ink. 'If we send to Shelton tomorrow there is a chance we might also be able to purchase some of their surplus flour for baking. Tell the cook to open the last remaining barrel of spices my father brought back with him. It is time we put them to good use. We will have ourselves two feasts, one for the tenants and one for the gentry the next day.'

'Thank you, my lord,' Neesh said as sincerely as she could, 'you are very generous.' The girl looked at the letter and noticed there was something crucial missing. 'Should you not add your seal to this?'

Rufus frowned and Neesh thought he must suspect her.

'Of course,' the Norman laughed, reaching for the wax and his seal and shaking his head. 'You are right.'

A few moments later he had lit a little candle under a small brass bowl full of wax. As soon as the red substance had melted he tipped it out over the page and pressed his seal down onto the paper to make a clear impression in it.

'There it is,' Rufus declared, handing the letter to Neesh. 'Thank you for giving me another opportunity to help my people.'

'The tenants will be so grateful,' Neesh replied politely. 'I can think of one or two who will be overjoyed that you have come to their rescue.'

The young FitzWilliam looked at her quizzically, unsure whether he had caught the full meaning of her words. But then he shook his head, telling himself he was exhausted.

'Very well then,' Rufus yawned. 'You have my leave to go about your business. I am about to retire. If there is anything else I can do, speak to me tomorrow.'

'Thank you, my lord,' the girl repeated, bowing as she

made for the door. 'I will let Eilish know of your generosity.' She stood for a second in the corridor, savouring her victory and trying to calm her racing heart. Now it was time to put the second part of her strategy into play.

'I must do what I can tonight,' Neesh told herself in a whisper, 'while the lord sleeps. If I wait too long, I may not get another chance.' With that thought in mind the girl made her way to the strongroom on the other side of the keep, where Braonin had been held since his capture.

The only entrance to the strongroom was from the courtyard. A guard stood sentry by the door in the falling snow. He looped an arm around his spear and rubbed his hands together. Beside him was a brazier full of turf and kindling. He stood as close to it as he could. Neesh swallowed her fear, went straight up to the warrior and asked to see his prisoner.

'It is more than my miserable life is worth to let you in,' he laughed. 'Quicktoe would rip out my heart with his bare hands if he knew I had allowed anyone to see that fellow.'

'Please,' Neesh begged. 'I have heard they are going to hang him tomorrow.'

'The day after tomorrow,' the guard corrected her. 'No rush.'

'Would Master Quicktoe let me in the strongroom when he returns?'

The guard sniggered. 'That is about as likely as each of these snowflakes turning to pure silver coins and finding their way into my pockets. Quicktoe has not got a reputation for kindness, my dear. His heart is as rotten as the centre of a blue cheese.'

Neesh had expected this answer, so as soon as the guard turned back to his brazier she threw herself into his arms, crying loudly. 'What am I to do?' she bawled. 'I will never see my lover again.'

'There, there, lass,' the guard admonished her, embarrassed at her open show of grief. 'Be quiet now. You don't want to wake the whole castle, do you?'

'If only I could see him once more,' she sobbed. 'Just one last time. I would not speak of it to anyone. It would be our little secret. Just between you and me.'

'I have strict orders, lass,' the man pleaded.

'I will be but a minute,' Neesh cried, 'I promise. I just want to see his face once more before they hang him. Quicktoe will never let me near my lover. This is my last chance while the sergeant is off on his patrol.' A great tear rolled down her cheek and the sentry groaned when he saw it.

'I cannot resist the tears of a woman,' he stated with defeat in his voice. 'Stop your crying and let me think.'

Neesh wiped her nose with the end of her sleeve and sniffled loudly. The guard looked around the courtyard and then up to the window of his lord's chamber. There was no light coming from the room so he knew Rufus was very likely asleep.

'Five minutes,' he said in a whisper. 'Not a breath longer. And if I am caught, I will swear you sneaked past me and I knew nothing of your visit.'

'Thank you,' she replied and in a second had brushed past the guard to open the heavy oak door to the cellar. It was locked and would not budge.

'You will need these,' the guard laughed, holding up a great iron ring on which hung a bunch of keys. The warrior came over to the door and selected a key. He turned it in the lock and the door swung open.

A lighted torch hung on the wall. She grabbed it to see her way down the stairs as the guard shut the door again behind her. After no more than twenty steps she came to a room strewn with fresh straw. There did not seem to be anyone about so she lifted the torch high in the air. There was a little flash as some cobwebs caught in the flames and exploded in fire. Then Neesh heard a sound. The noise of chains clanking together.

'Who is it?' a man's voice grunted. 'Come back to give me another beating, Quicktoe? This time let me out of the chains and I will show you what I am really made of.'

'It is Neesh,' the girl said, her voice full of emotion. 'I only have a few minutes.'

'How did you get in here?' Braonin exclaimed. 'Are you a captive too?'

'I have come to rescue you,' she explained.

'Have you brought a small army with you?' the hunter quipped. 'For there is no way I will be leaving this castle but in an unmarked timber box.'

'Do not speak so!' she berated him. 'There is still a chance we can get you out of here.'

'We?' Braonin asked. 'Who are these people you refer to?'

'Me,' Neesh admitted, stepping closer. The room filled with light and she saw Braonin seated on the floor with his knees up around his chest. He lifted his head and Neesh gasped at what she saw. One of his eyes had been battered so badly it was swollen as big as a new apple. His fair hair was matted with blood and there were cuts all over his face.

Without hesitation she knelt down beside him and touched the wound on his head. The hunter winced.

'If Cinneach and his outlaws have no chance of rescuing me,' Braonin sighed, 'what chance do you think you have?'

'Be quiet,' she countered. 'And be thankful someone is willing to risk their neck for you. The day after tomorrow they will be stretching yours unless I help you.'

'I am sorry,' Braonin said, realising he was behaving selfishly. 'It is difficult to think of anyone but yourself when you are awaiting execution.'

'I do not have much time,' Neesh cut in. 'Listen carefully. The day after tomorrow Eilish will be distributing alms at the castle keep. I will try to get a message to Cinneach and his men in the hope they will be able to get into the castle. They are not going to hang you until after the alms have been distributed.'

'He is a Christian gentleman, our Rufus,' Braonin smiled.

'Shut up, will you!' Neesh barked. 'Do not be surprised at anything that may happen. But be ready to make your escape.'

'How are you going to do it?' Braonin exclaimed.

'I have no idea yet,' Neesh admitted, 'but at least someone has you in their thoughts.'

The heavy oak door swung back with a thud as the guard stepped down onto the cellar stairs.

'That's it now, lady,' he called out. 'You have had time enough for your goodbyes.'

'I am just coming,' she called back, then dropped her voice to a whisper again. 'I will not let you hang.'

'Maybe it is my time to die,' Braonin sighed, 'for I swear I saw Donal on the road today. He was ragged and old like they say folk are who journey back from paradise to haunt this world. His eyes were weary and he had the scent of death about him.'

'You were dreaming!' Neesh insisted. 'The knock on your head has damaged your judgment. Donal's ghost has not come for you. Your cousin is dead now. The only thing you need fear is the hangman's noose.'

She looked behind her as she heard the guard descending the stairs. In the next breath the glow of another torch added to hers.

Without thinking, Neesh grabbed Braonin by the back of the neck. She drew his lips to hers to kiss him long and passionately. The hunter moved back from her in shock at first. But as she did not show any sign of pulling away from him, he relaxed.

'Come along, my lady,' the guard insisted, 'or you and I will also know the chafing of chains about our ankles!'

Neesh let go of Braonin and looked into his eyes. 'Farewell, my love,' she said. 'We will meet again soon.'

'You are too young to say such things, my lady,' the guard cut in. 'In a year or two you will have forgotten him.' Then the soldier reached down to grab her arm and drag her out of the cellar.

Long after the torches had been taken away and the great door secured again, Braonin sat in the straw, reliving the parting kiss Neesh had given him. He wished with all his heart there truly was a chance of her coming to his rescue. He wished he had been wise enough to hold his tongue when his rage had driven him to oppose Rufus.

'I may have had a chance, in time,' he told himself, 'to strike the tyrant down. What use am I in chains?' His thoughts returned to Neesh; how he longed to hold her once more before the hangman's noose tightened round his throat.

As his eyes adjusted to the darkness his thoughts cleared and he knew there was no hope of escape this time.

His fate was sealed. Rufus was determined to have his life. Resigned to his lot, Braonin rolled over in the straw, shut his eyes and forced himself to sleep.

Neesh went to find the victualler to hand him the young FitzWilliam's letter authorising the purchase of further supplies from Shelton Abbey. The victualler ran a critical eye over the document and agreed to send a cart off the next morning to bring back more oats as well.

'If this letter were to get into the hands of Cinneach O'Hare,' Neesh said slowly to make her point clear, 'it might cause all sorts of problems.'

'How do you mean?' the old man asked, not quite understanding what she wanted.

'Well,' Neesh went on, 'if the Culdees knew there was to be a great alms-giving, they would probably risk coming to the castle to receive food. I have heard it has been a hard winter out there in the forest.'

'Are you saying the Lady Eilish would like to contribute to the rebels?' the victualler asked in shock.

'Not necessarily,' Neesh answered slyly, 'but she would like to help the most needy inhabitants of the estate. And it would seem the outlaws are among the most needy.'

'I have no quarrel with the Culdees myself,' the victualler whispered. 'I can remember the days when they were numerous in these parts. But the landlord is Norman and you know how the Normans react when they think they smell a whiff of heresy. Is it safe for the Culdees to come here?'

'They will want to come to Bally Raine when they find out what Rufus has planned. As soon as the alms-giving is finished, Braonin O'Regan is to be hanged.'

The victualler's eyes widened as he rolled the letter tightly into a scroll. 'Indeed, there are some who would be grateful of that knowledge. Many of his kinfolk may wish to witness the execution. What is the charge?'

'Rebellion,' Neesh replied.

'Disloyalty?' the victualler countered. 'That is what the Normans mean when they speak of rebellion. Old Mathúin would wake from the dead if he heard this.'

'It will be enough that his kinfolk find out,' Neesh pointed out.

'I will see they know immediately,' the victualler assured her. 'We would not want the lad to dangle on a rope without some of his family around to cheer him on, now would we?'

Neesh smiled at the old man, confident he would spread the news across the estate. Then she bade him goodnight and returned to the chamber she shared with Eilish.

By the time she got into bed Eilish was already fast asleep and Angus was curled up at her feet, purring as loud as any man might snore. There was no sleep in Neesh though. She was awake half the night trying to work out how to get the keys off the guard so she could rescue Braonin from his chains.

Chapter Twenty-Five

Neesh may have had trouble sleeping but Eilish rested better than she had done in many months. This night the healer's dreams were vivid and colourful. All the events of the past two years seemed to mingle together in her mind so that everything was confused and muddled beyond any sense.

A figure appeared again and again in her slumbering thoughts. He was a strange man whose face she could not look on. He was dressed in the garb of a knight, his hands were dry and dirty and his hair thickly matted. But despite this the surcoat he wore was immaculately clean and his mail-coat shone like silver.

The stranger took Eilish by the hand to lead her down a muddy track. But she was not eager to go with him. His appearance frightened her. He was uncanny and otherworldly and an unusual scent followed after him.

The stranger looked directly at her when she resisted him and she heard him tell her that all would be well. Though his lips never moved.

The track they walked led up to a group of empty houses. Eilish immediately recognised the settlement as the clachan of Cúil Ghréine. The largest house was freshly thatched and there was fragrant smoke sifting up in billows through the roof.

The door to her old home opened then and a man stepped

out. All of a sudden the sun shone down on this scene. The man from the house strode over to her with arms outstretched.

'Eilish!' he called in a mellow, resonant voice that was welcoming and warm.

'Mathúin,' she answered, though until that moment she had not recognised her dead father-in-law. 'How are you?' she added. 'I have missed you so much.'

'I know,' the old man soothed, 'but everyone has their allotted time. Mine was well passed so I had to leave.'

'Is Donal with you?' Eilish inquired in the hope she would see her husband once more.

'Alas,' Mathúin replied, 'I wish he were with me for this is the most wonderful place I have ever been. There is no hunger or pain and best of all there are no Normans,' he joked.

'Where is Donal, then?'

'He is with you,' the old man exclaimed. 'At least, I know he is not on this side of the river. I do not get much news from your world any more.'

'Cúil Ghréine was burned to the ground,' Eilish said, confused at seeing the clachan in a pristine condition.

'Burned down,' Mathúin repeated incredulously. 'Who would have thought it. You are welcome to stay here with me if you wish,' he added. 'I would be glad of the company.'

Eilish felt a chill breeze against her face. She noticed the sun was shining brightly and there was sweat on Mathúin's brow. Her instincts told her that if she opted to stay with the old man even for one day, she would never be able to return to the world of flesh.

'You have not seen Donal then?' she asked once more just to make sure she had understood the old man.

'He is still with you,' Mathúin repeated softly. 'If he had come to us, I would have seen him.'

The doors to the other houses all opened and out stepped

a multitude of folk. Many of them were familiar to Eilish, though she could not place names with all the faces. The crowd gathered around her as Mathúin held out his hands to wish her well on her journey.

'You must leave now,' he informed her, 'or stay among your kinfolk here forever.'

Eilish felt a hand on her shoulder. She turned to see the stranger who had led her to this place. His face was no longer obscured but she found she could not focus properly on his features. The stranger took her hand again and led her away from the settlement of Cúil Ghréine.

Eilish cast a glance over her shoulder as they walked down the muddy track but the houses were all gone and the rise was smooth. To her surprise there were sheep grazing on ground where houses had once stood. The healer realised she was witnessing a vision of the distant future.

'Who are you?' she asked the stranger but before he could answer her they were back in the castle. The man led her up the stairs but they did not enter her chamber. Instead he led her to the room which Rufus occupied.

The stranger beckoned to her to follow him as he passed through the solid door as effortlessly as if he were passing through a waterfall. Eilish felt herself shudder as he disappeared but without hesitation she followed him, passing through the timbers just as easily.

At the window Rufus was looking out on the courtyard. In a chair by the fire sat the slumped body of Lonan the chamberlain. Eilish felt another chill run through her from head to foot. She was suddenly frantic to escape. But the healer found her feet would not do her bidding. Eilish reluctantly looked on the scene, realising she was viewing a past event. Lonan was dead from the shock of the news of Lord Robert's death. Spurred on by curiosity, Eilish made her way across the room to stand beside the old chamberlain. He seemed to be breathing lowly.

The thought crossed her mind the old man might live. As if he had heard her musings, Rufus went to the bed to grab a pillow. Lonan opened one eye and looked directly at her. The old man was about to speak when the young Fitz-William covered his face with a pillow and pressed down hard. Lonan offered no resistance and in moments he had ceased to breathe altogether.

Eilish was stunned. She had never suspected Rufus of murdering Lonan. She could think of no reason why he would have done so. Then she recalled Braonin's suspicions about the chamberlain's death.

'I am dreaming,' Eilish said aloud. 'This is just a dream.'

The stranger's hand on her shoulder told her it was time to leave again and Eilish found herself standing in the corridor with a lighted candle. The stranger had disappeared and she seemed to be entirely alone. Down in the courtyard Eilish could hear a great noise as if a large group of horsemen had suddenly arrived. But it was the middle of the night, she told herself. No-one travelled during the night hours in such bad weather. The healer decided to investigate.

At the foot of the stairs Eilish scanned the hall for any movement. She thought it unusual that the fire had been stacked with precious timber and was burning like a furnace. A man sat alone in a chair by the blaze. He looked up at her as she passed by. It was the tilecutter.

Eilish greeted the craftsman politely. He smiled back at her in his characteristic manner.

'I am surprised you are still here,' she said to him. 'Work on the chapel finished ages ago.'

'I am waiting for Donal,' Balek explained. 'There will be another tomb to be decorated before I am given my leave to depart.' The craftsman continued smiling at her, nodding gently.

'Have you seen my husband?'

'Donal?' the tilecutter asked in an affectionate tone. 'I have not seen him yet. But some men take longer to reach home than others. Perhaps he lost his way. Or maybe he is still travelling.' Balek smiled again.

'Where is Donal?' Eilish asked once more, sure this craftsman knew the answer.

'If you listen to the sound of the river,' Balek advised her, 'you will catch a fine salmon.'

The healer was about to ask for an explanation when a warrior in full battle gear stepped into the room. His face was covered by a helm which he proceeded to remove as he addressed Eilish.

'You will meet with your husband soon enough,' the soothing voice informed her. When the helmet was gone from his face, Eilish struggled to identify the warrior but she could not focus on his features.

'Who are you?' she begged. 'Tell me what you mean. Am I to die soon?'

The stranger laughed, replaced his helm and made to leave again. Eilish was determined not to let him go until he gave her some answers. She rushed at the warrior but he disappeared into the air.

The next thing she knew she was hammering at the door with all her might but it would not budge. A woman's voice called out her name.

Eilish turned to see Neesh rushing towards her with a blanket in her hands. The younger woman threw the warm cover over her friend. At that precise second Eilish awoke to find herself in the hall. The fire was not burning brightly. The seats were all empty. There was no tilecutter to be seen.

'Eilish!' the younger woman cried. 'What is wrong with you?'

'I was dreaming,' the healing woman said, only half believing that it was merely a dream. 'I dreamed Mathúin was living in Cúil Ghréine and Rufus had murdered Lonan.'

Neesh looked around at the staircase to make sure they were not being overheard. 'Be quiet now,' she soothed. 'It was only a dream. We will go back to bed now and forget all of this.'

'Yes,' Eilish muttered. 'Back to bed.'

'And we will talk of this tomorrow.'

Eilish nodded and allowed herself to be led back to her chamber where she lay through the rest of the night without closing her eyes once. In her troubled mind she went over every detail again and again so she would not forget any of it. As the sun rose she finally allowed her eyes to shut and then she slept. When she awoke, all memory of her adventures in the realm of dreams was gone.

The old monk ran down the corridor as fast as his fat legs could carry him. He decided to try searching in the large chamber which dominated the north wing.

'Where is he?' the brother puffed to himself. Then the monk turned around to see if the strangers were still following him. 'This way!' he called out to them. 'Down this way.'

The warriors strode heavily on the hard stone floor, holding their helms under their arms as they walked. Their spurs clattered at every step and their swords dragged along the paving.

Abruptly the monk stopped in his tracks, scratched the naked crown of his head and turned around.

'He will be in his own chamber,' he recalled, 'for it is after noon.'

Then the venerable brother took a passage to the right

and in a short while was knocking at a small wooden door.

'Brother William!' he called. 'Brother William. I am sorry to disturb you . . .'

The door swung open and a grey-bearded monk stuck his head out. 'What do you want, Brother Ignatius? I am busy at my books.'

'Brother William,' the old monk gasped, 'you have visitors.'

'Send them away!' William snapped and slammed the door immediately.

'A prefector of the order of the Temple wishes to speak with you!'

There was no answer.

'A prefector—' Ignatius repeated and the door swiftly opened again.

'I heard you the first time,' William stated as the two visitors turned into the corridor.

Brother William came out of his room when he saw them and stood with his arms folded. Ignatius proudly waited to hear what business a high officer of the Temple might possibly have with a monk of this abbey.

'Which one is the prefector?' William asked.

Ignatius pointed to the man with black hair. 'He is, brother.'

William looked at the white surcoat. Then he surveyed the long unkempt hair and beard. He spent a few seconds searching the warrior's eyes. The knight returned the gaze without flinching.

'That is no prefector,' William announced and Brother Ignatius's jaw dropped open in surprise.

'That man,' William went on, 'is my son, Robert Fitz-William.'

Ignatius stepped back as old Lord William approached his son, reached out a hand to him and smiled almost imperceptibly. Robert took his father's hand and held it in the grip he had been taught would identify his rank and status within the order.

'The abbot told me there had been a letter,' William said finally, 'from Outremer. They told me you were dead.'

'There were many times when I wished I was,' Robert replied and his father laughed a little.

'Why have you come here?' William asked gruffly to disguise his emotions. 'To disturb my contemplations?'

'To ask your help,' Robert answered and at that moment Donal stepped forward.

'It is Rufus,' Donal explained.

'Of course it is,' William sighed. 'I half expected I would have to ride out and deal with him. Shall I fetch my cloak and mail?'

Chapter Twenty-Six

The dark clouds of winter refused to retreat to the onset of spring. The River Clonough was still iced over and the snow was falling as if God had decreed there would be no warmth in Bally Raine ever again.

'It is a sign,' an old woman explained to Eilish on the morning of the alms-giving, 'that Banrigh na h'Oidche is not happy with us.'

'The Queen of the Night is a pagan deity,' Eilish gently rebuked the old woman. 'No-one worships her any more. She has no power over the seasons.'

'That is exactly what I mean,' the old woman chided. 'If we took a little more notice of her, the cycles would fall into their old patterns again. The winters are getting longer every year and colder. If we do not honour Banrigh, the snow will begin to fall all year long.'

'We should be praying to God,' Eilish explained, 'and keeping the sacraments. Father Conlan says the Banrigh na h'Oidche is a servant of the Devil.'

The old woman looked Eilish squarely in the face, a deadly serious expression in her eyes. Then suddenly she burst into uproarious laughter. 'You have spent far too much time among the Normans, you foolish girl!' she exclaimed. 'Why, I'll wager you've been locked up in that castle so long you don't even know which moon we're in!'

The healer was about to protest but then she realised the woman was right—she was not sure of the moon's phase.

The old woman shook her head. 'You're becoming a Norman,' she laughed.

'Are you ready to give your alms?' Rufus inquired in a friendly tone as he approached Eilish.

The old crone showed the whites of her eyes and hissed at the young FitzWilliam. 'You will be usurped by one of your own household. A male unwashed by water and unshaven will snatch your lands away from you. Beware the hunter. Your sins will be exposed for all to see. Blood will spill before this day is out.'

'You silly old hag,' Rufus laughed nervously but Eilish was as shocked at the prediction as she was at the Norman's reaction.

'Show some respect for her,' the healer urged her future husband.

'She is a stupid old crone without any senses,' Rufus protested. 'She has lost her wits.'

'I am as clear headed as when I was a young girl like her and tended the cows in the high hills,' the old woman grinned.

'You have moved me to pity,' Rufus replied, 'for the cows. Now move yourself along and eat your broth before we come to the main part of the feast.'

The woman shuffled off, chuckling to herself and shaking her head as if she were having a conversation with some invisible soulmate.

'My God!' Rufus declared. 'She has certainly spent too much time alone in the hills, hasn't she?'

'Can you not find any respect in your heart for the old and the wise?' Eilish asked.

'Age is something she certainly can lay a strong claim to,' the young FitzWilliam replied. 'But it is not wisdom she has been touched with,' he quipped. 'I applaud your sentiment in wishing to share our joy with those less fortunate than ourselves. It is a Christian act and the people are obviously grateful. But old soothsayers with sombre views of the future should not, as a rule, be taken seriously.'

'What if she does have the sight?' Eilish countered.

'What that blind hag sees of the future,' the Norman said, 'would fill a book with empty pages.'

The healer realised Rufus had borrowed that line from her father-in-law. 'Mathúin used to say that,' she replied, 'only he reckoned the shortest manuscript ever written was the Norman book of wisdom.'

The young FitzWilliam did not smile.

'We are expecting more folk from the outlying clachans,' Eilish informed him, changing the subject. 'Are you going to stay to help hand out the food?'

'I was going to ride over to Cúil Ghréine to search for traces of Cinneach,' Rufus told her, 'but with so many strangers in the castle I have decided to stay behind and see to final preparations for the wedding. I will be in my chamber if I am needed.'

'Have you thought about the matter we discussed the other night?'

'What is that?' Rufus asked.

'Is there a chance you might find it in your heart to pardon Braonin?'

The young FitzWilliam frowned. 'I thought I explained to you already that it would be dangerous to let his crimes go unpunished. The rebel outlaws are still at large in the countryside. Not even the sincere efforts of my sergeant-at-arms have been successful in that regard. It is my duty to send a clear message to the Culdee. He should move off these estates or face the same fate as Braonin.'

'You do not think the hag meant Braonin,' Eilish inquired, 'when she told you to beware the hunter?'

'That is ridiculous,' Rufus muttered, seeing the connection for the first time.

'When will he hang?' the healer asked.

'At noon,' came the reply.

'I understand you cannot pardon him,' the healer continued. 'He took up arms against his lord and that is a crime, but would you stay his execution until after we are married? I would be very grateful for that consideration. I do not want our wedding day to be marred by the memory of my cousin's death.'

It occurred to the young FitzWilliam to deny this request immediately. But he hesitated and did not speak. Rufus was suddenly surprised at his own willingness to bend to the healer's words. 'I will think seriously about it,' he said finally. 'You are probably right. It would be best to wait until after we are married.'

Eilish smiled as Rufus walked off toward the door to the keep. Neesh came over to her cousin as soon as Rufus had disappeared out of earshot.

'Braonin will not hang today,' Eilish announced, 'I am fairly confident of that. But none of us can know what the future holds.' The healer recalled the old crone's words to Rufus but could not work out what her prediction meant.

'Thank you,' Neesh squealed in delight as she wrapped her arms around Eilish.

'Now we must prepare to feed the people who are our guests today,' the healer announced. 'So it's back to work.'

By midday there was a growing crowd milling around outside the castle on the opposite side of the frozen moat, waiting for the drawbridge to be lowered. Some of them were dressed in little more than rags. These folk stood huddled together, shivering in the sleet.

Eilish ordered a collection be made of all the spare cloth in the household to give to them. Then she told the sentries to light fires outside the castle for the tenants to warm themselves by. Neesh went about organising this as the soldiers on duty at the gate began to lower the drawbridge.

Once the bridge was down, the people tried to push their way inside. But the warriors had strict instructions not to let anyone within the fortress until Eilish was ready for them.

After the fires were lit the tenants seemed content to stand beside them, warming their hands and talking amongst themselves. None of these folk could ever remember having been refused entry into the fortress. Not since the days of Lord William's first arrival. What they didn't know was that Rufus was unwilling to take any chances with the safety of the garrison. The ambush on the Shelton road had frightened him. That such a small group of poorly armed peasants could have driven off a dozen of his highly trained warriors was unbelievable.

Eilish arranged for those wanting to be fed to line up at the courtyard entrance to the kitchen after crossing the drawbridge. From there they were to take their food back over the moat to eat around the fires. The old crone and others who had arrived very early finished their food and lent a hand with preparations.

Jon Quicktoe was in charge of ensuring the people remained orderly while waiting. And that they left the castle grounds as soon as they had their food. From the courtyard window of his chamber Rufus watched the entire proceedings, retreating to his fireside now and then to keep warm.

Neesh returned with a small bundle of clothes and remnants for Eilish to give to the most needy of her people. The young girl's eyes widened when she saw just how many folk were lining up on the bridge for entry to the castle.

'There aren't that many people living on the whole estate,' Neesh whispered to Eilish.

'I would reckon,' the healer replied, 'that Cinneach has sent most of his outlaws up here for food. It must be very tough for them out in the forest.'

'Aren't you afraid Rufus will set his men onto them?' Neesh asked.

'I am not sure Rufus has any idea exactly how many tenants he has. I am hoping he will not cause a scene. Some of those folk look as if they are half starved and might perish without this meal.'

'They will need more clothes than we have in store,' Neesh observed. 'There are barefoot men and women in the crowd.'

'They can wrap cloth around their feet to keep them warm,' Eilish suggested. 'Bring me a cauldron to set on the fire outside. We will heat some water to bathe them in.'

Neesh rushed off again to get a cauldron. She passed by the soldier on guard duty who had let her visit Braonin in the strongroom. The warrior smiled at her. She nodded her head in reply and then noticed the warrior did not have his keys about his belt. Neesh did not want to look too closely for fear of raising the sentry's suspicions.

When she passed by him again she was lugging the kitchen cauldron all alone. She dragged it as far as she could in the snow, until finally she stopped near where the sentry was standing.

'Could you help me with this?' she pleaded.

The guard shook his head and waved her on.

'I cannot carry it alone,' she added.

'The lord will have my skin if I leave my post,' he replied under his breath. 'Ask one of the other men.'

'They are all on the parapets or at the gate,' Neesh pointed out. 'You are the closest.'

The guard looked up at the window where the familiar red-haired form of Rufus was watching over the courtyard. The sentry gestured at the iron pot and the lord nodded his head, then withdrew into the shadows.

'Very well,' the guard conceded. 'He doesn't seem too upset. Where do you want it?'

'Outside by the fire on the other side of the moat.'

The guardsman huffed and lifted the cauldron onto his shoulder.

'And when you're done,' Neesh called after him, 'you can fill it with fresh water.'

The warrior grunted but Neesh did not hear him. She had already found the keys hanging from a nail at the doorpost outside the strongroom. The girl stood back to watch the soldier as he passed through the gate and over the drawbridge.

The second he was out of sight she made her move. Trembling with fright, Neesh unlocked the great door and dashed down the stairs in the dark.

Her fingers fumbled about for the smallest key and she prayed it would be the one to unlock Braonin's chains. When Neesh found him she had to search for the lock that held the chains about his feet.

'What is happening?' Braonin asked her, but Neesh hushed him.

'Wait until the door opens again and then make your escape,' she advised him. 'The drawbridge will be open and Rufus is in his chamber, so he probably isn't expecting you to escape.'

Braonin nodded to indicate he understood. Then the leg irons opened and he rubbed his ankles. A few moments more and his wrists were free also. Without another word Neesh took the keys and ran up the stairs again. She opened the door slowly. When she was satisfied the guard was nowhere in sight, she slipped out, leaving the door unlocked. Then she hung the keys back on the doorpost before she headed back to Eilish.

With a glance up at the window to make sure Rufus had not seen anything, Neesh crossed the courtyard. She had nearly reached the table where Eilish was preparing the food when she looked up at the window again.

The young FitzWilliam was looking directly down at her. Neesh shuddered, overcome by the uncomfortable feeling that he had glimpsed her emerging from the strongroom. But he did not seem to be taking any action, so she convinced herself to relax.

'You are rather flushed,' Eilish noticed when Neesh came back to stand beside her.

'It is this weather,' Neesh explained. 'I wish the sun would return.'

'They are going to usher the people in now,' Eilish informed her. 'I want you to stay here and help if you can.' The girl nodded and went about placing ladles out on the table ready to serve the broth.

Father Conlan had his small stone altar set up about fifteen paces away from the food table. It was his intention to administer a piece of sacramental bread to each of the peasants. The first men to arrive dutifully knelt down before him to receive his blessing.

'This is the body of Christ,' the priest intoned.

'Amen,' the man replied.

Father Conlan slipped the bread onto the peasant's tongue. The man got to his feet, making the sign of the cross as he did so, and then moved on to get his broth. Before long the courtyard was full of chattering as people filed in to receive the blessing of the Church and of the Lord of Bally Raine.

Father Conlan had administered the sacrament thousands of times since he had been ordained and it was a chore which no longer held any excitement for him. Bored, the priest allowed his mind to wander as the faces presented themselves to him. At one point Conlan was surprised by the overwhelming stench of one of the peasants. But in his time he had smelled folk who were in a worse state, especially after a long winter, so he thought little of it.

It was not until his attention was caught by a tiny glint of metal on one of the tenants that he woke out of his half sleep. The priest looked intensely at the face before him. The features were haggard and old. The long beard was a light grey but the eyes were unmistakably familiar.

Conlan was suddenly shocked to realise he knew these features very well, though he could not put a name to the face. This disturbed him greatly for he had a good memory and the face really was extremely familiar. The priest gave the old man his bread, waited for him to stand, then grabbed him by the arm.

'What is your name?' Conlan inquired.

'I am called William,' came the answer in Latin. The priest gulped loudly as he recognised the resonant commanding voice.

'Sweet Jesu!' Conlan gasped. 'What are you doing here, my lord?'

'I am accepting the sacrament,' old William answered. 'I have a little surprise waiting for my son,' he added. 'Be careful you do not let on. I would hate to think of what might happen to you in the confusion of any fight. It would be terrible to see you cut down by a friendly sword.'

'My lord,' the priest swallowed as his body began to shake in fear, 'this is madness.'

William leaned in close. 'Have you heard the story of the prodigal son?'

Father Conlan nodded, his eyes darting up to the window of the keep where Rufus had been standing earlier. 'Of course I have,' he replied.

'Well, I am the prodigal father,' William announced with

a smile. 'I have returned to institute a few changes in the FitzWilliam household. Now go back to your work. Some of these fine men would doubtless be comforted by the sacrament just before they engage in a good scrap.'

'A fight?' the priest spluttered and he reached out to grab William's sleeve. 'You must not,' he cried, looking over his shoulder at the parapets. 'There are archers lying in wait.'

'For God's sake, man,' the old lord whispered, scanning the battlements as he grabbed the priest by the shoulder, 'calm down or you will give the whole game away. I would like to be able to surprise my dear son Rufus. You would not want to spoil a surprise, would you?'

William smiled when the priest shook his head and then added, 'The Abbot of Shelton sends his regards, by the way. He is hoping to have your company this evening.'

Father Conlan's face changed from a ruddy hue to the palest grey in a matter of seconds as William passed by to stand in line for his meal.

'The Abbot of Shelton?' Conlan repeated under his breath, certain he was in deep trouble now.

One ahead of William in the line a particularly ragged beggar held out his wooden bowl for Eilish to fill. She hardly looked at the man as he stood before her. But then he spoke.

'I would like to pay you for your meal, my lady,' the beggar offered, his voice gravelly and his accent rustic.

Neesh saw her opportunity when the man struck up a conversation with her cousin, and she hurriedly left the table to take a bowl of broth to the strongroom guard.

Eilish noticed her friend slipping away but paid little attention. She was distracted by this bedraggled man who obviously could not afford to pay her for the food at all.

'Keep your money,' the healer laughed, sensing he was teasing her. 'You might need it before the spring sets in.'

'I will keep it,' he replied, 'for it is not even a full coin I carry. It is only half a penny.'

Eilish's eyes widened in astonishment as the beggar held up his half-coin for her to inspect. She looked past the token into the man's eyes, not daring to examine the penny. She did not want to believe this man held Donal's coin. But her gaze was drawn inextricably to the flat bronze token. The healer could clearly see where it had been neatly cut from its other half.

As Eilish was facing the beggar Neesh handed the guard his broth.

'And Lady Eilish wants you to take this letter to Lord Rufus,' the girl informed him, handing the sentry the parchment she had stolen from the young FitzWilliam's desk. 'Immediately,' she added.

'I can't leave my post,' the warrior objected.

'Lady Eilish commands it.'

The sentry looked up to the window. There was no sign of Rufus.

'Let me finish my soup first,' the sentry begged. 'I have been waiting the whole morning for a bite to eat.'

Neesh frowned and the warrior gulped his broth. 'What is this letter anyway?'

'I don't know,' the girl answered. 'I can't read or write.'

The sentry shrugged to let her know he could not read either and then he set off across the courtyard towards the keep.

'Where did you get this coin?' Eilish was asking the beggar as she opened the pouch which hung around her neck. The healer drew out her own bronze half-penny.

'A craftsman from the city of Acre gave it to me as a charm,' the man said as Eilish looked once more into the beggar's eyes. She held her own half-token up beside his.

The two pieces fitted perfectly.

'Mine was also a gift,' she mumbled, feeling suddenly

faint. 'A tilecutter gave it to my husband, Donal O'Regan, before he left to go off on the crusade. He promised he would return within a year but he did not come home. A letter arrived to say he had been killed at the battle of Arsuf.'

'I was at that battle,' the beggar cut in quickly, just as Eilish was beginning to realise there was something familiar about this man. His beard was thick and filthy. His skin cracked and parched. The eyes were those of an old man, not of the youthful warrior who had left her side.

'Donal O'Regan did not die at Arsuf,' he went on.

'Where did he die?' she asked haltingly, fearing to hear the news first-hand from someone who had known her husband.

'He lives still,' the beggar whispered. 'And after all that I have seen and done, I live in hope that I will die in my own home by my own hearth.' As he spoke these last words his voice changed.

Eilish recognised her husband at last.

'Donal!' she cried out, her head spinning. 'I thought you were dead.'

'I was sure that I was a dead man once or twice also,' Donal laughed. In a second he had his arms around her and she was sobbing harder than she had when she received the news of his death.

'You're alive!' she cried joyfully. 'Alive!'

As the two of them were caught in their powerful embrace, several things happened at once. First, the drawbridge began to rise and many of those who were still outside the castle rushed to get over it before they were shut out.

Then Rufus could be clearly heard bellowing orders from the window of his chamber.

'Throw down your arms!' the young FitzWilliam barked. 'There are archers all about you on the walls. You cannot hope to escape. I have been waiting for you to return to my castle, Cinneach O'Hare.'

'A bloody trap!' Donal cried. 'I might have expected it from that bastard.'

In that instant Robert threw back the old cloak he was wearing and stepped forward to stand by Donal. Eilish felt her knees weaken from the shock of seeing him with his long beard and his white surcoat.

'I am the rightful Lord of Bally Raine,' Robert declared. 'You are a usurper and a traitor.'

'Who are you?'

'I am Robert FitzWilliam, your brother.'

'My brother is dead,' Rufus scoffed. 'He was killed in battle in the Holy Land. You are a filthy vagabond who would like to install yourself in his place. You cannot prove your identity to me.'

Another man stepped forward and threw back the covering from his head. 'I will vouch for him,' William stated. 'He is my son and he is the rightful heir to my castle and estates.'

Rufus looked on his father in horror. Then years of anger gushed forth from him in a mighty torrent. 'Kill the bloody lot of them!' he screamed wildly to his soldiers as he slammed the wooden shutters of his windows closed.

Within seconds there was utter mayhem in the courtyard. The archers on the walls began to shoot their arrows down on the outlaws below. The guards at the drawbridge fended off attackers from all sides who sought to open the gate again to let more of their comrades into the castle.

William, Robert and Donal drew their swords and carefully chose their opponents from among the garrison who were in the courtyard. Women and children fled this way and that, seeking cover from the flying arrows. Some quick-thinking soul let the pigs out from their enclosure to add to the confusion.

The guard from the strongroom had just opened the door to the keep when Lord William appeared from under a beggar's cloak. The sentry drew his own sword and ran toward Neesh as she pushed open the unlocked strongroom door and out stepped Braonin.

Without hesitation Braonin grabbed the guard by the rim of his helm and twisted the man's head until he heard a loud snap. The soldier fell dead from a neatly broken neck.

In the twinkling of an eye Braonin had grabbed the sentry's sword and was headed for the kitchen door. Neesh understood what he meant to do immediately and followed after him, dodging the flying arrow shafts.

Conlan saw the two of them making for the kitchen and decided this was his best route of escape. If he made it into the keep and then into the lord's chamber, he reasoned, the outlaws would not be able to get their hands on him. Nothing could break down that great door at the top of the stairs.

William had the same thought. He knew many lives could be saved if Rufus were dealt with quickly. But the fight in the courtyard had disintegrated into a bloody push where there was barely enough room to swing a blade. William was caught in the melee.

Donal fended off an attack from a tall warrior who had lost his helm. In the confusion arrows were landing haphazardly on the cobbled stones of the yard. Eilish stayed close to her husband, not wanting to lose sight of him amidst this mayhem. She crawled under the table which already had a dozen arrows stuck into its surface and waited for the situation to calm down.

The healer had just settled when she noticed old Lord William locked in a bitter struggle with the grinning Quicktoe.

'Donal!' she cried, but her husband had driven his opponent towards the gate and was out of earshot.

Eilish looked back at the old lord in time to see an arrow strike the knight high in the right shoulder. William dropped his blade and fell backwards over the body of one of Cinneach's men. Quicktoe roared with pleasure as his opponent fell.

'I'll have father and son both!' he cried in delight as he held the point of his blade at the old man's chest.

William looked up at the huge warrior, expecting to die any moment, but to his surprise there was a dull thud as Quicktoe's helm slipped forward off his head. The warrior dropped his sword and fell down onto the ground beside William.

The old man looked up and there before him was Eilish grasping a large iron ladle she had snatched up from the table.

'Thank you,' William muttered as he sat up. 'That is the second time an O'Regan has saved my life. It is about time I repaid the debt.'

Without a word Eilish dropped the ladle and grasped at the arrow shaft, twisting it out of the old lord's shoulder while he stifled a scream. Once she had the shaft in her hand and could see the wound was not too deep, she held out a hand to help William to his feet.

While Eilish was guiding William through the throng towards the keep, Braonin and Neesh got to the door of the lord's chamber. But they found it already locked and barred. Behind them on the stairs Father Conlan was puffing from his run but obviously still hoping to be able to take refuge with Rufus.

As soon as he saw the old priest, Braonin devised a way to get Rufus to open the door to them. The hunter held the sword he had taken from the strongroom guard at the churchman's throat. The priest trembled uncontrollably but Braonin showed no mercy. 'Knock on the door, Conlan,' he hissed.

'Lord Rufus?' the priest called in a feeble voice. 'It is I, Father Conlan. I beg you, my lord, to let me in that I might find sanctuary with you.'

'Are you alone?' Rufus yelled back.

'There is no-one else here,' the priest stammered as the point of the blade pressed into his throat.

'Were you followed?'

Braonin pushed the sword hard against the priest's neck. 'No, my lord. I beg you to hurry before the outlaws catch me.'

There was a short pause. Then Neesh and Braonin heard the key being turned in the lock. Suddenly the door swung open and Braonin rushed through it, forcing his way into the chamber. Rufus was knocked backwards and fell heavily on the stone floor near his bed. Neesh dragged Father Conlan in after her.

'You stupid bastard!' Braonin laughed. 'That was a very costly mistake.'

'Not as costly as yours,' Rufus snarled and two warriors stepped out from behind the door, their swords levelled at Neesh. A third slammed it shut and turned the key.

'You would be well advised to drop that sword, Braonin O'Regan,' Rufus directed. 'I do not wish to see this young girl's blood spilled unnecessarily.'

Father Conlan broke away from Neesh to sit on the edge of the bed, puffing and panting, distraught at all that had happened. Braonin let the sword fall from his hand. Neesh stood her ground, proudly defiant.

'You had the chance to kill me years ago,' the girl declared. 'You lacked both the competence and the ability to do the job. Why would you have changed?'

'You were very lucky,' Rufus agreed. 'In those days I was a green youth with no ambition in life other than conquering pretty maids such as yourself.' The Norman smiled at her and Neesh recalled how she had been at first taken in by his false charm.

'But the little incident at the well, of which you speak,' Rufus went on, 'taught me never again to take chances with anything. That is why I had all my soldiers waiting and ready for the outlaws to turn up today. I knew they would come and I was certain that if Robert and Donal had truly arrived back in Ireland, they would be here too. But unlike the debacle at Shelton a few days ago, today everything will go exactly as I have planned it.'

'Donal is alive?' Braonin exclaimed. 'I thought I had seen a ghost.'

'You are a very superstitious race,' Rufus sniggered. 'Perhaps that is why it was so easy for us to trample on your people in the first place.' Rufus went to the window and flung open the shutters to observe the fight.

At the same moment William found the door to the concealed passage which he had incorporated into the design of this keep when it was first built.

'No-one else knows about it,' he told Eilish as he disappeared up the hidden stairs. Not wishing to be left behind, she followed after him.

At the top of the stone steps there was an iron plate set within the arch of an empty fireplace. William held his finger to his lips, gesturing to Eilish to remain perfectly still. She did so and almost immediately realised she could hear every word that was spoken in the chamber on the other side of the iron plate.

'It would seem your ill-armed rebels have been defeated,' the young FitzWilliam was sneering, 'It was very thoughtful of them to bring my father along to help. His death in this insurrection will ensure that I ascend to the lordship without any impediment.'

'Cinneach and his men outnumber your soldiers three to one,' Father Conlan observed nervously.

'Oh ye of little faith,' Rufus quipped. 'I have archers all along the walls. Those bowmen were chosen for their expert marksmanship. They will simply pick the outlaws off one by one until there are none left. No-one can break into this room. My father designed it as a last refuge against attack.'

Then Rufus laughed again. 'The old bugger must have had you heathen Irish in mind when he built it. He may have pretended to respect you all. But in truth old Lord William considered your folk little more than a disorganised band of wandering heretics, traitors, cowards and superstitious fools. It may have been the only thing my dear father was ever right about in his life.'

On the other side of the fireplace William felt his resolve harden. His fingers gripped the hilt of his sword and his knuckles turned white.

'The tenants will not stand behind you,' Braonin scoffed, 'and you need their support if you are going to hold this estate and sow the fields.'

'I will simply bring in more warriors,' Rufus replied, unconcerned. 'The tenants will sow at the point of a sword if necessary. Peasants soon learn it is better to bend to the will of their lord than break under the strain of punishment.'

'And if the tenants refuse to acknowledge you,' Braonin asked, 'will you treat them in the same way you did Lonan?'

'Lonan was an efficient chamberlain,' the young FitzWilliam recalled. 'Unfortunately he was a little too efficient. He objected to my plans for Bally Raine and the surrounding estates. No matter how much I tried, I could not convince him to support me.'

'So you strangled him,' Braonin spat. 'An old defenceless man sitting in a chair by the fire.'

'Yes,' Rufus grinned, 'I killed Lonan. He challenged my leadership. He stood in my way.' Then the young FitzWilliam sighed heavily. 'It is a pity,' he went on, 'that you and I became enemies. You have a quick mind. We could have done wonders with this estate together.'

'I am sorry I had to spoil your little dream,' Braonin spat sarcastically.

On the other side of the fireplace Eilish looked on in dismay as William's eyes filled with tears. The healer reached out to touch the old man's hand and he instantly stood up straight.

'You have not spoiled my dream,' Rufus laughed. 'In a few hours order will have been restored to this castle. All the outlaws will have been eliminated and there will be no-one to challenge my authority. Tomorrow you will hang. I will marry Eilish and establish my own FitzWilliam dynasty.'

'Eilish will not marry you now she knows Donal is alive,' Neesh cut in.

'Donal will not be breathing by the time the sun sets,' Rufus retorted confidently. 'And Eilish will do as she is told, like a good Norman wife.'

William looked at Eilish quizzically and she turned away in shame at her own bad judgment.

'Those letters from the Holy Land reporting Donal's death were forgeries, were they not?' Braonin asked. 'It was your intention to use Eilish as a means to gain complete control of the estates. You knew the tenants would do anything she asked of them.'

'Of course,' Rufus shrugged his shoulders. 'And when we are married, that is exactly what will happen. I have had a guardian spirit watching over me,' the young FitzWilliam added, 'ever since I first conceived of a plan to bring the estates under my dominion . . .'

He had not finished speaking when there was an almighty crash that seemed to originate in the corridor outside. The three warriors rushed to the door and Rufus turned around from the window in shock.

Then, with a rumble that shook the floor, the iron sheet behind the fire fell forward across the glowing turf. A knight dressed in white charged out with his sword at the ready. Braonin seized the opportunity to snatch up his own sword from the floor. In a flash he had stabbed the point of it into one of the guards and the man fell backwards.

A second warrior slumped over William's blade but the third man had no wish to die. He dropped his weapon and begged for mercy. William granted it.

As they were dealing with the warriors Eilish stormed through the secret entrance behind the hearth and strode directly over to Rufus. By this time he was cowering in the frame of the window, speechless.

'You bastard!' she screamed. 'You murdering bastard! You killed Lonan. You burned my house to the ground. You lied to me and everyone on the estate!'

Rufus put up his hands to stop her from striking out at him, retreating all the while back into the window recess. Eilish stopped right in front of the young FitzWilliam, then raised her hand intending to hit him hard with the back of it.

'Curse you,' she hissed and with that Rufus moved back a little further. But the stone which he was sitting on moved under his weight and the old mortar disintegrated.

Then the strangest thing happened. Angus, the cat the old lord had kept since a kitten, jumped up onto the young FitzWilliam's chest, hissing and sticking his claws deeply in between the rings of his mail shirt.

Rufus screamed in fright. But before anyone could reach out a hand to save him, the stone he was sitting on dislodged. The Norman slid silently backwards out of the window. Angus leapt off his chest just in time and landed at Eilish's feet.

There was no sound as Rufus fell. He did not scream or

call out. No-one in the chamber heard his body hit the cobblestones below. The noise of men fighting drowned all other sounds out. And after the young FitzWilliam was gone, everyone in the room kept perfectly quiet, shocked into silence.

The cat rubbed his back against Eilish's leg and purred loudly, begging to be picked up.

The stunned silence lasted a long while. It was not broken until Robert, Donal and Cinneach began to pound at the door to the chamber, demanding to be let in.

'We have won the castle!' Cinneach cried out to them. 'Rufus is dead!'

Chapter Twenty-Seven

Balek rolled the wide parchment tightly and began packing away his drawing tools, rulers and angles. He had almost finished tidying up when the door to the chapel of Mary Magdalene swung open and two figures entered.

'Balek,' Donal called, 'how goes the new work?'

'Very well, brother,' the tilecutter answered with a smile.

Cleanly shaven, washed and dressed in a new brown tunic, Donal went straight to his father's tomb. With Eilish by his side he knelt, crossed himself, said an 'Ave' and then turned to speak with his friend again.

'Have you decided upon a theme?'

'It proved a more difficult task,' Balek admitted, 'to choose a tale to depict than the actual tilework is likely to be. But I have settled on a theme.'

'Will you tell us?' Eilish asked.

'The old lord,' he began, 'is determined the crimes of his son Rufus FitzWilliam not be forgotten. But I believe it would be too easy to emphasise the faults of such a man. Too easy to portray his darker side and rely on fear to teach the lesson.'

Balek looked toward the far end of the chapel where the body of the young FitzWilliam had been laid to rest.

'The challenge for me,' the tilecutter went on, 'is to show how adversity can bring rewards of its own. I am of the opinion that in times of hardship our individual spirits reach out to one another in ways which are not possible when times are good. Rufus did many destructive things in his life. He injured many innocent folk. But in the end we are all still here. Our spirits have not been diminished at all.'

'What about Lonan?' Eilish cut in. 'Rufus took him away from us before his time was up.'

'Lonan is not gone,' Balek smiled. 'The dead are always with us. They live on and we all must join them someday. When our friends pass on, they watch over us and keep us safe.'

Eilish recalled the dream in which she had met with Mathúin. 'I believe you are right, Balek,' the healer answered. 'Perhaps Lonan and Mathúin were looking after us.'

'I am certain of it,' the tilecutter retorted. 'But I have not been able to translate this great theme into a story which could be depicted on the tomb. Perhaps you could help me in this task.'

'I would be happy to aid you in any way I can,' Eilish agreed, 'if you will teach me to judge how many tiles it takes to cover a wall.'

The tilecutter laughed. 'That is easy. Only as many as the wall will hold,' he bowed. 'I will take my leave of you now,' he went on. 'I have much work to do preparing a new firing of tiles.'

Donal bowed, wishing his friend a good day, and the tilecutter made his way out of the chapel to leave the two of them alone. The chieftain leaned against the wall to study the decorated ceiling of the small building. Then he let his gaze take in the walls and floor.

'Balek of Acre is indeed a great craftsman,' the chieftain told his wife. 'When he showed me the drawings for this place, I never imagined how magnificent the finished work would be.'

In the beautiful blue shades of the tiles edging the floor Donal was reminded of the clear indigo sea near the port of Acre. The chieftain scanned the splendid map of Outremer which the tilecutter had created from tiny chips of ceramic.

'Balek has captured something of his country in this chart,' Donal noted. 'The heat and dust are there,' he said reaching out to touch the tiles. 'I can even sense the conflict and the common ground between the faiths who call that land home.'

'How fitting that this map is set above old Mathúin's grave,' Eilish noted, turning to her husband. 'He would be proud of you and your achievements.'

'I did not do anything,' Donal protested. 'I was but one sheep among the innumerable flock. King Richard did not need me. Nor did the cause of Christianity.'

'Tell me about the places you visited,' the healer asked as she threaded her arm through his.

Donal pointed to a line on the map which represented the west coast of Outremer. 'This is the city of Acre,' he told her, 'where we landed. Nearby is the village of Arsuf where Robert and I fought in the army of King Richard. It was a terrible battle,' he went on, 'thousands of men were killed. Their bodies were left to rot upon the field until nothing but sun-bleached bones remained. That action turned the tide of the war. A short while afterwards Saladin sued for peace and Richard returned to Acre.'

The chieftain shifted his hand to an empty spot on the map, north-east of Jerusalem. 'This is where we were held captive in the mighty castle of Mont Salvasch. It is not marked on any map. I learned a great deal in that place. And I met a man who may one day head the most powerful military order the world has ever seen. Robert decided to become a Templar while we were there.'

Then Donal shifted his finger to touch the place marked

as Jerusalem. 'After the Templar army, under Henry St Clair, rescued us from our prison, Robert, Geoffrey and I rode to Jerusalem. It was the lord's dream to visit the Church of the Holy Sepulchre in that city and to take his vows as a knight in that place.' Donal paused to look about him.

'That building is very like this one in many ways,' the chieftain realised. 'Though this chapel is much smaller, of course. But I can see Balek's decoration must have been influenced by that on the walls of the Holy Sepulchre. Robert made his own private vows of renunciation in that church because the Templar order was not permitted to enter Jerusalem. Saladin discovered they had been responsible for the desecration of the great mosque, so he refused to allow their leaders within the city walls. When we returned to Acre he took off the green surcoat of the FitzWilliams and he has worn the Temple white ever since.'

Donal drew his wife closer to him and kissed her forehead. 'From there we sailed to France and on to Scotland where Henry St Clair has his estates. He is a Norman in many respects but his mother's family were Gaelic-speaking Scots. Henry put a ship at our disposal so we could sail home.'

'Home,' Eilish sighed. 'Only to find your home destroyed. What will we do now that Cúil Ghréine is gone? Will Robert stay on here to administer the estates?'

'Robert is going back to stay with Henry and Geoffrey in Scotland,' Donal told her, 'but the Temple will be taking over these lands. We will rebuild Cúil Ghréine and settle back there again in the place of our ancestors. Now that the weather has broken and the sun is shining, it will not be long before we can begin our lives again.'

Eilish took Donal's hand, placing his index finger on the mosaic design that bordered the map. 'Do you remember this?' she asked him. 'Follow the knotwork maze until you return again to where you started.'

Donal smiled as his finger traced around the panel, coming to rest at last in the spot where he had first touched the design. 'I remember,' he smiled. Then he took out the half-penny from his pouch and laid it on the top of the tomb. Eilish put her half down beside it.

'They will never be apart again,' she promised.

'Never,' Donal agreed.

As he spoke they both heard the doors to the chapel opening and in strode Lord Robert followed by Cinneach the Culdee.

'How goes your father's wound, my lord?' Donal inquired as he and Eilish stood up.

'He has a tough skin,' Robert laughed. 'It would take more than an arrow shaft to kill him.'

'It is his spirit which has suffered the greatest wound,' Cinneach added.

'My father never held much hope of Rufus maturing into a warrior like himself,' Robert explained, 'but he surely never imagined my brother would turn out to be cold-blooded murderer, a thief and an arsonist.'

'Will Lord William return to the abbey?' Eilish asked.

'As soon as he is able to travel,' Robert replied. 'I will be departing soon after,' he added. 'Cinneach and his wife will accompany me. In the Kingdom of Scotland the Culdees are not persecuted as they are in Ireland under Norman rule. And I have realised I have much to learn from this man.'

'Lord Robert and I were talking about returning to Outremer together on another pilgrimage.'

'If the prior of my order allows it,' Robert cut in.

'Who will take over the running of the estates?' Donal asked. 'Has that been decided?

'My father and I have spent the morning discussing that,'

the lord informed him. 'That is why I am here.' Robert cleared his throat and Donal immediately recognised the gesture. Whenever his master had to make an announcement of any kind he always coughed nervously before speaking.

'Donal,' the lord began, 'and Eilish,' he added, remembering that she had served as chancellor in his absence and was a chieftainess in her own right, 'the estates of Bally Raine are to be handed over to the Order of the Temple. Cúil Ghréine is not to be rebuilt.'

'What?' Donal exclaimed.

'You cannot do that!' Eilish insisted. 'Cúil Ghréine is the ancestral home of the O'Regans.'

'The O'Regans will have to find a new home,' Robert went on sternly.

Donal frowned deeply as he heard those words. He had not travelled halfway round the world in the entourage of this man, he thought, risked his life and fought to uphold the rule of the FitzWilliams, only to be stripped of his home by them at the very last.

'Where will we go?' Donal hissed in outrage.

Robert smiled broadly but the chieftain did not take the gesture well. He suddenly thought that treachery might be a FitzWilliam family trait.

'Calm yourself, sergeant,' the lord commanded, realising Donal was fuming. 'The new residence of the O'Regan family will be the castle of Bally Raine. The Temple will own this estate but you two are to be the stewards of the holding. From this day forth the O'Regans will administer all the lands formerly held by the FitzWilliam family. You will answer to the Temple but you are free to set the rents and taxes as you see fit. May God bless you and aid you in your task.'

Donal could not believe his ears. 'Live in the castle?' he repeated, stunned.

'More than that,' Robert went on. 'The stronghold and chapel belong to you and your heirs.'

'It was William's idea,' Cinneach explained. 'He reckoned the only way to ensure he was never disturbed again from his quiet life in the abbey was to put you two in charge of everything.'

'There is a cask of ale left over from the winter,' Robert told them. 'Would you be interested in sharing it with me and a few of the servants?'

Donal smiled broadly. 'I believe that would be most enjoyable,' he replied, taking his wife by the arm.

'Then let us retire to the hall,' Robert sighed, 'and maybe Cinneach will tell us one of his tales.'

'Which one would you like to hear, my lord?' the Culdee asked.

'The one about the Holy Grail,' Robert laughed and Donal could not help smiling a little either.

When they had gone the chapel fell silent again. The light began to fade as the sun made its way across the sky. All the bright mosaics gradually lost their lustre in the gathering darkness.

In the hall of Bally Raine Donal and Eilish sat drinking, laughing and listening to travellers' tales. Neither of them noticed they had left the two halves of their precious penny lying on the tomb of Mathúin O'Regan.

Epilogue

It is not wise to ignore the words of an oracle. The best among them have an uncanny talent for plotting a steady path through the mists of confusion and delusion which fog the mind. Some among their number can describe every event that will unfold in a lifetime, from birth to burial.

Make no mistake, there is a force at work within these folk, greater by far than the impotent rantings of a celibate priest. But it is not Satan who grants people this power of foresight. For the Devil, if he is any more than a mere invention concocted to frighten children, surely does not have the skill to fashion these favours. Only God bestows such good fortune. Our fate is in the hands of the Creator, not a misshapen fiend of legend.

At a village fair in my early years, long before I was sent to the Holy Land, I met an old woman who plucked me from the crowd. She sat me down to tell me all she could about my future. The aged crone cradled my hand in hers and stared earnestly at the lines upon my palm. She spoke of bloody battles won by a brave and reckless king. Of voyages over monstrous seas and a castle concealed deep within a mountain range.

She spoke of a mystical quest which would end in cruel imprisonment at the hands of an unpitying black knight. And a test of faith that would lead me on to a new life of service to the true doctrines. The old woman embellished her tale with a warning. She told me that my insatiable yearning for knowledge would be my downfall; that it would lead me to uphold a creed which many men would judge to be a heresy.

She told me not to falter in my convictions, to stand by those who shared my beliefs. A heretic monk, she claimed, would be my greatest friend and that he, like myself, would end his days as a prisoner of the Inquisition. At the last she murmured that fire would release me from the clutches of my tormentors. Of course I did not understand then exactly what she meant by that final prediction.

It was a good story. As a youth I enjoyed nothing more than the singing of songs and the telling of tales. So I paid her well for her talent. Naturally I did not believe a word she said. Would you?

Now as I sit bound in chains in a dank stone cell I have plenty of time to ponder her words. It is plain to me the old woman truly had the faculty of foresight. And she must have known I would not heed her advice. For if I had better understood her esoteric skills, I would never have taken ship to the Holy Land after my father's death. I would have ignored my brother Godfrey's summons to join him in Acre.

Had I known where the path of the Templars would lead me, I would have shuddered in fear and refused to go to Scotland with Henry St Clair. Had I realised I would later become embroiled in the Cathar revolt I would have thought twice about my sacred vows. I would have found myself a wife and raised a brood of children to carry on my memory through the generations.

If I had held the slightest inkling of what detestable atrocities would be committed in the name of the Bishop of Tournai, I would have cut his throat when I had the chance. But that is another story and I fear I will not have the chance to tell it before they lead me to the stake.

With the hindsight of experience it is easy to wonder what could have been. It is much more difficult to act upon the foresight of an unwashed old woman who spins a fantastic tale and then demands a farthing for her eloquence.

It would not take a wise-woman to see what lies before me now. There is nothing more certain but that my life will come to its end in this, my fortieth year. I have learned much and lived longer than many of my peers. I have been entrusted with the greatest secrets of the Temple. I have counted among my friends the most influential men and women of our time.

And now I feel their spirits gathered about me, hovering near, waiting to lead me on to new adventures. And I take heart that the secret I hold dear will not perish with my passing.

Somewhere in the cold northern kingdom of Scotland, my successor, a new Guardian of the Scrolls, is waiting for the day when it will be safe to disclose his knowledge to the world.

Notes on Pronunciation

Words of Irish Origin

Bally Raine	ballee rayn
Banrigh na h'Oidche	ban-ree n-oy-keeya
Beltinne	bel-cheena
Broanin	brenan
Cinneach	kin-ack
Clachan	clah-han
Clonough	clon-oh
Columcille	kolm-kill
Cúil Ghréine	kool-greeny
Cuilgne	kooly
Daoine Sidhe	dun-shee
Donal	doh-nal
Eilish	aylish
Emain Macha	e-han mah-ha
Fidach	fee-dak
Gioll Martin	gill martin
Maelruan	mal-roon
Mathúin	mat-choo-un
Ochone	oh-hone
Poteen	po-cheen
Seanachie	shen-ah-hee

Caiseal Mór
The Circle and the Cross
Book One of the Wanderers

A rich historical drama that blends fact and fiction in a sumptuous feast of storytelling.

Imagine that you sit warming yourself by a fire in a tiny settlement lying deep in snow. Sweet peat smoke scents the chill breeze and an old song-maker raises a keening cry for summer's long absence. Here amongst folk who call themselves the Feni was a young lad born and there passed his first years on Earth.

Raised as the son of a blacksmith, Mawn, this very lad, knows little of the world outside his sleepy village.

But Eirinn, his island home, is in turmoil. Black-robed monks have made their way across the tempestuous sea from Rome and have set the people at war with one another.

The High-King and his Druid Council know they cannot survive the furious might of the Roman Empire so they must find other ways to save their ancient magical traditions from the evils that threaten to engulf them.

For this great task the Council has named a young boy who amongst the Feni was born and there passed his first years on Earth . . .

'an immensely satisfying fusion between early Celtic history and fantasy' Dr Colleen McCullough

Did you enjoy this book?

Would you like to receive information about other Caiseal Mór titles?

Would you like to receive information about Caiseal, his music, and the real-life Angus?

If so, simply clip out the form below and send it to:

Caiseal Mór Information
Random House Australia Pty Ltd
20 Alfred Street
Milsons Point NSW 2061

....✂

NAME: ....

ADDRESS: ....

....

STATE .... POSTCODE ....

EMAIL (if applicable): ....